DESTINY AND DESIRE

Kelly could not fall asleep. Her mind was full of the strange fantasies she'd been having. She remembered every detail, right down to the last fringe on the hem of her doe-skin robe, the smallest bead on her moccasins . . . and the look in Wolf's eyes as he made wild, passionate love to her. Not to mention the exact timbre of his husky voice, telling her she would be his for always . . . always . . .

There *had* to be a logical answer to all of this, she thought, badly frightened. Was she *really* reliving actual memories of a former life — or — was she going crazy? No! It was impossible.

But when she closed her eyes, Wolf's lean, handsome face at once filled her mind, his eyes smoldering with desire for her.

With a cry of denial, Kelly force her eyes to open, determined now not to sleep and give way to her delusions, or her fantasies, or whatever the things were.

Yet, before too long, fatigue won out. And, inevitably, with sleep came the dreams. Or was she really still awake, and the things she saw not dreams, but memories . . . ?

PASSIONATE NIGHTS FROM ZEBRA BOOKS

ANGEL'S CARESS   (2675, $4.50)
by Deanna James

Ellie Crain was a young, inexperienced and beautiful Southern belle. Cash Gillard was the battle-weary Yankee corporal who turned her into a woman filled with hungry passion. He planned to love and leave her; she vowed to keep him forever with her *Angel's Caress*.

COMMANCHE BRIDE   (2549, $3.95)
by Emma Merritt

Beautiful Dr. Zoe Randolph headed to Mexico to halt a cholera epidemic. She never dreamed her caravan would be attacked by a band of savages. Later, she refused to believe that she could love and desire her captor, the handsome half-breed Matt Chandler. Captor and slave find unending love and tender passion in the rugged Commanche hills.

CAPTIVE ANGEL   (2524, $4.50)
by Deanna James

When handsome Hunter Gillard left the routine existence of his South Carolina plantation for endless adventures on the high seas, beautiful and indulged Caroline Gillard learned to manage her home and business affairs in her husband's sudden absence. Caroline resolved not to crumble and vowed to make Hunter beg to be taken back. He was determined to make her once again his unquestioning and forgiving wife.

SWEET, WILD LOVE   (2834, $3.95)
by Emma Merritt

Chicago lawyer Eleanor Hunt was determined to earn the respect of the Kansas cowboys who openly leered at her as she was working to try a cattle-rustling case. The worse offender was Bradley Smith—even though he worked for Eleanor's father! She was determined not to mistake passion for love; he was determined to break through her icy exterior and possess the passion woman who lurked beneath her.

Available wherever paperbacks are sold, or order direct from the Publisher. Send cover price plus 50¢ per copy for mailing and handling to Zebra Books, Dept. 3115, 475 Park Avenue South, New York, N.Y. 10016. Residents of New York, New Jersey and Pennsylvania must include sales tax. DO NOT SEND CASH.

FOREVER AND BEYOND

PENELOPE NERI

ZEBRA BOOKS
KENSINGTON PUBLISHING CORP.

ZEBRA BOOKS

are published by

Kensington Publishing Corp.
475 Park Avenue South
New York, NY 10016

First printing: September, 1990

Printed in the United States of America

We have shared a
Hundred lifetimes —
Bittersweet, but ever fond.
Through eternity I'll love thee,
'Til forever and beyond . . .

Prologue

His uncle Lomahongva, Clouds Standing Straight in the Sky, was waiting in the abandoned *kiva* when Wolf returned from his vision-seeking on the high mesa, which had lasted three suns.

In the dark hours before dawn, White Wolf found the Hopi medicine man sitting cross-legged before the ashes of a small fire, his chin sunk upon his scrawny chest in sleep. It was as if the *shaman* had not moved since Wolf had left, although the sacred sand paintings he'd carefully created and placed the woman and child upon before Wolf's departure had been ritually destroyed. Their colored sands had been buried, along with the evil their magic had drawn from the sick ones.

Lomahongva's eyes, once black as the midnight sky, were no longer bright with health and cunning. Over the past winters of his long life, they'd become cloudy and inward-seeking. They saw little of this world any longer, White Wolf fancied, but looked to the World Beyond. His *naa's* skin had grown leathery, too, dry as the wings of a bat. His fingers were swollen at the joints, like the curved talons of an eagle. Nonetheless, White Wolf knew that despite his frailty, Clouds Standing had the gifts of wisdom and magic, and with them the knowledge to explain the visions of men. If any man could restore his woman to him, Lomahongva was the one!

Respectfully, Wolf went to stand before him. In silence, his head bowed, the young warrior waited. It was the way.

At length, Clouds Standing's chin lifted from his chest. With a small gesture of a clawlike finger, he motioned Wolf to seat himself on the dirt floor of the *kiva*, reaching into a beaded parfleche worked with sacred symbols at his side.

The medicine man cast a pinch of sacred cornmeal and

golden pollen onto the ashes of the dead fire and muttered a prayer. There was a hiss. The embers rekindled. The air about them was suddenly filled with a sweet, pungent smoke that was intoxicating to White Wolf's starving senses. His weary head reeled as blue flames became yellow. They writhed in the predawn chill, scattering the shadows and spilling warmth over the painted walls of the sacred *kiva*. White Wolf grunted with pleasure as their heat also danced over him.

"By your eyes, I know that Sotuqnangu, the Sky God, smiled upon you, my son," Clouds Standing observed in a low, reedy voice. "Tell me of your dreaming!"

White Wolf grunted assent. He was eager to begin, for his vision quest had confused and troubled him. But when he spoke, his tongue was as dry as the desert wind, his voice hoarse as the cawing of ravens.

"For two suns, Wise Uncle," he began, "I felt only the heat of Tawa, Father Sun, as he tested my body in that barren, shadeless place. By night, I heard only the cry of the wind and the singing of the stars. I saw only ghosts, the spirits of those who cannot find the Star Path. There was nothing more."

The Old One nodded sagely. "So it is for all men, my nephew. The Sky God tests a warrior's courage before He grants him visions. But, go on!" he urged.

White Wolf wetted his parched lips on his furry tongue, considering how best to describe what had come next.

"On the third night, I stood on the rim of the mesa and raised my hands to the heavens," he began. "I heard a mighty voice asking the Sky God to accept offerings of sacred tobacco and cornmeal from the warrior White Wolf. At first, I did not recognize that mighty voice as my own, and I was afraid," he admitted sheepishly.

The old man smiled and nodded, rocking back and forth very gently, as if nodding his entire body in agreement. "Yes, yes. And then? What came then?"

I asked for the gift of guidance, as you instructed, Uncle. I asked the Sky God to send me a vision—one that would tell me if my woman would be restored to me. So-

8

tuqnangu's answer came swiftly out of the starry sky!

"A great wind rushed through me, and at once, I felt my spirit soar free of its earthly shell, and whirl away as a leaf is whirled! When stillness returned, I found my spirit-self wandering in the canyon of the little red river—that holy Place of Emergence which is sacred to our People?"

Lomahongva nodded

"I saw the wisps of orange mist that our legends say are the souls of the unborn, floating between the canyon walls. I saw also the gray mists that are the spirits of those who have already lived and died, and now seek to enter the After World. My heart was heavy, for I believed that the Sky God had chosen this means to tell me that my woman would die!"

Looking up, Clouds Standing saw that White Wolf's handsome copper face was drawn with worry. Worry for his wife, Blue Beads, whose spirit had fled her living body, and worry for the little son who also hovered between two worlds.

White Wolf wetted his lips once again, wondering how best to explain the next part of his vision. It was unlike anything he'd heard recounted by other young braves around the camp fires of his Black Hawk band after they'd returned from their vision quests; so strange and frightening, he hesitated to tell it aloud, fearing Clouds Standing might call his dreaming false—the fabric woven of an empty belly and a light head.

He continued hesitantly, "Then, in the manner of visions, everything changed! Suddenly I was no longer floating between the little canyon's walls, but journeying on foot, running through the blackest night I have ever known, along a narrow pathway that led to the little canyon's highest ledge. I stood there, as still and silent as if carved from the mountains, waiting for . . . *something*, though I knew not what! Soon I heard a great sound in the sky above me—a roaring, screaming sound that was louder than any I have heard before. Truly, my uncle, it was as if the very skies had been torn asunder! Covering my ears, I looked up.

9

"Darkness had now fled. Out of the mouth of Tawa, the setting sun, flew a mighty hawk! Its wings were silver against the blood red sky, and it screamed as it swooped toward me. My heart—hiyeeah, my heart quaked in terror as its passage fired the sky with a jagged scar of light, for I saw—" he gulped, "I saw that on its back rode a great black *beetle!* Hiyeeah, yes! A hideous beetle! It was large as any man, and in its legs—by the Spirit, I swear I do not lie!—in its legs it held my—my woman! I saw this, I saw how she struggled, and yet I, White Wolf, could do nothing to help her! I stood there, and trembled like a coward—!" he finished with a grimace of self-loathing.

Clouds Standing saw that as his nephew relived the terrible vision, he had paled beneath his coppery skin. His powerful hands trembled.

"When I'd found the courage to look again, both monstrous beetle and silver hawk had vanished! I was again on the mesa, my spirit returned to my body. Only my shame remained—and these."

So saying, Wolf held out his hand to Clouds Standing. He uncurled fingers that had guarded their secret for many long, lonely hours to reveal their contents.

The fire's light winked off the pair of glass beads that White Wolf held cupped in his palm: the two blue beads that his woman had once carried in a medicine pouch about her throat. He shivered, and the hackles rose on his neck, for the pouch had been stolen by the one named Pale Eyes many winters ago, and he had no inkling of how the beads had come to be there, cupped in his hand!

With a grunt, Clouds Standing leaned over and took them from Wolf. He held each bead reverently to the firelight in a bony pincer-grip, before setting them carefully upon a smooth, flat altar of rock. Again, he delved into his parfleche. This time he withdrew a pair of sacred rattles, fashioned from the dried scrotal sacs of a white buffalo. They were filled with the humpback's magical powers!

Shaking them rhythmically in his gnarled fists, Clouds Standing rocked back and forth. Then, after what seemed an eternity to the waiting man, he began to chant:

"Hiyeee — aahh! Hiyeee — aah! Hiyeee-aahh! Hiyeee-aahh . . ."

His old voice rose and fell eerily in an ancient, one-word prayer, crooned in an ancient, half-forgotten tongue. Its pitch was part-beseeching, part-wailing, and his quavering entreaty stirred the hackles on White Wolf's neck once again, although darkness had now fled, taking with it both ghosts and shadows. Golden morning light spilled through the narrow opening in the ruined pueblo above the *kiva*.

Clouds Standing appeared drained when he fell silent again. The power the chanting had suffused him with drained like water poured from a gourd. In return, the blue beads had the lambent glitter of sapphires in the ruddy shadows. They reflected hidden fires and hinted at powers unknown, and as yet unrealised!

Taking up the beads, the old medicine man folded them carefully in a circle of soft doeskin. He added to them pinches of pollen and sacred cornmeal, a small, fluffy down feather taken from the breast of an eagle, the broken claw of a coyote, and a child's bone whistle. He tied the new medicine bundle with a slim cord of rawhide to form a small pouch, then knotted the cord loosely about Wolf's neck, so that its magic lay close to his heart.

"Your vision tells me much, my nephew," the old *shaman* revealed in a grave tone.

With a start, Wolf realised that the *shaman's* eyes were no longer cloudy. They were black as berries in fall now; brighter than wet stones in the bed of a river.

"Through it, the Sky God has given you a sign," Clouds Standing explained. "As the Great Spirit returned these beads to your hand, so will your woman's lost spirit be returned to her body! She will once again share your robes. She will once again be the one-above-all-women who shares your heart — *if* you have the courage to destroy the evil that keeps her from you!"

"What is this evil?" Wolf demanded hoarsely. "Name it, and it shall be destroyed!"

"The evil is that of one whose spirit — like the Two-Hearts of our legends — cannot enter the After World! It is the evil of one who searches, but can find no peace. This, my

11

nephew, is the Evil One, the black beetle of your vision!"

"*Him!*" Wolf breathed, knotting his fists at his sides. His jaw hardened. "How can my courage save her? Tell me, Lomahongva! Tell me, and I will do it!" he swore, his blue eyes steely with purpose in the murky light.

"How?" Clouds Standing echoed, and shook his head. "How was not revealed by your vision, alas. How is known only to the Sky God! But—of one thing I am certain. What will happen will happen soon! In the coming suns, our people will celebrate the rites of Wuwuchim—the night when all fires are extinguished in our villages, and all roads but one are closed, until the god Masau rekindles the fires. Is this not the blackest night of all? The one of your vision? A night without fires to brighten the shadows, and but one road open?"

"Truly, it is so," Wolf acknowledged, dry-mouthed. "But—can you tell me nothing more?"

Lomahongva shrugged fatalistically. "When the moment comes, you will know it in your heart, my nephew, and be ready to do your part. Then your great love will conquer all fear. It will vanquish all evil. You will not tremble then, but will do what is needed. Trust me, nephew. Trust in yourself, and believe that your prayers *will* be answered. I have received many visions concerning you, the son of my sister Yoyokee Mana, since you were taken from us," he disclosed. "*Haliksa-I!* This is how it is!

"It was revealed to me that he whom I gave the secret war name, Child of Lightning, and his chosen woman would have many offspring; children and grandchildren and great-grandchildren. Through them, the love of Blue Beads and White Wolf would live on forever, be remembered always in the minds and hearts of men.

"And, many winters from now, it is promised that one of your line will become a chief of this land, a chief of greatness and wisdom. This One Who Comes will have the gift of eloquence, the power to move men's hearts by his words. His talks for peace will be heeded, where the words of other chiefs have been ignored. His voice will soften the hatred of the bitterest enemies, and teach them how to live in brotherhood, be they white or red, black, or yellow of skin. This seed of your seed will be called the Peace Bringer Chief, the one to unite all tribes in brotherhood!

"In that time—which comes after the Third Great War of Mother Earth—the red men will be few. Hopituh and Navajo, Comanche and Cheyenne, Lakotah and all others will be scattered to the four winds, as the sands of the desert are scattered. And yet, because of one who carries the blood of White Wolf and Blue Beads, *all* men shall become as brothers. Their tribes will take the warpath no more. This is what my visions told me!

"Do you not see, my nephew? It is in order to fulfill this great prophecy that your woman's spirit *must* be returned to her body, for if yesterday is altered, so must tomorrow also be changed, neh? And if this should happen, the prophecy can never be fulfilled! Do you understand?"

White Wolf nodded mutely, shocked into silence by the old man's telling of his visions. Truly, there was great medicine stirring here, for the prophecy of Lomahongva was the same as that foretold him by the *shaman*, Semanaw!

"Then, it shall be," Clouds Standing ended simply, tottering stiffly to his feet.

"But—can you tell me nothing else?" Wolf persisted, unsatisfied with the shadowy promises of future greatness the old one had made him. In his sorrow, he could think only of the present: craved only the recovery of his little son, and the return of his beloved woman to herself. "How shall I find my woman's spirit?" he demanded. "Where does it wander now? If you would have me conquer the Evil One, I must know where she is!"

The old man looked at him long and hard, as if measuring him. Then he said in a low voice that sounded like the rustling of dry leaves:

"You must be strong, my nephew, for my visions have shown that your woman will be returned to you from tomorrow, borne on the wings of the silver hawk of your vision!"

"From—tomorrow?" Wolf echoed, his heart thudding ominously now, like the hooves of a galloping horse.

"Hiyeeah, it is so, my nephew. Her spirit is lost in the canyons of time. It wanders the world, searching through space. It cannot find its mortal shell, nor return to this moment, as it *must* to fulfil the destiny for which she was given life. The Sky God has chosen one to go after her. I, Lomahongva, will be her Guardian, the one to show her the way!

"Blue Beads is the daughter of the future now, Child of Lightning! She is the daughter of days yet unborn, and of dreams yet undreamed!"

Chapter One

Phoenix, Arizona, July 1988

"Kell? *Kelly?* It *is* you!"

"You were expecting someone else?" Kelly teased, pushing a heavy wave of dark brown hair out of her eyes and smiling at Barbara as she exited Customs and ran to meet her.

Simultaneously, the two young women laughed and fell into each other's arms, hugging fiercely.

"Oh, God, Kell, it's been so darned long!"

"Three years, one month, and ten days—I figured it out," Kelly admitted, blinking back tears. "Oh, it's wonderful to see you again, Barb! And?" she asked, holding her friend at arm's length and pretending to inspect her critically. "How are you, little mother? Happy with that great redheaded brute you married?"

"Look at me! The signs of wedded bliss are plastered all over me—though some people unkindly prefer to call them fat!" She rolled her eyes and sighed. "Saddlebags, love handles—I've got 'em all, but yes, I'm really and truly happy with Bill. Don't I look it?" Barbara grimaced horribly, but couldn't hold onto the scowl for more than a second. She giggled, hazel eyes merry in a very pretty round baby-face framed by short wisps of brown hair.

"Same old Barbie-doll, still fishing for compliments, hmm?" Kelly teased. "But honestly, Barb, you do look fantastic! If that's what three years of marriage and a brand-new baby do for you, maybe I'll try it myself!"

"Well, I'll tell you all the secrets of my success—and my size-sixteen figure!—just as soon as we find your bags, I promise. Through here, I think. Baggage carousel seventeen. God, it's good to see you again, Kell!" Barbara said

15

fervently as they walked with linked arms through the crowded Sky Harbor International Airport terminal to the baggage areas. "Phone calls just aren't the same as being together, are they?"

"Not at over two dollars a minute, they aren't! I knew I either had to come back or file bankruptcy, after all the long-distance charges I ran up. So, here I am!"

"Oh, you! I don't know what made you stay on in Europe anyway, after—oh, you know, after your divorce. There! I told myself I wouldn't bring it up first, but now Loose Lips Douglas has said it, and that's that! But—why did you stay in England, Kelly? Your friends are all here, on this side of the Atlantic, for heaven's sake. You needed us nearby at a time like that, after Tony turned out to be such a bastard."

"I know, Barb. And you don't know how badly I sometimes needed to talk to you about everything that had gone wrong in my life. But I guess—I guess I just needed some time alone more. Space to regroup, get myself together, find out who I really am and what I really want out of life," she finished in a mad-professor voice. "You know how that stuff goes?" she smiled a little wistfully, her deep blue eyes sad. "And then again, maybe you don't!"

Barbara snorted. "We'll see if you feel the same about my perfect life tonight, when Bill comes roaring through the door demanding food, and precious little William Junior starts squalling for his supper. Three weeks old, and the kid's a miniature tyrant already!" Barbara groaned, but was unable to keep the love and pride from her voice. "I forgot to ask, Kell—what color are your bags, anyway?"

"Those burgundy ones coming out now. That one, there—and that big one, too! Oh, get it, Barb!"

The two young women made a lunge for the suitcases, squirming their way between the other waiting travellers with breathless apologies, in order to snatch the bags off the carousel before it continued on.

"Is this *it?*" Barbara looked disgusted as she hefted a heavy case up onto the luggage carrier she'd commandeered from a startled student. "Just these two cases?"

"The sole sum of my worldly possessions!" Kelly confirmed. "By the way there's a little souvenir from England for you in that case so don't bang it around, kid! Baby William's present from Auntie Kelly is in the mail—the biggest teddy bear I could find in Selfridge's Toy Department. Every cabbie in London did a U-turn when they saw me coming with *that* one, so I didn't think at his age he'd mind if I posted it. I got Bill an Aran sweater. He's still into skiing?"

They made their way outside, Barb shaking her head to the taxi driver who sprang forward with a hopeful expression from one of several Courier Cabs lined up outside. The two women were still talking with hardly a moment's pause for breath, so engrossed in catching up on each other's lives, Kelly hardly noticed the transition from cool, air-conditioned terminal to the scorching ninety-five degree heat and dazzling blue skies of an Arizona July as they made their way to the parking lot.

"Skiing? Silly question! Wherever there's enough snow, there you'll find my Bill," Barbara said a little ruefully, softening her tone with a shamefaced grin as she fished her car keys from an enormous battered brown leather shoulderbag. She drew out a chain of diaper pins with a puzzled frown, before finding the key ring on her second try. "Oh, I know, don't say it—I shouldn't be down on Bill's hobbies just because I hate sports, especially since Bill's such a fantastic husband. He'll love the sweater, Kell, honest he will. No, this way! I parked over there—the gray station wagon, see it? If we leave now, we can be home before the rush hour, and you can fill me in on everything over a glass of wine, while I fix dinner." Barbara smirked a little and eyed Kelly expectantly for a reaction. She wasn't disappointed.

"You can cook now, too? *The* artsy craftsy Barbara—domesticated? I don't believe it!" Kelly exclaimed.

"I didn't say I could cook, exactly," Barbara corrected, her hazel eyes bright with merriment. "Just that you can watch while I *fix* dinner. You know, open a gourmet frozen entrée or two, toss a salad, throw some frozen dinner rolls into the oven—it's fixed! There's nothing to it!"

"I should have known," Kelly said ruefully, shaking her

head in exasperation. "Lead the way!"

Moments later, they were headed north on Forty-fourth Street to Indian School Road, and Scottsdale.

Despite Barbara's airy dismissals of her cooking skills, and although not gourmet fare, supper was a far cry from frozen dinners!

Kelly was suitably impressed as a delicious tomato salad with a homemade vinaigrette-and-herbs dressing that was out of this world, and crusty rolls as light as cotton balls, were followed by thinly sliced London broil, faintly pink and swimming in Burgundy wine sauce, *au gratin* potatoes, and tender asparagus tips, the latter cooked to a turn and crowned with a creamy topping of Hollandaise.

"Coffee?"

"Please. Lord, I'm so stuffed! I'll have to let all my clothes out if I stay with you for long!"

"Serves you right. You did have seconds of everything," Barbara reminded her with ill-concealed satisfaction. "But then, you probably won't gain a darned ounce. You never did, remember, not even when we pigged out in college, while I only had to look at food to put on a ton. It wouldn't hurt for you to gain a pound or two, though. You look far too thin to me."

"Dear Mother Barbara, everyone looks far too thin in your eyes!" Kelly came back quickly, true to form. It was an old joke between them, but at heart she knew Barb was right this time. She *had* lost weight, and on her those few pounds showed. She sighed. She was five-feet-eight in her stockinged feet, and Barb's bathroom scales said she weighed one-hundred-and-twenty pounds. At one-hundred-thirty, she had boobs and a bottom. Right now, nothing! A Living Bra, if she wore one, would have died of starvation . . .

"Ignore her, Kelly. I always do," Bill suggested with a grin that set his blue gray eyes crinkling up at the corners, and was forced to duck as a soapy dishrag came flying his way. "All right, pest, I can take a hint! I'll take care of loading

18

the dishes tonight, while you girls catch up on things—but no diapers, understand? I don't do diapers or windows," he mimicked in a squeaky, girlish voice that was so at odds with his tall, broad frame.

"Deal," Barbara agreed quickly, relinquishing the huge ceramic-tiled kitchen and dishwasher with an eagerness that made Kelly and Bill exchange quick, amused smiles. "Come on, Kell, I'll help you unpack—then you can give me my present."

"And I thought you loved me for myself," Kelly protested as Barbara dragged her away down the hall of the sprawling ranch-styled house.

They looked in on baby William en route to the guest room. At three weeks, little Billy's wrinkled new baby/old man appearance was fast filling out. Smooth pink and white cheeks, delicate wisps of chestnut-colored hair, tiny clenched fists and a puckered rosebud of a mouth—he was adorable, and Kelly fell instantly in love. Why, even in sleep, his lips moved, and he seemed to be nursing, she noticed, fascinated. She inhaled the wonderful smell of baby, powder, shampoo, and lotions that filled the room, and felt a catch in her throat and the weirdest longing for a baby of her own. Lucky Barb. Oh, lucky, lucky Barb!

"Enough of the kid, I want my loot," Barb insisted, ushering her out of the nursery with its teddy bear motif. There were bears everywhere: on a frieze running around the sunny yellow-painted walls like wainscotting, on baby blankets and quilts, the bright blue and yellow honey-jar lamp—everything was bears! "You can play with him soon enough. Those feedings seem to come around with incredible frequency."

The large guest room Kelly'd been given was decorated in pale orchid shades, with a few black-framed watercolors artistically scattered here and there on the walls. Barbara had the eye, and no mistake, but then, she always had. Give her a bare room and free rein for her imagination, and she'd transform it, Kelly thought. The headboard, twin night stands, and dressing table were fine black-lacquer wood; the satin bedspread and ruffled pillows shams, the

19

drapes, all a deeper shade of orchid, with silk throw pillows in contrasting pastel hues that had oriental-style flowers appliquéd to their muted backgrounds. The deeply piled carpet was creamy off-white. The closet doors had become an oriental flower mural, and looked like Japanese screens showing delicate blossoms on a misty orchid background—Barb's artistry again. A black shoji screen with white rice-paper panes discreetly concealed the door leading to the adjoining bathroom. Before them sat her two somewhat battered, non-oriental burgundy suitcases.

"*Very* nice," she commented for the second time that evening. "Bill's practice must be doing well."

"Dr. Bill's *and* yours truly, I'm happy to say! The boutique's a roaring success, even if I do say so myself. Six months, and we're out of the red. Not bad, hmm?"

"Oh, Barbara, I really am so happy for you, all joking aside," Kelly said softly, hugging her friend.

"Not half as happy as I am! Everyone said me and Mom were crazy, opening yet another boutique here in Scottsdale. Remember, I wrote and told you? But it's working out better than even we had expected. We have an artist from Tucson who does these wonderful stained-glass pieces for us on consignment. And a Navajo lady and her two daughters who're all weavers, and whose rugs are really well-respected in the local arts and crafts circles and sought-after by collectors. They're designing exclusively for us, as are a select handful of Hopi potters and painters and wood-carvers and kachina doll-makers and so on. Their work's just terrific, Kelly! Raw, natural colors and mediums, stark beauty, incredible eye for detail—you know the kind of thing."

"Sounds pretty hectic!"

"Oh, it is. And soon to get busier, all going well."

"And little William? Where does he fit into all of this?"

"Oh, just perfectly, Kell. Of course, I don't plan on going back to work full-time until Billy's eight-weeks-old at least, but I don't see any reason why he shouldn't come to the boutique with me, do you? With Grandma and Mommy both working there, the kid'll be spoiled rotten. So you don't need to worry, Auntie Kelly—I have no intention of

20

neglecting your one-and-only nephew. Is that for me?"

Barbara's eyes lit up as Kelly withdrew a cardboard box, wrapped in air-bubble wrapping paper, from amidst the layers of neatly folded clothing in the case she was unpacking.

"It is. Enjoy, brat!"

Kelly pulled out a dresser drawer and began stowing underthings inside them while Barb unwrapped her gift. Oohs and aahs of delight followed as an exquisitely crafted English cottage appeared, complete with tiny roses trailing about the door.

"It's signed and numbered by the artist, the genuine article. Nobody fools this kid," Kelly added, warmed by the broad grin on Barb's face. "You're still collecting miniature houses, I take it by that greedy smile?"

"Didn't you see them in the curio cabinet in the dining room? Never mind, I'll show you later. The little castle you sent me from Germany last Christmas is in there, too. Oh, Kelly, this is just perfect. Thank you!" Barb crossed the room and hugged her again.

"Don't mention it, m'dear," Kelly, embarrassed, dismissed in her best British accent. "Now, getting back to the boutique, are you sure you need me working there? This isn't a mercy hiring, is it?"

"No question about that, we need you, kid! Remember, I wrote and told you about Aunt Mary back in Illinois?"

"Your aunt who was ill?"

Barb nodded. "Right, my Aunt M. Well, the poor thing's taken a turn for the worst, apparently—cancer, I suspect, though Mom seemed vague about the details—and they decided to operate. Mom was only waiting for me to hatch before she flew back there to take care of her and Uncle Gene. She said with you coming home, she knew her grandson and I'd be in good hands. As usual, she was right. God, Kell, it's so good to have you here."

"And it's good to be here! So, where do you want these empty cases?"

"I'll have Bill store them in the attic first thing tomorrow. Oh, I know—! Don't look at me like that, Kelly, I know

21

you're planning on getting your own place as soon as you can, but there's no point in rushing things, is there? I thought after breakfast tomorrow, I'd take you to see the boutique. You've just got to meet this old man Mom hired to help out in the store before she left—he's incredible! Sam Cloud's his name, and believe me, he's quite a character!"

"Sam Cloud? With a name like that, he'd have to be!" Kelly grinned. "Don't tell me—he's Indian, right?"

"Full-blooded Hopi from the tribal reservation lands, and proud of it, too!" Barbara confirmed. "Anyway, his niece or some relative or other makes these beautiful coiled clay pots, and one day he shows up with a half-dozen of them at the store, and the rest's history. The next thing I know, Mom's telling him the story of her life—you know how Mom is?—and before the day's out, Sam's hired to help out around the store and Mom's making airline reservations! Our Sam's apparently a respected medicine man among his people, so not surprisingly he's heavy into mysticism—you know the type, surely? Sand painting, curing, the whole bit. A sort of poor man's answer to Shirley MacLaine! We'll have to have him do you, Kell—find out what's in the stars for you. Who knows, maybe our Sam'll see a tall, dark, and handsome millionaire coming your way!"

Kelly wrinkled her face in disgust. "After Tony, I can live without tall, dark, and handsome, thank you. I'll settle for a sweet, gentle, totally nonpossessive, totally nonviolent millionaire, if it's all the same to you."

"Was it that bad?" Barb murmured, her expression pitying.

"Worse! And I'll tell you all the lurid details some other time, promise. For now, let's go rescue poor Bill from the chores, before he starts wishing I'd never come!"

Chapter Two

After Barbara's glowing descriptions of Sam Cloud the evening before, Kelly fully expected the man to be something out of the ordinary, in some way eccentric-looking. After all, in their college days Barb had always possessed the knack of hooking up with the strangest people and mothering them, numbering among her more memorable protegées smuggled into their dorm at considerable risk, a tobacco-chewing bag lady named Corkie who swore colorfully and constantly, and spat just as often and as indiscriminately, a defrocked priest with a penchant for the bottle and nubile young college women, and a hooker whose dream had been to get a degree in veterinary medicine — a dream that had lasted all of eight months, when Barbara's enthusiasm for good works and spare cash had simultaneously run out, and with them, Candi!

But the following morning, when they arrived at Barbara's new boutique, the Paloverde — primely situated in the heart of the Old Scottsdale Shops on Scottsdale Road — Sam Cloud himself looked disappointingly ordinary at first glance.

Standing maybe five-feet five-inches tall, the diminutive Sam was a skinny, ordinary-looking Indian man of between sixty-five and seventy, or thereabouts. His straight white hair touched his shoulders, and he wore it cut in bangs across his brow and falling loose from beneath a floppy-brimmed black reservation Stetson that had seen better days. The crown boasted a band of huge silver *conchas* set with turquoise stones, and a black and white feather drooped over the brim. Despite the summer heat, he wore a long-sleeved, red-and-black-plaid flannel shirt buttoned up to the neck and at the wrists, and faded baggy denim jeans tucked into scuffed brown cowboy boots with worn-

23

out heels. He had the barrel-chested, slim-hipped build of his people. His eyes were arresting, though, Kelly decided; fine, black eyes that were bright with intelligence, amidst a welter of wrinkled brown skin. Their almond shape gave him the almost oriental look of a full-blooded Hopi, and his once-handsome, high-cheekboned face also boasted the broad, flattish nose of his race.

"You said he was a character," Kelly whispered reproachfully to Barbara when Sam, introductions completed, volunteered to fetch them coffee from the storeroom in back of the boutique. Coffee, apparently, was Sam's only discernible vice. He brewed and imbibed pot after pot of it, thick and dark, without eating anything—or at least, so Barbara had confided last night. "I expected a witch doctor's headdress or a feathered war bonnet at the very least, knowing your fascination with eccentrics!"

"He is *too* a character! Just give him a chance to warm up to you, then you'll see," Barbara promised. She turned her attention back to baby Billy who was cradled in her arms, clucking and cooing to him.

While they waited for Sam to bring the coffee, Kelly looked around the boutique. She admired the hanging stained-glass pieces Barb had raved about the night before, holding her hand behind them so that the sunshine falling through the door and windows patterned them with rainbow spectrums of color. She fingered the finely woven Navajo rugs and wall hangings that echoed the colors of the Painted Desert in all its vivid hues, sincerely impressed by the infinite patience and artistry that had clearly gone into their creation, and smiled at the curious little Zuni fetishes.

Thanks to Barbara's long-standing interest in Native American arts and crafts, and her relentless determination to immerse her dearest—if reluctant—friend in her own pleasures, Kelly'd been dragged to numerous arts and crafts shows, and had seen countless similar pieces in other boutiques before going to England with Tony. Inevitably, some of Barb's ability to discern good from bad or outright awful had rubbed off on her, with no voluntary effort at all on Kelly's part. She realised instinctively now that each of the special things Barb had filled her shelves and tables with had been chosen with love, and a discerning eye for authenticity, simplicity, and sheer beauty of design, color, texture, or craftsmanship. It was small wonder the Paloverde was drawing customers like bees to honey, despite the numerous other craft shops around it!

"Cream, no sugar, right, Kelly?" Barbara asked.

Turning around, Kelly saw that Sam had returned with a tray bearing two mugs.

"Here. This one is yours, Ms. Michaels."

"Thanks, Sam." Kelly reached out to take the cup Sam indicated with a grateful smile for the old man, at the same time stifling a yawn that popped out of nowhere.

"Too much talk and too little sleep last night, I think, eh?" Sam Cloud observed in his husky voice. He smiled. "It is the way of women."

He stood with the wide arc of sunlight pouring through the display window at his back. For a moment—as Kelly looked straight at him—the old man's features lay in heavy shadow, although the light surrounded his body like a golden aura.

Kelly frowned, rubbing smarting, gritty eyes. *Was* that Sam Cloud standing there before her, after all—or a customer she hadn't seen come in, whom she'd mistaken for the Indian man? For as she stared at him, Sam's hair seemed different, somehow; longer and darker. His huge hat had gone and was replaced by a narrow band of buckskin binding his brow. The plaid shirt and denims had gone, too, and a short kilt of antelope skin now covered his scrawny loins, leaving his chest bare. The snapping dark eyes had vanished as well; they were no longer bright and clear, but cloudy with cataracts. Why, it was as if someone else—someone who was not Sam Cloud—stood there in his place!

Look, my daughter! Look with the eye of the spirit, not the body! See me as I truly am! Alas, we have so little time, and much to accomplish!

The old Indian's mouth never moved, and yet . . . peculiarly, his voice seemed to be whispering strange words in

25

her ear. No, not in her ear. In her *mind!* In her confusion, Kelly flicked her head and blinked rapidly. At once, the fleeting impression of another man was gone, and with it the compelling voice. There was only Sam standing there, the coffee tray in his hands, his expression concerned.

"Are you feeling all right, Ms. Michaels?" he asked in his hoarse voice.

"Yes, Kell, you did look a bit pale for a minute there," Barbara added in concern. "I thought for a moment you were going to pass out on us! You're not coming down with anything, are you?"

"No, really, I'm fine!" Kelly covered. "Please, excuse the yawn! I think the jet lag must be catching up with me, or maybe it was the travel-sickness pills or something? Lord! I can't remember ever feeling this tired or—or disoriented!"

With a self-deprecating laugh, Kelly took a mug from Sam and gulped a swig of the coffee. It was very hot, strong, and felt wonderfully reviving going down. "Mmm, wonderful! I think I needed this more than I knew!"

"Mmm. Probably. It was a long flight, and we were up talking for hours, remember?" Barbara airily dismissed the matter; there was a gleam in her eyes now that Kelly recalled from the old days only too well. Barb, if she was not mistaken, was about to indulge her endless fascination in the occult in one of its weird and varied forms! Sure enough, she added too casually, "I think I mentioned last night that Sam's a highly respected medicine man among his people, didn't I? And that he does curing and sand paintings and stuff?" Barb asked, giving Kelly a hefty nudge in the ribs to remind her to play along.

Kelly nodded and tried to look suitably impressed. "I believe you did mention it, yes," she acknowledged dryly.

"Well, he promised to take a look at Billy's palm, didn't you, Sam, and see what the future has in store for him?"

Sam nodded gravely. "I certainly did. And what a fine little rabbit he is, too, Barbara! Big and strong and handsome as a bear—much like his father! Come to Grandfather Cloud, little friend, and let me see what life has in store for you."

26

Sam took Billy into his scrawny old arms with a grandfather's ease, and murmured some guttural words in Hopi as he smiled down at the infant. "Hope of the future," he translated for the two watching women, glancing over at them. "I called him Pride of his Father."

The baby focused his murky newborn eyes on the bobbing feather that trailed over Sam's hat brim, stirred gently to and fro in the draft from the air conditioner. He stared at it, fascinated as a baby rabbit as Sam took the baby's tightly furled fist in his gnarled brown hand and gently uncurled the fingers. They closed tightly about the Indian's own instead.

"Aah. I see a long life for this little rabbit, and a happy one, too," Sam said at some length in a quavering voice, looking intently into the infant's face. "Great riches will never come to him, not in the sense of material wealth as measured by the white man's world, but his life will be rich in other ways. I see him surrounded by family and friends, wrapped in a blanket of love and happiness all his days! To be loved is a great gift, is it not, Barbara? A mother could ask for no better for her child."

"There, you see, Billyums? Grandpa Sam Cloud says you're going to be loved to pieces, always and always. Thanks, Sam," Barbara said warmly, delighted by the old *shaman's* prophecy, judging by her expression. "Say . . . maybe you should tell Kelly her future next? See if there are any sweet, gentle husbands with a big, fat stock portfolio, and a future in oil, in the offing!" she teased, taking the baby from the old man and giving Billy a smacking kiss on the cheek that made him squeal and throw out his tiny fists in protest. "Excuse me a minute, you two—I left some paperwork back there the day I went into labor—taxes, unfortunately! I really should take them home to work on, before the IRS catches up with me. And, Master William Reid Douglas, I do believe I have someone's soaking wet bottom to diaper, too! I'll be right back, Sam, Kell. It'll just take a minute."

Kelly wasn't deceived by Barbara's tactful exit, and neither, she doubted, was Sam. Old he might well be, but he was certainly no fool. *Oh, Barb, darn it!* she groaned silently, wishing Barbara hadn't been so obvious, *Why can't you leave well enough alone, for once, and count me out of your harebrained fortune-telling!*

She felt curiously uncomfortable with the old man now that they were alone, badly in need of something to say to fill the sudden silence Barbara had left in her effervescent wake.

"I can't believe Barbara's accomplished so much in so little time, can you?" she gushed to ease the tension, looking about her in what she hoped was friendly pride and enthusiasm. "Six months, and already the Paloverde looks so — so thriving and — and permanent," she finished lamely.

"It is so. Barbara is a woman who embraces life eagerly and without fear, and with rather more emotion and enthusiasm than careful thought. Her heart, though, is a loving and caring one, and so she is surrounded by others who steady and guide her. But — enough of Barbara, for the time being! Let us speak instead of you, Kelly Michaels, and of your present life."

"You mean you want to tell me my future, right? Thank you, Sam, but no. There's really no point. You see, I don't believe in all that palm-reading and astrological nonsense!" She smiled, not wanting to hurt his feelings.

Sam appeared not in the least put-off by her refusal. "Perhaps you don't," he allowed amicably, his dark eyes fastened intently on her face. "But often, I've found a refusal to believe in anything but the obvious and the proven is nothing more than fear."

"Fear!" she exclaimed. "Fear of what?"

"Fear of the truth?" Sam posed. "Fear of discovering something about yourself that you have tried to deny? Fear of facing up to whatever it is, of dealing with it, before it destroys you?"

Ah ha. So that was it! Barb's Sam was really just another homespun pyschologist rather than a mystic! she realised, smothering the tiny burst of anger his glib and ambiguous explanations had detonated in her. Fear, indeed!

"Look at me, Kelly!" Sam said softly, and so suddenly

that Kelly jumped. "I have been waiting for you to come to me for a long, long time. Now that the moment is here, we have no time to lose. Look at me, and give me your hand!"

Despite his level tone, his voice suddenly had a distinct firmness, a compelling ring of authority to it. To Kelly's surprise, despite her reluctance she found herself turning to gaze deep into his eyes, into shimmering liquid depths that were like a bottomless, fathomless pool. Her will to resist him ebbed like an outgoing tide, and like a puppet, she extended her hand to him, letting Sam draw her down beside him onto one of the two chairs placed behind the antique cash register without protest.

"You have no parents, isn't that so?" Sam murmured. "Until you met Barbara, you were very much alone."

His voice seemed muffled and yet crystal clear all at once. His words penetrated her cottony thoughts. She jumped and jerked the hand Sam clasped between his leathery brown ones in surprise at his accuracy, before realising dimly that Barb or her mother, Margot, must have mentioned the fact that she was an orphan to the old man at some point. She smiled dreamily, feeling foolish for her childish reaction to his little parlor trick, and relaxed.

For a moment, she'd actually wondered if the funny old man didn't have some psychic powers after all.

"That's . . . that's incredible! You're absolutely right," she acknowledged in a patronising, sing song voice, deciding with part of her remaining will power to humor him. After all, great age should have some privileges. "That's me exactly—Little Orphan Annie in the flesh. A social worker told me that according to their records, I was found abandoned as a baby. I was raised by a steady stream of foster moms, shuffled from place to place, never really belonging anywhere. Margot—Barb's mom—and her husband Roy before he died, were my last foster family—and the very best I could have asked for. I guess that's why Barb and her family are so special to me. Barb's been like the sister I never had, and Margot's about the closest I've come to having a mother . . ."

Sam nodded, his attention riveted, Kelly noticed, not on

her words at all, but still gazing deeply into her eyes, as if plumbing the very depths of her soul. A darned peculiar way to tell fortunes, she thought uncomfortably, unable to deny the niggling feeling of unease gathering in her stomach now, but so sapped of strength she couldn't seem to find the willpower to stand up and walk away.

"The past two years have been unhappy ones for you, no? The man you thought you loved proved cruel, overly possessive. His is a violent, troubled spirit! He is perhaps what my people's legends call a Two-Heart—one whose spirit cannot find peace! He is no longer your man—but neither is he cast out of your life, despite what you believe. His past and yours return again and again to haunt you both, my daughter. You cannot escape it, and neither can he. You must fight, or the Evil One will destroy you!"

Damn that Barb and her big mouth! Kelly thought, annoyed as she realised that Barb must have betrayed her written confidences about Tony, too. *What else has she told him?* she wondered uncomfortably.

"Please, Sam, the past is over and done with," Kelly murmured sharply, her irritation rapidly building, though in all honesty she was angry at Barbara rather than Sam. "If it's all the same to you, I'd rather not rake it all up again. Read my palm or whatever, if you must, but stick to the future, please." Embarrassed by the sharpness of her words, she added almost apologetically, "You know, can't you tell me my destiny or my fate or something, instead?"

"Alas, I can tell you nothing of your destiny in this life, Kelly," Sam said in a voice laden with regret, "for in this life, my daughter, you have no destiny—no future! You see, your destiny still lies in the past. It is as yet unfinished."

"Oh, really? Well, I think I've had just about enough of this—this rubbish," Kelly snapped. Suddenly, she found the strength and the will to tear her hand from the old man's grasp and spring to her feet.

Her lovely face was pale, almost white about the lips, the only color two flushed spots of pink high on her cheekbones. "The very last thing I need right now is all this talk of doom and gloom. Please, Sam, that's more than enough! Obviously Barb's told you about my divorce and everything, so you must know enough to realise how painful it's been for me, and why I'd—I'd rather leave it buried."

"Ah, but we can't bury our past mistakes, child, however much we may want to. Don't you understand?" Sam Cloud said earnestly. "They follow us! They become the burdens we must bear in future lives, unless we understand them and deal with them. I can teach you how, daughter. Trust me! I have the power to help you, if you'll let me. That is why I'm here. That's why I've been waiting for you to come to me. Together, we can make the past right, and with it, restore hope to the future.

"Don't be afraid, my daughter! If you'll only step backwards and remember how it was, it can be done! We have so little time left to us now, for there are only a few short weeks remaining until my people celebrate the rites of Wuwuchim. Then the gateway between past and present will close, and it will be too late to go back—too late for both of us!

"Look, my daughter! Look into the face of Tawa, the Sun, and remember. Remember!"

Kelly heard the hypnotic drone of the old man's strained, sing song voice as if through a layer of batting. It sounded like the somnolent, rusty buzzing of a thousand bees. Eyelids drooping, she found herself drawn against her will to look at the silver disc he cupped now in his gnarled hand, and at the etching of a sun there. She couldn't look away! She felt her knees give as she resumed her former seat beside the man, and the warmth of Sam's hands enfolding her own and holding them tightly, tightly, strength and courage flowing from him to her.

Then the boutique was gone. The walls receded, like the walls of the Haunted House at Disneyland, flying back, back, and away. There were other walls surrounding her now; walls of stone, painted with ancient symbols. She could smell the scent of sage scattered on the flames of a fire, pungent and grassy; feel the warmth of the fire on her limbs. She lay on a hard rock floor, surrounded by paintings worked in lines of colored sand. And, as she gazed up above her, she could see the frosty glimmer of stars through a narrow chimney that led to the heavens above; hear the sound of voices chanting, chanting, and a muted heartbeat that was the throbbing of drums:

> "Past, present, and future, they are one!
> Woven together,
> In the cord of life.
> Grandmother, Mother, Daughter,
> Woven together.
> No past without present,
> No future without past.
> No Daughter without Mother.
> Without beginning,
> No end . . .

Then there was only Sam's voice; the hypnotic voice of Clouds Standing, her guardian spirit sent from Sotuqnangu, the Sky God. Lomahongva, Clouds Standing, leading her down the paths of memory. Leading her to the moment of her birth — and beyond.

Chapter Three

"How old are you, little lost one?" old Sam Cloud asked.

His quavery voice reached her as if echoing down a long, dark tunnel. Struggling to throw off the disorienting sensations that enmeshed her like the sticky filaments of a web, she tried very hard to remember . . .

"Six," came Kelly's drowsy reply after an endless pause. Her voice was as piping as a little girl's now as she proudly held up six fingers.

Barbara, about to return to the front of the boutique, stopped short in the doorway, a freshly diapered William tucked in the crook of one arm. Her mouth dropped open in shock as she heard the lisping, childish quality to Kelly's voice. Frowning, she darted Sam a questioning glance, obviously intending to comment, but the old man silenced her with a finger across his lips.

"Six!" Sam echoed approvingly in the same lulling voice. "And what a grown-up girl you are for only six winters, neh? Tell me, little one, where do you live?"

"At the fort," came the sing song child's voice again, and Barbara felt gooseflesh raise on her neck and down her arms as Kelly began swinging her legs slowly back and forth, and squirming her bottom in the chair like a fidgety first-grader.

"Ah. Then your father is a trooper?"

"Nope, he ain't, mister. My Pa's a blacksmith for t'fort, an' Mama takes in laundry and mendin' for the troopers. We live on Suds Row, y'see? Ma's hands is always rough an' red, jest like a chicken neck." She wrinkled her nose.

"She must work very hard," Sam acknowledged, nodding sagely. "And what about your name, little one—can you tell me it?"

"I surely can. I was baptized Mary Margaret Rose Kelly,"

the girl quickly supplied as if by rote.

"Good, very good. And where were you born, Mary Margaret?"

"Independence, Missouri, sir."

"And the year?"

"The year of our Lord, 1843."

Sam ignored Barbara's shocked gasp from across the boutique and with an admonishing hand raised to silence her once again, continued in the same level, calming voice, "And where is this fort where you live now? Is it also in Missouri?"

"Heck, no!" Kelly grinned, as if the very idea of the old man not knowing was an amusing one. "It's in Arizona Territory, sir! Fort Agave, Arizona. Aw, you knew that! You was jest funning me!"

"Ah, it is so, you're quite right, I knew it all along! But tell me, Mary, are you a happy little girl?"

"Yessir, I reckon so—'cept when Ma takes a switch to my tail. Then I ain't, much." She grimaced and her legs swung faster.

"Do you have any brothers or sisters, Mary?"

"Yes, sir—a passel of 'em!"

"Tell me about them, would you?"

"I reckon so," she began slowly, considering. "Well, first comes Sean, 'cos he's sixteen, see, an' the biggest of us Kelly kids. Then come the twins, Mikey and Patrick. They're always braggin' that they're gonna be Injun fighters some day soon, but Ma says, 'An' sure they will—over my daid body!' Then comes Brian—he's twelve—an' next comes me!

"The leprechauns—that's what my Pa calls 'em 'cos they're just little!—come next. They're twins, too, Seamus an' Bridget. They're only three, and they still bawl fer a sugar-tit nighttimes, when they're fretful," she disclosed with patent disgust. "Pa told 'em the 'Paches eat babies, an' that they'll come an' gobble 'em up, they don't quit their fussin'," Kelly grinned. "But Ma said 'That's more'n enough of that whisky talk, thank ye, Mr. Kelly. I'll not have ye scarin' my wee babes!' an' so Pa don't say it no more." She

34

grinned again, adding, "Leastways, not in Ma's hearin', he don't!

"Ma birthed another girl baby after me, but Deirdre didn't live more'n a day and a night after she was borned. She's an angel in Heaven now, rocked in the arms of the Virgin in Heaven."

Sam nodded. "What a fine, big family you have! But — let's move on now, shall we? Let's go on through two whole years, to your eighth birthday. Can you remember your eighth birthday, Mary Margaret?"

"No! I cain't!" It was said in a small voice; a little girl's voice, true, but a markedly defiant, whiney one now.

"Oh, but I think you can, if you try really hard, Mary. Won't you tell me about it?"

"No! Don't *want* to!" Kelly's childlike voice had gone from shrill to a hoarse whisper. She sounded terribly frightened, almost choked with tears, and it was all Barbara could do to keep herself from flying to her friend's side to comfort her.

"Come, come, you're only remembering, child! Whatever happened that day no longer has the power to hurt you. It is past, done with, and you are here and safe. Tell me about that day, Mary. Describe everything that happened on your eighth birthday to Grandfather Cloud. I know, you can tell it as if it was a story — as if it happened to another Mary Margaret, neh?" Sam suggested softly.

To Barbara's surprise, she saw Kelly shudder and slowly nod. There were tears glistening on her cheeks as she drew a deep breath and began:

Ma Kelly had unexpected company that hot July morning and Mary Margaret was sulking.

It was her birthday — her eighth — and Ma had been promising for weeks that on that special day, they'd cut out the length of blue-and-white gingham Pa'd got from the trading post up north, and sew her a pretty new dress for her First Communion.

But now, now that stuck-up Missus McHenry'd come calling, an' Ma was boiling tea and baking soda bread and setting out the company dishes and the good teapot 'stead of

35

the reg'lar cracked old brown one. There'd be no dress cut out today, t'be sure, and the old one'd have to do for church on Sunday yet again!

Mary's lower lip quivered with a mixture of disappointment and anger. Friday afternoon, she'd boasted her head off to all the girls in the fort's one-room schoolhouse that she'd be wearing a fine new dress come Sabbath morning— one that'd make Liza Yorke's new pink one look downright shabby. But now she'd have to wear her stifling old gray linsey-woolsey, and they'd all poke fun at her and taunt her with, "Liar, Liar, pants on fire!"

Her piquant face set in a furious, red-cheeked scowl under a dishevelled mop of thick, dark hair, Mary Margaret scuffed her booted feet through the dust outside the Kellys' quarters. Built of stone plastered with adobe, it was one of a row of dwellings inhabited by the fort's laundresses and their families, known as Suds Row. Before the Kellys' dwelling, there was a rickety pig sty containing a half-dozen hogs and a dusty wallow, and a few scrawny chickens scratching half-heartedly in the sand, looking for lizards.

Mary was peculiarly satisfied as her actions raised red, powdery clouds all about her like smoke, before the dirt settled again. She pretended she hadn't noticed the two lines of snowy wash her mother'd slaved hours over, bleaching and steaming as it dried in the desert heat.

The day offered not even a breath of wind, and the air was clear and dry. The distant White Mountains shimmered under a shifting blue heat-haze, and the fierce desert heat also made the cacti seem to jiggle about as if they were dancing, seen through rifle-slits in the stockade's adobe walls. The vault of azure sky arching over the fort was brilliant blue, unmarred by even a wisp of cloud, and the sun was a bright white ball that hurt your eyes so bad, you couldn't look at it without goin' stony blind, Brian'd told her once. If only it would rain, she thought petulantly. If only somethin' would change, somethin' exciting would happen . . .

"Mary Margaret, shame on you, ye young divil! You just stop that dust-raisin', ye hear me? If I have to scrub that laundry over, I'll

36

take a strop t'your tail, ye little imp o' Satan, jest see if I don't!"

"Sorry, Ma," Mary responded by rote, without even turning to glance over at the doorway through which her mother had thrust her head like a turtle to scold her. If she had, she'd have seen how exhausted Kathleen Kelly appeared. There were sweat-sodden wisps of hair framing her pretty face, and her heavy belly—already swollen again with another child beneath her dark skirts—pained her, although she caressed her burden with reddened hands.

Instead, Mary stuck out her tongue as she caught her brother, Brian's shining, laughter-filled eyes, as bright blue as morning glories over the rim of the pig trough. He was slopping the hogs, his first chore of the day.

"Eight years old, t'be sure, an' still the wild look of a banshee and the bogs about ye! When will ye become a proper lady, Miz Mary Margaret Rose, instead of a rat-tailed hoyden?"

"When you're a man, Brian Kelly—which like as not won't be 'til the moon turns blue!" she retorted, making a horrible face at him.

"Happy birthday, Mary Margaret. Many happy returns!"

Mary Margaret turned around, Brian and his teasing instantly forgotten. A grateful smile lifted the corners of her mouth and poked merry dimples of pleasure in her plump little cheeks on hearing that someone—anyone!—had remembered her birthday.

But the smile faded to a frown when she saw who her well-wisher was. 'Faith! 'Twere only that horrible Dane McHenry, Missus McHenry's pampered sissy of a son!

He had curly, wispy hair the waxy color of saguaro blossoms. His complexion was the same ghastly shade as curdled milk, and his tall, gangly twelve-year-old frame was dressed in knee britches, like a much younger boy. Oh, he was a prize package, was Dane, the butt of all the cruel teasing and name-calling Fort Agave's schoolchildren could dream up, Mary among them!

"I can do without your well-wishes, God rot ye, Dane McHenry," she said rudely and with huge relish. She'd been wanting to say God rot ye aloud for weeks, ever since hearin' one of Pa's soldier friends say it to Captain McHenry's Injun scouts, but without a suitable victim on hand—'til now!

"And if God don't, me boyo, then our Mary Margaret surely will!" Brian observed, grinning infuriatingly.

Mary flashed him a look of pure fury. It was one thing for her to bad-mouth Dane, but quite another to have Brian join in and make sport of the one and only person who'd wished her well on her birthday.

"Take no notice of *himself*, Dane," she advised the McHenry boy, eyeing Brian scathingly. "He spends so long with the hogs, he don't know how t'act 'round people no more. Acts like a hog hisself, he does—an' smells like one, too!" she shot over her shoulder as she dragged a bewildered Dane away.

Dane, although none too bright, was nevertheless smart enough to know that somehow the tide of Mary Margaret's temper had turned favorably in his direction. He shut up and let her lead him off without a squeak of protest.

The two children plodded down the hard-packed dirt streets that had been marked off between the fort's hastily erected adobe walls. As they went, they passed the corrals, the commissary, the guardhouse, the parade ground, the sutler's, the barracks, the armory, the officers' quarters, the stores, and her father's forge and the like. An occasional trooper nodded or winked at them as they trotted along, but although Dane beamed at these signs of recognition from the men he so admired, Mary never even noticed.

Her thoughts were occupied in thinking up ways to make everyone sorry for neglecting her on her birthday!

'Twould serve them all right if she fell into the horse trough and drownded. Aye, 'twould serve the lot o' them right if she strayed away from the fort's tall adobe walls in her upset, and got captured and horribly killed by wild savages—*then* they'd be sorry and cry, and wish they'd been nicer, t'be sure!

She frowned, suddenly unconvinced that even such dire measures as her death would wring the guilt she craved from her Ma. She and Pa had so many children, maybe they wouldn't even notice one was missing? She gulped and choked back tears of self-pity. It was a sobering thought if you were only eight, that no one would miss you if you were drownded to death, or chopped into bloody, gooshy little pieces . . .

"Let's go in here," Dane suggested, his pale blue, red-lidded eyes reminding Mary of an albino rabbit she'd seen once. "I—I got somethin' to show you."

"In the stables? Oooh, whatever is it?" she demanded, all ears now.

"I can't show you out here, Mary Margaret. It's a—it's a secret."

"For my birthday? Oh, goodie!" Her blue eyes suddenly brightened.

"Er—sort of," Dane agreed vaguely. "Come on, if you're coming!"

Childish avarice won out over common sense and her innate dislike of the McHenry boy. Mary allowed Dane to take her grubby hand and lead her inside the stables, where the bales of fodder only added to the heat.

It was dark inside the lofty building after the bright glare of outside. Mary blinked like an owl in the gloom for a moment or two before getting her bearings. Stalls ranged either side of the stables, each one with an opening onto the parade ground beyond to let in air; each one boasting a well-groomed bay or gray mount, ample evidence that the men of the Bay, or the Gray, troop respected good horse-flesh. Pitchforks and shovels were ranged tidily to one side, and rough shelves held brown glass bottles of smelly horse liniment and such. Another wall was hung neatly with well-oiled tack, and bits and bridles gave off a dull wink in the meager light. A calico cat uncurled from a hay bale and stretched lazily, walking aloofly away from the intruding pair to find a new spot in which to doze undisturbed.

"All right. Where's my surprise?"

"Up in the loft. Come on!" Dane urged, his pale blue eyes sort of glittery-looking now.

Mary had never seen Milksop McHenry's face so animated! It must be quite some present, she thought eagerly,

39

to make that ole Dane McHenry so all-fired lively! She obediently clambered up the loft ladder after him, hoisting her white pinafore and scratchy gray serge frock way above her scabbed little knees to do so.

"Well? Can I have it now?" she demanded impatiently when the two of them were seated amidst the piles of hay in the loft. It was scratchy but sweet-smelling there in the fort's granary, and sunlight flooded through the rectangular opening. Dust motes swirled lazily in its rays, like gold dust in a miner's sieve, reminding Mary of her father and older brothers' departure several mornings ago.

The fort had been built just a year ago as an outpost and way station, to supply and shelter the rush of would-be miners headed west over the mountains to California by the Gila River Route in search of gold. Just a few weeks ago, there'd been reports of gold nuggets being discovered along the Gila itself, and Pa had been itching to join the placers and try to raise a little "color" for himself.

"Ah, Kat'leen, mavourneen, with just a wee nugget or two t'me name, I'll be after clothin' ye in the foine silks an' satins your fresh young beauty deserves!" he'd said dreamily, bussing Kathleen Kelly's cheek. But her mama had been less enthusiastic.

"Gold nuggets, indaid! Foine silks an' satins, indaid!" she'd scoffed. "Just have a care them red savages don't put an end t' yer wild schemes, Mr. Donovan Kelly!"

Still, Mama'd laughed and wished him well. She'd even given him a farewell peck on the cheek as he rode off with his strapping sons to spend a fortnight trying his luck alongside the other placers on the Gila.

A winch and a pulley dangled outside an opening in the hayloft, like a noose from a gallows. It was operated as needed to raise or lower heavy bales to and from the ground below. Hanging onto it, Mary angled precariously out of the upper storey. From here, if she squinted some, the distant mountains were a hazy lavender blue, rugged and craggy as fresh-baked biscuits, topped with swirls of whipped cream clouds.

"Close your eyes, Mary Margaret, and I'll give you a big

40

surprise!" Dane promised unsteadily.

Coming back inside, Mary obediently closed them.

"Ready yet?" she asked seconds later, her dark lashes quivering against rosy cheeks as she fought the urge to peek. Inside her tummy, she was all trembly with excitement.

"Almost," Dane promised again, breathing heavily as he fumbled with something.

"Now?" she demanded, squirming with impatience.

"Soon," Dane panted, and she thought he sounded strangled, somehow. "First, you gotta promise not to tell anyone 'bout this, all right, Mary? No one, never!"

"No one?" she asked, her eyes tightly squeezed shut, her little body quivering all over with anticipation. A present she couldn't show anyone? What could it be? "Never? Why not? Why can't I tell?"

"Never mind why not, just swear you won't. Cross-your-heart-and-hope-to-die-stick-a-needle-in-your-eye!"

Mary quickly crossed her heart, hoping nothing of the sort. "Aren't you ready yet, Dane?"

"All right. I—I s'pose you can look now."

Expectantly, a pair of wide, deep blue eyes blinked open. It took Mary a full ten seconds of glancing this way and that about the hay-scented loft to realize that there was no present in sight. Rather, Dane McHenry was standing proudly before her with his breeches' buttons unfastened and his boy's thing exposed.

"Well?" he asked breathlessly, his pale eyes excited. "Do you like my surprise, Mary?"

"That's *it?* That's all?" she squeaked, almost in tears with disappointment as visions of new hair ribbons or a fluffy baby kitten or a striped peppermint humbug twist popped like burst soap bubbles. "That—that ugly-looking ole thing is my—my present?"

His boy-thing looked like a small, pointy finger standing out from the front of his blue bib-pants, as if he'd cut Mister Thumbkin off his hand and stuck it there with paste instead! Oh, Jumpin' Jaysus an' all t' saints in Heaven, that awful Brian would *never* stop laughing at her if he found out

41

about these shenanigans, she thought ruefully. She silently vowed he never would, not from her, so help her God! Not even wild Injuns could make her tell!

"Ugly?" Dane protested. His feelings were hurt, his pride utterly destroyed by her scornful tone and withering scowl. Worse, she hadn't even seemed shocked or frightened. That, at least, would have been something!

Scowling horribly, he flipped his rejected member back inside his dungarees with a wounded expression, fumbling over the buttons in his haste as he argued, "It is not ugly!"

"Is too! T'ugliest ever—and the smallest!"

"An' how would you know, you stupid little baby? You don't even have one!"

"Aye, to be sure, but I've got brothers, ain't I, ye blathering idjit? An' compared to them, Dane McHenry, your little willie's purely dyin' of starvation, an' that's a fact!" she goaded triumphantly, her hatred for him even fiercer now that he'd made a fool of her. Present indeed!

"All right, maybe it is a mite small—but that's 'cos I ain't finished growin' yet! It's—it's different for boys', see." He paused. "Mary?"

"Aye?"

"Let me see what you got down there instead, hmmm?" Dane suggested unsteadily but slyly, wetting his lips. "Come on, Mary Margaret, show me—*please?*"

He suddenly sat down in the hay beside her, and reached for the ruffled hem of her pinafore, intending to peek up her skirts. He withdrew his hand quickly when she soundly boxed his ears and his wandering paw.

"Oh, c'mon, please, Mary, show me? Go on . . . pretty Mary . . . pretty, pretty please?" he begged. "You're so cute, Mary, and I ain't—I ain't never seen how a—how a girl looks—down there—before. I showed that Lucy Langtree mine last Christmas. She said she'd show me hers back, but she never did. That stinkin' snot-nosed little liar, she just shrieked and ran away. Oh, come on, Mary, let me peek! Just a little peek, an' I'll kiss you, an' tell you where babies come from, an' how they get made . . . *promise!*"

"Why, you stinkin' old buzzard, Dane McHenry! The

divil I'll show you me—me personal parts!" Mary exploded, springing to her feet with her little fists planted on her hips and her deep blue eyes flashing her outrage. "You jest wait 'til my Pa and big brothers get back from the Gila! I'll tell 'em all what you wanted me to do—an' your snooty ole' Mama, too! My Pa'll nail your pink coyote hide t' the corral fence—aye, and that lil' old pink worm with it, t'be sure!" She stuck out her tongue just as far as it would go, then crossed her eyes horribly.

"Oh, yeah? Well, just you go ahead and try, Miz Smarty Pants Kelly, an' I'll tell them *you* wanted to see it!" Dane countered triumphantly, at his most vicious when cornered. "Everyone knows you're a brat, always up to no good—my Mama's said so, dozens of times. I'll tell 'em you just kept on bugging me to show you, and they'll believe *me,* not you, 'cos *my* pa's a Captain! 'Sides, my mother won't believe a word you say, anyway," he crowed, " 'cos her folks were St. Louis quality, an' you Kellys ain't nuthin' but a bunch of stupid Irish 'taters' an' pig-farmers. Everyone here says the Kelly brats are dirty little snot-nosed Catholic heathens who—!"

He never managed to complete his insult. A furious heathen Kelly fist shot out of nowhere and slammed hard into his nose, sending eye-watering pain exploding through him. Blood spurted and dripped onto the golden hay at his feet. Abruptly, Dane sat down, tears filling his eyes.

"You—you broke my nose, Mary Kelly!" he wailed nasally, strings of pink-tinged snot pouring down over his lips and chin. "I hate you!"

Mary tossed her head, about to retort in kind. But in that same moment, she heard sounds from outside—terrifying sounds she'd dreaded hearing almost half of her short life: bloodthirsty whoops and curdling yells . . . shots being fired . . . horses screaming in terror . . . and men and women's panicky cries . . . !

Dane forgotten, Mary flung about and scrabbled on hands and knees to the edge of the hayloft, kneeling at the edge of the winch opening—which commanded a view clear across the fort's compound—with her fingers arched like claws over the splintering wooden edge.

Oh, please, no! Let it be a false alarm! Oh, no, no no nonono—!

As she'd feared, the Apaches—ever a threat to the isolated outpost—had finally attacked! Somehow they'd gotten through the high gates or scaled the cactus-topped adobe walls to overrun the fort and its compound!

Spotted mustang ponies, each one bearing a dark-skinned savage, were careening down the main street of Fort Agave. Apache riders leaned low from their mounts' backs to let loose a deadly hail of arrows or a few bullets as they whooped their savage war cries.

A handful of troopers had taken up positions behind the shuttered windows of the barracks, the general store, and other buildings. They were returning the Apaches' fire through the firing slits, but even an eight-year-old girl could count, and Mary knew the soldiers were desperately outnumbered. Two of the fort's three troops had left Fort Agave a little over a week ago, acting as escort to some beleaguered miners headed for Old Spanish Crossing—the pass through wild, hostile mountain terrain that led to California. Confident the small outpost offered no enticing prize for an Apache raiding party, Colonel Nicholls had left only a handful of troopers and civilian families behind to defend it.

Ma! The twins! And Brian—! Oh, Blessed Mary in Heaven, she had to get home. She had to be with them, whatever happened!

Her mouth working soundlessly, Mary whirled about and started scrabbling backward down the hayloft ladder, taking two rungs at a time.

"Don't leave me, Mary! Please! I'm scared!" Dane blubbered, his face an ashen moon in the instant before she'd clambered too far down the ladder to see him any longer. But Mary didn't heed him. She didn't even hear! Her every thought was on home, on reaching the cabin at the end of Suds' Row, on finding Ma and hanging onto her just as hard and as tight as she could. Ma could make the terror go away with just a touch of her rough, red hands, Ma could. Ma could make things safe and right again. She

44

could do anything, Ma could. Oh, she could, she could, she could—!

The fervent prayer became a litany as she fled for home, running like a wild thing down the hard-packed earth. With a whoop of glee, an Apache warrior rounded a corner and spotted the small girl. He wheeled his nimble pony about to follow her, his lance raised.

Mary sensed rather than saw or heard the savage coming up fast behind her. Reacting blindly, she flung herself off the open street and through the sutler's door, hoping the sturdy walls would offer sanctuary.

Recoiling in horror, she saw the sutler, Jedd Turnbull, impaled by a feathered lance through his belly to the saw-dusted floor. His dead eyes were still wide with the agony and horror of his final moments, his scalp raw and bloody where a tuft of his curly black hair was missing!

Mamaaaa! she screamed, but no sound came out of her mouth.

As she stood there, stunned into immobility, someone padded silently out of the whisky shadows and trailed a gruesome trophy across her cheek, leaving a sticky trail of what had to be blood on her face.

Mister Turnbull's scalp!

Mary let out a shriek and spun about as brown arms clawed for her hair, her clothes. Copper-skinned male bodies—reeking of bear grease and smoke and Jedd Turnbull's liquor—jostled around her, whooping raucously. She twisted and squirmed, evading the cruel hands that reached for her, and somehow managed to get free, diving between a forest of wiry brown legs, baggy white pants, and dangling breechclouts.

Despite all odds against it—or maybe because the braves were reeling drunk—she broke free and managed to reach the rear door of the sutler's store. She tumbled through it and spilled out into the blinding sunlight on a tide of guttural voices raised in whoops of drunken laughter, narrowly missing tripping over Mrs. Turnbull, fat Mrs. Turnbull, lying in the dirt with only a bloody expanse of raw meat were her long, frizzy blond hair used to be. She was having

45

her clothes cut off her by yet another Apache brave, who crouched over her with a huge skinning knife in hand.

The brave leered wolfishly at Mary from a red-and-black-painted face as she pulled up short, tottering in shock, before careening on down the row of buildings until she reached the Kelly cabin, silent screams pouring from her little mouth every step of the way.

But what she found at the cabin made her want to close her eyes and never open them again.

To plug her ears and never hear again.

To sew up her lips and never speak or laugh again.

Brian lay in the hog pen, surrounded by slaughtered hogs stuck through with so many arrows, they looked like porcupines. Her brother'd taken a single arrow through the chest, and his linen shirt was soaked with blood and crawling with shiny blue flies. His morning glory eyes were closed, and he was so still—so very, very still—she knew he had to be dead.

"No! No! It can't be, it can't!" she sobbed, and turned and ran for the cabin; ran for it as hard and as fast as she could, as if it were her only hope left, the only sanity remaining in a world gone crazy. Ma was there. Ma, with her big red hands and her tired smile. She'd be all right soon, she'd be safe, if only . . . if only . . . if only she could . . . just get . . . to Ma . . .

But Ma would never cuddle her again, nor scare away the nightmare monsters from her sleep. She'd never do any of the loving mother-things she used to do, because Ma was dead, too. Mary saw it the second she entered the cabin, and knew in that instant that her childhood was over, and that nothing and no one could ever bring it or her mama back again.

Ma and Rachel McHenry lay sprawled across the freshly sanded cabin floor on their backs. Their throats had been cut, their calico dresses had been torn from their bodies, their naked legs were bloody and obscenely spread. Mrs. McHenry's sapphire necklace had broken as she struggled for life, Mary observed with a tiny, still-thinking part of her mind. The sapphire beads had rolled every which way over

46

the hard-planked floor. *Better pick 'em up, Miz McHenry! Ma's mighty houseproud, aye, t'be sure!*

She reeled away and vomited onto the braided rag rug, her little belly heaving over and over until only bile remained to sting her throat. She ground her clenched fists against her stomach until there was nothing left inside her but the roaring agony in her little heart—and crushing, enormous guilt.

Logic had no place, no, not here, not in this suddenly illogical world. Somehow, in her shock and terror, the naughty things Dane McHenry had wanted her to do in the hayloft seemed inextricably entwined with all the horror and death about her. If only she hadn't gone with him, greedy for a gift, maybe she'd have spotted the Apaches sneaking up on the fort, and could have sounded an alarm . . . ? Maybe she could have gotten back to the cabin sooner, done something—*something!*—to save Ma and poor, poor Brian? Oh, Brian, Brian—! He of all her brothers had been her favorite, the one who teased her and taunted her, but always, always made time for her . . . !

Silent sobs wracked her. Her little face contorted, she sank to her knees in the puddle of congealing blood beside her mother's body with her head bowed, her shoulders heaving. Summoning all of her courage, she gripped the hem of her mother's skirt and pulled it down to cover her shame. The Apaches had surely gone, leaving the mother she loved violated and dead, her brother with an arrow through his chest, and the twins—!

Her heart skipped a beat.

The twins.

Where on earth were they? What had happened to them? Had the Apaches ridden away and taken little Bridget and Seamus with them? Or were they, too, horribly dead somewhere? She swallowed the enormous knot in her throat. Oh, there were so many things to be afraid of, to worry over, each one taken alone overwhelming of itself. Together, they seemed insurmountable to the child!

But then, suddenly, she realized that muffled sounds were echoing her own sobs. They were coming from somewhere nearby, she realized. Rising slowly to standing, a spark of hope kindling in her breast, she softly called, "Seamus? Bridget? Oh, please, dearlings, tell me where you are! 'Tis only me, Mary Margaret! For the love o' God, where are ye?"

She followed the heartrending sobs, ducking under the cloth partition into her parent's sleeping area in the second room of the cabin.

The crying had stopped again now, and she stood there, looking about her as she waited for further sounds. A rough-hewn ladder ran up to the small loft above where her older brothers, Sean, Mike, and Pat, made their bed. The younger twins had slept in a wooden drawer alongside their parents' rawhide bed, while she'd always had the cosiest corner, a straw pallet by the hearth. She shuddered. She doubted she'd ever feel cosy again.

"Mamaaaa!"

There it was again, that same muffled whimpering! It seemed as if it were coming from the barrels at the rear of the room. Stuffed with straw, they'd carried the Kellys' few pieces of stoneware from Independence to Arizona two years ago when her Ma and Pa'd made the long journey west by wagon train, Brian'd told her. But now, emptied of their former contents, they served as little tables on which to stand the lanterns of a night, so that Pa could read his Bible, and Ma her poetry. The whale-oil lanterns were still standing on them.

Certain of what she'd find beneath the barrels, knowing without a shadow of a doubt that Ma had hidden the twins inside them moments before she'd lost her life, Mary started toward them—but then some sixth sense froze her in place. Pa had always claimed she was the fey one of the family, and now that intuitive quality served her well.

"Shut up, you two!" she hissed sternly, rapping her knuckles on the side of one of the barrels. "Make so much as a squeak, I'll see our Pa whups ye good, d'ye hear me now?"

Turning about, she saw that her instincts had not played her false. Even as she looked desperately about her for a

48

hiding place of her own, an Apache brave's threatening silhouette filled the doorway, and her heart stopped beating with terror.

His face was garishly painted for war in blood red and sooty black stripes, as his savage brothers' had been. His shoulders were as broad as her Pa's, and he stood near as tall as her brother Sean. The top of his head grazed the lintel. A red bandanna had been wound about his forehead and knotted to one side, the ends left trailing. Thick blue black hair fell unbraided to his shoulders. He wore a leather vest, adorned with silver *conchas*, over a spotted dark blue shirt with long tails, which he'd left loose and belted with another strip of red cloth at the waist. Below, he wore a breechclout over loose white cotton pants, and thigh-length leggings of soft, tan-colored doeskin.

Mary swallowed, her throat muscles frozen so tight in fear that not even a scream could escape it. Her heart thudding so loud and so fast it seemed it might explode, she somehow managed to remember the twins, silent and frightened, hidden only inches behind her. Her thoughts were all on protecting them as the Apache padded silently toward her. She daren't think of anything ese, or she knew she'd scream . . .

The Apache halted, towering over her like a painted demon straight from hell.

"Please, mister," she managed to whisper hoarsely. "Oh, please, mister, please, please don't hurt me! I'm the only one left — !"

Whether he understood her words or no, the brave's glance darted from her pale face to the cabin. His glittering black eyes travelled over the straw pallets, the ladder, the two barrels, before returning contemptuously to her face.

Hush, little ones! Not a sound! she prayed silently, and to her relief, there was none. In the uneasy hush, she could hear her own heart beating, and the rush and roar of the blood in her veins . . .

The Apache grunted something and stepped closer. Bending, he thrust his cruel face full into hers, so that she could smell the grease with which he'd oiled his body and

49

painted his face; male, bloody, and smoky, too, like half-cooked meat. Fighting the urge to gag, she closed her eyes and swallowed her terror as he gripped her chin and turned her face this way and that.

For moments that seemed endless, he inspected her with eyes almost as black as coal; eyes without a shred of either compassion or pity. Then he released her to look about him again, his keen hunter's instincts warning him that something was awry.

She saw his attention shift, and panic filled her. Tales she'd heard—of how bloodthirsty, murdering Apaches slew little babies by taking their ankles and dashing out their brains against a rock—filled her with nightmare visions of that fate befalling Seamus and Bridget. Ma and Pa would never forgive her if that happened!

Thrusting out her fist to the brave, she uncurled her fingers to reveal two blue beads lying on her palm. Damp with her sweat, they glinted in the meager light falling through the slitted window.

With a start, Mary realized numbly that they were two of the dozens of spilled blue beads from Mrs. McHenry's broken necklace. But, still in a stupor of sorts brought on by shock, she was unable to recall picking them up. In her horror, she must have done so without even knowing it!

The Apache warrior took the beads from her, and gave a guttural laugh. The beads were the exact same color as the paleface child's eyes, as deep blue as the sky when the Thunder Spirit spoke!

"Is this all you have to offer in trade for your pretty scalp, Blue Beads Girl?" he jeered, but the blankness to her expression showed she'd not understood his tongue, and he grunted again.

Mary felt a little ray of hope spread through her. He hadn't killed her—yet. Would he accept her trade, then? Would he spare her life, in return for the two blue beads she'd offered him? *God, please, please make him accept!*

The Apache added the beads to the drawstring medicine pouch at his throat, then jabbed a brown finger at her chest. Seeing her confused expression, he gripped her upper arm and hauled her to standing. Pointing to the pouch and then to her, he made signs, and her flicker of hope fizzled and died. His meaning was all too clear; he had decided that both she *and* the beads now belonged him! And, if she wanted to put up a struggle — well, the finger he drew slowly across his brown throat before touching the long sheath at his thigh was easy enough to understand . . .

Close to fainting from fright, Mary swallowed and tottered on her heels. Before she could fall into merciful oblivion, the Apache gripped her roughly by her thick brown hair, dragged her outside into the blazing sunlight, and tossed her up onto the back of his waiting pony.

As they galloped away, Mary clinging to the Apache's waist for grim death, she thought she heard the twins. Little Bridget's plaintive sobs and Seamus's whimpers seemed to echo over and over in her ears, long after the Apaches had carried her far from Fort Agave:

"Mary, come back! Mary, don't leave us! We'll be good! Mary! Mareeeeeeee!"

Then there was only the vast silence of the open desert. . . .

Chapter Four

The Apache warrior behind whom Mary rode didn't seem to care if she was there or not! He just rode and rode, obviously fearing pursuit. All the terrified eight-year-old could do was cling to his waist, and hope and pray she didn't fall from the pony and become trampled under its galloping hooves, and that he—the Indian she'd silently christened Rattlesnake—didn't intend to kill her when they stopped—*if* they ever stopped, which she was beginning to doubt . . .

It was dusk when they finally halted. The fiery sun had slipped bloodily over the rim of the mountains to the west and disappeared, leaving the desert silent and purple all about them. In the dusk, the gray green cactus looked like dwarves with their arms raised, as if trying desperately to trap the vanishing light. Stars came out one by one. Their frosty wink was the diamond glitter of demon eyes, peering slyly down at the world below through a curtain of dark sky. When the milky moon rose, her cold light painted the foothills, arroyos, and stark mesas with gray and silver, picking out the shimmer of evening dew on a patch of grass here, the wicked gleam of an Apache eye there, or the glitter of a knife blade.

Other Apaches escaping the fort had joined the one she called Rattlesnake as they galloped away. Many of them had also taken captives and loot, along with the dozen or so horses and mules they'd stolen from the fort's corrals and her father's smithy, which they drove before them.

Mary recognised twelve-year-old Liza Yorke from school, clinging desperately to her Indian captor's waist, and fourteen-year-old Hiram Turnbull who'd helped in his father's sutler's store, flopping unconscious over the back of another pony. Pretty Missus Whitman, the doctor's wife, was there, too, her face dazed and empty-looking and white as a winding-sheet in the moonlight. There were two other women and three men who were familiar to Mary by sight, but she didn't know their names. Two of the men were troopers. They wore blue uniforms and remained grim-faced and silent. The other, a civilian, cried a lot and called on God to help him, until the Apache who'd captured him silenced him with the butt of his tomahawk. Somehow, the utter silence that followed seemed worse.

The Apache ponies and mules flew over the stony ground, headed for what looked like a shadowy forest of thorns in the foothills of the mountains. When they reached it, they rode single file through a narrow opening in the thorny wall that soon became a tunnel leading through a growth of tangled chaparral, herding the stolen horses and mules ahead of them.

The thick growth opened up into a large clearing littered with brush lean-tos or wickiups, the dwellings of the Apache, surrounded by prickly, concealing walls. The chaparral offered a well-concealed hideout; one the Apaches obviously considered a haven safe from either retaliation or discovery by the paleface long-knives, for they immediately relaxed their guarded manner and whooped and laughed in triumph, strutting like cocks as they appraised the booty their raid had yielded; iron kettles, lengths of calico cloth, red trade blankets, military jackets with shiny gold buttons, horses—and captives.

The Apaches, Mary saw now, were clothed in bright calico shirts they'd obviously stolen on other raids, or in the loose white cotton *calzones* or breeches of Mexican peasants, while others were bare-chested and wearing breechclouts and vests. Some of them immediately donned the stolen jackets and peacocked about, aping the stiff-backed stride of paleface cavalry officers and growing steadily more raucous and wild as they passed jugs and bottles of liquor about their band.

Rattlesnake dragged Mary to the ground by her hair like all the others had been dragged, jolting her so roughly from his mustang's back that her feet—which had long since gone to sleep—were slammed against the hard ground. Needles of pain exploded through her scalp and her legs, and she cried out in agony.

Seeing her pained expression, hateful Rattlesnake shot her a pleased, malevolent grin which quite froze the whimper on her lips. Oh, Blessed Mary! His face was terrifying—like something out of her darkest nightmares! He was flat-featured, his reddish brown skin stretched taut over high cheekbones. Narrow, glittering black eyes and thick, sneering lips gave him a savage, inhuman cast that was so terrible and fascinating, she couldn't look away, but only stared at him mutely from wide, deep blue eyes that hardly blinked at all.

Rattlesnake touched the little pouch he wore at his throat—into which he'd tossed the two blue beads she'd offered in trade for her life—and uttered some guttural words, jeering as he did so, and eyeing her speculatively from a garishly painted face in which his dyes glittered like a snake's.

"You be my woman soon, eh, Blue Beads Girl? Young girl, she sweet like ripe peaches, not tough and bony like old mule meat!" And he threw back his head and roared with drunken laughter.

Mary sensed from his tone that he was goading her—maybe hoping to force some reaction from her that he could answer with blows. Something of her obstinate Irish nature reasserted itself, driving out a little of the fear—or maybe, just maybe, it was pure childish outrage at his cheating her, after a lifetime of being taught that fair play was everything? Whatever the reason, he was a dirty liar, aye, t'be sure he was! An' a doublecrossin' cheat, too, t'take her beads and then refuse t'let her go. *God rot him* if she'd let this—this ugly spalpeen see she was afraid of him!

"Laugh at me all y' want, y' yeller-bellied son of the Divil!" she shouted fiercely. "I'm a Kelly, and the Kellys ain't afeared o'the likes o'ye, ye godless, ugly, double-dealin' heathen, so there!"

Her desperate tactic had the desired effect. When she simply stood there, scowling and wide-eyed, yelling furiously at him from a dirty, tear-streaked face with her little chin pugnaciously raised and her fists planted on her hips, he roughly shoved her to the ground, spat in disgust, and flung about on his moccasined heels to join his fellows, who whooped with drunken laughter and taunted him mercilessly about his fierce little prisoner's defiance.

Soon after, the whisky ran out, and the liquor-sodden braves quickly grew bored. Inevitably, they turned their attention to the silent captives huddled in the shadows. Drawing their long-bladed skinning knives from their belts, they stripped them naked, before staking out all but one of the troopers on the hard, stony ground. They spread-eagled their arms and legs, lashing them to short pegs which they pounded into the hard dirt with the butts of their tomahawks. Each peg was placed far apart, so that the prisoners' limbs were stretched to the limit. Then—as if that wasn't enough—they ran a rawhide thong across each of their prisoners' throats, with a stake hammered into the dirt on either side of their necks so that movement of any kind was impossible, and breathing a shallow luxury.

Huddled on the ground, Mary stiffened. Her belly squeezed painfully as she waited for her turn to come, as sooner or later she knew it must. Oh, Blessed Virgin, they couldn't take off all her clothes, she thought with a shudder of horror, she'd die of shame! No one had ever, *ever* seen her naked 'ceptin' Ma, when she took her bath on Friday nights. She swallowed, but terror gagged her. Oh, poor Liza an' Missus Whitman an' the others! They looked so—so darned *shameful* that way, she swore she'd rather die than be pulled open and made to look like them!

She stifled a sob, turned her face away so that she wouldn't have to see, and buried it in her little hands, covering her mouth to keep both her fear and the sob tightly clamped inside her. She was afraid if she let out the tiniest sound, after her earlier outburst she wouldn't be able to stop. A whimper would become a howl, a howl a shriek, and then an agonized wail, and then for sure the 'Paches'd slit her throat or strip her naked! Maybe if she was real, real quiet, they might forget she was here at all, they were that drunk . . .

The terrified child's effort to stay quiet, to remain a small, inconspicuous ball in the hopes they'd forgotten her, was a painful one. Her muscles were screwed up into achy knots around a bladder that was agonizingly full. It hurt so bad to hold it in! She just knew she'd disgrace herself and pee all down her chapped legs if they didn't let her use the bushes. Dare she ask them before they tied her up? Or would asking them anything mean they'd kill her? Would they kill her anyway, if she peed herself?

She gnawed at her quivering lower lip, torn with uncertainty, paralyzed by terror, so wrapped up in her own fears that she hardly noticed when they strung up the remaining trooper by his thumbs, dangling him between two sturdy saplings planted in the ground. Soon after, they began torturing him. Each drunken, staggering brave took turns at scarifying the trooper's body with his skinning knife, until the soldier's blood ran dark as a black river against his pale body in the moonlight, and pooled beneath him on the powdery soil. Leaping and staggering and cavorting about him in the ruddy light spilled from the huge fire they'd lit, they looked like masked demons, driven straight from the pit of hell.

The poor trooper was a brave man, Mary thought tremulously, her little heart going out to him. Despite their torture, he made hardly a sound, 'cepting for a few groans and drawn-out moans of "Oh, sweet Jesus, deliver me!" even though Mary knew he must be hurting so bad. Who wouldn't be, having the skin carved off them inch by inch like he was, she thought, trembling and sick to her stomach, her eyes brimming over with tears. Shivering, she tried to say a prayer for him, that God would hear the soldier's moans for deliverance and make him die soon, please, oh please, *soon!*

But she gave up after a few minutes, uncertain anymore if God really existed, or if He and the Blessed Mary were not some fantastic tale her Ma'd made up, like her tales of howling banshees and leprechauns and fairies. After all, He surely hadn't heard any of her other prayers today! Ma was

56

dead, and Brian, and maybe the twins, too, by now, she reminded herself with a sniffle.

She looked timidly about her, suddenly wondering why Rattlesnake hadn't come to tie her up, too? Had they—oh, had they left *her* untied like the trooper because they meant to do the same awful things to her that they were doing to him? Or would they do that other, hateful thing some of the braves were doing to poor Liza and Missus Whitman, who'd had clods of dirt stuffed into their mouths so they couldn't even scream as the Apaches drew aside their breechclouts and climbed on top of them, one after the other? Mary could tell by the way the women's eyes were almost bugging out of their heads and by the strangled, gargling sounds they made that they wanted to scream, but couldn't. She turned her face away, unable to bear watching them do to the two women what they surely must have done to her own poor Ma . . .

She happened to look back just as Rattlesnake knelt between Liza's thighs in response to the raucous hoots and jeers of the others who'd already had their turn at the moaning captive girl. When Rattlesnake began riding back and forth atop her and grunting like a constipated bear, Mary knew what she must do.

While the Apaches' attention was riveted on the women and on their pitiful victim, Mary began edging backward, squirming on her bottom inch by slow, agonizing inch toward the narrow opening that led through the chaparral thicket. Whoops of laughter from the 'Paches told her they hadn't noticed she'd moved, not yet. There was a chance that, as she'd prayed, they just might have forgotten all about her . . .

Her heart thudding so loud she was convinced they'd hear it, she uncurled to standing, turned, and ran.

She flew like a fawn before the snapping jaws of a forest fire down the tunnel of chaparral, scraps of scattered moonlight illuminating her path, her terror lending her new-found strength and speed. The scratches and bruises that crisscrossed her little body and the raw chafing of her inner thighs from the long, wild ride from Fort Agave were forgotten. Her little feet flew over hard, stony ground and cactus thorns.

She'd run less than a mile when from afar off, she caught the silvery notes of a bugle. Sound carried a great distance on the still, cold night air across the flat wasteland of the desert, and hope surged through her. Swallowing her sobs, she ran even faster. Could Cap'n McHenry have returned to the fort and discovered the massacre? Were he and Major Nicholls and his men even now riding after them to free them all—and her own Pa with them? *Oh, please, please, let it be so!*

She'd gone only six hundred yards when she heard a pony coming up fast behind her, Rattlesnake astride its bare back. At the same time, she saw the cavalry crest the rise up ahead; close to fifty men and horses with the bright moonlight silvering their metal buttons, bridles and bits, and turning to ghostly white the pennants that riffled in the nightwind above them. They seemed deceptively close, to Mary's eyes. Surely they could see her, hear her, from there? Surely she could reach them before the Apache reached her . . . ?

"Help me! Oh, please! Please, help me!" she screamed, and began running wildly toward them.

But her small, tired legs were no match for the sturdy, rested mustang. Rattlesnake drew alongside her and, leaning low from his mount's back, he plucked the little girl up before him and raced on across the desert, his pony fleeing like the wind before the long-knives had spotted either the solitary Indian rider or the pathetic little figure, or heard her desperate screams for help.

Rattlesnake carried her swiftly away, far from all hope of being rescued any time soon. His fleeing brothers joined him as they rode, numbering a dozen in all.

Before dawn broke over the mountains, they'd covered many miles and had left Arizona far behind them. They were now deep in the territory the white men called New Mexico, and had lost their pursuers.

* * *

"There'll be no respite for those godless, murdering bastards! No hiding place they can crawl into to escape our vengeance!" Major Nicholls vowed through gritted teeth, looking bleakly about him as he slapped his white gauntlets against his thigh. "We'll scour these damned deserts to north, south, east and west, until the last devil's spawn among them is planted six feet under!"

Major Nicholls, Captain Elias McHenry, and the rest had returned to the fort after escorting the prospectors safely over the Old Spanish Crossing, to find the captain's wife, Rachel, and twelve-year-old Dane McHenry, brutally slaughtered, his remaining men and the civilians in his care slain to the last man and woman, the stock driven off or stolen. Most of the fort's buildings had been looted, then fired, and were still smoldering when the major and his men had returned.

"They leave one, two hours mebbe," one of the Apache scouts had informed them. "That way!" he'd added, pointing toward the foothills.

"Can we trust him, Eli?" Nicholls had asked the ashen-faced captain in a low voice. "After all, he's one of those bastards, by blood!"

"Do we have a choice, sir?" McHenry'd asked bitterly, his voice hoarse with grief.

Accordingly, Nicholls had picked a score of his best men — many of whom had lost friends or loved ones in the attack and had volunteered — and set the remainder to burying the dead and beating out the smoldering ruins of the fort. He'd ridden out at the head of the pursuit detail, and soon after, the fort's scouts had picked up the trail that led to the clearing where the Apaches had rested their horses; a vipers' nest hidden deep within a huge thicket of thorns. Within the thorn clearing, the soldiers had found fresh cause to lament. Before the Apaches had fled, they'd murdered and scalped the remaining captives.

"No, by God, I ain't letting up, no sir!" Elias McHenry vowed, locked in his own private hell, his fists clenched as he silently echoed the major's sentiments of moments before. He'd never give quarter, nor take respite from his quest, not 'til he'd killed the last of those bloody, murdering, thieving savages; obliterated their kind from the face of the earth! And, when they were good and dead, he'd personally lift every one of their cursed heathen scalps and deny their bloody souls their Injun Paradise!

Like the other two men, Mary's father, Donovan Kelly, was in shock as he looked about the moonlit clearing at the pathetic bodies of the dead women and the three men. In the aftermath of returning from the Gila River to find his wife slain and his twelve-year-old son grievously wounded, his babies scared witless, he didn't know whether to feel relieved or regretful that his beloved little Mary's body wasn't among the others. If she wasn't dead, where in God's Name was the poor child, he wondered with an aching heart and a cold sense of dread that went far beyond his fears for her life? What bloody horrors and atrocities had his wee colleen, the apple of his eye, witnessed or experienced firsthand since those animals had taken her? And what more would she be forced to suffer before he found her, or she joined her sainted mother in heaven? One way or another, Donovan swore, he'd find her, even should it take 'til his dying day!

He drew off his battered hat, wiped the tears from his cheeks on the back of his huge, callused fist, and gazed grim-faced out over the moon-washed gray terrain before him. He could see nothing but the pale sheen of boulders, the inky silhouettes of cactus, and the spiked bayonets of the agave clumps, but his little daughter was out there somewhere, and alive, Donovan was certain. Aye, he could feel it in his gut! She wasn't dead, not yet. Maybe the Apaches'd split up—as they often did following a raid to throw off pursuit—and had taken their captives in two different directions? Whatever, Mary Margaret was out there somewhere, he knew it, and he'd find her.

"Pa's coming for ye, Mary, me wee darlin'!" he murmured, scalding tears blinding his eyes, sobs constricting his throat. "Just you hold out an' be me own brave, darlin' wee girl, mavourneen. Yer Pa's comin' fer ye!"

The following week became a hellish blur for Mary, with the soldiers from Fort Agave harrying her captors' heels. Blazing days ran into frigid nights, each one colored by a blaze of pain from either too much heat or too much cold, thirst or hunger. Each day seemed worse than the last. And with each passing day that went with her prayers unanswered, her hope of being rescued faded. Her spirit died a little. Her defiance ebbed.

When the Apaches slaughtered one of their stolen cavalry mounts for meat three nights after her capture, she grovelled weakly in the dirt like a starving little animal for the half-raw, sizzling scraps they contemptuously tossed her way amidst gales of cruel laughter. Her former proud defiance was utterly destroyed by hunger as she devoured the horseflesh, her first meal in four days.

On their brief halts to rest or to briefly water the horses at some river or creek, she was led about on a noose of rawhide like a dog, for Rattlesnake—more malevolent toward her than ever since her attempt to escape—was obviously fearful she would try running off again. The others wanted him to kill her, she could tell by the arguments they had, the murderous looks they gave her. They snarled angrily at him in their guttural Apache tongue and jerked their chins in her direction, but Rattlesnake staunchly refused to slaughter his captive. He met their arguments in stony silence and with drawn knife, shaking his head.

Why he bothered to keep her alive when she knew she was slowing him down, and why they hadn't killed her already, as she guessed they must have killed the others after she ran away, Mary didn't understand, and couldn't begin to guess, unless that toady Rattlesnake hoped to ransom her to the soldiers if they ever drew too close for him to escape?

In the end, she gave up trying to figure out the whys and wherefores of it all. Child that she was, she'd already decided that dying quickly, painlessly, had to be better than this endless, excruciating captivity, for to her horror, her worst fears had been realized. They'd stripped her of her gray serge dress, her white pinafore, her bodice, petticoats, and boots the very first time they'd halted after fleeing the chaparral thicket, ignoring her hoarse screams of protest and her desperate writhings and flailings to free herself and hide her nakedness and shame.

Now, after seven long days of riding, the pitiless sun had burned her pale white body until blisters formed, burst, then formed again, leaving angry scabs in their wake. Raw, red chafed areas were everywhere on her little body. Too little water to drink had made her lips swell as if they'd been stung by bees, and also left them cracked and bleeding. Her tongue was huge and furry in her mouth, and lack of food had hollowed out her already slender, finely boned body. Her hair was filthy and matted, gnarled with twigs and filled with sand. Her eyes were bloodshot from wind-blown grit and from squinting against the fierce, cruel sun. Her arms and legs were scratched and bruised. Even her own Pa wouldn't have recognized her as his pretty little Mary, she doubted, gulping dryly. She wanted badly to cry, yet she was too dried out to shed even a single tear! Dully, she stared up at the merciless moon, floating on high like a silver balloon. Death wasn't her enemy, no, not anymore. He was a friend whose coming she would welcome, for it was the thought of going on living that terrified her now.

Nevertheless, they were on the move again the next day long before dawn broke, just like all the days that had gone before it, with no end, no final destination, no place these savages called home, anywhere in sight.

Perhaps . . . she thought, her little head lolling with the pony's jarring trot and her bone-deep weariness . . . Perhaps . . . perhaps they'd ride forever?

Unknown to the Apaches or their exhausted captive, trouble lay ahead as well as behind them now.

A band of young Comanche braves had left their people's summer camping grounds in the lands the white-eyes' maps named Texas a moon earlier, to ride west in pursuit of wild horses. They'd followed the pony herds deep into New

Mexico, where the mustangs roamed free for the taking.

Of a marriageable age, and belonging as they did to an Indian people who counted a man's wealth by the number of ponies he owned, the young braves had ridden far and wide in order to encircle the wild mustangs they'd cut out from the main herd. They'd chosen as their holding corral the same blind canyon that the weary Apaches were now entering, and had bottlenecked the ponies within it.

The canyon was an oasis of sorts in this wild terrain. Three miles deep, it had a creek running like a vein clear through its heart which, although it was the height of summer, still contained several inches of murky water, tall sere grasses for grazing and a few mesquite bushes, *manzanitas*, and cottonwoods for shade and kindling. Though panthers and wolves also called the canyon home, there were mule deer and cottontail rabbits, bear and antelope aplenty for hunting, too, so a warrior's belly need not growl with hunger when he lay down to sleep.

White Wolf, a Comanche brave of eighteen winters and the adopted son of their band's chief, Black Hawk, was their lookout that morning. He lay flat on his belly atop a high bluff at the mouth of the canyon. When he saw the interlopers eagerly and boldly trotting their ponies into his domain, he scowled in disbelief. Those sons of scorpions known as The Enemy, or Apache, had grown bold indeed, to trespass so carelessly and so deeply into the lands of the true People!

Cupping his mouth, Wolf uttered a low "Pew—iit! Pew—iit!", the nighthawk's cry that was his signal for danger, and heard the same cry returned and acknowledged from deeper in the canyon.

Eyes narrowed, he withdrew an arrow from the deerskin quiver at his back, and nocked it with the easy grace of a born hunter against the string of his bow. His corded muscles rippled down shoulder and arm as he sighted on his target—the last rider—and drew back the string.

But then, he hesitated and lowered his bow. He'd spotted a small, disheveled little girl-child clinging to the last Apache's waist—a white-eyes' child, to all appearances, though from such a distance, he couldn't be certain! She was so exhausted, she could barely stay upright, and lurched from side to side with every jarring motion of the worn-down pony.

Seeing her, White Wolf was forcibly reminded of another child torn from the arms of a loving mother twelve winters past; another child—this one a half-breed boy-child of the peace-loving Hopituh tribe—carried off to a new life he knew nothing of nor wanted any part of. Of a sudden, his spirit shrank from inflicting further pain on this innocent little one by his actions.

He, White Wolf, had once feared as she must be fearing now. He had once reeled with exhaustion behind a Comanche master, a hated one who'd bought him from his captors in exchange for horses and robes, almost as she was reeling now behind her Apache master. He had known what it was to be bruised and dirty and quite alone among enemies. But—he had been fortunate. He'd managed to find a new family and carve out a new life amongst the very people who'd bought him. Would she? Wolf thought not. He doubted she'd even be given that chance, not at her present captors' hands! The Apaches were far from their own territories, and it was rare that they treated captives well. Rape, torture, and death was their usual fate—aiee, by the Great Spirit, the Apache dogs were masters of torture!

There were, too, signs that this raiding party of Apaches was fleeing from someone. Their horses carried the mark of the long-knives' brands on their rumps, an upside-down moon and a snake standing on its head. They had been ridden too long and too hard and moved dispiritedly, sides heaving, heads lowered, mouths sagging open. They would need to be replaced, and soon, if their riders were to escape their pursuers. And, when the little child ceased to be valuable, when she was no longer needed as a hostage to trade for their freedom or their lives, White Wolf knew she would be slaughtered without second thought . . .

His people, the Comanche, were little less forgiving of the white-eyes who were invading their sacred hunting grounds in droves, and scaring away or slaughtering in great numbers the sacred buffalo on which their very lives depended, and ravaging the face of Mother Earth. And yet, children were precious in the eyes of his people, whose women seemed cursed by infertility and rarely were fortunate enough to birth more than one babe. Each new little life was considered a gift from the Great Spirit, one to be cherished. Accordingly, children—even the children of the enemy white-eyes—were rarely killed when taken captive on a raid, unless the blood madness possessed the attackers, or the children proved too young or too weak to survive the ride back to camp.

Wolf thought of his father's sister, his favorite aunt, Spotted Pony, and her empty arms and her empty lodge, and knew what he would do . . .

Casting aside his bow and quiver, he nimbly clambered down over the boulders unhampered, until he was on a level with the unsuspecting Apache riders on the narrow path below. Biding his time, he waited until the last pony had passed him, and then ran lightly, swiftly after it on soundless moccasins.

His knife raised and at the ready in his right hand, he boldly swept the child from the rump of her captor's mustang with his left, and—holding her under his arm like a rolled bed-robe—he sprinted for cover! He'd not made a sound as he did so, and neither, to Wolf's surprise, had the child.

So swiftly and silently did he act, it was several heartbeats before Rattlesnake realized that the little hands which had clung so desperately to his waist for seven sleeps had now suddenly released his belt. With a snarl, Rattlesnake twisted around to discover where she'd gone, barking in his guttural Apache tongue, "You, Blue Beads Girl? Where are you?"

But it was as if a spirit had snatched up the she-cub and vanished! And, in the same moment that Rattlesnake shouted an alarm, White Wolf's companions swept full tilt down the canyon and attacked, their feathered lances raised, their arrows nocked, their wild whoops filling the air.

In minutes, the short but fierce battle was over. The dozen Apaches had fought with courage, but had been tired and outnumbered, and soon their bodies littered the ground. They'd proven no match for the fresh and well-rested Comanche braves, who whooped in triumph and lifted the required tufts of flesh and hair from their enemies' scalps to dangle from their lance points as trophies of war. Their bodies thus mutilated, their Apache foes could not join their ancestors in the afterlife. So be it! Such was the way of things when dealing with one's enemies. Mercy was only for fools — or white-eyes!

Mary came around to find a pair of morning glory eyes gazing down at her.

Puzzled, she frowned, for the eyes did not match the savage, high-cheekboned face in which they were set; jewel eyes startlingly at odds with their owner's pale copper complexion and thick, glossy black hair, which swung like the iridescent tail feathers of a raven to his shoulders.

"Brian?" she whispered through cracked lips. "Am I dead, too, Brian — is that it?"

White Wolf smiled. "You croak like a frog, Skinny Lizard," he teased her in a gentle, bantering tone. "And smell as sweet as my little brother, the skunk!"

He could not understand what she'd said any more than she understood him, but he tried to make his tone convey that he was a friend, and meant her no harm. It seemed to work, for the tension in her fragile little body lessened a fraction. He drew a water horn from his belt, unstoppered it, and held it to her swollen lips, letting a few precious drops trickle down her parched throat. *Too much will make you sick*, he signed, making gagging motions when she tried to grab it and drink her fill.

She nodded, then looked him up and down. He saw her stormy-sky eyes widen in amazement as she noted his bare scarred chest, his breechclout and leggings, his beaded moccasins, before, with a heavy sigh, she sank back down to the soft buffalo robe on which he'd lain her, and fell deeply asleep.

"What's this you have here, Osolo?" Broken Claw, friend and cousin to White Wolf, demanded, coming to stand beside his Comanche blood-brother. With a curling lip, he inspected the child Wolf had risked his own life to save, and grunted in open disapproval and disgust when he was finished. "Pagghh! Have we become midwives to the whelps of the white-eyes, that you would make a pet of this she-cub? You grow desperate for a woman to warm your lodge, I think, my brother! Surely this dirty little vixen is too young to have seen her first blood. What then will Osolo do with the child upon his sleeping robes? Play at dolls, perhaps, or find-the-button?" he teased scornfully, and their watching companions joined in with his laughter.

White Wolf grinned good-naturedly and shrugged. They did not know of his feelings of pity for the girl-child, and nor would he try to explain to them. His brothers had never been captured as he had been captured, nor taken from all they held dear to live in foreign territory with a warlike, alien people. How then could they understand what lay in his heart, or indeed, in the heart of this small girl? The white-eyes were weak in battle, true, unless armed with their wonderful shooting-sticks. They were greedy to own the land his people called Mother. They spoke with forked tongues that told only lies and broke the promises made by them, every red man of the plains knew that. But should their children—who knew no better—be made to suffer for the wrongdoings of their fathers?

"You know well that I have women aplenty to please me, and I think you're jealous of my good fortune, eh, friend Broken Claw, and of my mighty lance, which is never idle?" Wolf retorted, gesturing to his groin with a boastful swagger. "However, I thought to give this little one to my aunt for mothering—just until she ripens to my taste, you understand," he bantered, rolling his blue eyes wickedly. "Spotted Pony is already past child-bearing age, and has never felt her belly quicken with child, although she's longed for a little one since she became Many Horses's woman. This one is in need of a mother, just as my aunt is

67

in need of a child! They will gladden each other's hearts."

"But you'll have to ride double, and she'll slow us down on the ride back to our camp, my friend," Hawakakeno, Wide River, grumbled, joining the pair now. "It's a long ride, and we'll need help with the horses, you know that."

"Never fear, I'll do my share, as always," Wolf promised them. "But—should I fail to do so—you and the others may divide my ponies among you. Agreed?"

"Agreed, Osolo, my brother," Hawakakeno accepted readily and with a broad, greedy grin. The greater number of the best, swiftest mustangs corralled in the blind end of the canyon belonged to Wolf, whose skill with the lasso allowed him to pick and choose only the best from among the mustangs running free in the wild herds! Such a suggestion was unheard of, and for his own part, Wide River hoped Osolo would find himself shirking his share of the work. There was a fine pony or two in Osolo's bunch that would make pretty Kianceta's father look on him with greater favor as a mate for his daughter!

"Then let us return to our camp, before whoever was chasing our enemy, the Apaches, decides to chase the sons of the Comanche instead!" White Wolf declared, scooping up the child and vaulting easily astride his pony as if he were empty-handed. "Sahonkeno! Kansaleumko! Fox! Rolling Thunder! Hiyyeaah! We ride, my brothers!"

Chapter Five

The Sun Dance rites were a time for giving thanks to the Great Spirit for the blessings he'd bestowed upon the People over the past year, and to ask Him to smile upon them once again in the months to come.

For those twelve days of summer, Comanche bands from all across the Great Plains came together after the long winter, in order to celebrate the ceremony and to witness the courage of those warriors who had chosen to sacrifice their flesh to the One Above in the climactic ritual, which took place on the twelfth day.

Suspended from tall cottonwoods by sinews attached to sharpened stakes, which were then thrust through flaps cut into their chests on either side, the warriors endured great pain. They hung, sometimes for several hours, beneath the fierce sun, blowing on their whistles of eagle bone to sublimate the agony when it threatened to engulf them, while below them sacred dances were performed. They remained in this fashion until the skewers that pierced their flesh ripped free and they slumped to the ground. In return for their sacrifice and the strength exhibited by withstanding such self-torture, they attained great honor in the eyes of the People, garnered blessings for their tribe, and—it was hoped—experienced a personal communion with the Great Spirit in the form of powerful visions.

For the common people of the tribe, the Sun Dance ceremonials served an additional purpose, becoming a time when relatives who had married into other bands visited each other to renew their blood ties, to admire new babies, to rekindle old friendships and catch up on the juiciest gossip!

Old women who had feared never to see another summer in the long, cold moons of snow found new life in the warm, golden summer days, and their old chins wagged incessantly. The children, naked as pups, romped and gambolled, shrieked and laughed, in and out of the vast Comanche camp of over six hundred tepees, whose lodgepoles looked like a small forest when seen from a distance. The young men showed off the paces of their finest horses in races, gambled outrageously with their bone dice, and boasted of the coups they had counted and the feats of bravery they had performed since last coming together, while the old men bent their heads and congregated in serious discussion, passing the sacred pipe among them.

Babies strapped into cradleboards viewed the busy world about them through round, sloe-dark eyes of wonder, while their proud mothers boasted of their little ones' teeth, their hair, their prodigious size, or the length and difficulty of their births, none wanting to be outdone in the telling.

Storytellers sat cross-legged before their lodges and acted out the old, favorite tales for the new crop of children, sitting wide-eyed in circles about their feet. The *shamans* chanted and offered songs to the Great Spirit, asking for guidance in the selection of those favored ones who would be asked to dance the sacred Buffalo Dance, or to participate in other ways in the solemn rituals of the Sun Dance. It was a busy, happy time for all.

In her eight years among the Comanche of Chief Black Hawk's band, Blue Beads Woman, as Mary Margaret Kelly was now known, had witnessed many such Sun Dance ceremonies. This year's celebrations, however, would have a special significance for her, for on the fifth day following Black Hawk bands' arrival at the gathering place, one of the *shaman's* assistants came to Many Horses' lodge.

He informed her proud foster father that, along with several other virtuous, unmarried girls of the tribe, Blue Beads had been chosen to chop down the sacred cottonwood tree. It was a great honor to be chosen, for a tall, straight cottonwood would form the focal point for the final, most sacred days of the ceremonies, when the warriors sacrificed their flesh to the Great Spirit by hanging from the sacred cottonwood's highest fork.

Even more exciting, to the young girl's mind, was the rumor that White Wolf had been chosen from amongst the finest braves to select the cottonwood that would be used, and to capture it by putting his mark upon it with red paint!

This tidbit of news especially thrilled Blue Beads, for it meant that Osolo, White Wolf, must be here among the People for the first summer in many years, and she would finally get to see him again after all this time!

Would he remember her at all after so many winters had passed? she fretted as her mother helped her to comb out her hair on the morning of the sixth day of the celebrations. She'd been only eight winters old when he'd last seen her, a forlorn, frightened girl-child with the trails of her tears crisscrossing her dirty cheeks, imploring him not to leave her. A child he'd scornfully called Skinny Lizard, moreover, though she hadn't understood his teasing name for her until much later, when she'd mastered some of the difficult Comanche tongue! Oh, yes, she certainly remembered him! Ever since he'd swept her from the Apache's pony and into his safe arms, she'd known she'd always love him! True, she'd been only eight winters then, and eight more winters had come and gone since, turning her from gangly child to budding woman. But although her body had changed dramatically, her feelings had remained constant. She'd thought often and with aching fondness of the blue-eyed Wolf, and longed to see him again.

Would White Wolf think she'd grown pretty when he saw her again—or would he find her fair complexion as ugly as the white belly of a snake? Had he already chosen a woman to share his lodge? Was it already too late for her? she agonized, then sighed heavily. Probably she was just being vain and foolish to think he'd even notice her, much less feel for her as she felt for him!

Oh, Great Spirit, let the answer to my questions be no! she thought fervently, clasping her hands tightly together. Let White Wolf have found no woman as yet to share his lodge—and let him have eyes for no other but Blue Beads when he comes here!

71

She felt almost sick to her stomach with excitement and the giddy uncertainty of it all, a fact her mother noticed and scolded her for, although with shrewd brown eyes that were more fondly amused than stern.

"Aiee, daughter!" Spotted Pony remonstrated. "Must you squirm like a newborn prairie dog? How am I to brush the knots from your hair, if you won't sit still!"

"But I can't help it!" Blue Beads cried, the words bubbling from her. "I'm too excited to sit still!"

"For what reason?" her mother chided. "You've seen the Sun Dances before, child. What is it about this summer that makes it all so special, eh? Tell me that."

A pink tinge filled the lovely young girl's cheeks. She turned her head shyly aside so that her thick, shining curtain of wavy dark brown hair fell half across her face. That way, Spotted Pony could not read her expression and guess her thoughts, as she was always so adept at doing!

"There's no special reason, Mother," she said with exaggerated nonchalance and a casual shrug. "I'm just—glad—and—and—proud—that I was chosen as one of the maidens to chop down the sacred tree. That's all."

"Paggh! A pretty lie, but a lie nonetheless!" her mother guessed shrewdly, raking the porcupine-bristle brush through her daughter's shining hair with a callused brown hand that was gentle despite its work-roughened appearance. "Chop down the tree, indeed! Do you forget that I was young once, too? I remember what it is that makes a young maiden blush, and her heart beat a little faster— even her eyes shine like the stars in the night sky—and it is *not* the reason you gave me, daughter! No, not a tree at all, I think, but a—young man!"

Blue Beads shrugged noncommittally again, but Spotted Pony knew her guess had been correct by the little smile that now played about the girl's lips.

Aiee, surely this one was a beauty, Spotted Pony thought, her heart filling with love as she caressed her adopted daughter's dark head. In the eight winters since her nephew White Wolf had deposited the child on the floor of her lodge with the casual order to, "See that this skinny

72

lizard finds a mother, my aunt," she had loved the girl with all her heart, and knew that in turn, Blue Beads had gradually come to love and accept her, in place of the white mother she had lost to the Apache.

Spotted Pony had always been patient with the frightened child Blue Beads had been then, gradually teaching her all she needed to know to survive in her new life. The girl's quick mind had absorbed it all swiftly and well. Little by little, she had become one of the People in all but blood. The nightmare of her capture and the unspoken longing for her slaughtered white-eyes' family that had once stalked her dreams and awakened her from sleep each night, no longer troubled her.

And surely, by her hard work and the adjustments she had made so well, this precious daughter had earned the right to choose whomever of the young men she wanted for a husband, Spotted Pony determined obstinately. She remembered only too well how her own greedy father had browbeaten her into accepting Many Horses as her man, just to increase his own vast herd of ponies!

True, she'd come to love Many Horses with time, and to respect him as a husband should be respected, for he was a good man, a fine provider, and she'd lacked for nothing but children since their marriage. But—in her own, secret heart—her blood still moved a little faster when she thought of that other one, the handsome, tall, laughing-eyed one she'd loved with all a young girl's first longing. No, Blue Beads would not be disappointed in her mate as she had once been, Spotted Pony promised herself firmly. She would speak to Many Horses herself, and tell him that there was a young man the girl had set her heart upon. She'd insist that he accept the young man's offer for their daughter when the time came. And, if he argued—as Many Horses was overly fond of doing, just for the sake of arguing—he would find his sleeping robes lonely, chill ones in the long darkness of night, with no Spotted Pony Woman to warm him! A man could quickly be brought to reason after a moon spent sleeping alone with a swollen manroot . . .

"There! You are ready! Go now, wriggling one, and find your friends! Aiee, I am tired of you! Go!" So saying, Spotted Pony shooed Blue Beads from the tepee.

Wearing her second finest fringed, tan doeskin shift, her long hair lifting about her like a dark veil in the sultry breeze, Blue Beads hugged her mother in thanks and left their lodge, unaware that Spotted Pony was watching her as she went.

Stepping gracefully as a young deer picking its way delicately through a leafy forest, her hips swinging in a way that drew men's eyes, Blue Beads made her way across the flattened grass between the double row of conical tepees, calling a greeting to those she knew and stopping to exchange a few words here and there with women friends she had made among other bands in past summers.

Her footsteps faltered as she spied a group of newly arrived young men boasting and bantering with each other before Elk Horns's tepee. Sahonkeno, the Fox, was there, as was Kansaleumko, Rolling Thunder, and Hawakakeno, Wide River. Her heart skipped a beat. White Wolf and his closest friend, Broken Claw, must be among them, too, for these young braves were known to be close friends, and were rarely seen apart!

Yes, she was right, she saw. As she drew closer, she recognised the spotted mustang hobbled outside her uncle Chief Black Hawk's tepee nearby as Wolf's own horse, the stallion he called None Swifter. She had ridden before him on that very pony after he'd stolen her away from the Apaches!

Nervous as a skittish mare herself now, Blue Beads suddenly wanted to turn away and run; to choose another path to Wounded Doe's lodge—one that would not take her past the young men, nor expose her to their inevitable teasing! But to turn away at this point would have been too obvious, and so she walked on, her head shyly bowed, her heart thudding.

"Well, well! What have we here, my brothers?" a deep, teasing voice rang out. "A pretty white fawn who's become a doe since last I saw her!"

It was Broken Claw who'd spoken. Yet even as he did so, Blue Beads saw White Wolf turn his head sharply to look at her, his bright, shining eyes—their color so vivid and startling against his coppery skin—kindling with frank curiosity.

Warm color flooded her face, turning it crimson to the hair roots as she felt his eyes upon her. Aiee! The painted symbols that marked her as a maid of marriageable age and status—a fiery red crescent moon above each brow and the full red moon in the center of her forehead—seemed to burn like brands!

Careful not to look at White Wolf, she forced herself to smile shyly up at Broken Claw instead, and murmured some words of welcome—*what* words she could not remember, even a heartbeat after she'd uttered them!

From the tepee opening, Spotted Pony saw the exchange. She noted the way her daughter blushed on meeting Broken Claw's admiring eyes and looked at no one but him, and grunted in satisfaction. So! That was the way of it! Blue Beads had eyes for the brave, Broken Claw, it would seem, and Spotted Pony heartily approved her choice in men.

But for the one maimed finger on his left hand which had given him his name—the result of a shooting-stick that he'd stolen on a raid having misfired—Broken Claw was a fine young man. He stood tall and straight as an arrow among the often short and stocky Comanche people, and boasted a virile, lean warrior's body that would sire many strong sons on a woman. And despite his youth, Broken Claw was already wealthy by the standards of their people, owning a herd of four score fine horses and a lodge of his own. If he wanted her pretty Blue Beads for his bride, then Spotted Pony would see that Many Horses put no obstacles in his path. The girl had ripened this past year since the time of her womanhood ceremony. Like a flower bud in the days before it comes fully to blossom, she trembled on the threshold of womanhood. There was an aura of expectancy about her, an innocently sensual awareness of her changing body in the graceful, feminine way she moved. All of this spoke of a young woman's readiness to mate and enjoy a man upon their sleeping robes, to become his companion and the maker of his lodges, the mother of his little ones. Aiee, it was high time that one was married! With the happy expectancy of a mother with a wedding to organize in the near future, Spotted Pony ducked back inside her lodge, humming.

Blue Beads mumbled some excuse or other and quickly fled the group of teasing, flirting young braves, seeking out Wounded Doe's tepee instead. Her friend from old chief Sawasaw, The Bear's band, was coming out of her lodge as she entered, but let out a squeal of delight as she caught sight of Blue Beads, and ran to hug her tightly.

"Sister! How good to see you again!"

"And you also, my sister! Aiee, but you have such a glow about you! Can it be that you're with child?"

"I am!" Wounded Doe confessed, patting her gently rounded belly with pride. "He will be born in the Moon of Deep Snow. And you, my sister?" she asked eagerly. "Are you yet any man's wife?"

"Not yet," Blue Beads confessed, shaking her head shyly. By Comanche reckoning, sixteen winters was old for a girl to still be unmarried, and her condition embarrassed her. "Though there is a man I find more pleasing than all the others!" she added mysteriously.

"Really? And who is this one-among-men who's caught the fancy of my fickle friend, Blue Beads?" she teased. "Tell me all about him while we fetch water from the creek."

The two young women, one short and sturdy, the other tall and slender as a reed, but with a woman's soft curves rounding out her doeskin shift, made their way to the creek. Finding the highest point along the banks, where the water remained unsoiled by horses and the swimming, diving children who'd stirred up the muddy bottom, Doe filled her waterskin while Blue Beads dreamily confessed her feelings for White Wolf.

". . . and so each year I've come here, hoping to see him again, and at last he's here, too! He's the one called Osolo, White Wolf, and he's more handsome than any of the other braves," she said, sighing.

"It is so. He's even more handsome than my Little Cougar! Tell me, does he find you pleasing, too?" Doe asked, her cinnamon brown eyes bright with curiosity.

"How could he?" Blue Beads grimaced. "I was just a baby when he left me with Many Horses to be raised, and today was the first time he's set eyes on me since that day. Aiee, my sister, my poor heart beat so fast when I stood close to him, I dared not steal so much as a glance at him!"

"Aah, but did *he* look at *you*, that's the question?"

"He did! But I pretended I didn't see him, and stared at Broken Claw instead!"

"Well done, little sister!" Doe approved wholeheartedly. "To snare a clever warrior such as your Wolf, a woman must use all her weapons, no? The hunter that lives in all men relishes most the quarry he cannot easily bring down." Doe grinned. "Take my advice, sister, and run away very fast whenever your Wolf comes near—but make sure you give him *such* a look of longing over your shoulder as you flee him!" Doe pouted and fluttered her thick black lashes coyly to demonstrate, before ruining the seductive expression by sticking out her tongue and crossing her eyes horribly.

The two talked together companionably as they strolled back to the camp between thickets of cottonwoods and juniper, coarse rabbit-brush and a few straggly willows that swept low over the brown waters of the creek. Blue Beads carried Doe's heavy waterskin for her, although her friend insisted she was quite strong enough to do so, and that the coming child did not drain her strength.

"White Wolf has been chosen to capture the sacred cottonwood, has he not?" Doe remarked.

"So I had heard. And I—I've been selected as one of the maidens who will chop it down," she revealed modestly.

"Really? Oh, what an honor! I'm so happy for you, my friend!" Doe said approvingly. "Then that handsome one—your Osolo—cannot fail to be aware of you in the next few days, can he?"

"Believe me, my sister, I will make certain he is not!" Blue Beads said with unusual determination.

Doe laughed aloud and rolled her eyes, hugging her friend. "Aiee, poor White Wolf! I could almost pity the quarry with such a scheming huntress after him!"

Chapter Six

Two mustang ponies—one black, the other a spotted gray—stretched out their necks. Manes and tails streaming, their hooves thundering, they galloped like the wind across the flat red plain under the afternoon sun. Behind them rose a cloud of reddish dust that drifted slowly to ground again in their wake.

The riders, both expert horsemen, needed neither saddle nor bridle to control their swift mounts. They hooked heels over their horses' backs, slipped arms through the single, braided-horsehair loops woven into their mounts' manes, and rode laying dangerously along their mustangs' sides, Comanche fashion. Or else they stood upright on their ponies' rumps, all the while urging the racing ponies on with wild whoops of encouragement and hurling insults at each other. Their excited cries were echoed by the anxious onlookers who had wagered their prized belongings on the outcome of the race. Now they hoped to spur their favorite on to victory with their yells, and collect their winnings!

White Wolf felt Broken Claw's mount draw level alongside him. They were galloping neck and neck now, and he knew with a single glance at the younger pony that the race already belonged to his friend. Whereas the black gelding was yet fresh and eager to run, None Swifter was lathered and tiring. He had grown too old to live up to his proud name. But, since he'd sired many fine colts in the past for his master, and since, with care, would live more winters to sire others, Wolf had no wish to see his loyal friend and companion of many long journeys and many fierce battles fall dead, his brave heart burst in the effort to win. It was not his way to press a tired pony to exhaustion like a careless Apache, just so he could later bask in the admiration of some giggling female! Perhaps Broken Claw had a need to prove himself. He, Wolf, did not . . .

"Enough, my old friend," he whispered in his pony's ear. "I would sooner lose this race than you. You have done your best, as always. I am content."

None Swifter slowed in answer to his commands, and as White Wolf had expected, Broken Claw swiftly drew ahead, his black mustang streaking past the older, spotted gray horse like the arrow for which he was named.

"Plodding tortoise! You're slower than an Apache virgin!" Broken Claw flung over his shoulder as he pulled ahead, insulting his friend Osolo and the enemy tribe's women in one breath. He grinned in triumph as his pony skidded to the winning post—a strangely formed rock—a full three lengths ahead of None Swifter, amidst the wild cheers and yells of their companions who had backed the black.

White Wolf reined in his pony and sprang lithely from its back to the hard ground, praising the tired animal before good-naturedly joining the crowd of others who were thumping Broken Claw on the back in congratulations, or haggling furiously over their winnings.

"You speak truly, my friend of many winters," he told Broken Claw solemnly, but laughter danced in his piercing blue eyes, which looked to Broken Claw like circles of fallen summer sky, "when it comes to these races, my None Swifter is no longer a match for your Black Arrow. But—" he added with a wicked sparkle in his gaze now, "—thanks to the mighty manroot of White Wolf, nor are there yet virgins in the wickiups of the Apache! I, White Wolf, have taken them all, and have made them mothers and grandmothers, instead! Win your races if you must, Broken Claw. I will win hearts!"

Bawdy guffaws greeted his outrageous boast, and Broken Claw grinned amicably amidst the teasing insults flung at him in return. "Sample all the Apache lovelies you wish, my friend," he said with a smug, secretive little smile on his long, angular face. "I have no envy in my heart for you. I have eyes for only one maiden—and she is not of the Apache."

White Wolf gave him a quick, searching glance, and saw that his friend was not joking, but deadly serious. What was this? He'd never seen Broken Claw so obviously smitten by any woman before! Accordingly, he asked, "So? Who is she, this unfortunate maid who's captured the eye of my ugly friend?"

"She is the one they call Blue Beads Woman among Black Hawk's band—your aunt Spotted Pony and Many Horses's captive daughter. Remember the blue-eyed beauty we teased this morning as she walked through our camp? The one who wore the painted moons of a virgin on her brow? That's her! Surely you can't have forgotten how you stole her from the Apaches, my friend! Or that you once called her Skinny Lizard?" Broken Claw smiled. "Now, she is a woman grown, no longer skinny, but very pleasing to my eyes!"

White Wolf's broad grin wavered a fraction, for he had also been strongly attracted to the lovely captive maid that morning, and had recalled very well the circumstances of their first meeting. In complete honesty, he'd thought of little else but her since then, until Broken Claw had diverted his thoughts by challenging him to a race! When she walked shyly toward him and his friends, he'd been openmouthed and silent, struck dumb by the transformation the past eight winters had worked in the girl. Since he'd seen her last, she'd become a woman, as Broken Claw had pointed out—and a lovely woman, at that. Ah, well, so be it, he thought resignedly, his shoulders slumping in disappointment. As Broken Claw's friend, he could hardly put his feet where another's moccasins were already planted, and still remain a worthy companion! He would have to set his eyes on another young woman, he decided, and forget the shy, gentle beauty that Blue Beads had become.

"Let me take your pony to water, my friend," he offered, adding roguishly, "You can use the time to daydream of your blue-eyed paleface, while I ogle the brown-skinned beauties bathing in the creek—all plump and ripe and sweet as chokecherries!"

Vaulting astride None Swifter, he led Broken Claws's black pony behind him to the creek and water.

But once there, he found the dusky charms of the Comanche beauties no longer tempted him to spy on their bathing, nor felt so much as a stirring of lust in his man-root for their generously curved bodies.

Instead, if he closed his eyes against the golden afternoon sun winking through the fluffy yellow boughs of the cottonwoods, as he rubbed the ponies down with handfuls of grass, he saw the storm eyes of Blue Beads as they'd looked this morning, gazing adoringly at his friend. As if her face were painted against his eyelids, he could see the glistening red moons painted on her brow, the curve of her cheek glowing pink as a wild rose from the mountains as she hid her face in her hair; the smile of soft lips like the arc of a rainbow as she looked up at Broken Claw, rather than him . . .

And, for an instant, he tasted the sting of jealousy, bitter as gall.

Hiyeeah! What had become of the reeking, snivelling girl-child he had taken pity on, and stolen from the cruel Apaches eight winters ago, to become the daughter of his barren aunt, Spotted Pony? Where was that child now in the slender, pretty young doe she had become? Where the Skinny Lizard in a ripe young maiden whose body moved beneath her doeskin as fluidly as water?

Dismayed by the treacherous direction of his thoughts, he stoutly tried to force his mind away from the young woman his friend desired by thinking of other, more serious matters.

With the horses hobbled and quietly grazing now, he sprawled lazily on the creek banks with his arms folded beneath his head, and gazed up at the brilliant blue sky while he considered the Sun Dance rites yet to come, and his important role in them. Or rather, he *tried* to consider them, for more often than not, he found his thoughts straying back to the captive white maiden . . .

When, some while later, he felt someone's eyes upon him, he looked up, startled, to find Blue Beads standing there, gazing down at him.

By the Great Spirit, it was as though she were a vision; a dream woven from the images that swirled in his head, he thought, amazed! She stood there quietly, watching him with her head tilted to one side, dark hair the color of an otter's pelt cascading down over her shoulders in heavy waves. Glinting strands bleached by the fiery plains' sun shone like threads of sunshine caught in its dark fall. She appeared breathless, poised for flight, astonishment mirrored in her eyes, as if she'd not expected to find anyone there. Had the reeds and tall grasses of the creek bank concealed him from her as she clambered up the slope, he wondered slowly? They must have!

"Forgive me!" she flustered. "I didn't mean to disturb your thoughts. I was looking for my medicine bundle. Oh, here it is, you see!" she suddenly exclaimed, retrieving something from the tall grass and holding it up triumphantly. "I must have dropped it here this morning, while drawing water. I—I will go now that I've found it." She turned as if to hurry back down the slope.

"Wait!" he commanded sharply, not knowing why he'd said it even as the word leaped off his lips.

"Yes?" she asked, turning to look back at him as he sat up, his knees bent, his bare, muscular arms dangling casually between them.

He was very handsome, she saw. Even more handsome than her memories had painted him. His long, blue black hair fell thick and glossy to his shoulders, and his scalp lock was bound in otter fur and adorned with the single, fluffy, white down feather of an eagle; the symbol of the breath of life. Indeed, everything about him shouted life, virility, vigor, strength, and beauty! Oh, aiee, yes—beauty, too!

His features were strong and sculpted. His aquiline nose was bracketed by the jut of high cheekbones and a firm chin that gave his face a pleasing arrogance. His lips were slim and chiselled, sensual lips with an intriguing hint of cruelty to them that his warm smile fiercely belied. It was his eyes that fascinated her the most, though. Blue eyes, bright as the Indian paintbrush flowers, they made a striking contrast against his coppery skin. Those eyes were searching as he gazed at her, liquid blue stars under brooding black brows that slashed like bird wings across his brow. How had he come by those pale eyes? Had he, like her, once been take captive by the People, or was his birth the result of a mating between a trader squaw-man and his Indian woman, or a Comanche brave and a captured white-eyes' slave? Postponing the asking of such an impudent question — though truly, she burned to know the answer, as well as everything else about him! — she considered the rest of him.

His torso was naked, save for the deerskin medicine bundle at his throat. Muscle and cord rippled across his shoulders and down his back in a fluid shimmy as he flexed his powerful arms, the upper portions of which were bound with slim bands of rawhide, hung with more eagle down-feathers and beads. His chest was dark from the sun and gleamed as if oiled. A residue of sweat from the race he'd ridden and the effort of rubbing down the two ponies still clung to it. Somehow, those tiny beads clinging to that gleaming, powerful body fascinated her! Two terrible scars marred his smooth, beautifully delineated chest; proud reminders of his own sun-gazing several years before, she noted, proud of his courage.

"Do you fear me so, you must run away at first sight of Osolo, Skinny Lizard?" he asked curiously, a grin tugging at his mouth. "Or has the sight of me frightened the speech from your tongue?"

Her face turned pink as she realized how openly she had been appraising him. The transformation fascinated Wolf! Was this some magic that only white women possessed — this delightful, chameleon trick of changing the color of their faces? If so, he wanted to see it happen again! Better yet, he'd make it happen!

"I'm not afraid of you!" she retorted, bridling at the

insulting name he'd called her. "Nor have I been struck dumb." Her deep blue eyes sparkled with indignation as she added scathingly, "And neither am I called Skinny Lizard, for that matter! If you must call me something, Rude One," she said tartly, "my name is Blue Beads."

"Oh, I know that already," he admitted with a wicked expression, and his sensual mouth quirked up in a grin. "After all, it was I, White Wolf, who named you! I also see very clearly that you are no longer skinny, but as soft and pleasingly curved as a girl should be . . ."

She could make no comeback, could find no ready retort to put him in his place, for his bold, teasing words sent funny little tremors skittering through her belly like stones skimming over the surface of a lake. She looked quickly away, unable to meet his eyes. Did his words mean he found her pleasing? Oh, surely they must!

"It is not proper for us to be here alone. I will leave you to your thoughts now," she said hurriedly, and turned to leave the creek bank.

"I had none—except for thoughts of you, Blue Beads Woman," he called after her in a deep, teasing voice, and even as he did so, he wondered what madness had possessed him to voice the truth? There was no honor in what he was doing, none at all, and at one-score-and-six winters, Wolf had always considered himself an honorable man—'til now! Of a certainty, this was not the act of a true friend, this flirting with the woman his brother, Broken Claw, had chosen, he knew that only too well!

And yet, some evil spirit inside him no longer cared what Broken Claw might think or feel, nor what this dallying with the girl might do to the bonds of friendship between them. His attraction to this lovely one was too fierce and strong, too unexpectedly sudden to deny. At the sound of her voice, his blood had begun to pulse hot and sweet through his veins, like sun-warmed honey flowing inside him with the stirring throb of a drum. At the sight of her loveliness, his manhood had stirred, his groin growing heavy and aching with the fiery yearning to carry her off, and explore with hands and mouth the slender curves that swayed so enticingly beneath her deerskins.

Sweat broke out upon his brow, his back, and began a slow, trickling path down his spine. By the Great Spirit, had she bewitched him? Her allure was powerful medicine, indeed—stronger than that of the magic rock, which could draw a metal arrowhead to its bosom and hold it fast. Or the raging current of some swift-flowing river, that could snatch up a mighty log and swirl it away like a fragile twig. For in that moment, Wolf *was* that arrowhead, that log, drawn and held fast, snatched up and swirled away . . .

"I speak truly, little one," he repeated in a softer, gentler tone. "Since I saw you this morning, my thoughts have been only of you! Tell me, what of your thoughts?" he asked eagerly, certain of her answer, for her eyes and her blushes betrayed her feelings. "Have you thought of me? Do you remember White Wolf at all?"

Did a bird remember its nest? Did a wolf remember her cub? Aiee, she remembered him, *how* she remembered him! He'd been the only gentleness, the only promise of protection and security, in a seven-night hell filled with terror and horror and uncertainty, following her capture by The Enemy, the hated Apaches! How could she ever forget him? He was pricked into her thoughts like the tattoos of the northern People were pricked into their skin. He was branded into her heart like the brands with which the white-eyes scarred their horses. He was gouged into her very spirit and soul like the grief wounds of those who'd lost their loved ones to Death! But—she could never tell White Wolf that.

"Forgive me, no! I don't remember you at all," she insisted curtly. "Though your name seems somehow familiar, yes? But, please, enough talking. I—I really I must go now!"

And with that, she ran lightly back down the slope, leaving White Wolf staring after her, more disappointed by her denial than he would have believed possible.

He was more intrigued than ever as she shot him one last, bewitching glance over her shoulder, lashes beckoning him through her curtain of hair, before Blue Beads disappeared from view.

A grin curved his lips, and he threw back his head and roared with merry laughter, startling the mourning doves that preened in the cottonwoods above him into frantic flight. That blue-eyed vixen! That bewitching little doe! Oh, she'd remembered him all right—and not, he was certain, unkindly!

A puff of gray cloud suddenly came from nowhere and dimmed the sun. Beneath its shadow, White Wolf's grin abruptly faded. His skin prickled, and he touched the medicine bundle at his throat, filled with sudden foreboding.

Some powerful magic he'd never felt before had flowed between himself and Blue Beads as their eyes met, for all that she'd run from him. Some powerful force that was driving them toward each other, like wild horses thundering out of control! Was the cloud covering Father Sun an omen of grief to come if he followed his heart's desires and pursued the girl, he wondered uneasily—or the way the Great Spirit showed his displeasure with a dishonorable one who would betray a brother's friendship?

He thought of Broken Claw's glowing expression and heated eyes when he'd spoken of the captive maid, and was filled with foreboding.

That night, as Blue Beads sat before the fire with her parents in their lodge and discussed the final four days of the Sun Dance ceremonies that would begin the following morning, the haunting music of a flute floated to their ears on the still night air.

The woodwind notes seemed to be coming from somewhere very close to their tepee. Sad and silvery, the song rose and fell, trembled and soared. It sounded, Blue Beads thought breathlessly, her heartbeat quickening, like a little bird crying for its lost mate; as mellow and sweet as the cooing cry of the desert mourning dove.

"Aaah! Ha! I knew it! Someone has a sweetheart who

comes courting," Spotted Pony observed smugly with a sly glance across the fire at her daughter, and then another, prodding glance at her dozing husband.

Many Horses jolted awake and sat up a little straighter on his rawhide couch, blinking rapidly as he digested his wife's observation while rearranging the hang of his breechclout as he did so.

"It seems someone has caught the eye of a man looking for a bride!" she added slyly.

Many Horses grunted. "Paggh! Someone's father will see who this other someone is!" he growled, and lumbered to his feet. "Someone's father will chase away this bold one who sniffs about his lodge like a coyote after a female!"

The music ended abruptly on one high, squeaky note when her father rose to standing. No doubt the player had seen Many Horses's silhouette through the walls of the tepee and fled, Blue Beads thought with a muffled giggle, for the glow of their fire would have revealed his movements to someone standing outside in the darkness. For all their daring and courage in battle, Comanche braves were truly bashful when it came to courting!

Nevertheless, Many Horses left the tepee, determined to discover who his daughter's admirer might be, the young pup! Blue Beads was not surprised when her father ducked back inside their lodge moments later, with the disgruntled declaration that the flute player had vanished into thin air.

"Someone has a sweetheart who fears her father!" he growled, giving his wife and daughter a disgusted look. "Someone has a *cowardly* sweetheart who admires her in secret, and fears to show his face!"

"And someone will never become a wife or a mother, if her father chases her lovers away!" Spotted Pony scolded, furious with her husband.

But as Blue Beads lay on her sleeping robes that night, a warm deerskin pulled up to cover her from the chill night air, Spotted Pony saw that her daughter was smiling as she slept.

Perhaps, she thought fondly, the haunting song of the courtship flute still filled Blue Beads' ears as she drifted on the river of dreams?

Chapter Seven

All of the People crowded about the central gathering place in the midst of the huge camp the next morning, as White Wolf prepared to seek out and capture the sacred cottonwood that would be used for the Sun Dance rites in the coming days.

Purified in the sacred smoke of a sweat lodge at dawn that same day, White Wolf was now dressed in his finest garments. His face and torso had been painted with magic symbols. His lower body was clothed in white breechclout, leggings, and moccasins of soft skins, beautifully worked with dyed quills and sewn with beads. None Swifter had also been honored for the special occasion. White Wolf had braided eagle feathers into his pony's charcoal mane and painted handprint symbols on his gray rump to show his bravery in battle.

Blue Beads's heart swelled with secret pride as she gazed at the magnificent picture the pair made. She smiled to hear the admiring comments of the other young women, more than one of whom had eyes for White Wolf, she knew.

Rider and horse sat motionless as statues while the lesser of the *shamans*—each wearing the headdress of an animal or bird, and robes with the dew claws and tails of the beasts left dangling—chanted their medicine songs, shook their sacred rattles, and danced.

Meanwhile, the one known as the Mentor—an old medicine man named Yellow Beak—who'd been chosen to lead the *shamans,* held aloft the sacred buffalo skull. The huge horned skull would occupy a place of honor within the Sun Dance bower, and preside over the rituals. Its bleached bones had been painted with spots, its cavities stuffed with grasses which were an offering to the

90

buffalo's spirit, asking it to bless their rituals.

The *shamans* circled White Wolf and his pony time and time again, as Sun climbed higher and higher into the blazing blue vault of the sky. Their whirling gyrations and rhythmic stampings in time to the heartbeat of the gourd drums was calculated to frighten away any evil spirits or ghosts that might be lurking nearby, which might try to accompany the chosen one's search and misdirect his choosing of the sacred cottonwood tree.

At last, White Wolf was judged ready to set out on his quest of honor. Amidst the prayers of the *shamans* and the well-wishes of the People, he rode proudly from their camp.

Sun was beginning the ride to his lodge in the Great Waters to the west, when the camp lookout ran to spread the news that Wolf had returned.

His expression was triumphant as he rode between the lodges, his wild, ululating whoop a signal to all that he had been victorious. The cry ran through the village that the chosen warrior had captured a sacred cottonwood taller than any in past years, with the prized fork at the top of its trunk. He had marked it with red paint, and had returned to tell the People of his success.

The welcome news resounded through the encampment, borne on the throbbing beat of the drums as the Buffalo Dance began. Dancers who'd been chosen days ago and secreted away until this very time now burst into the gathering place and performed their sacred dances, giving thanks for home and family and the blessings of fertility.

The dancing continued long into the sultry night, until well after moonrise. The pounding of the drums carried for many miles across the flat, open plains, a throbbing heartbeat on the stillness and darkness that coccooned the over six hundred lodges of the Comanche camp. In the torchlight, the dancers took on a magical appearance, becoming one with the spirits for whom they danced in their fantastic costumes of feathers and pelts and horns.

But Blue Beads grew more and more nervous as night

inched toward dawn like a crawling snail. When Sun rose again, it would be her turn to take part in the summer rituals. Would the People accept a white captive as one of their sacred maidens, she wondered apprehensively? True, she'd lived among the Comanche for eight winters now; had learned their tongue and loved them and called them her family for almost as long, but had they truly ever accepted her? Many had, she knew without a doubt—but not all. There were some, she believed—those who'd lost loved-ones in attacks by the whites—who would never fully accept her; to whom she'd always be an outsider, and an untrustworthy enemy. She would have to do especially well tomorrow—better than her friends—in order to prove she was worthy of the honor despite her white birth. If only she could do her part as well as White Wolf had done his, she would be well content . . .

Looking up, she happened to catch Wolf's shining, brilliant azure eyes upon her. She saw him touch the little flute in his hands to his lips as he returned her gaze between the writhing flames of the huge fire that blazed in the center of the open area, touching copper-skinned faces with its ruddy light. *Oh, if only she were that flute, cradled in his hands, pressed to his lips!* she thought giddily, her heartbeat quickening.

Her immodest thoughts frightened her. They sparked a slow, pleasurable warmth in her veins that spread silkily throughout her body; an excited, tingly, skittish feeling which resembled no sensation she'd ever felt before. The soft doeskin of her robe seemed suddenly rough and irritating against the budding peaks of her breasts. The chastity cord running between her thighs felt suddenly uncomfortable and confining, and she chafed to tear it from her body. Confusion filled her. She quickly looked away, unable to meet Wolf's lambent blue eyes any longer, feeling scorched somehow by the heat of his smoldering gaze, as if she'd leaned too close to a crackling fire.

Spotted Pony saw the delight and confusion that filled her daughter's face in quick succession, and guessed their source. Turning her attention in the direction Blue Beads had been staring, she saw her rascal of a nephew, White Wolf—the womanizing foster son of her brother, Chief Black Hawk and his third wife, Red Bird—seated close to his father. And, as she'd expected, sitting cross-legged beside him was his closest friend and blood brother, Broken Claw, who was staring across the circle at Blue Beads as if his black eyes would devour her—and to the very last morsel, too. So! She had been right, Spotted Pony thought smugly.

"I have spoken with your father, my daughter," she confided to the girl in a whisper, and chuckled as she heard Blue Beads's gasp of surprise. "I have told him who it is that looks with fondness upon our daughter, although he is too bashful to show his face."

"You did?" the girl squeaked. "And what did my father say?" Blue Beads asked anxiously, her heart in her mouth, her deep blue eyes wide and expectant in the firelight.

"Your father said he will allow someone to become the woman of her secret admirer, *if* this bashful suitor should ask for her," Spotted Pony divulged with the smug air of someone whose plans had succeeded—as well they had!

Spotted Pony remembered the hours of darkness last night, when Many Horses had tossed aside his warm buffalo robes and reached for his woman—only to be refused a husband's pleasure of her body! Aiee, how quickly he had agreed to allow his daughter to choose her own husband! Many Horses had been as easily molded as wet clay in her hands, thanks to the rutting fever in his blood and the firmness of his manroot! She chuckled slyly as Blue Beads exclaimed in delight, flung her arms about her mother and hugged her so hard, Spotted Pony feared her ribs might crack, and laughingly protested.

Blue Beads was like one in a dream for the remainder of the evening. When next Wolf came to stand before her father's lodge and play his flute for her, she would go outside to welcome him, she planned happily, now that

93

she had her father's blessing. She would take with her a red trade blanket, and she and Wolf would stand very close together and whisper secrets beneath it, as was the People's custom in matters of courtship. And someday very soon, White Wolf would ask her father for her, and she would be carried on a blanket to his lodge to become his bride!

A shiver of anticipation shimmied through her. Soon, she would know the caress of those morning glory eyes upon her. Soon, in the moonlight that fell through the smokehole to silver the inner walls of their bridal lodge, her body would take wings under the touch of Wolf's powerful hands as he took her innocence, and made her his woman-above-all-women. In the many winters that they would share as man and wife, her heart would beat with his always, always—oh, she just knew it would! Had she not loved him for eight long winters and eight long summers already, with never a thought nor a glance given any other brave?

To her surprise, her nervousness about the ceremonies tomorrow had vanished, replaced by the pleasant antici- pation of being seen in her finest garments by the man she loved and admired, and of making him proud he had chosen her.

Six lovely maidens of the People—each one of spotless reputation—ran out from the huge encampment the fol- lowing morning to begin their search for the sacred tree which White Wolf had marked with red paint.

Giggling and laughing, the girls ran along the banks of the creek, winding between the cottonwoods, junipers, and willows there, making an exaggerated search for the chosen cottonwood. But the creek beds did not hide the tree White Wolf had chosen.

They ventured some distance from the camp to the crest of a nearby, low-lying hill, then turned their efforts to another clump of cottonwoods beyond it, both times without success.

Three times in all the girls made a search for the chosen cottonwood, and each time—amidst much pretended wailing and dismay—they failed to find it, for such was the custom! Then, on their fourth try, the captured tree was miraculously discovered, standing taller and straighter than all others as White Wolf had promised, with a red mark painted upon its trunk.

Amidst glad shouts, a procession poured from the village, winding like a long, bobbing snake to the chosen tree. Several times en route, the *shamans* performed their dances to scare away evil spirits, rattles clack-clicking, chants wailing and quavering from old throats, moccasins pounding the hard red dirt and raising puffs of rusty dust.

Only after great ceremony and the counting of coup upon the valiant tree by the strongest among the braves was the cottonwood felled by the six lovely young maidens who'd been chosen for the task. It was then stripped of its bark and hauled triumphantly back to the Sun Dance bower, a short distance from the main camp.

Blue Beads's shoulder and arm ached from swinging the axe as she'd helped to chop down the tree, but she was content nevertheless. Spotted Pony and even Many Horses had praised her. Doe had declared that she'd performed wonderfully. Even the stern brave, Broken Claw, had given her an unexpected nod of approval—a rare gift from a noted warrior such as he, for the habit of warriors was to remain aloof from the ordinary goings-on in their camp, in order to protect their war medicine from becoming contaminated by the weakness of women.

Oh, she hadn't been able to stop smiling all day as her mother and other relatives gifted her with necklaces of linked and beaten silver discs, fine hair ornaments of feathers and beads, a buffalo-tail quirt, a winter robe of creamy white wolf skins with the paws left intact, and the hems adorned with ermine tails, a new sewing parfleche already supplied with steel needles, awls, paintbrushes and dyed quills, and from her friend, Wounded Doe, a pretty belt with turtles worked in tiny colored trade beads. The turtles were amulets, good-luck charms to bring her many children and a long life, and she wore it spanning her slender waist this afternoon.

What a shining day this sun had proven, she thought happily. She was humming as she made her way to the creek late that afternoon, to draw water with which to cook the evening meal. Yes, and a very special meal it would be, too, in all likelihood!

When Spotted Pony had returned from the ceremonials that morning, she'd found a slab of fresh mule deer meat skewered on a pointed stick set before their lodge. There had been no clue as to who the giver of this generous gift might be—though Spotted Pony had her suspicions, as did Blue Beads!

Blue Beads, Spotted Pony instructed, was to prepare a rich, savory venison stew for supper, one cooked in the prized black kettle that Many Horses had brought back from a raid on a white-eyes' wagon train last year. A stew thickened with acorn flour. A stew afloat with fat, succulent hunks of venison and tangy wild roots, such as onions and turnips, to add flavor. And perhaps, her mother'd added mysteriously, they might have guests for supper that night; important guests who would be curious to learn if Blue Beads Woman was as skilled in the duties of a wife as she was beautiful . . .

It was already beginning, Blue Beads thought happily as she leaned low over the creek banks to let the water flow into her waterskin, seeing a smiling reflection looking back at her. Today Wolf had placed a gift of food before their lodge. And tonight, he would come forward to speak with her father. Surely her happiness was secure!

She hurriedly scrambled upright as the sweet notes of a flute reached her ears. Smoothing down her dress and tidying her hair, she rose expectantly to standing, looking about her for the source of the sound.

Her mysterious serenader rose from his hiding place—amidst a clump of ripe chokecherry bushes nearby—and came toward her still playing, his moccasins silent on the coarse grass. The song he'd chosen to woo her with today was very different to the melancholy song he'd played the other evening, she noticed. It was as light and playful as a butterfly dancing over a field of wildflowers; as trilling as the merry song of crickets at dusk. Her heart racing, she waited for him to reach her, her blue eyes shining with pleasure to see him again so soon and so unexpectedly.

White Wolf halted only when he stood very close to her, their bodies almost touching. He lowered his hand, letting the flute fall forgotten to the grass. This close, Blue Beads could smell his male scent. He smelled wonderful, like cold creek water, fresh and clean, she thought, inhaling deeply, and knew he must have gone swimming before lying in wait for her. He also smelled of the fresh grasses on which he'd lain while he waited, and of the sunshine that had warmed his body — a warmth that rose from him and enveloped her, mingling intimately with her own body heat, they stood so very close to each other.

"I will carry your waterskin as far as the outskirts of camp," he offered gruffly. The sudden huskiness to his voice stirred something deep and yearning inside her.

"There is no need," she began to say, remembering Doe's advice. "Drawing water is women's work." But instead, she followed her heart and murmured softly, "My thanks. You are kind, White Wolf, and your strong arm is welcome."

"I saw how the maidens played their part this morning," he told her as they set off down the long, sloping hill together. His loose, pantherlike stride was one her slender, shorter legs were hard put to match! He added simply and with a frankness that startled her, accustomed as she was to the obliqueness of the People, "There was none among them more pleasing than you. My heart swelled with pride."

She blushed and lowered her eyes modestly, thick dark lashes hovering above the pinkening curves of her cheeks like dusky moths. "As did my own heart, when I saw the

97

warrior who was chosen to capture the sacred tree. There was—there was none finer in my sight," she murmured in a rush, for her tongue felt suddenly awkward and clumsy.

"Perhaps because there *was* only one?" Wolf teased her, and she glanced up to see that his blue eyes were twinkling with laughter, and that his black brows were raised in inquiry.

"Perhaps," she agreed seriously, adding, "But—I think not. Even among a hundred others, White Wolf would have drawn my eye."

She looked away, afraid she had confessed too much of what lay in her heart, wondering if he would find her too bold, too outspoken and forward, for an unmarried maiden. Oh, she should have heeded Doe's council, she knew it, and not seemed so eager to please as she'd been today!

But to her surprise, Wolf reached out and took her hand, drawing her close to him. Far closer than was proper!

"Truly?" he asked in an anguished voice that shook with a man's desire. By the Spirit, how his hands ached to roam freely over her woman's body! To learn the contours of her hidden breasts and stroke the sleek swells of her buttocks. He yearned to discover for himself the soft moss-texture of her skin, and enjoy the feel of her thick, glossy hair when he buried his fingers deep in its pelt.

"Truly," she whispered, and again shyly looked down, away from him.

Taking her hand, he drew her after him into a concealing thicket of junipers, and there cradled her face in his palms, touching her at last as he had longed to do. It was like cupping the opened blossom of a sun-warmed flower between his hands; so delicate and lovely, the slightest touch might bruise her fragile petals. Sunlight dappled her golden skin, its patterns shifting as the tree-tops danced and rustled in the warm breeze. He'd never seen anything lovelier than her, he thought, standing there with her face raised so sweetly to his, and the liquid golden light of late afternoon weaved its magic spell about them. Something tugged at the strings of his warrior's heart, infusing its strength with tenderness and longing. It was more than desire he felt for her, he realized. It was a yearning of the soul.

With his touch, dizziness swept over Blue Beads, for she'd dreamed of and longed for this moment so many winters. Now, seeing the wondering expression on Wolf's face and the light blazing in his eyes, feeling the gentle caress of his hands, she uttered a glad little cry, one that was quickly silenced as he began to speak.

"You fill my dreams, little dove," Wolf whispered hoarsely. "Even as I searched for the sacred cottonwood yesterday, my thoughts were of Blue Beads, and not on the solemn meaning of my quest. You've bewitched my soul, little stranger-to-our-camp! You've cast a spell upon me that makes my eyes search for you whenever you're not near. My ears strain for the sound of your laughter. My arms ache with the longing to hold you!"

He drew her against him, molding her willowy body to the sinewy hardness of his, his warm breath fanning her cheek, her hair. His sun-browned hand grazed the column of her throat, running up it to cradle her head and plunge his fingers deep into the heavy mass of her hair. As he'd imagined, its texture was as silky as the winter coat of a beaver to his touch; as sweet-smelling in his nostrils as a prairie scented with wildflowers and fragrant grasses. Overcome with longing, he lowered his dark head, intending to press his lips to her throat.

"No!" she cried, frightened by the intensity of his expression and by her body's immediate, fevered responses to his closeness and his touch upon her. Pulling away, she pressed her palms against his broad chest and pushed, resisting when he would have taken her in his arms yet again with increasing boldness. "You must not be with me here, alone like this. You shouldn't have lain in wait for me! You shouldn't speak to me in that familiar way!"

"Do you not like the things Wolf says to you?" he asked huskily.

"Yes, oh, yes—I like them too much! You know that I

do . . . But—you must not say them!"

"And do you not like being here, alone with me?"

"You know my secret heart, truly you do! I like being here with you, ˙es! How can I pretend otherwise, when my eyes betray me? But—please, Wolf, enough! Let me go back to camp now?" she pleaded. "I must go back, before my mother comes looking for me. It is not right for us to be here, like this. I wear the moons of a virgin on my brow! If someone finds us here, alone together, you will bring shame on my reputation! My father will throw me from his lodge, and my dishonor will be on everyone's tongue! Would you do this? Would you have me shamed, when I am blameless? No. It is not right!"

"Is it right for a man to suffer the tortures I have suffered?" Wolf growled, embracing her hungrily despite her pleas. He caressed the silken fall of her hair with an unsteady hand, and gazed deep into the wellsprings of her lovely dark eyes, conveying his hunger for her by the heat of his own blazing eyes.

Against her belly, she felt his manhood harden and grow eager with desire. The heat of his flanks was burning through her shift as he held her hips fast to his. Such proofs of his desire were almost her undoing! Her knees grew weak and trembly, as if she'd been contaminated by the breath of the trembling-sickness-spirit. And when his hand trailed down from her hair to cup her breast above her doeskins, she flinched as if his fingertips were the touch of hot coals upon her.

Gently fondling the soft mound and the little peak that rose firm against her doeskin blouse to fill his hand, Wolf added huskily, "Yes, I would mate with you, my lovely one. Were you willing, I would take you here and now in the soft summer grasses, for you know that I desire you as a man desires a female. But—I would bring no shame upon the name of the innocent one I would make my own. It is my wish to be provider and husband to you, not a dishonorable lover who comes and goes beneath the skirts of your lodge under cover of darkness. I would seek Blue Beads's smile to brighten my lodge always, instead of the light of a lamp, and the warmth of her woman's body instead of the warmth of a fire. But—I would honor her as my woman, the mother of my children, if she is willing—not use her as my plaything! Give me your answer, beloved one, or my heart will shrivel and die, like the turtle's eggs left to roast in the hot sun! Will you accept me?"

"Yes, I accept you," she whispered softly, tears of happiness shining in her eyes, "for you've captured my heart! Yes, Osolo, I will be your woman!"

The rich, savory aroma of Blue Bead's venison stew wafted over the camp that night, sending braves and children alike hurrying home to their lodges with growling bellies and watering mouths, and setting women to frowning and reaching for a tasting ladle to adjust and compare their own seasonings.

Blue Beads had gone to the river with her mother shortly before dusk fell, and with her help had bathed and oiled her body and washed out her long dark hair in yucca suds. Now sweet-smelling from the crushed mint leaves with which she'd rubbed her skin, and rosily aglow from her scrubbing, she sat expectantly beside her mother, watching as Many Horses greedily stabbed his eating knife into the stew kettle and slurped down juicy chunks of venison with approving smacks of his lips.

"Someone will make her husband a lucky fellow," he said with unaccustomed fondness, "one with his belly fat and always full!"

Blue Beads blinked and smiled, amazed by his rare compliment for her cooking skills. Perhaps after all, in his own way, Many Horses loved her as much as her adoptive mother?

Spotted Pony took the porcupine quill she was softening by chewing it from between her teeth and clucked agreement. "She will indeed!"

Just when an impatient, fidgeting Blue Beads had given up all hope of their mysterious guests ever arriving in time to share the evening meal with them, she heard a voice at the opening to their lodge, asking for permission to enter.

"Come, come inside, my brother! And you, too, my sister!" Spotted Pony greeted politely, springing to her feet and hurrying to usher her guests into the tepee's large, cozy confines.

She glanced about her with pride as the man and woman ducked inside.

All was tidily in its place, a credit to her skills as wife and mother. The many parfleches she had sewn with her own hands from hides she had herself first fleshed and tanned were hung neatly from pegs set in the tepee walls. These hide containers were filled with herbs, or sewing implements such as her best bone needles, thread from the white man's trading post, quills and glass beads and pretty ermine tails, as well as bone-handled awls and fleshers, and all the other many items needed every day in her woman's busy life.

Quivers held both her husband's hunting and war arrows, and his battle shields and medicine shields hanging with honor alongside them filled her with pride. The sleeping robes had been neatly rolled and stacked against the rear tepee walls. The willow backrests had been placed close to the fire, above which the black kettle hung from a tripod of three stout sticks, the stew Blue Beads had prepared bubbling heartily within it.

It was a lodge to be proud of, Spotted Pony thought with satisfaction, and along with the five score of horses she and her husband owned together—hobbled in the communal corralling area with all the other thousands of ponies belonging to the gathering—her guests could not help but see for themselves that the girl their son had chosen came from a rich and honorable family; one who would bring no shame on their own name, but would add to its standing among the People.

"Please, warm yourselves at our fire, and share the food my daughter has prepared for your visit," Spotted Pony urged, and with a nod the man named Elk Horns took his seat across from her husband. The men would sup first, and only after they had filled themselves would the women satisfy their hunger. It was the way.

Spotted Pony led Elk Horns' wife — a hefty, dark-skinned woman named No Bones Showing — to one side, motioning her to sit alongside Blue Beads. As No Bones Showing ponderously took her seat, Spotted Pony smiled down at her daughter and fondly patted her head. She was surprised to see a puzzled, troubled expression on the girl's face as she looked up at her mother, rather than the happy smile she'd expected.

"Someone within our lodge finds the daughter of Many Horses and Spotted Pony pleasing to his eyes and dear to his heart," Elk Horns began solemnly in the old, oblique fashion of the People, once they had eaten. Names were one's personal magic, and not to be worn out by over-usage. "Someone would take this woman as his wife. He would give her father many horses as a gift in return for such an honor, if her father should agree to the match?"

"How many horses?" Many Horses asked shrewdly, for he had not come by his name frivolously.

"Four hands of horses," Elk Horns said proudly, opening and closing his fist four times. Spotted Pony beamed.

"And does this someone love my daughter?" Blue Bead's father pressed. "Will he be a good provider for his woman and the little ones they make together?"

"He will, and more. But — let us speak now of your daughter! Is she skilled in the work of women? Is she healthy and strong for the bearing of children?"

"It is well known among the People that the daughters of the white-eyes are more fertile than our own, is it not? She will be the mother of many little ones, and make her husband smile upon his sleeping robes. And yes, she is a daughter who brings a mother honor with her women's skills, and makes a father's eyes shine with pride for her virtue."

"Then there is nothing more to discuss. It is agreed between us!" Elk Horns declared with obvious satisfaction at a business transaction speedily and profitably concluded.

Many Horses drew his everyday sandstone pipe from its rawhide case, filled it with fragrant tobacco, and lit it with a coal taken from the fire between a pair of sticks. He solemnly offered the long-stemmed pipe to the four directions of the wind—north, south, east, and west—before taking a puff or two. When he'd finished, he passed the pipe to Elk Horns, who drew on the stem deeply to signify that a bargain had been sealed between them. The sweet-musky scent of tobacco rose on blue streamers of cloud to escape through the smokehole above them, blurring the triangle of star-spangled sky framed by the lodgepoles.

"Only the consent of your daughter is still lacking, my friend," Elk Horns observed after a moment or two. "Ask the girl what lies in her heart. If her answer is the one I expect, I will tell our someone to come inside out of the night wind and smoke with us, and maybe speak for himself to the one who will be his woman!"

"Well, my daughter?" Many Horses asked, smiling with rare indulgence as he turned to Blue Beads. "Would it please you to become the wife of Broken Claw?"

"Broken Claw?" Blue Beads exclaimed in dismay, the words choked from her. Her worst fears were now confirmed, her dread a reality. She had hoped—on seeing who their visitors were—that the couple had come to act as go-betweens for the parents of White Wolf and herself, as was often the case. But now, it seemed she'd been wrong—terribly wrong! It was not Wolf they had approved as her husband, but Broken Claw, the son of Elk Horns and No Bones Showing!

"Forgive me, my father, but I cannot be his wife!" she exclaimed. "Broken Claw is a fine warrior, but—but he is not the one my heart has chosen! I—I have already promised myself to another."

"What is this?" Many Horses thundered, his loud voice filling the lodge as his anger roiled swiftly to the surface. He shot his wife a threatening scowl.

But Spotted Pony ignored him as she also sprang to

her feet, her expression one of bewilderment as she echoed, "What? Not Broken Claw? But—how can this be? I saw with my own eyes how you looked at each other!"

"Be that as it may, it is now too late to change what has already been agreed upon," Many Horses said sternly, giving his daughter a warning glare, for the stubborn girl seemed ready to argue the matter. "You are but a young girl whose heart changes each sun, as the winds change. You will obey your father's wishes in this, and honor the match that Elk Horns and I have agreed to! Would you bring dishonor to my lodge by refusing this young brave without reason? Be obedient to your father, daughter, and accept him, I say! Broken Claw would make any maiden a worthy husband. I will not allow you to disgrace his lodge or my own by refusing!" Nor willingly relinquish the gift of twenty fine ponies, he added silently.

"But I must refuse him!" his daughter cried, her voice sounding strangled with tears but determined despite them. "I have no choice, Father—don't you see? You've always been kind to me, and I've always tried to please you and obey your wishes. Aiee, I would do anything rather than bring you shame, Father—except this. I don't love Broken Claw—and I will never marry him!"

So saying, she sprang to her feet and ran across the tepee, ducking swiftly through the opening and rushing outside into the cool evening air. She ignored the angry threats of her father and the pleadings of her mother that followed her hasty exit.

Broken Claw was pacing outside their lodge. She almost ran into him in her haste to escape, to be anywhere but there. His brown, almost black eyes lit up when he saw her, mistaking her breathlessness for eagerness to see him, rather than anxiety to escape her father's lodge.

"Is it agreed so swiftly then, storm-eyes?" he bantered, grinning broadly with pleasure. "When have the old ones decided you're to become my woman?" he asked, his eyes shining with love for her, and no little desire.

"Never!" she told him hoarsely, bluntly, tears streaking down her cheeks in the starlight. "It is another man I love. My heart cries out to belong to him, not you! I am sorry if you thought otherwise."

"What?" Broken Claw growled, stepping forward and gripping her by the upper arm. His expression was ugly now in the patchy gray light, and his fingers bit cruelly into her tender flesh so that she yelped in surprise and pain. "What is this you say, woman?" he sneered. "That you'll never become my woman? Ah, but I say you will! I will not permit you to ridicule me before everyone by scorning my offer of marriage! The gossips have whispered all over our camp of how Broken Claw played the flute for you, like one of our lovesick coyote-brothers who yips at the moon."

"It was you who played the flute—?" she whispered.

"It was," he growled. "And many know of the deer meat I left as a courtship gift before your lodge, too bashful to make myself known to you. Clacking tongues have already spread the word that tonight, the parents of Broken Claw come to ask a special someone to be his wife. I say you *will* be my woman!" he insisted, shaking her roughly as if by so doing, he could also shake reason into her. His eyes blazed with the dark fires of polished jet in his anger, and in the murky light, his face was that of a hateful stranger who frightened her. "And, as my woman, you will soon forget this tricky weasel who's blinded your eyes to one who truly loves you!"

"No," she argued, shaking her head obstinately. "Forgive me, but I'll never forget him, never! I cannot—I've loved him too long!"

"Who is he, then? Tell me!" Broken Claw demanded roughly, determined to discover his rival's identity. "What is his name?"

"I cannot! You would kill him!" she whispered, and knew it was no lie.

With that, she jerked herself free of his punishing grip on her arm and fled through the Comanche encampment, leaving a seething Broken Claw staring after her, his expression murderous, his black eyes deadly with purpose in the starlight.

Before this moon grew old, he would discover this other one's name, Broken Claw swore, his heart curdling with hatred and the bitter bile of jealousy. With his brother White Wolf at his side, he would track his rival down — and bloody his knife on a weasel's heart!

Chapter Eight

Wounded Doe, Blue Beads's friend from the Bear clan of the Comanche who'd married Little Cougar, a brave of old Iron Kettle's clan, was returning from the perimeters of their camp when she saw Blue Beads running toward her tepee. Since the baby had begun to grow inside her, Doe was feeling the need to empty her bladder far more often than usual. It was to relieve herself that she'd left her lodge after dark.

Hurrying to catch up with Blue Beads, she called breathlessly after her, "Ho, my sister, wait for me! What's wrong? Why are you running? No one's hurt, I hope?"

"No, it's nothing like that. Is your husband within his lodge?" Blue Beads asked huskily, and as she slowly turned to face her, Doe saw the sheen of tears on her friend's cheeks, the frantic working of her mouth.

"No, he's gone for now. We can talk alone," Doe reassured her gently, frowning with concern as she took Blue Beads's arm. Her plump little face was serious for once, her merry, sloe black eyes shadowed with apprehension. What could have caused such upset in her friend, the one she called sister, she wondered? She was trembling beneath her hand, and seemed more distraught than Doe had ever seen her before. "The men sit in council in the talking lodge of your chief, Black Hawk. Tonight the war societies are deciding what action to take against the white-eyed Rangers who raided chief Iron Kettle's village last moon, and killed many of the old ones, women and children. Tonight, they'll vote on whether to take the warpath against them in retaliation. They will not quickly decide such a grave matter. They never do! We have plenty of time to talk."

Doe blushed, yet it was a pleased blush, for her knowledge of what was to be discussed at the war council came directly from her husband, Little Cougar, and it was rare that a brave discussed matters of war with his wife, even in the intimacy of their sleeping robes. "Come inside, and tell me what's upset you so!"

Doe's tepee was smaller than Blue Bead's father's, but still a tepee to be proud of, Blue Beads thought. All the women had helped to raise it when Doe had married Little Cougar last Moon When the Leaves Change Color, and the couple had begun their life as man and woman together within it, she recalled, her eyes smarting with fresh tears. True, she might soon share a bridal tepee with a man, but if that man were not Wolf, there would be no joy for her within its walls . .

Her voice choked, Blue Beads stared into the fire as she brokenly told her friend everything that had happened in the past few days; of how her mother Spotted Pony had mistakenly believed that Broken Claw was the brave she'd lost her heart to; how Many Horses had passed the pipe and smoked with Elk Horns to seal the match between his son and herself; even how Broken Claw had been waiting outside her lodge when she ran from it, and his fury when she'd scorned him and told him she loved another.

"And now what am I to do—?" she cried when she'd finished her short but disturbing story. "My father is more angry than I have ever seen him, and will disown me if I refuse to become the mate of Broken Claw! And yet, how can I become his woman, when it is Wolf that I love with all my heart?"

"Come, come, all is not lost yet," Doe comforted her, making a soothing, clucking sound as she took her friend in her sturdy arms and let her cry out her fears on her shoulder. "First, White Wolf must be told what has happened tonight. He's the one to decide what must be done, not you. If—as you say—you hold his heart, then dry your eyes and stop your worrying. He is clever, your Wolf, and will have a plan. True, he's always been a rascal where women were concerned. Why, half the women in our camp would crawl under his lodge skirts at night, given an invitation by your handsome Wolf—and the other half *want* to, but are too cowardly to admit it! And yet, although he loves to play the stallion and considers all women eager mares for the taking, I have yet to hear it gossiped that he's made any woman promises he didn't intend to keep. If he's told you that he loves you and wants you for his woman, then it is so. Trust him, my sister. Believe in him. Let him take care of this problem, as a man should. When the council is ended, I will send him word that you must speak with him. Where would be a good place for you to meet?"

"The juniper thicket—the one by the path leading from the creek. He—he will know where to find me." Oh, yes, he would know, she thought, remembering the feel of his arms about her that afternoon, the warmth of his body against hers.

Blue Beads stayed with Wounded Doe until the sound of men's loud voices warned her that the war societies had ended their council for the night and were returning to their lodges. Soon Little Cougar would also return to his lodge, and Blue Beads had no wish to be there when he did so, for then everyone would know that Doe had taken her in and hidden her.

Earlier, as they sipped the delicious coffee Doe had brewed and sweetened with yet another gift of the trading posts, the sweet white sand the white-eyes called "shoogah", they'd heard the sound of an angry voice, going from tepee to tepee demanding knowledge of Blue Beads's whereabouts. Her outraged father had been scouring the encampment for her—no easy task when any one of the over six hundred lodges might harbor his defiant, disobedient daughter! Surprisingly, Many Horses had not come to ask for her at the opening to Doe's lodge, and she was relieved. She did not want Many Horses's anger to fall on her friend and her husband, however vehemently Doe might protest that she didn't care.

"Your husband will return soon, so I will go now. If

110

you can send a message to Wolf, then I would be grateful," Blue Beads whispered. "Tell him I will wait for him in the place I told you of."

Shortly after bidding Doe farewell, she stood shivering in the thicket of junipers, waiting for Wolf. Would he come in answer to Doe's message, she wondered? Would he even care? Did his heart truly beat with hers — or had his words been empty and false, a trickster's ruse to make her give herself to him, as so many others had before her?

If so, what would become of her, she wondered bleakly? Now that she had told Broken Claw what lay in her heart, his pride was injured, his anger and resentment high as a river at the spring thaw. She knew he would prove the cruelest of husbands if they were forced to marry, under such conditions.

Reluctantly, she thought of Crooked Woman, a woman of her own Black Hawk band whose patched and tattered lodge lay on the outskirts of camp, denoting her husband's low status among the men of the tribe. Crooked Woman had been young and lovely once, Spotted Pony had said, whispering behind her hand, but she was neither now. Her husband, lardy Big Bear Sitting Down, was a hateful, jealous man, a suspicious one who saw wrongdoings on his wife's part where none existed, and who heard rumors that had never been whispered. On some pretext or other years ago, he'd chopped off the tip of his poor woman's nose, publicly — and falsely — condemning her for adultery. He loved to beat her, too, and did so often, and had broken her bones many times. Her hurts had healed poorly, and because of them she'd been given her name, Crooked Woman. And yet, she'd remained with Big Bear, and had never taken the People's way of divorcing herself from a cruel husband by piling his belongings outside their lodge as a sign to all that she was no longer his woman. Why not? Blue Beads wondered. What made a woman stay with such a brutal beast as that one, and accept his beatings? But in her heart, she already knew the answer to that question. Pride held Crooked Woman there; pride, and a feeling of unworthiness, and the fear that life's path held nothing better for her as a woman alone among the People. Without a husband—any husband!—who would provide her with meat in the hungry moons of deep snow?

She sighed and hugged herself, trying to peer through the patchy gloom to see if she could see Wolf coming through the shadows to find her.

Old Woman Moon sailed out from behind a banked mountain of silver-edged clouds, and flooded the thicket with her ethereal light, glinting like new coins off shiny leaves and pouring over the topmost branches in a river of silver. Looking down, Blue Beads saw Wolf's courtship flute lying forgotten in the dew-frosted grass, where he'd let it fall to take her in his arms that afternoon.

In the moonlight, the stem gleamed like a slender ivory bone, shiny from many hours of careful polishing with a smoothing rock in Wolf's careful hands. The hole where the sound escaped was shaped like a little bird's head with an open beak, and a stallion—the most ardent and passionate among all the animals—had been painted upon the polished stem. She bent and picked it up, hugged it to her breast. And, when she looked up once again, he was standing before her, tall and strong and silent, as if he'd materialized from the night.

"Wolf, oh, Wolf, you came!" she cried, and a moment later she was in his arms. Her heart sang with joy as his arms enfolded her, for she knew by the way he held her that he'd not played her false. Burying his face against her hair, he tightened his hold, and she could feel the strong, measured throb of his heart next to hers.

"I am here, my dove. Don't be afraid," he reassured her huskily.

"Did Doe tell you—?" she whispered.

"She did. And I went to your lodge to speak with your father before I came to find you," he announced, his expression stern in the moonlight, his chiselled features etched as if from dark glass. "I offered many horses and fine gifts to make you my bride, but my offers fell on deaf ears. Your mother's husband is too angry to hear

112

reason. His pride is smarting too sorely from your defiance for him to accept that a mistake was made. In a voice of thunder, he bade me be gone, and speak of you no more. He has sworn you will join with Broken Claw, or he will disown you. And so, we have no choice, my heart. I have decided we must leave here tonight. Together."

"Run away?" She uttered a little cry of denial, and her hand flew to cover her mouth. "By the Great Spirit, is there no other way?"

"No, beloved. It is the only way," Wolf told her grimly. "Many Horses will never willingly accept me as your husband until his anger has cooled. And nor will Broken Claw forgive me for betraying our friendship, I know. When he learns it was his blood brother White Wolf who stole your heart, he will live only to kill me and take you for his own. Such is the way when the deepest of friendships sour and love becomes hatred! If we stay here, you know what must happen, do you not? The council will be called upon to settle this matter between us and return harmony to our camp. They will agree that Broken Claw has been wronged, and that he and I should fight to decide who will claim you. They will insist upon a duel with cord and blade—a duel that can end only in death for one, or even both of us. Broken Claw was as a brother to me from when we were both children—my closest friend among men, my companion of both war and peace. I cannot take his life—and yet, nor will I ever give you up! And so, we must go. In time, your father's anger will cool, and we can rejoin our band."

"And what of Broken Claw? Will his anger also cool?"

"That I cannot say," Wolf admitted evasively, for he knew in his heart that it would never be so. Broken Claw was a man of simple emotions, ones that were all the fiercer for their lack of complexity. He loved, or he hated. He warred, or he lived in peace. There was no gray in Broken Claw's life—all was either black or white, and never were the edges blurred by emotions. "We can only wait, and hope that in time his anger softens."

He put her away from him, and instead took her hand in his large one. Her skin was cool and clammy with fear, for all that the night was warm and the breezes sultry. "Come now, we must be gone long before anyone suspects what we're about and tries to stop us. Your father will send warriors after us, I know it."

He led her from the juniper thickets and out onto the narrow path. There, to her surprise, she saw that four ponies waited. Two were for riding, one her own little paint mare, Badger, the other Wolf's spotted gray pony, None Swifter; another pony pulled a heavily laden travois of poles behind it, and another was laden with still more belongings. Someone held the ponies' halters, and as they drew closer, Blue Beads saw who it was and ran to her.

"Mother!" she cried, "Oh, little mother, what's to become of us?"

"Hush now, hush," Spotted Pony insisted firmly, sniffing back a tear of her own as she patted Blue Beads's shoulder and set her from her, "if you love this rascal, everything will work out, I know it! When you return in a few moons with his grandchild growing in your belly, Many Horses will forgive and forget this night. I know his heart better than any woman, after all! He is stern and proud, true—yet he loves our daughter. He will accept your husband, when the time comes, for he will miss your smile in our lodge and your place in our lives, and want to dandle your babe upon his knee.

"There are a few things I thought you might need on the travois, my daughter—things I've been making in secret and saving for your marriage. As for the lodge cover, it is not new, but it is sound. The rains will not find you beneath it, nor the snows pierce its skirts to gnaw at your bones. It is yours now, child, until the time comes when you have buffalo hides, and are able to sew a lodge cover of your own. My nephew is your man henceforth, his voice the only one you must heed hereon. Go in love and with the blessing of the Great Spirit, my daughter. Follow your Wolf—and may you find happiness always with he who fills your heart."

114

With a bone-crushing farewell hug, Spotted Pony turned and ran back to camp, and Blue Beads was alone again with Wolf.

"Soon, I will make you my woman," he murmured, clasping her by the waist and lifting her up onto the tall wood and rawhide saddle on her pony's back. "Is there no smile for that small blessing?"

"My hearts sings with gladness to be your woman," she whispered truthfully in answer to his teasing tone, and somehow managed a tremulous smile before adding, "But—my soul shudders with fear for the moons to come. Our love has made a bitter enemy of Broken Claw. Aiee, I saw it in his eyes! How they glowed with the lust to kill, my husband! When he learns that you are the one I've chosen, he will try to slay you!"

Wolf grasped None Swifter's mane-loop and vaulted lithely astride his bare back. Turning to Blue Beads, he leaned down and fondly pinched her cheek. "First, little worrier, he will have to find us, no? And your Wolf is not easily found, unless he wants to be! Come. We will go now! We'll set our eyes to the trail of the future which leads onward, filled with promise, rather than cling to the trail of the past, which can never be changed. I am eager to make you my woman, but we have many miles to ride before it will be safe to halt, and I can hold you in my arms . . ."

With that sensual promise, he touched his heels to None Swifter's flanks and led the way from the camp.

Blue Beads took up her reins and rode after him, following him into the inky darkness that lay like a blanket over the desolate plains. Following the man she loved toward the future—and into the uncertain promise of tomorrow.

The stars were already paling from the sky when White Wolf finally called a halt. The Old Woman hung like a polished abalone shell in the charcoal heavens, translucent and pale as glass.

The place Wolf chose for their camp nestled in the heart of a small valley. Blue Beads could see star and moonlight reflecting twisted black-diamond ropes in the flow of a stream, which was bordered by smooth black boulders. Many dead branches and small logs littered the banks and the shallows, debris left stranded there by a spring flood when the stream had risen and overflowed its banks. It would provide plentiful kindling for their fire, she noted with a shrewd eye.

Cottonwoods grew close by the stream banks, and willows dipped their graceful tresses into its gleaming black flow. Further away grew what looked like pecan trees in the gloom, and there were a few *piñons*, too, as well as ample grazing for the horses. A smooth, flat area with an outcropping of boulders at its back appeared dry and easily defended, if the need arose, for the raising of their lodge. All in all, it was a wonderful place to camp, from what little she could see of it in the moonlight, and it promised to be a pretty spot, too, by daylight.

Some of her earlier apprehension lifted. There had been no sign of anyone riding in pursuit of them as yet. Perhaps she'd overestimated Broken Claw's anger? Perhaps he would accept that her heart had chosen elsewhere, and leave them alone, once his initial outrage had cooled? Or—perhaps he'd yet to discover that she'd fled their summer camp, and the identity of the rival who'd accompanied her! Did that explain why no one had ridden after them? The latter, she reluctantly had to admit, was far more the likely answer.

While Wolf scouted the area to make sure there were no hidden dangers, Blue Beads dismounted, and set about unloading the things her mother had thoughtfully loaded onto the travois. There were rawhide containers filled with pemmican, two warm buffalo robes, and several smaller ones of doeskin and pieced rabbit skins, a paunch for the cooking of stews, a pouch of healing herbs, as well as many of Wolf's belongings and all of her own personal possessions, including the gifts she'd been given following the felling of the sacred cottonwood.

She had to unload the travois first, for the long poles which had been lashed together to form the frame of the litter were also the lodgepoles over which her tepee cover of buffalo skins must be fastened. Working quickly and methodically as Spotted Pony had taught her, she began setting up their little camp.

When White Wolf returned a short while later, satisfied that the camp he had chosen was a safe one for the night, he found his lodge had been speedily and efficiently erected, facing east as was proper, the ground within it strewn cosily with robes, and a new fire already burning beneath the smokehole. Some distance from the solitary lodge grazed the three ponies, hobbled by long rawhide halters, and before the opening to the tepee, gazing up at the stars, sat his woman, Blue Beads.

Pride filled him when he noted how quickly and efficiently she had completed her woman's tasks. Surely this was a woman above all women, one to be cherished and respected for her womanly skills, as well as her uncommon beauty? No, he told himself with a fierce sweet sense of joy, his heart had not played him false. Whatever the cost, the price had been worth it, to make this special someone his . . .

Silently, he staked out None Swifter with the other ponies, and made his way to their lodge, only to find that Blue Beads had finished her stargazing and gone inside.

Ducking under the low opening, he entered the tepee and closed the weighted flap behind him. He saw Blue Beads curled beside the fire like a little cougar cub, her head modestly bowed, her legs tucked under her. As befitted a bride upon her wedding night, she had bathed in the stream and prepared herself for his return. Except for the mantle of her unbound hair, she was now quite nude, except for the chastity cord that ran between her legs and was fastened at both back and front to a slim band of rawhide about her waist. The cord would be loosened by Wolf when he was ready to take her maidenhead.

The flames cast their ruddy glow onto her face, and reflected hidden fires in the inviting darkness of her storm blue eyes. Amber firelight picked out the threads of gold in her flowing sable brown hair, and flickered over the pearly, rounded curves of her shoulders and the snowy hillocks of her small yet lovely breasts, which were crowned with small buds the color of sunrise. Ah, yes! It would be good for them, the life they would make together, he thought with pleasure, for she was lovely, innocent, all that a proper wife should be.

"Welcome, my husband," she whispered huskily, tilting her face up to his and holding out her hands to him, palms uppermost. Nervous now, she bit her lower lip and added in a small, nervous voice, "I hope that you will find me pleasing?"

Looking down at her, White Wolf felt his loins tighten in response. Pleasing? Aiee, he found her pleasing indeed! The ache of desire roiled through him like a river at the flood, making his groin heavy and full. Striding across the lodge like a dark, graceful panther, he dropped to his haunches beside her. Smiling, he ran his hand caressingly down the length of her rippling hair and over her body.

"More pleasing than I'd ever imagined!" he murmured, and drew her against him, cradling her against his shoulder. Kneeling and facing each other, they embraced, and he could feel the flutter of her heart against his chest, like the wings of a frightened bird.

His buckskins smelled of smoke and night dew, and of the masculine essence that was his alone. Trembling, she buried her face against his chest, fully aware of the warmth and virility of the man who held her in his arms as she did so. She could feel the steady throb of his heart beating against her palm, and the play of a warrior's powerful muscles under flesh as he lowered his head to hers, cupping her face in his palms. The balls of his thumbs caressed her cheeks. His eyes, blue as a jay's wings in the ruddy shadows within their lodge, dove deep into hers as he repeated gently, "More pleasing than any other maiden in the eyes of White Wolf."

Releasing her, he grasped the fringed hem of his buckskin shirt and drew it up and over his head. Leggings, moccasins, and breechclout followed, until finally he was as natural and free as she. His lean, well-muscled body gleamed as if oiled. His shoulder-length black hair was as glossy as a raven's wing, and alive with bluish highlights in the fire's golden circle.

Turning to her, Wolf gathered her again into his arms. He bore her down to the heap of buffalo robes she had spread before the fire in readiness. Their softness pillowed the hard ground, and cradled the lovers in luxurious warmth and comfort.

"You will have no regrets, Blue Beads Woman" he promised her solemnly, his voice husky as they lay side by side, their limbs entwined. "Your Wolf will prove all you could ask in a husband."

She shivered with pleasure as he stroked her shoulder, his fingertips trailing possessively, casually, down the length of her bare arm and then behind to trace her spine. She was afraid of what was to come, for she knew that there would be pain the first time Wolf took her. And yet, there was also an overwhelming need in her to be taken and possessed by this man; a female's natural desire to submit and yield her body to the male she held dear above all others; to discover the pleasures and joys of mating that could unfold for two whose hearts beat as one.

Wolf's hand enfolded her breast, gently weighing its soft firmness in the cup of his palm. Dipping his raven's head, he suckled gently at a deep pink nipple, teasing it between his lips. She shivered and gasped as the bud stirred and grew firm and sensitive against his tongue. An arrow of desire sung clear through her, piercing deep and sweet before lodging, quivering, in her loins. Oh, his every touch was the caress of a feather, the flutter of bird wings, teaching her skin new ways to feel, her heart new rhythms by which to beat!

"I have followed the bee, and found a honeycomb," Wolf whispered teasingly against the creamy velvet of her skin. Joy danced in his eyes, and his warm breath made her shiver as he lapped delicately at the sensitive little nubbin of flesh with the very tip of his tongue, until it grew wet and slippery and as hard for his mouth to capture as an eel in the shallows. Under his playful caresses, she grew breathless, dizzy with delight.

"And here, another, just as sweet!" he declared moments later, sampling her other breast. Leaning up, he cupped the twin mounds in both his hands, pressing them high as he buried his face like a greedy child between them. He mouthed her tender flesh with teasing lips and teeth and tongue, until little birdlike cries and whimpers escaped her parted lips.

When she could bear no more, his palm swept downward, skimming over her abdomen, firmly stroking and pressing against her flat belly. He drew her over onto her side so that she now lay facing him, their chests and bellies meeting. In this position, he could fondle at will the little globes of her buttocks, which had twitched so seductively and gracefully beneath her doeskins as she made her way about camp—and driven him to madness with the desire to have her! He could also draw her hips against the hardness at his flanks, and by so doing make her fully aware of his desire for her, and of his intentions. One hand resting possessively upon the swell of her hip, he told her tenderly, "Do not be shy, little one. Soon, you will become Wolf's woman, and you must learn to touch me, too. Come, beloved, give me your hand."

So saying, he took her hand and pressed it to his face. Tentatively, she traced the outline of his cheek and jaw with long, slender fingers, feeling the strength of bone beneath firm, supple flesh. She skimmed the margins of his lips like a blind woman, learning to see him through her fingertips for the very first time. She wondered how it would be to touch her mouth to his as she'd heard the white-eyes did before mating, or to welcome those they were fond of? Perhaps, when they were comfortable together, they would try that strange custom for themselves?

Meanwhile, her touch told her what her eyes already knew; that his body was all masculine beauty and strength, a strength leashed now and gentled by superb self-control—and the constraints of love that tempered lust. Where another might have used her body cruelly, roughly, and taken her gift of innocence without thought, Wolf was all patience, all gentleness. She shivered with excitement. Touching him so intimately sent a tingling awareness through her fingertips that, mysteriously, travelled the nerve paths through her body to quiver in the very tips of her breasts, to spread heat through the pit of her belly, and flutter maddeningly in that secret, hidden woman's place between her thighs.

Down her hand travelled, learning the broad expanse of his smooth, broad chest, skimming the silvery knots of his Sun Dance scars, and the tiny cactus buttons of his male nipples. Further down, she encountered a flat belly that was hard as rock, with the muscles clearly delineated beneath her fingers in overlapping ridges. Still lower, she caressed twin thighs as strong and powerful as lodgepole pines, with sinews and cords running down their backs like bowstrings. Between them rose the proud length of his manroot, mantled in a pelt of soft black wolf's fur, and below, his weighty seed sacs. With just a moment's hesitation, her palm enfolded his length, curiosity overwhelming fear. She felt his manhood buck in response to her hesitant touch, as if given life and movement independent of his. She gasped and tore her hand away, hearing his low chuckle as she did so.

"Do you see what powerful medicine you possess? Aiee, woman, he feels your touch, and grows eager to hide himself in the softness and warmth of your woman's body," Wolf murmured teasingly. "Tell me, little bird, do you grow eager and ready to hide him?"

So saying, he slipped his hand between her thighs so smoothly, she had no time to protest his actions. Circling the silky inner flesh there, he moved his fingertips around and around, circling higher and higher until his hand brushed the mossy maidenhair that shielded her treasures, and caught against the slim length of cord that impeded his taking of her innocence.

Wolf reached for and took up his skinning knife. Careful not to touch the razor-edged blade to her skin, he cut

121

the cord that prevented more intimate caresses, as was his husband's right. The severing of the chastity cord rendered her totally defenseless against his male advances. He was aware as he tugged the strip of rawhide free of how her body had begun to tremble uncontrollably beneath his touch. She'd not answered his question, he realized. Yet he knew from experience that in this moment, a maiden was more frightened, more apprehensive than eager, and his heart filled with tenderness.

He would take her gently, like picking a delicate flower he had no wish to crush or bruise in the plucking. He would awaken her fully to pleasure before they mated, for a woman whose body was ready and whose heart was eager to give herself to a man felt little pain, even the first time she was mounted. And, after such a pleasurable first coupling, a woman would always be eager and willing to play with her husband upon their sleeping robes!

Accordingly, he covered her soft, fleecy mound with his hand, and let the warmth of his body suffuse her treasure to its core. He made no attempts at a more intimate caress until she'd accepted this gentle, nonthreatening one. But, as he'd half-expected, she still grew rigid with fear beneath his palm. Her slender fingers encircled his wrist, attempting to tear his hand away. Her breathing came harsh and labored from between her lips as her nails sank deep into his flesh.

"Please, my husband, don't—!" she rasped shakily, some long-buried resistance to his invasion of her body suddenly surfacing. She loved him. She wanted him, and yet—if he continued to touch her there, she thought irrationally—something terrible would happen, she knew it! Something dreadful that she had no control over . . . "Please, no, my husband. Wait! I—I need a little longer to—to—"

"If you would become my woman, then I must touch you here, and still more, my dove. Surely you knew this? Surely your mother explained such things?"

His tone was still gentle, yet it was also firm, reminding her without words what he expected of her; reminding her

122

that he was her husband, and that he would take her—as it was his right to take her—this very night.

"I know, my husband. I know!" she cried softly, beginning to tremble uncontrollably as he delicately invaded her most secret self, and readied her with his hands for their first mating.

Little by little, he explored the tightness of her body. His enflaming touch and deepening caress elicited a dewy response that he knew would ease his passage. And, little by little, her hands fell away, yielding him all. Despite all protests, she melted, surrendered, became all liquid fire and passionate female heat beneath his hand. Panting shallowly, her fingers twined in his glossy black hair. She sought to hold him fast against her, arching her hips upward to meet his flanks, to mold herself to them and rub against the hardness of him.

He increased his rhythmic strokings until she was gasping his name aloud, over and over. Her fingers were tight in his hair now, almost painfully so. She was ready to receive him. It was their time.

In one fluid move, he parted her thighs with his knees and lifted himself astride her, pinning her to the buffalo robes beneath them with his weight.

With the moment hard upon her, she came briefly to her senses and stiffened beneath him, thrusting her palms against his chest to dislodge him, arching her slender length to hold him at bay when he would have entered her and claimed her as his own.

Wolf knew that in a matter of seconds, she would surrender to the sweetness of the fire blazing between them, her fear and resistance forever forgotten in the world of pleasures she would soon discover. But for now, he must be her master, the one to conquer and take control. Gripping her by the thighs, he raised her hips and plunged deep into the warmth of her body, burying himself to the hilt in her tightness and warmth.

Her innocence was swiftly, expertly taken by a man who was no stranger to women, having taken his first soon after receiving his manhood vision at the age of twelve winters: by one who loved her dearly, besides, and wanted all unpleasantness soon finished with. It was accomplished with little pain for Blue Beads, other than a sharp burning sensation that was swiftly past, and the hot trickle of her virgin blood against her upper thighs. Then, to his delight, her cry became a drawn-out sigh of pleasure, and her whimpers of resistance, little aahs and oohs of female satisfaction. He withdrew and thrust, flexing his hips, slowly working himself ever deeper and fuller into the sheath of her body as it expanded to welcome him.

"Now, beloved! Fly with me to the stars!" he urged her some while later, grinning tenderly down at her transported face. In the silvery moonlight that spilled through the smokehole to drench them both with magic, she looked as if she'd discovered paradise! "Soon, you will soar like the she-hawk, my woman!" he promised huskily. "You will flutter like a moth to the light of a lamp! Old Woman will singe your wings with her light!"

Delicious sensation gathered within her. Although it centered in her belly, it filled every pore of her body, as if her skin would burst open like a ripened fruit to spill its seeds. She was like a cloud that grows swollen with rain in the face of a storm! An arrow poised for flight against the tautened string of a bow! A doe tensed for flight in the second it spies the hunter!

On and on Wolf rode her, each powerful, fluid thrust of his pelvis to hers building the need within her, fanning the fires of her passion until the promise of fulfillment towered like a fiery wall above her, threatening to consume her in hungry conflagration.

She gasped and gave a strangled cry as the storm cloud burst; as the arrow sung free, as the doe bounded, as the fires engulfed her!

Soaring, gliding, they climbed to the stars as one, and the moon's magical light singed her wings—gloriously! Gloriously!

"You are mine, woman," Wolf growled, holding her fiercely, jealously, to his chest as his seed sprang deep into her womb. He would never relinquish her, *never!* he swore. She was his woman, and would belong to no other in their lifetime.

"Yes, my beloved!" she sobbed. "Always . . . always!"

Chapter Nine

"Kelly! Kelly? It's time to come back now. Time to return to the present. Do you hear me, child?"

"Nooo! Please, Old Grandfather . . . I don't want to . . ." Kelly mumbled, curling dreamily into a ball on the straight-backed chair and cradling her cheek on her arms. In her coffee-colored gauze blouse and calf-length matching skirt, she looked like a little girl dressed in her mother's clothes, perched there that way, her knees drawn up, her stockinged feet resting on the chairseat. "Just . . . let me stay here . . . with Wolf."

She sighed heavily, and mumbled some words in a strange tongue that Barbara had never heard before.

"Ah, yes, I know. It's wonderful there in the past with Wolf, isn't it, Kelly? There's so much happiness, so much love between the two of you, you never want it to end! But for now, child, it must. The time is not yet here. You must come back, Kelly," Sam insisted gently. "Barbara's here, and she's waiting for you, you know. Come back to the present . . . but remember everything you've seen and heard and felt in that other place, as if it happened just yesterday. Now, your eyelids are growing lighter . . . lighter . . . The sun has gone, and you want badly to open them, yes, Kelly? You *can* open them. Wake up, child, when I give you the word. One. Two. Three. Now, you will wake up!"

Obediently Kelly opened her eyes, and looked about her with obvious confusion.

"Wolf?" she began uncertainly, and then stopped, a look of bitter panic on her features. "Who—?" Dear God, where was she, she wondered for an instant? Where was Wolf, and their lodge, the four ponies . . . ? And who

126

was the old one bending over her?

But then the disorientation lifted like fog burned off by the morning sun, and she remembered. No, she wasn't back in England, nor with Wolf, nor in college. She was in Phoenix with Barb and her family. That's right. She'd come to stay with them, and they were at the Paloverde, Barb's boutique. Barb was standing wide-eyed by the door, with little Billy, her baby, beginning to fuss in her arms. The old man was Sam . . . Sam Cloud. She must have fallen asleep—from the jet lag, probably—and had dreamed that—that strange, wonderful other life that had seemed so very real.

Relieved, she blinked a few times to clear her head and looked up to see Sam Cloud leaning over her, his dark eyes bright and shining as lumps of polished coal amidst their bed of wrinkles and lines. Sam! She needed no help in recalling that strange, pushy little man now! The last of her confusion abruptly cleared, driven out by annoyance, indignation—perhaps even anger! Yes, she was damned well angry at the interfering old man's arrogance!

"Sam, would you please back off and leave me alone? I've had quite enough of this mystical mumbo jumbo for one morning. I told you I didn't believe in that stuff, didn't I?" she snapped, jumping to her feet. "And I meant it! And yet you deliberately ignored my feelings and went ahead with your wierd little experiment! Well, unfortunately, I was right, wasn't I? It didn't work on me, just as I said it wouldn't. I fell asleep, and you wasted your time!"

She turned toward Barbara, giving her a rueful smile. "I'm sorry, Barb, but I find Mr. Cloud here just a bit too forceful for my liking. You go ahead and talk or do whatever you have to do. I'll wait for you outside."

Barbara opened her mouth to protest that it was noon, and scorching outside, then thought better of it. Kelly needed space to cool off in ways that had nothing whatsoever to do with air-conditioning or soaring temperatures! She let her go, and the door slammed behind her with a noisy thud that set the old-fashioned bell hanging above it jangling violently.

"Oh, dear!" she said afterward. "I'm so sorry about that, Sam. Kelly's not usually so touchy or so rude. It's unusual of her to overreact that way. I guess it was a mistake bringing her here, but I thought she'd get as much of a kick out of your fortune-telling and hypnotism stuff as I do! Obviously, I was wrong. I'm sorry if she upset you. I'm sure she'll feel terrible about snapping at you later, when she's had time to cool off and see how silly it all was. She's really very sweet, you know."

"Barbara, you have nothing to apologise for! I took advantage of your friend's good manners, you know! I suspected she would be far too polite to tell me outright to—get lost, I believe the expression is?" He grinned toothily. "But—I could sense how unhappy and confused she is, and I wanted to help her . . . Perhaps—yes, I think I was too forceful about it."

"But I know you meant well, Sam, and I'll tell Kelly that, okay?" Barb frowned, deep in thought for a moment before brightening resolutely, "Well, I've got the tax papers I came for. I guess I really should go after Kelly and see if she's alright—she was pretty upset. I left your paycheck in back, Sam. By the way, Myra called me and said she plans on dropping by tomorrow, around two-thirty, threeish. She has a few more of those wonderful Navajo blankets her mother weaves that she wants us to take on consignment. Can you handle it yourself, or should I drop by?"

"Navajo blankets, huh?" Sam repeated with a disgusted expression, and Barbara remembered belatedly that the Navajo and Hopi peoples were none too fond of each other. "I guess I can handle it. You run along and enjoy your leave. Walk in beauty, little one," he told baby Will, caressing his little head fondly with a gnarled brown hand that was surprisingly gentle. "It is a Navajo saying, but for them, a good one!"

"Great!" Barbara hitched William more comfortably into the crook of her arm and headed for the door, almost reaching it before turning back to Sam. "Oh, and one more thing—will Kelly remember any of what she said?"

"She should. Maybe not all at once, but I think it'll all come back to her, when she's calmer, yes?"

Barbara shook her head, her expression bemused. "It sure came as a surprise to me, hearing all that stuff! I'd no idea Kelly was such an expert on Indian life and lore. She should be writing books if she can come up with all that romantic fantasy stuff, don't you think?"

"Ah, but what you heard wasn't imagination, Barbara, nor fantasies that Kelly was creating. It was her own *past* you heard her describing. Her former life as a little girl named Mary Margaret Rose," Sam insisted quietly.

"Sure!" Barbara said with a broad, amused grin. "And I'm Napoleon Bonaparte! See you, Sam. If anything comes up here, just give me a call."

She waved and left, stepping out into the sun-drenched street and brilliant light that made her screw up her eyes and rummage through her purse for her sunglasses.

Kelly was some distance down the sidewalk, a fairly tall, attractive young woman with the leggy, willowy look of a high-fashion model—an impression enhanced by her gracefully casual stance with one hand crammed into her pocket. The window she was staring into was a travel agent's, judging by the glossy posters of faraway places.

"Ready to go for lunch?"

Kelly jumped, startled, and turned to face her, her lovely face framed by a poster of the Painted Desert in all its glorious colors. It suited her somehow, Barb thought with an artist's eye.

"Oh, Barb, I didn't see you! You startled me."

"Sorry, but here I am, in the flesh!" She grinned wryly and added, "In rather *more* flesh than I care to be in, to be honest, but here nonetheless! Are you hungry, kid?"

"No, not really. I feel more sleepy than anything. That flight over is a killer! I've been close to falling asleep all morning, and I guess Sam's hocus-pocus finished the job . . ."

"I can imagine! But even if you're not hungry, I am — as usual! I guess the ritzier places are out, with my Sweet Willums here. How about a salad at Romeo's? The food's good, and the prices are reasonable, and we can relax there."

"Sounds perfect! Here, let me take Master William Douglas Junior, while his Mommy finds her keys and gets herself organised, mmm? Up we go, sweetie," she cooed, taking the baby from Barb. "Auntie Kelly'll hold you, and we'll be on our way!"

Romeo's was packed with the lunch-hour office crowd, and it took a while to find a parking space, and still longer to get a table. Barb charmed her way into — and a portly gentleman out of! — a plush booth with a window view where she could sit comfortably opposite Kelly, with William asleep in his infant carrier beside her. He'd nodded off on the drive here from the boutique, she saw with relief. This was the perfect time for a heart-to-heart with Kelly, to find out what lay beneath her unusual short-temperedness, and she didn't intend to pass up the opportunity.

They ordered seafood salads, then nibbled on hot rolls and sipped icy white-wine coolers while they waited for the food to arrive. Barbara chatted on about inconsequential matters until she saw the tension drain from Kelly's face, and her rigid shoulders finally relax.

"That's better," she said approvingly. "For a while there, I was expecting you to reach for a pack of cigarettes and light up!"

"After what we went through trying to quit back in college?" Kelly grimaced. "No way! I did start smoking again for a while, though. Before Tony and I were — when it was rough going."

"Feel like talking about it?" Barbara said casually, offering Kelly the opening she sensed her friend badly needed.

"I guess I should tell you all about it, sooner or later." She sighed. "It can't be helping me any to keep it all bottled up inside." Her fingers rubbed and tugged at the hem of her dusty rose napkin. "But it's—it's still not easy talking about it, Barb—not for me, anyway. I guess admitting to myself that I screwed up—excuse the French!—and royally, is the hardest thing. You know me better than anyone! I thought—I really believed—that I loved Tony, and that we'd have the world's best marriage. He seemed like exactly the kind of man I'd been searching for all my life—you know, the handsome Air Force pilot in a dashing blue uniform, all tall and tanned and dark and moustached, and with that flashing smile for a bonus! He was attentive and romantic and he—he seemed to really need me, Barb, and no one had ever needed me before! Oh, lord, I just about ate him up, remember?"

"I remember," Barbara said with feeling, and rolled her eyes. "After just one date, you had the worst case of in-love-itis me and Bill had ever seen! You were crazy nuts about the man!"

"Mmm. And it really seemed as if it was going to work out. First, there was that lovely wedding you and your mom arranged for us, and then Tony getting assigned to a tour of duty in Europe—I'd always wanted to go to England and Ireland, remember? I was so excited about going! Everything seemed perfect."

"Of course I remember. We were both going to marry English earls and become duchesses. How could I forget?" Barb quipped with a rueful grin. "But then, what went wrong? Between you and Tony, I mean?"

"Oooh, nothing concrete I can really look back on and pinpoint as *the* moment when everything started to slide. It was more subtle—an ongoing thing that somehow escalated so quickly, it was out of control before I realized what was happening."

"Other women?" Barb hinted guardedly. With his dark good looks, women had fallen all over Tony, she recalled.

"Oh, no, nothing like that. After we arrived at Mildenhall Air Force Base—that's in Suffolk—we found an adorable cottage just outside of this town called Ipswich in only a matter of days. We took out a mortgage and moved in, and it seemed as if we were all set for a typical, happy-ever-after life. I used to spend my time cooking for Tony, doing minor repairs needed on the house, or driving around the countryside looking for antique pieces to furnish our home with, while he was flying. You see, Tony said he preferred I stay home and play housewife, rather than get an outside job," she explained.

"And the liberated Kelly I know and love agreed to that chauvinistic idea?"

"She did—and without a whimper of protest, too! Oh, you must know how it is, Barb! We were newlyweds, and I loved Tony so damned much, I would have done anything to please him—even walked through fire if he'd asked me to! Staying home seemed the only way to go. Besides, I enjoyed being there whenever he came home, and my little trips into the countryside—at least, for as long as they lasted."

"Oh? What stopped them?"

"We started having problems with my car." Her voice sounded strained.

"So? Cars can be fixed, can't they?" Barb took a sip of her wine cooler.

"Usually. But not this one! Tony finally made it clear that in his opinion, the car was beyond hope, and that we should sell it. By then, we'd fixed brakes, transmission, block—you name it, we'd done it! It'd spent more time in the garage than out of it, so I agreed, and he seemed relieved. I thought it was because he'd been afraid I'd have an accident, but I realized much later that Tony must have been doing something to the car for it to keep breaking down that way, though at the time I never dreamed he would do anything like that! Anyway, the car went, and my antiquing ended. I was more or less housebound."

"Round one to Tony, hmm?" Barbara observed. "I think I see what was happening already. Underneath all that dark charm and poise, he was Mister Insecurity, hmmm? And working hard at turning that wedding ring

132

into a ball and chain, right?"

"That's putting it mildly! Soon, he didn't like the clothes I wore—too revealing, too short, too bright—oh, nothing could please him! He gradually got so jealous and possessive that he started accusing me of being interested in other men—not any one in particular, *all* of them! He accused me of flirting with the newspaper boy—a kid of fifteen, for crying out loud! *And* the milkman. *And* the postman. *And* the village bobby! Oh, Barb, it was so crazy! I tried to laugh it off as a new husband's insecurity, because it all seemed so ridiculous, but Tony—oh, lord, he didn't see the funny side of it, not at all. He came home one day to find me talking to a door-to-door salesman—trying to get rid of him, to be honest, and he—"

"Don't tell me, he hit the roof, right?"

"Right! The roof, first, anyway. Then he hit the salesman, and then—then he decided to hit me." Her voice had dropped to almost a whisper.

"Oh, Kelly, no!" Barbara exclaimed, horrified. She'd known things had been rough for her friend, but had never suspected this.

"Oh, yes! From then on, it was all downhill. I finally admitted to myself that loving Tony and telling myself he'd change one day wasn't working. He needed professional help that I couldn't give him, or else I had to get out of the marriage before he ended up hitting me again. I still loved him, in a funny sort of way, so I tried to talk him into seeing someone at the base hospital, but of course, Tony wouldn't hear of it. It was all *my* fault he was the way he was, according to him. He said if I'd be a good wife instead of a goddamned little tramp who had the hots for every man who came knocking at her door, he wouldn't have to be so violent and punish me. You see, in his mind, I'd really done all the things he accused me of! He really believed I'd had all the affairs he suspected me of having!"

The corner of her napkin, although made of sturdy linen, was in shreds now, Barbara noticed, swallowing.

133

And Kelly's poor, tortured hands were moving, fidgeting restlessly, betraying more eloquently than words her innermost anxieties. The long, slender well-manicured fingers Barbara remembered were a thing of the past now. Kelly's nails were clipped brutally short and the edges were bitten and ragged. She'd always prided herself on her hands, too, disclaiming her looks as average, her friend remembered sadly.

Reaching across the table, Barbara clasped Kelly's hand and squeezed it tightly. "You must have been half out of your mind, Kell," she said huskily, tears smarting behind her eyelids. "I wish I could have been there to help you through it, really I do. Why didn't you tell me you needed me, you idiot? You know I'd have come running!"

"Oh, I wished you were there, too—God knows how many times! But—you and Bill had just bought your house and had moved here to Arizona. You had your own lives to live, without having to deal with my problems. And besides, I felt it was something I had to handle myself."

"There's more?"

" 'Fraid so! You see, it all came to a head one night after we'd been to a dinner party at the base officers' club. It was a farewell party for one of the pilots who worked with Tony—he'd been rotated back to the States. It was a lovely dinner, nice people, and I really thought I could get to be friends with a couple of the wives. But then, Tony insisted we leave early, and I knew as I watched him driving home that I hadn't misread the black looks he'd been giving me all evening.

"The minute we got inside the house, he started in on my dress—it was too revealing, according to him. I'd had just one glass of white wine with dinner—just one!—but he said I'd drunk too much, and called me a lush! When we'd made our strained good-byes, I'd wished the guest of honor good luck in his new assignment, but Tony had misinterpreted that as a come-on, and insisted that we'd planned to get together while Tony was at work! Oh, the list of crazy things he said that night is endless! I knew then that he really was sick—he had to be!—and that I should just be quiet and wait 'til he calmed down, and then get myself out of there as soon as possible. But—I couldn't just stand there and take his abuse, or let his sick accusations go unanswered any longer! Something inside me snapped, Barb—it just snapped! I started screaming and screaming at him, all the misery and anger and hurt of the past months coming out of me at once. He looked at me with a wierd, glassy expression and said in this sort of stilted voice, 'You will be silent, woman! You will not scorn me again!' I've never forgotten what he said—I thought it sounded like a line from an old movie! Anyway, he lunged toward me, and the next thing I knew, I was waking up in the base hospital with a nice concussion and the mother-and-father of all headaches, plus assorted scratches and bruises and so on. The neighbors had heard the ruckus and screaming, apparently, and called the police, luckily for me. They said—they said he meant to kill me, Barb," she ended in a whisper.

"Oh, lord, thank God they heard you and helped! And what happened to—to him?"

"Tony? Oh, Tony was put in the hospital, too. The emotionally disturbed ward, as it turned out, though the medics called it the cracker factory. When I was well enough to handle it, the doctors came and told me Tony'd had a complete breakdown, in their opinion. He'd also been diagnosed as suffering from paranoid schizophrenia—claimed he'd lived before as a Comanche warchief, one nurse told me in confidence. Oh, you name it, Tony had it with bells on, according to the shrinks! They suggested—very tactfully, of course—that I seriously consider starting a new life alone. I knew they were trying to tell me they were convinced Tony'd never completely recover from his illness. But by that time, I didn't need their suggestions. I knew what I wanted—I wanted *out* of that nightmare!"

"And you never saw Tony after that night?"

"Once. I decided I'd do the decent thing and tell him face-to-face that I was divorcing him, rather than having the papers served on him without warning. That was a bad mistake on my part. The minute I walked into the room, he reacted violently, ranting and raving that I'd betrayed him. They finally calmed him down, but then he wouldn't stop insisting that he loved me, crying and begging me not to go, asking me to wait for him. In the end, I promised I would. I left — and I never looked back, never saw him again." She took a long, thoughtful sip of wine.

"You didn't come back to the States, though. Why not?"

"The doctors had told me that Tony would be flown stateside and hospitalized at a military institution here — San Francisco, actually. I decided I liked living in England, and that I'd stay there until I got myself together. It seemed the further I could get from Tony, the better and safer I'd be," she finished with a shudder. "So. There you have it all! My whole sordid little story. So much for happily-ever-afters," she said bitterly.

"Hey, don't knock it, kid — you got *out!* So many poor women don't," Barbara observed sadly. She paused for a moment, and then decided to dive in head first and mention what had happened that morning, rather than mince words. "Sam said that he could sense how unhappy you'd been. It seems he was right."

"Oh, yes, the amazing Sam Cloud! I'd almost forgotten that crazy old man!" Kelly remarked with unusual sarcasm, a flicker of irritation crossing her lovely face. "I know how concerned you were about me, Barb, but please, no more heart-to-hearts with Sam about my washed-up marriage, okay?" she asked, trying to sound firm and yet keep her tone light and friendly. "It's over and done with anyway, and I'd sooner not dredge it all up again — with anyone."

"Me? But I haven't said a word to Sam about you or Tony — other than that you were coming to stay with me and Bill, and might possibly be working at the boutique for a while," Barbara protested, hurt that Kelly would think otherwise.

"Hmm. Really?" Barbara nodded indignantly. "Well, then, Momma Margot must have said something, and Sam put two and two together. I'm sorry, Barb."

"Mom? I really doubt that! She loves to talk, true, but she wouldn't normally discuss a friend's personal life with someone else—her own maybe, but never a friend's, and certainly not yours! She thinks of you as her daughter. You know that!"

"I know, bless her, but someone must have told Sam about my lurid past, right? If you and Marge didn't, who did?"

"Mmm. Maybe Mom did say something then, in passing, and Sam put two and two together, like you said. I'll ask her when she gets back from Aunt M's. Remind me, okay? Meanwhile, talking of getting back, you'd better hurry up and finish that salad so we can get out of here. Bill's bringing a friend home for dinner tonight, and I'm planning on making veal cordon bleu *if* I can get to the market—unless you'd rather have peanut butter and jelly sandwiches?"

"You wouldn't be trying to matchmake again, would you?" Kelly asked, suddenly suspicious and giving Barbara an accusing look across the table. Barb had been famous for her attempts to play Cupid back in college, and now she had that transparently innocent look on her face that Kelly remembered only too well!

"Hardly!" Barbara retorted, trying to look wounded. "Devin is sixty if he's a day, balding, and with a potbelly that would make Santa look skinny."

"Liar!"

"Oh, all right, I confess, I'm lying! Guilty as charged, your honor!" Barbara admitted with a sneaky grin. "Devin Colter is one of the few true hunks left on the face of this planet—six-two, sexy brown eyes that have a delicious come-to-bed-with-me droop, crisp black hair, and a smile that would melt an iceberg. And not only is he good-looking, he's warm and sensitive and one of the sweetest men I've ever met, with a zany sense of humor—*and* a thriving pediatric practice. I just *know* you'll love him!"

Chapter Ten

"More wine, Kelly?"

"Mmm, please, Bill!"

Kelly took the refilled glass and smiled her thanks at Barbara's husband. She was fond of Bill, a football player who'd never lost the tall, beefy build of the sport's rigorous conditioning of his college days. He was a big bear of a man who'd always treated her with the indulgent affection and concern of an older brother.

Bill Douglas had specialized in family practice while doing his internship and residency in Houston, Texas. That was where he'd met Devin Colter, Kelly discovered as the enjoyable evening flew by. Devin, Bill's best friend, was also a doctor, Kelly'd learned from Barb, and after meeting each other again two years ago at a medical conference convened to discuss the growing AIDS problem, Devin and Bill had realized how well they could work together, and had decided to become partners.

Accordingly, they'd opened their offices together, Bill pursuing his interest in family medicine, Devin specializing in pediatrics. The combination had been a successful one, and now—two years after they'd first hung out their shingles—Douglas and Colter found their appointment books crammed for several weeks in advance, with new patients coming in daily.

"Quit stalling, Kell. It's your turn to draw—no matter how many times you have that glass refilled!" Barbara goaded her, impatiently tapping the Pictionary game board set up on the table before them with a short but polished fingernail. With her elfin hairdo and wearing a short red dress with bright red earrings that looked like British gob-stopper candies, she reminded Kelly of a robin: perky, cheerful, bright-eyed.

Kelly grinned and winked at Devin sitting beside her. "Why, so it is! I'd almost forgotten! Are you ready, Devin? Now remember, it's *A* for an action word. Think verbs, okay?" she teased, raising her brows.

Grinning back, Devin Colter nodded and smiled his disarming smile.

He was all Barbara had promised, and more, Kelly thought, blushing under his twinkling, brown-eyed gaze. Six-feet-two-inches of athletic muscle and outdoorsman, packaged very nicely in a navy blue T-shirt under a white Miami Vice jacket, now discarded. Cool white cotton pants hugged his lean hips and long, powerful legs. From the belt spanning his narrow waist was clipped a black pager device, which had crackled ominously from time to time throughout the evening, reminding Devin of his young patients hospitalized at Phoenix General. His hair was stylishly cut short, inky black hair with unruly little wisps that softened the severe cut and gave him a boyish air, despite his thirty-one years.

Grinning at her solemn appraisal of him, he lounged back in his chair and drawled lazily in a broad exaggeration of his mild Texan accent, "Well? What's keepin' yer? Fire away, Miz Kelly. I'm all eyes!"

Barbara flipped over the timer and scrutinized the run-away grains of sand with an eagle eye as Kelly's drawing pencil raced over the white notepad.

"It's a pen, a pencil!" Devin guessed wildly, throwing himself enthusiastically into the almost frantic mood of the game. "No, wait up—it's a knife! A dagger! No, an arrow? Is it an arrow? A harpoon!"

"I said action," Kelly reminded him through gritted teeth, wanting badly to laugh. Harpoon, indeed! How dare he?

"Hey, you two—no talking, no verbal signals allowed!" Bill accused sternly. "Why, you're a couple of low-down, dirty cheats, that's what you are!"

Kelly laughed at his phony western accent and tore off the top sheet of paper. Armed with a fresh sheet, she began furiously sketching again, while Devin watched her intently and appreciatively—much to Barbara's enormous satisfaction.

What a gorgeous pair they made, she thought smugly, the timer forgotten. Kelly had dressed for dinner in an oversized, long-sleeved shirt tunic with deep cuffs, made of a slippery, deep blue fabric that matched her eyes. From Paris maybe, or possibly an Italian designer? Barb observed that she'd left the top two buttons strategically undone to reveal the tiniest glimpse of the darker golden valley between her cleavage. Sexy, but classy, she rated approvingly, and the fullness of the tunic made the most of what Barbara'd once considered Kelly's perfect figure—one regrettably grown far too thin by unhappiness, in her opinion. Under the tunic, Kelly wore narrow, matching pants that clung to her shapely calves. They did full justice to her long, slender legs, and ended in a short slit at shapely ankles, where high-heeled, strappy sandals began. Her long hair was a mass of wispy, flyaway curls tonight that framed her lovely face and gave her a sophisticated look. Half a dozen narrow silver chains, an equal number of fragile bracelets, and a pair of huge twisted-silver hoop earrings set off the effect to perfection. Classy but *elegantly* sexy, the perfect choice for an intimate little dinner and evening at home with a gorgeous hunk, was Barbara's private opinion as she glanced back at the timer—and noticed Devin's expression instead. The man was hard put to keep his mind on the game, she noticed happily, but was dividing his time between making dutiful guesses at the word, and in watching Kelly's lovely face, intent and animated now as she sketched.

"Gun!" Devin guessed wildly, but remembering Kelly's reminder that the word was a verb, hastily amended, "Fire! Shoot! Oh, no, folks—what's this critter she's drawing now? A donkey? No, no, it's a mule—? No, wait, I've got it—it's a rabbit, right? Rabbit, gun, spear—whoa, got it, it's *hunt!*"

He roared the correct answer as the last three grains of sand slipped through the narrow waist of the timer, and Barbara snorted in disgust.

"There's definitely some monkey business going on here! *No* body could get that one from Kelly's awful drawings!"

Kelly giggled. "Oh, come off it, Barb! You don't have to have majored in art like you did just to play this game! It only requires a modest amount of intelligence and—"

"—and the cutthroat instinct of born winners!" Devin finished in a wicked, bloodthirsty voice. He winked companionably at Kelly. "Well done, lil' pardner."

"You, too, pardner! I couldn't have done it without you!" she came back, thumping him in the chest. "Now, roll the dice, and let's wipe these losers off the board! A six should do it! Come on, six!"

It was after two o'clock when Devin finally said his good-byes and left. As he leaned forward at the door to kiss Kelly on the cheek in friendly farewell, he murmured huskily in her ear, "I really enjoyed this evening, Kelly. How about having dinner with me?"

"Thanks, Devin, I'd really like that," she agreed, the spot where he'd kissed her cheek tingling pleasantly.

"Me, too, pretty lady. I'll call you tomorrow to set up a time, okay?" he promised, touching her briefly on the shoulder, but his eyes lingered caressingly on her flushed face, and she sensed he wanted badly to kiss her properly. Thank God Bill and Barb are here, she thought, unable to quell the feelings of terror the prospect of such closeness to a man—any man, even this one!—engendered. The thought of Devin kissing her, or holding her in his arms, alternately thrilled and terrified her . . .

But shyly, she managed to nod. The wine had relaxed her somewhat, erasing the faint tension lines about her mouth and eyes and softening her lovely, delicate features. Laughter and good companionship had added a vivacious sparkle to her deep blue eyes. For the moment, Tony and their disastrous marriage was almost forgotten. She couldn't go on this way, she told herself sternly, avoiding men, sidestepping relationships, shunning intimacy on

142

any level. She had to take that first step to get back into the real world again, with all the vulnerability that involved. Tony was in the past—finished, ended. She had to make the effort to build a new life for herself, of finding someone decent to love who'd love her in return.

"I'll look forward to it," she murmured, and with one last, lingering brush of his fingers against her cheek, Devin was gone, whistling jauntily as he made his way out to his car.

"Ah ha! I do believe you made a conquest tonight!" Barbara declared a short while later, as the two of them gathered up glasses and half-emptied bowls of peanuts and cut vegetables and dips from the living room. They carried them into the kitchen to be stowed in the dishwasher.

"Conquest?" Kelly snorted. "I'd hardly call it a conquest. Poor Devin! He could hardly fail to be nice to me after you'd so obviously paired us off together, now could he? Subtle you ain't, kid!" she complained ruefully as she arranged wineglasses upside down in the top rack of the dishwasher, and added detergent to the well.

"He asked to see you again, didn't he—as he was leaving, I mean?"

"He did—as you know very well! God, Barb, I could almost see your ears flapping from across the room! Yes, he suggested dinner, *and* said he'd call me tomorrow. Satisfied?"

"And you said . . . ?"

"I said okay," Kelly admitted with marked lack of enthusiasm.

"Okay? The most gorgeous hunk in the western hemisphere suggests dinner, and you just said okay? Oh, lord! Where did I go wrong!" Barb wailed, clutching her chest theatrically. "Where did I fail you, my child?"

"Just count yourself fortunate I didn't send him screaming into the night," Kelly cautioned. "To be honest, after my bad experience with Tony, my initial reaction was to do just that. Luckily for you, I restrained myself."

"Mmm. I suppose I shouldn't expect too much of you, just yet," Barbara allowed generously. "It is early days, I

143

suppose."

"Thank you," Kelly said dryly. "Does this mean you won't try to marry me off again before Christmas?"

Barbara stuck out her tongue rudely, prevented from retorting further by Bill's appearance.

"Where do you want these, hon?" he asked, filling the kitchen doorway with his large frame. He was holding a bundle of soiled linen napkins in one hand, and an armful of scrunched-up papers in the other.

"Napkins in the laundry hamper, the drawing papers you can throw away—unless Kelly wants to keep her and Devin's winning artwork?"

"No, thank you! I don't need any reminders that we beat the pants off you, thank you very much! The warm glow of victory is quite enough of a reminder!"

"Humble, aren't we?" Bill retorted with a grin. "Must admit, though, I'm quite impressed by the detail in some of your sketches. Look at this one!" He unrolled and flattened out the crumpled sketch of an Indian lance, holding it up. It was incredibly detailed, complete with decorative eagle feathers, rawhide bindings, and medicine symbols.

"Yes, I noticed that one, too," Barbara acknowledged. "And by the way, I've been meaning to ask you all day— what on earth happened this morning with Sam Cloud, Kell? The things you came up with—well, they were amazing! All the years I've known you, I'd never dreamed you knew so much about Indian life! You should have been there, Bill. I think Kelly convinced Sam completely that his hypnotism worked!"

"Been where?" Bill asked, consigning the papers to the trash can and going through into the adjoining laundry room to add the napkins to the hamper.

"At the boutique. You see, Sam persuaded Kelly to let him put her into a trance, or hypnotise her or *something,* right, Kell? Well, when I came back from changing Will, she was recounting the most incredible story!"

"Really? He hypnotised you?" Bill looked at Kelly with new interest. "Personally, I'd have said you'd prove a difficult subject, especially for a layman. Too controlled, too uptight, and resistant to suggestion."

Kelly flushed and looked flustered, her former happy calm evaporated by annoyance that Barbara had brought the disturbing matter up. She'd overreacted this morning, she'd decided on retrospect, and she felt enormously guilty when she remembered how mean she'd been, snapping at poor Sam that way. "You're right—I was an impossible subject for hypnosis. Sam tried, but it didn't work, and I fell asleep instead," she insisted. "He also tried to tell me I'd lived before, and that my unhappiness now stemmed from a disappointment or something in a former life—I'm sure you know how that crazy nonsense goes? Channelling and past-lives regression and so on is all the rage in California right now, apparently. There're dozens of books out about it, I've noticed. Anyway, Barb's Sam tried the old 'your-eyelids-are-growing-heavier' number, and it plain didn't work. That's all there was to it, Bill, there's no mystery about it. I don't know what Barb's getting at. What story?"

"You mean you really don't remember? You didn't make that lot up for Sam's benefit?" Barbara almost squeaked.

"What lot?" Kelly demanded, her annoyance building. She hated lying to anyone, especially, Barb, but why wouldn't her friend let well enough alone for once?

"That story you told—the one about being a little girl named Mary Margaret Rose Kelly who lived in the 1800s? And about being captured by the Apache from Fort Agave—you do remember, don't you, Kell? You must! I had goose bumps all over me, listening to you!"

"Captured by the Apache?" Kelly looked across the spacious ceramic-tiled kitchen at Bill and rolled her eyes. "Time to take your wife to bed, I do believe, Bill. Fatigue and too much wine—and the trauma of losing, too, maybe!—have done her in, poor kid! She's making even less sense than normal!"

"Don't poor kid me, Kelly Michaels! I *heard* you! You told Sam all about how this Comanche warrior had kidnapped you from the Apaches and taken you to his people

145

to be raised by his aunt, Spotted Pony—and how you fell head over heels in love with him but this other Indian—Broken Hoof or something, his name was—wanted you for himself, and so the two of you were forced to run away. Surely you remember?"

"Spotted Pony? Apaches *and* Comanches, mmm? How can I remember anything, Barb? *Nothing* happened this morning—other than that pushy old man trying to work his witch doctor's mumbo jumbo on me, and striking out." She shuddered. "Quite frankly, Barb, your Sam Cloud gives me the creeps! I don't understand what you see in him, really I don't. Now, if it's all the same to you two, I think I'll be off to bed. Lord, I'm beat," she added, stifling a huge yawn. "It was a lovely evening, a wonderful dinner, and I'll see you in the morning. Good night, Barb, Bill."

They murmured their good nights in return, and Kelly left the Douglases alone.

"Well! What do you make of that?" Barb demanded in an aggrieved tone after Kelly'd gone.

"The fatigue? Oh, just jet lag, probably. Nothing to worry about, unless it persists," Bill diagnosed in his best professional tone.

"Not the fatigue, honey—her denial that anything happened this morning! I was there, Bill, and I heard her! Sam had put her into some kind of trance, I guess it was, and she was reeling off this long, involved story about Comanche life as if she was watching a movie or reading from National Geographic. After about half an hour, she came around, and was really short with Sam and ran out of the store. I asked Sam about it—sort of teased him a little, to be honest and he got quite defensive, too, and insisted Kelly was describing a past life she'd lived. Do you believe in that stuff—you know, reincarnation?"

Bill frowned and shrugged his broad shoulders. "In my business, you see some strange things every now and then, Barb—patients who recover complete health who should—by medical standards, at least—have died. Or at very best, remained alive as little better than vegetables,

146

kept going on machines. But the human spirit is strong, honey—far stronger than we give it credit for being. I suppose, given that, reincarnation is theoretically possible. The spirit or soul, or whatever you choose to call it, surviving the lifespan of its mortal shell. Half the world believes that reincarnation is a fact, rather than a theory, after all. Eastern religions teach their followers that this life is just one of many such lives, each one a level that brings them closer to a state of perfect wisdom or oneness with God, or whatever you choose to call it."

"I know all that, hon—but what do *you* think?"

"I don't know. But—if I had to make an educated guess in Kelly's case, at least, I'd say it was far more likely that in her exhausted state, her subconscious invented a nice, comfortable little story of a happy former life with a man she was wild about. A fantasy world as far removed from Tony and reality as she could possibly get."

"Wishful thinking, you mean?" Barbara asked doubtfully.

"You could call it that," Bill agreed. He slipped his arms around his wife's waist and kissed the top of her head. "Come on, Barb, give it up for tonight. It's too late for all this profound, philosophical whatnot, honey. Let's go to bed and catch an hour or two of sleep, hmm, before that son of ours wakes us up for his four o'clock feeding!"

"All right. You get the lights in the living room and check the front door, and I'll finish up here."

With a grin and a cheeky salute, Bill went to do as she'd instructed. They met again in the hallway five minutes later. After looking in on the baby, sleeping soundly in the amber glow of a teddy bear night-light, they turned into their bedroom.

"There is one thing I think I ought to tell you—nothing to do with reincarnation, though," Bill said seriously, slipping his arm about his wife's waist. "It's about Tony. I didn't want to say anything this evening, in case it spoiled the fun."

"Kelly's Tony, you mean?"

"Right! You remember Royce James, my old med

school pal who was in Denver when Kelly and Tony got married, don't you? He was the one your mom talked me into inviting to the reception at the last minute. She swore he looked lonely!"

"I remember — the tall, skinny guy with sandy-colored hair who'd become an Air Force doctor, right? Oh, unzip me, would you, please, babe?" she requested as Bill closed their bedroom door behind them.

"That's him," he agreed, complying, absently kissing the soft nape of her neck as the zipper skimmed down its track. "Well, Royce — Lieut. Colonel Royce James, he is now, by the way — is in town on leave. He stopped by the office to say hi this morning, and we ended up having lunch together and playing a game of racquet ball. Well, in the process, we got talking, and he mentioned Tony, and how tragic it was that his and Kelly's marriage had turned sour. You see, it turns out he'd treated Tony on a professional basis a while back, and he implied that he's pretty badly off."

"Yes, I know, isn't it awful? I gathered as much from Kelly over lunch today. We went to Romeo's," Barb said with a heavy sigh, stepping out of her dress and slipping it onto a hanger in the closet.

Taking a seat before her dressing table, wearing only a white slip, she removed her makeup with cotton balls and cold cream, then brushed her teeth and undressed for bed. Looking cute and silly in a skimpy sleep-shirt with penguins printed across the chest, she continued, "He went completely off the deep end, apparently. Accused Kelly of everything you can think of, and got pretty violent about it, too, poor kid. She's better off without him, if you ask me. Just think, he could have killed her, Bill!"

"That's what Royce implied, though he couldn't say too much, of course, without breaching confidentiality. There was one thing he did let on that disturbed me, though," Bill confided, his broad-featured face unusually serious as he unbuttoned his shirt.

"What was that?" Barbara asked, turning to face him inquiringly, and pausing as she brushed her hair. The

148

graveness of his tone alerted her that what he was about to say was serious.

"Tony discharged himself ten days ago—just walked away from the military psychiatric facility in San Francisco where he was being treated. He's out there somewhere, Barb—and Royce'd bet money he's looking for Kelly! He warned me that he might try to find us, and through you, her. It's unlikely he'll be able to get as far as Phoenix before he's apprehended, but I thought you should know, and be on your guard. Just in case."

"Is—is he considered dangerous, then?" Barbara's face was pale now, her alarm obvious in her shaky tone.

"Not to people in general, no, Royce didn't seem to think so, and he's no fool. But to Kelly—?" Bill shrugged. "I'd say Royce thought he was, judging by his expression when I told him Kelly had come back from England and was staying with us. Remember, hon, Michaels is mentally ill, and he's carrying a hefty grudge. He expected Kelly to wait for him until he got released from the hospital, like a loyal, dutiful wife, but instead, she divorced him—deserted him, he probably considers it, in his sick mind. Who knows what's going on in his head now?"

Who knew, indeed? Barbara thought anxiously as she climbed into bed and lay down alongside Bill. Despite her own fatigue, sleep wouldn't come.

Chapter Eleven

Down the hall in the pale orchid guest room, Kelly was also having trouble falling asleep, despite the lateness of the hour.

Barbara's questions before she'd turned in had reminded Kelly of everything she'd been trying to pretend hadn't happened.

Despite what she'd insistently told her friends, she remembered every detail of the fantasy life she'd described to Sam Cloud. Oh, yes, right down to the last fringe on the hem of her doeskin robe, the smallest bead on her moccasins, the precise way the sweat had collected like dew on Wolf's broad forehead as he made wild, passionate love to her. Not to mention the exact timbre of his husky, sensual voice, telling her she would be his for always . . . always . . .

Oh, Christ! she thought, badly frightened, there *had* to be a logical answer to all of this! She was an intelligent woman; one who'd certainly have remembered where she'd come by all her information about the Comanche people — *if* she'd come by it through normal channels.

Her mind churned, looking for an answer. She was no stranger to all the layman's self-help and pseudo-psychology manuals available nowadays in the book stores. Armed with the knowledge she'd gleaned from them, logic insisted that the images she'd seen and experienced as vividly as if they'd been true memories of her past *must* have stemmed from her subconscious. There was no other possible explanation for them, she told herself sternly! They had to be the result of a deep-seated need in her to find someone to love, and to love her unconditionally in return. Not an unnatural end result of being passed from foster home to foster home as a child, surely? She'd simply combined her fear of committing herself to a real-life relationship after Tony's cruelty into a romantic fantasy, it was as simple as that.

But—if that were the case, how on earth had her imagination managed to flesh out such vivid, detailed fantasies? She'd always hated western books and western movies. She'd had little interest in Native American Indians and their culture. *So where, Kelly Michaels,* she wondered, tossing and turning, *did all that information come from?* And what did having all this knowledge she knew she shouldn't—couldn't!—possess, mean? Was that bossy old Sam Cloud not so crazy after all? Had she *really* been reliving actual memories of a former life . . . or . . . was she going crazy herself? Was that the answer? *No!* It was impossible . . . too ridiculous . . . too frightening . . . to even contemplate seriously.

But when she closed her eyes, Wolf's lean and handsome face at once filled her mind. His morning glory eyes smoldered with love and desire for her, like blazing jewels set in a copper-skinned face, whose high cheekbones and strong jaw lent it an exciting, savage cast. Thick, glossy black hair as inky dark as a raven's wings swept down to meet broad, muscular shoulders, and, dangling from his scalp-lock hung an eagle's white down-feather, so soft and fluffy it trembled in the faintest breeze. The symbol of life!

With a cry of denial, Kelly forced her eyes to open, and remained that way, unblinking, determined not to sleep and give in to her delusions, or her fantasies, or whatever the damned things were—!

Yet before too long, fatigue won out. Her eyelids fluttered, growing too heavy to raise. She sighed heavily, buried her face in the pillow, and gave up the fight. Her body stilled, and her restless tossing ceased. Her breathing became the deep, even rise and fall of sleep.

And, inevitably, with sleep came the dreams. Or was she really still awake, and the things she saw not dreams, but memories . . . ?

* * *

151

They had been exiled from the Comanche band of Chief Black Hawk for three moons. The fierce heat of summer was fast mellowing into fall, Blue Beads observed, gazing up at the pale, gray-washed sky above as she arched her aching back and flexed her throbbing arms and shoulders.

In the foothills of the mountains, the trees had donned robes of yellow and red leaves. Damp, cool mists rose from Mother Earth each morning, and returned each night, drifting in smoky, wispy wraiths between the trees. Although it was still warm and sunny during the daylight hours, Sun had weakened and lost much of his fierceness. Darkness brought a damp chill that seeped deep through one's flesh to gnaw at the bones like a hungry dog, and Old Woman moon rose huge and bloody over the empty plains. Comanche moon, the white men had fearfully named it, for such bright, moonlit nights were favored by the People's war chiefs for their raids.

Brother squirrel was beginning to gather nuts for the harsh winter that lay ahead, and like him, Blue Beads gathered *piñon* seeds for roasting. So, too, were the brambles and bushes heavily hung with clusters of berries, ripe and sweet for the making of pemmican. The tasty mixture of mashed berries, dried meats, and fat fed the People when snow lay deep upon the ground, and game could no longer be readily found.

The humpback that roamed the land in vast herds had grown shaggier, thicker coats now, prime pelts that would make warm robes for the months of winter. From the perimeters of the white man's wooden villages they'd passed, the cool air rang with the sound of many axes felling trees and chopping them into great stacks of logs that were piled in the lee of every cabin. Sometimes the breeze bore on its current other scents from the white-eyes' villages— the smoky, herbal scent of leaves burning, and the coppery stench of blood as hogs were slaughtered and their meat salted or smoked or dried for winter. The palefaces, too, it seemed, were preparing for cold weather and the moons of snow.

Despite Wolf's fears—and her own—Broken Claw had not ridden in pursuit of the lovers the night they had fled the Sun Dance camp of the People. Nor, for that matter, had her father sent warriors riding after them to force them back to camp. The latter, Blue Beads suspected, she had her mother to thank for, although Wolf had said it was more likely Chief Black Hawk's warriors had voted to join Iron Kettle's war party, and that this explained the lack of pursuit. No doubt he was right, she thought. Broken Claw and her father Many Horses had probably taken the warpath along with Iron Kettle's braves, raiding far and wide to avenge the deaths of Iron Kettle's bands' defenseless old ones, women and children whom the paleface Rangers had massacred in the summer moons; the tragedy Wounded Doe had spoken of her last night in their summer camp.

With such grave business as war at hand, a seasoned warrior like Broken Claw would have postponed his lust to revenge himself on the brother who had stolen his woman—and the woman who had rejected him—in favor of taking fresh scalps to adorn his medicine shields.

Blue Beads sighed. *Aiee, Little Mother, whatever the reason, I miss you—especially now that Wolf's son grows in my belly. I have as many questions to ask you about the bearing and birthing of babes as there are stars in the night sky!*

Yet her happiness was too great to permit such wistfulness to linger overlong. Although she missed her mother, the past three moons had been deliriously happy ones for her—and, she knew, for Wolf!

The two of them had traveled at will and as their moods dictated, riding far and wide across the flat, endless stretch of Mother Earth that the white men called the Great Plains. From there, they'd wandered to this place, a narrow ravine with soaring walls of red and ochre rock that lay deep in the territory the white-eyes called New Mexico, where they'd ridden in pursuit of yet another herd of wild mustangs.

Their own herd now numbered thirty of the finest mares Blue Beads had ever seen, each one carefully se-

153

lected, then captured. No Comanche brave was more skilled with the lasso than her White Wolf, she thought proudly. Why, even the short, olive-skinned people the Mexicans called *vaqueros*—who herded vast numbers of cattle in these parts and were known to be skilled with *las riatas*—could not equal his skills with a rawhide noose!

From the back of None Swifter, Wolf could throw and loop his lasso over a galloping mustang's head. From there, it was but a simple matter to spring to the ground, and wind the rawhide line about the pony's front legs, hobbling it securely to prevent it from escaping. Then, Wolf would cup the pony's soft nose between his palms and breathe into its nostrils, speaking soothing words and calling the pony little brother and friend, until his scent was as familiar and natural to the pony as its own. Thus calmed, the pony would let him slip a halter around its nose and lead it.

Blue Beads smiled with pride and contentment when she thought of her husband, her thoughts flitting here and there like a butterfly dancing aimlessly over a meadow, as she laboriously scraped the flesher back and forth, back and forth across the inner surface of the deerskin before her. Spread over a log that had been flattened by Wolf on one side for just this purpose, the elkhorn-handled flesher served to scrape the remnants of tissue from the inside of the hide. It took skill and perseverance to scrape the hide evenly, and it was with well-deserved pride that Blue Beads counted the colored dots painted on the flesher's handle. Three red dots, five black, a tally of thirty-five hides fleshed and tanned by her in the eight years she'd been with the People! It was a large number she was justifiably proud of, for the work was unpleasant, long, and arduous. But, in almost two moons, she thought happily, when the deer hide before her had been tanned and seasoned and softened, she could add yet another dot to her count.

Some feet away, off to one side of their lodge—which Blue Beads had raised within a sparse grove of young oaks that served to buffer the chill night winds—thin strips of venison hung drying in the sun over racks made of peeled branches. When thoroughly dried, the strips would be stored in hard rawhide containers, making tasty jerked meat that quickly satisfied a hunter's hunger and could be easily consumed on horseback as he rode the hunter's trail.

And soon, if the Great Spirit willed it, her own hunter, Wolf, would return with the welcome news that he had slain a mighty humpback—perhaps more than one—and that she should bring a travois and come and butcher its carcass!

Ah, yes, there would be shaggy robes to warm them when snow lay thick upon the ground, *and* a fat hump for roasting, *and* a liver seasoned with drops of bitter gall, tasty enough to make anyone's mouth water, for although but one man alone, Wolf was more skilled at hunting than any brave she'd ever seen! The powerful medicine of his hunting songs encouraged even the most reluctant game to give up its spirit upon the sharp points of his arrows, in sacrifice to the hunger of its brother, Man. Thanks to Wolf's skills, their bellies had been full each night since she'd become his woman. When the Old Woman rose high in the heavens, they slept content under the star-filled smoke-hole of their lodge, or listened to the restless mutters of roosting birds, the reedy trill of crickets, and the blowing of their ponies, as they enjoyed the pleasures of mating upon their sleeping robes.

On one such starry night, her beloved Wolf had planted his seed deep in her womb, staunching her woman's bleeding for that moon and the ones that came after. She'd suspected then that the Great Spirit had breathed His sacred wind of life into her belly, and that she was carrying their child, and she'd offered the One Above a prayer of gladness and gratitude that she'd not proven barren. Truly, the turtle belt that Doe had given her had proven powerful medicine indeed!

When Wolf returned victorious from hunting this evening, or the next, she would tell him of her secret, and watch his eyes kindle with pleasure like a blue lake sparkling under cloudless skies, to hear that soon he would become a father . . .

"Well, well! Would ye jest lookie what we got down over yonder?" the white man whispered hoarsely to his companions. "Ain't that jest about the finest herd o' prime mustangs you ever seen?"

Tilting back his coonskin cap, his partner, young Mose, spat a stream of yellow tobacco juice to one side and wriggled forward on his belly to look down over the steep, rugged walls of the ravine into the little valley far below. The third man did likewise.

Tucked snugly between a thin grove of young oaks sat a solitary conical skin-lodge with meat-drying racks ranged before it, the crosspieces hung with enough strips of jerky to rival Monday's wash. Behind the tepee, deeper in the little valley, grazed a herd of the finest mustang mares the third man—one named Elias McHenry but nicknamed Cap'n—had ever seen, each one hobbled and staked out on a rawhide leash some twenty feet long.

McHenry chuckled, a cruel glitter kindling in his eyes. Those prime cayuses weren't going anyplace, no sir—leastways, not until he, Jonah, and young Mose were ready to take 'em! They'd have plenty of time to take care of the dirty savages who'd captured them.

His feverish eyes narrowed as he surveyed the valley, looking for signs of life below. The drying racks indicated a woman's presence—a dirty Injun squaw, he thought with contempt. Since the slaughter of his wife and son at the hands of them devil Apaches over eight summers ago, there was nothing McHenry enjoyed more than killin' Injuns. Apache, Hopi, Navajo, Comanche, Crow, Cheyenne, Sioux, old 'uns, young 'uns, squaws or babes in arms—it made no nevermind, not to McHenry. Hell, whatever tribe they called 'emselves, or whether they were young and brave, or old and weak, didn't mean horseshit to him, no sirree—just so long as he could plant a bullet between their sneakin' eyes, or carve their stinkin', oily black scalps from their dirty red hides. McHenry had a powerful fire of hatred burning in his gut for the red men, and it'd take a heap more dead Injuns than those he'd already killed to put out the blaze.

To his undying regret, he'd never caught up with the Apache sons of bitches who'd killed his family that blazing hot summer morning back in '51. The catharsis of avenging their deaths by his own hand had been wrested from him by yet another band of murdering Injuns—Comanches, his scouts had guessed, judging by the arrows they'd left behind in their victims. He and his troopers had found the Apaches' ritually mutilated bodies in a little valley not unlike this one, with no trace of the little girl they'd taken captive anywheres in sight.

McHenry had bought himself out of the Army soon after that, and had joined former blacksmith Donovan Kelly and his sons in their search for his daughter, without success. And eventually, after two long summers and two longer, harsh winters of futile searching, McHenry had given up, believing in his heart that Donovan's eight-year-old daughter, Mary Margaret, must be long dead. He'd said his farewells to Donovan, offered his hopes that someday they'd find her, and gone his own way, since then becoming a sometime trapper, a sometime Indian fighter, a sometime Texas Ranger, and even a sometime mustang catcher and breaker—like he was doing now.

Good mustangs, sound in wind and limb and suitable for training as cowponies, brought a fat price 'round these parts from the wealthy Mexican ranchers, who grazed huge herds of longhorns on their land, and needed a steady supply of fresh mounts for their *vaqueros* to ride. Soon, he'd have more gold stashed in his name in the vault of the new Agave Flats Bank back in Arizona than any man had a right to call his own! And, when he did, he'd file claim on some land of his own, maybe start his own spread, close by the place where he'd buried his loved ones, Rachel and Dane. Then and only then would he send for his remaining child, his daughter Sarah, who'd been living back east with his brother and family since she was five.

A low whistle emitted from between Jonah's misshapen yellow teeth brought him back from his reverie. Glancing sharply about, McHenry saw what it was Jonah had spotted below—a tall, slender young Indian woman ducking out of the low opening to her lodge. She carried a bundle of clothing under her arm as she padded gracefully toward the stream.

By the smooth boulders that fringed it, the woman halted and dropped the bundle at her feet. Seating herself upon a rock, she unlaced her moccasins and leggings and removed them, then lifted her fringed robe over her head, standing naked in the fading afternoon sunlight like a statue of pale gold for several moments, before wading thigh-deep into the icy flow. They heard her utter a little shriek as the cold water closed around her.

"Well, I'll be—!" McHenry exclaimed softly.

"Hell, you'll be anythin', my friend!" Jonah growled, licking his lips like a hungry old wolf. "I seen her first, pardners—an' I reckon it's only fair I get first chance at her. Ain't had me some of that sweet red squaw-meat in I don't know how long!"

"Then it's time you opened your goddamned eyes and took yourself a good, long look, Jonah," McHenry snarled, his lip curling with disgust as he eyed the filthy, wild-whiskered mountain man in his reeking coat of badly tanned skins, stretched on his belly beside him. "She ain't no Injun squaw, ripe for the taking—not with that color hide. No sir! That little gal's a white woman, or my name ain't Elias McHenry!"

"Paawgghh! White or red, black, yeller or green, it's been too danged long since I had me a woman, McHenry," Jonah spat back. "And I aim to have me this one, 'fore long! 'Sides, my friend, my old pizzle's purely colorblind, an' that's a fact."

So saying, Jonah began wriggling backward, obviously intending to sneak up on the girl from behind and surprise her as she bathed in the stream.

"Wait up, you dirty varmint!" McHenry hissed through

158

gritted teeth, aghast. "You mean t'tell me you'd rape one of your own kind?"

"If she is white—an' I ain't entirely certain she ain't just a half-breed—ain't no countin' the young bucks what musta climbed on top o'her afore now. You know Injuns, McHenry—mebbe better'n any man I knows—and you know I ain't speakin' off my head. So, pardner—what's one more needy man ridin' between her thighs, to a woman like that? She's ruined, anyways. She ain't never gonna be fit company for decent white folks agin. So, what's the gold-blamed harm in me having a poke at her too, I'd like ter know? Hell, McHenry, these captives ain't like white women no more, not once they've been mated up with them red-skinned bucks a time or two. Why, they're animals, nothin' but mewling she-cats, jest like squaws. They just cain't get themselves enough of it. You'll see . . ."

Jonah let out a yelp of pain as McHenry's steely fingers clamped down hard over his shoulder and squeezed. Hoarsely, McHenry growled, "Did you ever stop t'consider that maybe she's got a family somewheres, just a-hopin' and a-prayin' she'll come back to 'em someday—a family that'll pay good money t'have her brought back to 'em? Think of the money, you greedy, gold-sucking varmint, if there's no shred of decency left in you! And while you're at it, just consider those ponies, too, why don't you? I counted thirty, in all. Too danged many for a lone brave to have roped alone. Before you go clambering on down there like a damned fool, just ask yourself *who* corralled 'em all, and who shot that game she's drying on those racks, and what in the hell a comely captive woman would be doing way out here all alone? The answer is, she *ain't* alone, my friend! Chances are, there's a brave around within shoutin' distance someplace, maybe her husband and his brother or father, too—and maybe all three. Go sashayin' up to her, and you're likely to lose those stinkin' whiskers and that straggly thatch you pride yourself on! But—if you want your scalp dangling from some young buck's lance, you just go right ahead and get

159

yourself killed!"

"He's right, Jonah," Mose, the youngest and most taciturn of the three, agreed solemnly. "Yessiree, I reckon he's right!" and he spat a yellow tobacco stream again, narrowly missing McHenry's boot.

Jonah's body slumped in resignation beneath McHenry's grip, and the former cavalry captain grunted in satisfaction.

"All right, boys," he murmured, "it's agreed. We do this my way . . ."

Chapter Twelve

Blue Beads hummed as she cupped handfuls of sand from the creek bed. She used it to scour her arms and hands, feet and legs, then scooped up more of the muddy brown water to wash the grit away when she was done.

The creek had felt icy at first. Its chill had puckered her nipples into hard rose-colored pebbles and raised wild turkeyflesh all over her body. But now that she'd grown used to it, the water felt almost warm. She smiled with anticipation as she scoured herself, removing every trace of the blood and fat from the evil-smelling hide she'd been fleshing. Wolf would return soon, perhaps before moon-rise! And when he did, he'd find their herd of ponies safely hobbled, a fine venison stew with wild turnips and onions bubbling in a paunch over the fire, a new hide almost finishing fleshing, and their lodge tidy and welcoming for his homecoming.

And he will also find his woman, Blue Beads, freshly bathed and smelling sweet as any wildflower, with dried herbs perfuming her skin and hair, ready and eager to offer him a more intimate welcome home, she thought with a dreamy little smile. Three sleeps had passed, and she'd missed his strong, warm body beside her on their sleeping robes . . .

She glanced up, startled, as an alien sound intruded into her daydreams. Yes! There it was again, the sound she'd heard! Her mare Badger had whickered an alarm from where she grazed, hobbled on a rawhide tether close to the opening of the lodge!

She straightened and stood thigh-deep in the burbling water, every muscle tensed as she looked slowly about her, scanning the thicket of skeletal young oaks with narrowed eyes, then the rocky red walls of the canyon that towered all about her, while her mind raced.

161

Wolf's stallion, None Swifter, and her mare, Badger, were always kept tethered close to their lodge, in easy reach in case of attack. She'd come to know the sounds her horse friends made very well. And this was not the low, contented nicker her little mare made to welcome her companion None Swifter home from a day's hunting. It was a higher, shriller cry, signalling danger! A warning of some stranger or predatory animal approaching their camp . . .

Splashing clumsily through the shallows in her haste, she floundered to the sloping banks, intending to snatch up her doeskin shift from the huge boulder where she'd left it, and cover herself.

But even as her hand darted out, a hairy gnarled fist rose from behind the boulder and encircled her wrist in a noose of pain. The fist roughly tugged her forward. She screamed as she found herself jerked off her feet and spilled naked into the arms of some great, reeking, furry creature—a white-eyes trapper, clad in the stinking, greasy furs of an animal! Before she could cry out again in protest, his beefy paw clamped over her mouth, stifling her screams.

Eyes widened by horror, she tried to tear free of his grip, drumming at his face and massive shoulders with elbows and knees, using all the strength she could muster. But the white-eyes only snickered at her pitiful efforts to escape. He snaked his arms around her waist instead, squeezing hard and driving the breath from her belly with the force of his grip. His wheezing chuckles sent waves of foul breath billowing into her face.

"You got 'er, Jonah?" rang out a voice in the paleface tongue that she no longer understood.

"Sure do, Cap'n! Got the pretty lil' filly hog-tied, right here in my arms!" Jonah roared, rumbling with laughter at the slender, naked girl's furious efforts to wriggle free of his grip. He angled his head over her shoulder, meaning to plant a whiskery, wet kiss on her cheek before McHenry spotted him. Fleshy lips puckered, he wormed his free hand up to knead one of her hard little titties

162

while he did so. *Damn, she felt good! Smelled purty too — clean as a whistle an' jest as slippery as an eel!* he thought, chuckling thickly. *Titties like Navajo peaches, and a firm little tail that jest begged a man t'—!*

But his coarse laughter was cut short by an obscenity as the girl twisted violently around and sunk her teeth deep into his pouchy cheek, drawing blood.

"Goddamn yer fangs, ye lil' hellcat!" He yelped in pain. "Yore gonna be sorry you tried t'take a bite outta me, squaw-missie!" he hissed under his fetid breath.

"Let *go* of me, white dog!" Blue Beads spat at him in Comanche, and kicked backward, landing a heel solidly against his swollen groin.

Jonah yelped again, then abruptly released her to cradle his hurts.

Like an arrow, Blue Beads sang free of him. She raced across the shale banks toward her horse, her wet hair flying behind her. Her heart was thumping like a panicked jackrabbit as she fled, her feet flying over the colored drifts of leaves beneath the oaks and cottonwoods. The breath poured from her mouth like smoke on the chill air, forced from her lungs in agonized, wheezing gasps.

She was so intent on reaching her mare and escaping the hideous paleface whose scalp grew on his chin instead of his head, she never even noticed the second white man! He sprang up from behind her mare to cut off her escape, and she spotted him too late to evade him. Full-tilt, she slammed into his open arms, brought up short with a cry of anguish and fear as she found herself held fast once again.

"Easy, lil' gal, easy there!" McHenry crooned, fighting the girl's desperate efforts to free herself with ease. He was far taller than she, and had the strength of an outdoorsman to aid him. "Ain't no one gonna hurt you, honey. You jest calm down, ye hear me, Mary? It *is* Mary, ain't it, gal? Mary Kelly?" he demanded hopefully while trying to get a firm grip on her. But her expression remained blank, devoid of any understanding or emotion but rank terror and hostility.

He held her by the upper arms while his pale blue eyes searched her face, yet his grip didn't slacken by so much as a fraction as he said something to her, asked her a question in his complex tongue. Behind her, Blue Beads heard the scrape of moccasins and boots on the shale banks, then other sounds as men scuffed through the dry leaves, coming nearer. White men. Her dread mounted. There was not just one other man, but *two* others nearby, making three—maybe more—in all! *Oh, Great Spirit, send Wolf quickly to free me,* she prayed silently, spitting defiance into her captor's hateful face with her eyes, but saying nothing. *Let him come soon!*

"Don't reckon she understands ye, Cap'n," Mose observed, shuffling up to the pair with his long rifle angled downward in the crook of his arm. "How old did ye say that lil' Kelly girl was when the 'Paches captured 'er?"

"Eight, by all accounts. I reckon you're right there, young Mose. This gal don't understand a blamed word I'm sayin'! She's more Injun than white," McHenry agreed reluctantly. Yet despite the girl's blank expression, he was excited by her capture. That wavy, dark brown hair, those deep blue eyes, them pert little sun-freckles—be damned if the girl didn't look the spittin' image of his old friend Donovan Kelly's woman afore her death! Why, he'd bet a year's money he wasn't wrong, no sirree, not this time around! Damn those stinking redskins t'hell an' back, turning a decent, Christian little gal into a heathen savage like themselves!

Anchoring his hand around the little deerskin bundle she wore at her neck, he tore it off her, snapping the rawhide cord. "Goddamned heathen charms! You ain't gonna be needin' this hocus-pocus no more, little gal! You're goin' home to your Pa, and God-fearin', Christian folks!" So saying, he stuffed her medicine bundle deep into his dirty duster pocket, to Blue Beads's silent dismay.

To Mose, the man added over his shoulder, "Find any sign of a Comanche buck 'round these parts?" His pale, almost colorless blue eyes were shrewd and narrowed now.

"Nope! Spotted some tracks leadin' off down yonder,

though. One horse—unshod, Injun-style. Dung left maybe one, two sunups ago. Hard to say exactly, this time o'year. Ground's too blamed hard."

"Good enough. Chances are, her brave's gone off huntin' t'fill their winter stores, an' likely t'be headin' back this way real soon, wouldn't you say?"

Mose nodded doleful agreement. He was liking these doings less and less.

"Cut out fifteen head o'that pony herd fer our trouble, an' let's make tracks fer home. Oh, an' Mose—!"

"Yep, Cap'n?" Mose turned.

"—leave that black-and-white paint hobbled right where it is. Chances are that red-skinned devil won't notice nothin' awry 'til he's all the ways home, if her pony's still there. I figure it might buy us an extra half-hour's start. By the time our friend figgers out his squaw-gal's flown the coop and lights out after her, we'll be long gone!"

"You got it, Cap'n!" Mose agreed with a grin and a mock salute. "C'mon, Jonah. Let's do like the man says."

Still grumbling, Jonah ambled after the younger man. He cast a hard, cold stare at the girl as he passed her. She returned it with a curled upper lip and nostrils flared with loathing, coupled with blazing sapphire eyes that spat hatred at him like flint arrowheads.

"Sure you can handle that lil' wildcat all by yer lonesome, McHenry?" he wheedled sourly as he did so. "I'd be happy t'give ye a hand?"

"Jest git!" McHenry snarled, his pale eyes icy slits of contempt.

Jonah hurriedly "got."

"Well, well, Mary, ain't this a cryin' shame?" McHenry observed, settling himself on his haunches alongside where Blue Beads was now huddled, watching him with all the wariness and mistrust of a cornered animal. "See, I was thinkin' you'd be happy t'see us, and get back t' civilized folk," Elias McHenry said when he and the girl were alone. "But now—well, I reckon that jest ain't in the cards, is it? I suppose after the trials an' tribulations you musta bin through these past years, it ain't hardly surprising you don't even trust your own kind! So, we're jest goin' t'have to tie you up for a spell, until we can get you safe home to your pa—fer your own good, see?"

Gripping her tightly about the arm, McHenry bent down and retrieved a coiled lariat from where it lay in the grass in readiness. Taking her by the wrist, he jerked her to him. Quick as winking, he slipped the running noose over her hand and pulled it tight.

Realising he meant to tie her, Blue Beads tore her hand away and leaped back, but she was no match for the mountain man.

Like a snake striking, his arm whipped out again. He brought her up short by her long, loose hair before she'd taken even a single step. Twisting his meaty fingers in it, he yanked her roughly back toward him. And this time, he slipped the noose over her head and down over her body to encircle her waist instead, ducking when she spat at him and clawed at his face, uttering what sounded like curses in the guttural tongue of the Comanche.

McHenry said nothing in reply. Jaws clenched, he ignored her furious outburst as he looped the running end of the lariat about her wrists several times. "There! That should hold you for a spell, I reckon. Now, let's move on out, gal!" he ordered, and pushed her in the small of her back to show his meaning, and get her headed in the right direction.

"I'll kill myself before I go with you, paleface offal!" she hissed defiantly, throwing her hair over her shoulders. With a mutinous expression, she dug in her heels like a balky mule.

McHenry frowned and uttered a sigh of regret. "Heck, gal, I surely didn't want it to be this way, no sir, given half a chance t'be gentle! I'm real sorry you're makin' me do this, Mary Margaret, but we're pressed fer time, ye see, an' I don't have much of a choice!" he growled.

So saying, he chopped the side of his hand smartly across the base of her skull, catching the unconscious girl before she folded to the ground.

With Blue Beads slung over his shoulder, McHenry

made his way to where their horses and pack mules were hidden in a clump of chapparal, a short distance down the valley.

Moments later, the trio were riding hell-bent-for-leather across the empty plains, driving the stolen mustangs before them. Lashed across the back of one of the pack mules, Blue Beads's limp body—dressed now in her own doeskin gown by Cap'n McHenry—flopped this way and that, like a rag doll's.

When she came to, it was already full dark. The moon was up. The stars were out. Coyotes were yip-yipping on some distant hill. She lay beneath a mesquite tree, covered by one of her own buffalo robes. The tall white man who'd stolen her medicine bundle was crouched over her, bathing the lump on the back of her head with a water-soaked bandanna. Wiggling her fingers, she discovered she was still tied.

She tried to pretend she hadn't regained consciousness, yet could tell by the light that filled his eerily pale eyes that he'd noticed the change in her. She glared at him, willing him to leave her alone, her face a stony mask of hatred that hid the terror pounding in her heart. What did they mean to do with her? Where were the palefaces taking her? How would Wolf ever find her now? They must have ridden far from the little valley while she was unconscious.

"Reckon I laid into you a might too hard, Mary Margaret," McHenry muttered apologetically. His tone was gruff yet gentle, but it did nothing to allay her fears. "Had me frettin' you might never come to, for a spell there. Here, little gal, drink some! I reckon you could use a wet right now, ain't that right?"

He lifted a canteen to her lips, and braced her head with the other hand so that she could drink. Her head throbbed. Her mouth tasted foul. But the lukewarm liquid he trickled between her lips tasted worse. She let it fill her mouth, then jerked her head to one side and spat the

167

water in Pale Eyes' hated face.

"Keep your filthy poison, paleface!" she seethed.

McHenry ruefully cleaned his splattered face on his knuckles and restoppered the canteen, infinitely patient.

"Have it your way, then, missie. I reckon sooner or later, you'll be real sorry you did that. We have us some long miles to travel 'fore we make Agave Flats—an' thirsty miles they are, too. You'll come 'round by then, honey. Have to, I reckon, or die of thirst!"

He rose off his haunches and joined Mose by their campfire, rubbing his hands together and then holding them out to warm them. Jonah'd drawn the first watch, and was riding herd on the ponies they'd stolen. McHenry'd been relieved it'd worked out that way. He hadn't much relished the notion of leaving that son of a bitch alone with the girl.

"Don't bet money on it, Cap'n!" Mose answered his observation. "She'll die 'fore she takes anything from the likes of us!" He helped himself to a skewer of the meat spitted over the fire. He took a bite, tearing the blackened, half-cooked flesh off the bone like a wild animal. Chewing thoughtfully, he swallowed the wad in a giant gulp before adding, "Heard tell 'bout Injun women starvin' 'emselves to death rather than be a white man's prisoner."

"Ah, but this one ain't no squaw, I'm telling you, Mose," McHenry insisted stubbornly, going to hunker down by the warmth of the fire across from his companion. "She's a white woman—daughter of a man I used to know. She was took the same day my woman Rachel and our boy were butchered by Apaches. The only one what survived the massacre!"

"Hell, Cap, there's been more'n one young'un captured by the redskins over the last few years. That little Parker girl down in Texas fer one, remember? How ken you swear this here gal's your friend's daughter?" Mose reasoned between mouthfuls. In his coonskin hat, with several days of sandy stubble darkening his long jaw, he looked way older than his twenty-one years, yet he'd seen and done more than most men ever experienced in a lifetime. It showed in his eyes, which were as old and empty as McHenry's, though maybe a fraction kinder.

"How do I know, Mose, my young friend?" McHenry repeated, pulling the makings for a smoke from his pocket and shaking tobacco from a little pouch onto a thin paper. "Why, I've got me some proof, that's how! Here, take a look-see at this!" He delved again into his voluminous duster, and withdrew a small round stone. It caught the firelight in a blue streak as he tossed it across to Mose.

Mose caught it and held it up to the ruddy glow. "A glass bead?" His pale straw brows rose.

"More'n that, my friend," McHenry divulged with a knowing smile. He lit his smoke in the flames of the fire, dragging deeply on it before continuing, "See, that there's no ten-a-penny trade bead. That's a sapphire, son—one of *the* sapphires from my Rachel's necklace! The Apaches left it behind eight years ago, after they killed my woman. Didn't reckon it were valuable, I guess. When I rode into the fort an' found her that day, the Kelly's cabin floor was covered with these beads."

He dragged on his rollie, letting the smoke escape in twin spirals from his nostrils, before adding wearily, "Nope, there ain't no mistake, Mose, my young friend! See, I bought that necklace for Rachel—gave it to her myself back in St. Louis the day we were wed! Rachel never took it off, not from that day on. A man don't forget a thing like that, Mose. Yep, that there's a sapphire, I'd stake my life on it! I'd also stake my life on that gal being Mary Margaret Kelly, and that she came by those beads the day she was captured. She was wearin' em as a good-luck charm, or somethin'."

"Still, could be we're all risking our necks, taking her along, Cap," Mose pointed out carefully, tossing the blue bead back to McHenry. In his short life, he'd learned more about Indians that he cared to know. "T'my mind, she don't have the look of a run-down slave-squaw to me, no sirree! She's bin cared for—leastways, cared for as best those red savages care fer their own. Chances are, we've got us a lovesick Injun buck on our tails right now, Cap'n—one with murder on his mind! Way I see it, we'd be smarter runnin' off the mustangs, leavin' the girl behind, and high-tailin' it out o'here right smart!"

"No," McHenry refused stubbornly. "Nothin' can bring my loved ones back, but by God, I aim t'see Donovan Kelly back with his little gal here, an' that poor bastard's mind finally set to rest! The man ain't never forgiven himself fer leavin' his loved ones alone that day, Mose. I don't reckon he ever will, not 'til he finds out fer sure what happened to his daughter. So, any stinkin' redskin comes sniffin' after this lil' gal, he's lookin' t'find himself starin' down the barrel of my rifle, so help me God!"

With that, McHenry fell to work cleaning and oiling his Springfield by the light of the fire.

Mose, meanwhile—still convinced Cap was acting like a danged fool—fell silent once again. He stared morosely into the flames for some time, wondering if the morning's light would find them alive, or scalped and dead.

He was still pondering the same question when McHenry gruffly ordered him to turn in, and went himself to spell Jonah, who'd drawn the first watch.

Wolf was jubilant as he rode back through the deepening slate and amethyst twilight to the canyon where he'd left his woman.

Mist wreathed from the hard ground, rising like wisps of smoke from the drifts of fallen leaves. The air was chill and damp. But although Wolf's muscles screamed with pain and his body throbbed with exhaustion, a warm glow of satisfaction filled him. His hunting had been good! The winter moon would find his and Blue Beads's parfleches filled to bursting with all the dried humpback flesh they could hold! And, come the first snows, there'd be two new buffalo robes to keep the harsh bite of the blizzards from his woman's soft skin, for the spirit of the sacred buffalo had smiled upon his brother, White Wolf, and his hunting chants had proven even more powerful than usual.

"Hear me, sacred brother!" he'd prayed, seated cross-legged before a small fire that gave off the sacred smoke of the herbs he'd sprinkled on its flames.

"The snow moons await us!
Soon, the People will shiver
In their lodges.
The four winds will blow
Their cold breath in our faces,
And hunger will follow us
Like a stalking wolf.

We ask the gift of your life, sacred brother,
Your flesh to nourish our bellies!
The gift of your pelt,
To keep the cold's teeth
From our bones . . ."

For the two suns that had risen and set after bidding his woman farewell, Wolf had followed a small herd of humpbacks from grazing to grazing. Biding his time, he'd carefully thought out his every move. The herds had grown few and far between now, driven from the plains of Mother Earth by the coming of the white eyes. He could not afford the luxury of a second chance.

Little by little, using whistles and bone rattles to startle the buffalos he'd chosen, he'd gradually separated a pair of older cows from the rest of their herd. Since he hunted alone, the usual surround and attack that was his people's method of hunting the sacred beasts was impossible, and so Wolf had determined to use another, even older method, to provide him and Blue Beads with meat for the winter.

Scouting the nearby terrain, he'd at last found what he was looking for; a sheer yet shallow cliff that abruptly dropped away from the flat plain, forming a low shelf. Above, the unsuspecting cows he'd cleverly cut off from their main herd grazed peacefully, chewing their cud.

With prayers to make his spirit invincible, he'd made a great sound and ridden None Swifter straight at the two humpbacks, whirling a pair of flaming pine-resin torches above his head and yipping and yodelling and shaking his rattles until, in a panic, the cows had bellowed and stampeded.

As he'd planned, the massive shaggy beasts had bolted blindly from the path of the approaching danger—only to hurtle themselves over the edge of the shallow cliff, for although big and strong, the humpbacks' sight was poor. From there, it had been an easy matter for Wolf to quickly finish off the bellowing beasts with his sharp arrows, for with their legs broken, they'd been unable to flee him.

The remainder of that day he'd labored long and hard. It was a gruelling task to skin the enormous carcasses, even using None Swifter's wiry strength to draw the skins from the bodies once Wolf had made the necessary cuts around their massive necks and hindquarters. Then he'd butchered the rest, hanging great haunches of buffalo meat from rawhide thongs high in the branches of the tallest trees, far above the teeth and claws of hungry predators. The nights were chill, the days damp and cool, and the meat would keep without spoiling until he returned with Blue Beads and a travois at sunrise. Together, they'd carry it back to their camp for drying.

Wolf's success that day filled him with great pride in his manliness and in his hunter's skills. It also fired an equally great lust in his loins! Truly, he thought as he arrogantly rode his pony back through the gathering twilight to the little valley, his lance in one fist, his round shield looped over the other, he was a fine provider for his woman! Moreover, there was the added satisfaction of having her to provide *for,* a responsibility fulfilled that spread a warmth inside him he'd never felt before. How her storm blue eyes would shine with pride and happiness when he told her of his success! How her berry-ripe mouth would water when he showed her the tongues and livers of the humpback, delicacies that he'd brought her

172

for a treat! And, after they'd shared his feast, how eagerly she'd join him on their robes, and show her womanly pride in all his manly talents . . .

His blue eyes gleamed roguishly in the moonlight as the thought of Blue Beads's welcome hardened his manroot. By the Spirit! For all that they'd been joined for over five moons, he was as eager to mate with her now as he'd been the first time! His heart swelled with the great river of love he felt for her. His arms ached with the need to hold her, and fill themselves with her softness. And his manroot—? Aiee, how it throbbed with eagerness to find the soft sheath of her woman's body, and lodge itself snugly in the honeycomb there, he thought with a low, wicked chuckle. Accordingly, he slapped moccasined heels against None Swifter's sides, and urged the stallion to go still faster over the moon-drenched trail.

On the rim of the little valley, he halted, and sat his pony in stillness. As he looked down at the little camp below, it was as if man and pony were carved from obsidian.

He saw how their lodge made a dark cone-shape against the lighter, moon-washed terrain, but to his surprise, the hide walls did not glow as if a candle had been lit within them. Wolf frowned, his copper face perturbed now. Had his woman fallen asleep, and let the fire go out? Surely not! She was one who prided herself on her womanly skills, in seeing that all tasks were done well. She would never have let the fire go out—not willingly. His sharp eyes strayed further, missing nothing, picking out the white patches of her black-and-white mare, Badger, hobbled before the tepee. All seemed calm and as it should be, except for that darkened lodge. If some danger had threatened her, surely she would have mounted her horse and ridden away . . . ?

Fear squeezed at his vitals, gripping them like a painful flux. Perhaps—perhaps the sickness spirit had breathed upon her in his absence, and even now she lay in the thrall of a fever, too weak to ride away, or even call for help?

Apprehension thundered through him as he roughly turned his pony's head, heading it down a narrow defile that opened out between bushes along the ridge. None Swifter's nimble hooves picked the way delicately down a stony mouflon track that looped back and forth down the valley walls, leading to the wild sheep's watering place by the creek.

As he rode to their little camp, Wolf realized for the first time the great burdens that were inseparable from the great joys of loving one woman above all others. His belly was filled with dread at what he would find there — and with the fear of losing her.

Chapter Thirteen

"Don't scream, girlie!" came a phlegmy rasp of warning from the shadows. "One squeak, an' I'll slit yer pretty throat!"

Blue Beads came fully around from the fitful doze she'd fallen into, jolted headlong into a waking nightmare.

The whiskery man was crouched over her. He clenched a skinning knife in his fist held angled across her throat. His eyes hardbored a lust-filled glitter and an evilness of spirit as he looked down into her pale, frightened face. To add weight to his warning, he pressed the razor-edged blade lightly against her throat. There was a stinging sensation as it nicked the skin, drawing blood.

She understood none of his words, but his meaning was clear to any but a fool—and Blue Beads was far from foolish! Clamping her lips together, she stared mutely back at him, her face expressionless.

"That's right!" he crooned unsteadily. "That's the way of it, lil' squaw-missie. Ole Jonah here ain't aimin' t'do nothin' bad to yer—leastways, nothin' what ain't bin done a hunnerd times already, eh?" He sniggered, hawked thickly, and spat. "Hell, it'll be our little secret from fussy-old-woman-McHenry, eh . . . ?"

She moved her wrists experimentally, wondering with a sudden upsurge of hope if perhaps the other white-eyes had loosened her ties as she slept? But as she'd half-expected, her hands were still lashed together, numb now from sleeping on them. The one she'd called Pale Eyes had tied them with his lariat, which he'd then looped several times around the trunk of the cottonwood tree at her back. He'd done the same thing the first night they'd halted to rest the horses in a mesquite grove. Tonight was the second night. Had Wolf discovered she'd gone? Aiee, surely he must have by now! Was he tracking them even as she lay here, helpless and bound? Was he stalking the white-eyes' camp with all the stealth and cunning of his namesake? Half of her wanted desperately to believe he was, and that he'd rescue her — while the other half feared that if he came, the three white-eyes would kill him!

Whiskered One slipped his hand beneath the fringed hem of her doeskin shift. His fingers felt like sucking leeches crawling over her flesh. She shuddered in revulsion and shrank back against the rough bark of the tree, as his meaty paw squeezed and fondled her thighs. Drawing a wheezing breath, he thrust the skirt of the soft suede garment higher and higher, until it was rucked up about her hips, exposing her bare legs. Spittle shone on his fleshy lips in the grayed light, giving him the look of a slavering animal as he lowered his face to her throat.

She expected wet, hateful kisses — the joining of mouths in the white man's way. In short order, she discovered that Whiskered One had no taste for such pretty preliminaries. Instead, he clamped his teeth down hard into the soft web of flesh where her shoulder joined her throat, while he pressed the steel blade flat against her windpipe. An agonised moan escaped her and, despite his warning, she jerked away from his brutal mouth.

"Shut yore trap, girlie, an' be still!" he rasped. "I warned ya I wouldn't ferget ya takin' a bite outa me, remember?"

Tears of pain scalded behind her closed eyelids as she did as he'd ordered, for his meaning was plain. He drew the blade from her throat and, breathing heavily, used it to cut the doeskin shift from her shoulders. Yanking it clear down to her waist, he drew back to admire the pearly mounds of her dark-nippled breasts, licking his lips in glee.

"Pretty pair, ain't they? Mighty pretty! Too danged pretty fer a blamed savage! Come on, girlie! Open them long legs, real obligin', like, an' let ole Jonah inside ye, ye hear me?"

He levered himself atop her, straddling her captive body. His weight was enormous and smothered her. His foul breath, reeking of rotted teeth, nauseated her. The stink of his unwashed body and his coat of smelly furs suffocated her as he forced her thighs apart with his knee, prying them wider and wider with his bulk. Fighting for breath, she tasted the sour scald of bile in back of her throat and gagged as he ground his hips down hard against her belly. His free hand fumbled, poking and searching between their bodies, until he found the soft, vulnerable core of her with his stubby fingers. His small manroot prodded at her thigh, bruising as a blunt stick, clumsy as a blind mole as it sought out and missed its target.

"Help me, damn yore hide!" he growled sourly. "Let me inter yer, bitch, or so help me, I'll—*eeaagh—aah!*"

With a gurgling shriek, he suddenly slumped full-length across her. He smothered her under his dead weight as if she'd been pinned by a grizzlie!

Over his motionless shoulder, she saw the slim shaft of an arrow protruding from his back in the bright light of the full moon, still quivering with the impact. In almost the same moment, she felt the dead man's nerves spasm in one last twitch. The hot flood of Whiskered One's blood spewed against her breast from his slackened mouth.

Blessed Spirit, Wolf had found her!

He came then, slipping like a silent, dark wraith between the bare trees, keeping to the shadows beyond the circle of firelight where the one named Mose still snored upon his bedroll, unawares.

With a finger across his lips, a stern-faced Wolf silenced her glad cry. Going quickly on one knee, he knelt and hefted aside the body of the white-eyes dog,

177

before drawing his hunting knife to sever her bonds. While she chafed her numbed wrists, he knelt over the body. His eyes were filled with loathing as, with his blade reflecting the Old Woman's pale silver fire, he scalped and castrated the Whiskered One, tying his mutilated spirit to earth through all eternity.

With a grunt of contempt, he tossed the grisly trophies aside, and turned to face her. Jerking his head, he indicated curtly that she should follow him. His blue eyes gleamed, yet seemed somehow fathomless in the meager light—the eyes of a stranger, she thought with mounting apprehension.

His closed expression weighted her heart with dread as she padded silently after him. He had answered her prayers. He'd come for and freed her, true, and yet instinctively, she knew he carried a terrible anger in his heart, and that it was directed toward her. Did he think she'd gone willingly with the white-eyes—was that its cause? Did he believe she'd run away?

"You are angry with me, my husband?" she whispered, unable to withstand the doubt despite the danger.

"Later. Now is not the time to—!"

Yet even as he harshly silenced her, the other, younger white-eyes had wakened! At once, he spotted the pair and the hulking body by the fire. With a roared oath, he sprang to his feet, his firestick braced against his shoulder!

Wolf shoved her ahead of him, out of the way, then spun about like a whirling panther with his knife upraised.

Darting a glance over her shoulder, Blue Beads saw a sulphurous streak of fire blaze from the barrel of the white-eyes' firestick. The sound of the report thundered on the hush. Simultaneously, the blade sang from Wolf's fist. It thudded home, lodged deep in the white man's chest, and the one named Mose toppled.

Wolf was jerked backward as the paleface's bullet ploughed into his side. A white frisson of pain filled his

178

vision with hoops of red and white. He grunted in pain, yet somehow managed to stay afoot despite the impact. His gait abnormally clumsy, his hand pressed to his side, he loped crookedly toward her.

"Aiee! You're wounded!" she cried.

"It is nothing," he growled. "Hurry, woman! Our ponies are tethered by the bend in the creek. Bring them! We must ride, before the other one returns! I have watched him, looked into his eyes. He'll not die as swiftly as his brothers!"

Silenced by his cold, angry tone, she swallowed her fears and obeyed him.

Wolf lay on a couch of heaped young *piñon* boughs, softened by a buffalo robe spread over them. Another covered his sweating body. Although the night was chill and the wind carried a biting edge, his skin felt burning to Blue Beads's gentle touch.

The sun had risen and set several times since the night she had escaped the white men. Although she had staunched his bleeding and cut out the bullet, two suns later the fever had come upon him while he slept. Now it raged through his body, sapping his strength. He tossed and turned and muttered incoherent curses. At other times, he spoke to those who'd already become Star People, as if the Spirit Ones crowded the lodge all about him, clamoring to be heard. He also mumbled in an Indian tongue she didn't understand—perhaps the strange talk of the Peaceful Ones, the Hopituh, who lived in the land of the south and west winds and had given him birth?

"*Naa!*" he called, thrashing about. "Lomahongva, my uncle, where are you? Help me! Ogre Kachina comes . . . he is after me! Help me, *naa!* He'll whip me!" he whimpered like a frightened little boy. His legs flailed frantically, as if he were trying to flee some terrible monster, and his eyes moved beneath closed lids as if seeking an escape.

"Be still, my soul, be still!" She murmured soothing words, bathing his glistening copper-skinned face and chest with water from the creek, smoothing the burning flesh with her cool hands in a touch filled with love. "Please, my husband, don't! You'll open your wound!" She'd brought the edges of the ragged hole together with cobwebs — as Spotted Pony had taught her — before binding it, but the delicate mesh would soon break if he continued his restless thrashing.

But he would not obey, would not heed her in the depths of his sickness. And, in the end, she was forced to tie his wrists and ankles with rawhide cords, to keep him from harming himself. When he was bound fast, she finished bathing him.

Afterward, he seemed calmer, and fell into a deep, still sleep. She touched his brow, and thought it felt a little cooler to her touch — but only a little.

With a heavy sigh, Blue Beads put away her gourd basin and went to sit cross-legged before the small stone altar that was a part of the furnishings of their lodge. On it, she placed a pinch of sacred tobacco, offering it in the direction of the four winds before casting it into the fire. The fragrance of sage and other herbs filled the lodge.

"O, Great Spirit," she prayed, "you heeded my pleas for help when we rode from the camp of the white-eyes! You guarded our path as I brought my husband safely to our lodge! So, too, you guided my knife when I cut the bullet from his side. You made my hand steady, my actions swift and sure. Accept my offering, Great Spirit, and hear me again, I beg you! Drive the fever-spirit from his body! Help me rid his flesh of the white man's poison!"

For four suns now, she'd prayed the same prayer over and over, yet her husband still lay with one foot in the land of the living, and the other on the Ghost Path. She would bathe him with cool water, and his fever would ebb, only to rise again even more fiercely.

She bit her lip and swallowed a knot of useless tears. After all, what good would tears do? They couldn't heal Wolf, couldn't bring his spirit back from where it wandered! Oh, if only they had Yellow Beak, or Semanaw, the Wise One, or some other skilled *shaman* nearby; someone who knew the right medicine chants to drive the evil from Wolf's body! But alas, there was only her, and although Spotted Pony had passed on to her daughter her great knowledge of herbs, and although Blue Beads's parfleches were filled with the dried roots and plants she needed, her juniper berry and black willow bark tea had had no lasting effect on Wolf's fever.

Another night came. Another moon rose and set, the fifth since his wounding. Wolves howled in the distance, her White Wolf's spirit-brothers. Did they mourn him already, she wondered unhappily, adding dry pine boughs to the fire? Did they call to his sick, troubled spirit?

The kindling immediately caught and crackled. It filled the lodge with a pleasant rosin scent as, with a weary kneading of her aching back, she stooped to pick up the gourd of warm broth she'd been spooning between her husband's lips. In the ruddy firelight, a livid bite mark rode at the angle of her throat and shoulder, purple against the pale gold of her neck; a legacy of Whiskered One's cruel teeth.

There were stones heating in the glowing red embers of the fire, and a paunch of cold creek water hanging from a tripod of green sticks. When the rocks were hot, she would toss them into the water. The steam given off, and the buffalo robes she would heap over Wolf's body, might sweat out the fever. They must, she thought. It was her last chance, the only remedy she had left to try . . .

She leaned low over him, her unbound hair fanning out across his sweaty chest, and pressed her lips gently to his parched ones.

181

"Draw strength from my love, my heart, and grow well!" she whispered, running a tender hand through his long hair. It felt dull and lifeless now, his raven's glossy plumage as limp as dry as wild turkey feathers. There were new hollows beneath his unnaturally ruddy cheekbones, too, and the eyes he opened from time to time to stare up at the smoke-hole were abnormally bright and glittering. His ribs showed beneath the flesh of his abdomen in easily discernible ridges, and at his left side, an angry area, the shape and color of a red spider, had spread across his flesh. It extended beneath the drawing poultice she'd made with white clay taken from the creek bed and mixed with herbs: a sure sign that the poison was spreading through him.

"Fight, my husband!" she whispered brokenly. "Are you not a mighty warrior, a proud son of the Comanche nation? Did you not endure the trials of the Sun Dance when little more than a child? Aiee, it is so! Then you must fight this evil inside you! Fight it with all your strength! Do not let the white man's poison win, beloved one, for I and the child yet to come will be desolate without you!"

The rocks were hot. Seeing this, she began covering Wolf with buffalo robes and deerskin cloaks, tucking them close about him. When he was tightly swaddled, she lifted the rocks from the fire using two sticks for tongs, and dropped them into the pouch of cool water.

Hissing steam rose in thick, wet billows all about her, filling the lodge. Soon, sweat began to pour from Wolf's brow. Perhaps, she thought hopefully, it is draining the fever from him? Slipping quickly through the low opening, she dropped the weighted flap behind her, and went out into the cool, moonlit night.

The shale of the creek banks was an eerie, grayish white, like heaps of ivory bones. The ripples of flowing water were shiny black ribbons, threaded with silvery glints. The drifts of fallen leaves were dark red underfoot, but Blue Beads saw none of them.

Her head bowed, her hair a dark curtain that hid her pale face and haunted eyes in deep shadow, she wandered among the sapling oaks, her soul cast low within her.

For several moments, she wandered in silence, deep in troubled thought, until the chilling howl of a wolf came again, close by this time. She glanced up.

There, upon a narrow ridge cut high in the valley walls by the elements, crouched a huge white wolf, its thick fur standing out around it, limned with silver in the starlight. As she watched, it raised its nose to Old Woman moon, and uttered yet another drawn-out, mournful cry that chilled her blood. Her heart clenched in her breast, as if a fist had squeezed it.

"No!" she screamed, and a startled owl rose from its roost in a tree above her and flapped away, hooting. "No, Brother Wolf! He is mine! You cannot take him from me!"

The wolf turned its maned head, the ruff standing out about its muzzle like a war bonnet of silver-tipped feathers. For an instant, its glowing amber eyes seemed to gaze directly into hers, and reach down into the very depths of her soul, challenging her to deny it its human namesake—White Wolf, the one whose spirit it had come for.

"No!" she repeated softly, firmly, her fists clenched at her sides, her eyes blazing defiance. "Go now, my brother! Be gone! It is not your time—and nor will it be his!"

For a second more, their eyes locked, the woman's defiant, a blazing, stormy blue that was resolute with love and purpose, the wolf's glassy amber, otherworldly and unfathomable. Then the massive white beast turned and loped silently away. It vanished between the craggy ledges like a shadow, disappearing as if it had never been.

Blue Beads was trembling as she slowly turned and made her way back to the steam-filled lodge, yet her resolve had somehow been strengthened by her encounter.

No! she vowed, remembering the amber eyes of the spirit-wolf, *I love him! I will not let him die!*

Chapter Fourteen

That night, shortly before the pale yet lovely Morning Star appeared in the sky beside his mother, Old Woman moon, Wolf's fever broke.

He lay in rivers of sweat that ran down his body to soak the buffalo pelts beneath him. And, when his body was at last done sweating, he drew a deep sigh and opened his eyes to her, coming fully awake for the first time in many suns.

"Blue Beads?" he murmured, his voice hoarse with anxiety. "Where are you?"

"Wolf? Oh, Wolf, you're better!" she cried, roused thoroughly from the fitful doze she'd fallen into. "The fever's gone!"

She scrambled across the lodge to his side, and fell on her knees to embrace him. Tears of joy trickled down her cheeks to dampen his with salty trails. A broad smile curved her mouth in happiness and relief. She picked up his limp hand and kissed the tanned back of it, laying her flushed, teary-wet cheek against its coolness. "I was so frightened for you! I feared I'd lost you to the poison-sickness!"

"The bullet—it is out?"

"It is," she confirmed, and he nodded wearily and with obvious relief, his head sinking back down to the pelts in exhaustion.

He slept for many, many hours after that brief awakening, but she was no longer afraid for his life, for it was the true, healthful sleep of healing.

She let him rest, took up her smaller woman's bow and a few arrows, and went hunting up and down the little valley.

Far sooner than she'd anticipated, she brought down

an unsuspecting jackrabbit, with a single shaft before it could bound to safety, much to her surprised delight. It was the very first time she'd hunted out of necessity, rather than to improve her hunter's skills, and her success was unexpected but welcome. She thanked the plump animal's spirit for its sacrifice, for with the gift of its life, her Wolf would have the fresh meat and broth his body needed to regain its former strength.

Wolf didn't even waken later, when she rebandaged his wounds with cool mosses held in place by a length of buckskin wound around his chest. What she saw when she uncovered his wound was even greater cause for celebration. The white clay poultices had finally worked to draw out the last of the pus. The wound, though still deep and open, was no longer red and angry-looking, but clean and free of poison. It would heal leaving a scar, but he would recover, and that was all that mattered. Her heart sang with gratitude as she offered a prayer of thanks to the Great One Above.

The sun was setting before Wolf awakened again and declared in a stronger voice that he was starving.

Whirling about, she hurried to fetch him the gruel of boiled corn and honey she'd prepared in readiness for his waking. He ate it to the last morsel, but with a horrible grimace at every bite.

"Is it not good?"

"Good enough, but it is fresh *meat* I crave—not this babies' pap!"

He made such a disgusted face, she couldn't help laughing.

"Eat the corn mush, and then you shall have some broth and a little fresh rabbit," she promised sternly, like a mother with a finicky child, but her heart was lighter than it'd been in seven long suns of worrying about him. Even to hear him grumbling was now a pleasure—far more preferable to the profound silence or troubled thrashings and mutterings of his sickness!

"Oh, Wolf, how good it is to hear you complaining again!" she trilled, moving about the lodge and setting it

186

to rights with quick, graceful movements, like a small brown bird building a nest. The day's last rays of pale fall sunshine fell through the smoke-hole, and she raised the flap to let in still more of its rays, along with the cool, fresh breezes to rid their lodge of the lingering smells of sickness.

"Pah! You are crazy, woman!" Wolf growled, moving about to get more comfortable with little success. His left side still ached as if Apache torturers had stuck red hot knives into it. His head felt light, his limbs as weak as a cougar kitten's. What did that foolish woman have to rejoice about?

"Perhaps," his foolish wife agreed merrily, laughter bubbling up behind her lips and threatening to spill out. "But what I'm feeling is a good craziness, one with a very good cause! Here, eat your roasted rabbit, my husband, and grumble some more!"

Day by day, the nights became colder, and the days shorter, as fall drifted irrevocably toward winter, while Wolf grew stronger. The flesh returned to him, and his ribs were no longer so sharply defined as before. The luster returned to his hair, the vitality to his eyes and skin. And yet, he was different from the man he'd been before his wounding—remote, aloof, colder somehow—and it troubled Blue Beads.

Sometimes, she'd glance up from one of her woman's tasks to find him regarding her with an expression that was brooding and angry, his jaw clenched and hard, his morning glory eyes lit with some disturbing emotion she could not define—and was not certain she wanted to!

With this new strangeness about him, she couldn't bring herself to tell him the joyful news about the child she was carrying, and miserably hugged the secret to herself, feeling more guilty with every sun that passed without her sharing the happy news.

By now, he had to have noticed that she left her hair unbound each morning, instead of neatly braiding it, so surely he must have guessed, she thought? After all, it was the custom of the Comanche women to braid their hair at all times, unless they were with child. Then it was feared that tying or looping the hair in any way would cause the babe to be born with the cord looped around his little throat. But if Wolf had guessed, he said nothing of it to her.

In fact, he rarely spoke at all anymore—unless it was unavoidable, tending to their remaining horses in a taciturn, brooding way that made her want to scream, and eating the food she prepared with only a grunt instead of smiles and words of thanks. Nor did he offer invitations to join him as before, letting her eat after him, alone, as did other men. Perhaps he'd guessed her condition and was displeased? she fretted. Perhaps—oh, surely not! Perhaps he feared that the hateful Whiskered One had succeeded in forcing himself on her before he'd arrived to free her, and that the child was the white-eyes' seed—?

One morning, as she gathered up yucca root from her parfleche, a fresh deerskin shift, leggings, and new moccasins in readiness to go down to the creek to bathe, Wolf happened to glance up from his arrow-making. His blue eyes travelled over her, taking in the items she carried, before returning sharply to her face.

"Where are you going, woman?" he demanded, uncoiling to stand and tower over her. His expression was stern and forbidding.

"To the creek to bathe, as I do every morning."

Surely he could see that, she thought irritably. She'd not slept at all well the night before, plagued by the need to empty her bladder several times. Unable to sleep when she did finally settle down, she'd caressed Wolf's broad chest and stroked his face with feather-light fingers, pressed her lips to his warm, pliant skin. She'd hoped he would awaken to her seductive caresses and be eager to make love to her. They'd not joined since before his wounding, and she'd missed the intimate nights of love-play upon their sleeping robes. She wanted badly to resume them, now that he was stronger and the risk of reopening his wound had passed.

However, although she'd quickly determined by his breathing and by the stirring of his manroot that Wolf was not only wide-awake, but *very* much aroused by her touch, he'd turned over and offered her his cold back, pretending sleep! Consequently, in the face of such rejection, she was in no mood to answer any silly questions! She scowled at him instead.

"To the creek? Ah, yes, so I see! And where, then, is your knife, your bow and arrows, if you go alone to bathe?"

She scowled harder, glowering defiance at him. "I go to wash myself, not to take the warpath, my husband!" she retorted through gritted teeth.

"Ah! Then are you a reader of minds, that you can be certain no danger awaits you there? No Brother Cougar, perched to spring down at you from a ledge? No paleface trappers lying in wait, hoping to spy upon your nakedness and take you from me by force?"

She took his point, and her lovely mouth tightened. Her storm blue eyes flashed, then narrowed. Spotted Pony and Many Horses had taught her to use a knife and a woman's smaller bow and arrows when she was still a little girl of nine winters, for young Comanche women often hunted with their menfolk and were encouraged to know how to defend themselves should the need ever arise. Yet, knowing Wolf was right, and his pointed yet perfectly understandable reminder that her carelessness had been the cause of her capture by the three white-eyes and—though he'd never openly blamed her—his subsequent wounding, did not humble her as it normally would have! Perhaps being with child made her of a more contrary frame of mind than usual? Or perhaps—more likely!—her own guilt made her overly defensive? She knew very well she'd behaved irresponsibly that day, going to the creek to bathe without taking so much as a knife along for her defense. But, whatever the reason, in her present mood it seemed a fierce attack was by far the surest means of defense! She whirled on him

189

like a cornered she-wolf.

"So! Will my brave warrior-husband not defend me, nor see to my safety while I bathe, then?" she snapped at him.

"The first rule a warrior learns is to rely on no one but himself—or herself—and only after to expect his companions' help," Wolf gritted. "Of course I'm here, and I'll protect you as long as I am, and can still draw breath. But—what happens when I'm away from camp, hunting? Or if I am killed? What happened that other time, when I was not here to protect you, eh, woman? Your carelessness then cost us dearly! The two humpbacks I'd killed that day were left to hang rotting in the trees, their meat wasted, while our winter parfleches are still empty! And three hands of ponies belong now to the pale-eyes who stole them—ponies that took many suns for me to capture. Both time and wealth wasted! And—almost it cost us the life and honor of White Wolf's woman!"

"Huh! It's only fitting you'd count my life the last on your list of losses!" Blue Beads hissed, her voice breaking with hurt, tears springing into her deep blue eyes. "If I forgot my weapons that day, it was because my mind was busy elsewhere. All that day, I'd thought only of your return, my husband, and of my loneliness without you! I wanted to welcome you home, and show you how much I'd missed you. I wanted—I wanted you to find me beautiful and pleasing, and meant to—to bathe and perfume my hair and body with fragrant herbs for your delight. And so—yes! I forgot my stupid knife! And yes! I forgot my stupid bow and arrows! But it was because I was thinking of *you* that I did so!"

"Me? Don't lay your guilt at my feet!" Wolf bellowed, leaping forward and taking her by the arms to shake her soundly. "If you love me, as you say you do, and wish to please me, then it's your first duty to stay alive—to keep yourself from harm! That, my woman, is what would delight me most!" he rasped, his fury—held in check for many suns—bursting forth now.

190

"Perhaps not," she came back sarcastically, throwing off his hands. "Perhaps White Wolf finds having but one woman—a wife!—too burdensome for him? Perhaps the responsibilities of being a husband chafe him sorely? Perhaps he'd rather delight in many women, as he did before we were joined, rather than one such careless, stupid creature as me—?"

She stopped, hoping he would disagree, praying he would tell her she was foolish to even think such a thing, and that she was the only woman he wanted. Her heart sank when he did not. He simply stood there, his expression murderous, his mouth a hard, uncompromising slash, and his blue eyes glacial.

Wounded to the quick by the words he left unspoken, she stifled a sob and fled toward the sloping shale banks of the creek, her bundle stuffed under her arm.

"By the Great Spirit, your knife, woman!" he roared after her, his fists clenched at his sides, wishing that for once—just once!—he could be the kind of man who would thrash some sense and obedience into a defiant wife, while knowing in his heart he was not. "Do you forget my warnings so soon?" he roared.

She stopped abruptly, but remained standing on the creek bank with her shoulders stiffly squared and her spine held straight as a lodgepole pine. She kept her back to him as, no doubt, he thought with grim humor, she silently cursed him!

Then, after a few seconds of crackling silence, she flung the bundle down, spun about on her heel and stalked back to their lodge without looking at him.

She ducked inside it and came out moments later carrying not only her small knife, but his hunting knife, his club, his lance, her bow and arrows in a rawhide quiver, and a small stone tomahawk adorned with feathers—weapons enough for a small war!

"Satisfied?" she gritted, her eyes like thunderclouds.

Hiding a smile, he nodded brusquely, revealing no trace of his amusement to her, and said grudgingly, "For the moment, yes . . ."

Blue Beads was still angry with Wolf when she returned from bathing in the creek, and seemed not a whit less angered when they lay down to sleep that night.

So, she seethed! He regretted taking her as his woman did he? Yes, his silence had proved as much! He'd not even attempted to deny her accusations. And he found her foolish and irresponsible into the bargain, did he? Well, then, by the Great Spirit, she'd not be his woman a heartbeat longer! Let him find someone else to ease his male lust! She'd have none of him!

Wolf's temper was short-lived normally, and his capacity to forgive those he loved virtually boundless. He'd said his piece, and once he had he forgot the little incident entirely — until he found the first amorous advances he'd made toward her since his wounding curtly rejected that night.

When he ran his hand over her hips and bottom, she rolled over, away from him, offering no response but the stiff and hostile back she turned in his direction.

She'd washed her dark brown hair with yucca suds when she bathed that morning. When it dried, it shone with golden highlights in the fire's glow — highlights that he'd itched all day to trace with his fingertips, for their rare color and her hair's soft, fine texture continued to fascinate him.

Accordingly, he stroked her hair, gently, tenderly smoothing it down over her pale back. He fanned it out beneath his fingers and admired the way the ruddy glow of the fire was trapped in the fine strands. Perhaps, he thought hopefully, he'd misread her change of position as a rebuff when it was truly nothing of the sort? But rather than turning to him and coming eagerly into his arms, she jerked away from him as if he'd pricked her with his knife instead of stroking her!

Her actions almost confirmed his growing suspicion, but — with the heady lust he had upon him now — he was reluctant to give up so easily! Ignoring her flinching, he

192

slipped his arm around her waist and cupped the full curve of her breast. Gently, he rolled the nipple between thumb and finger to stand erect, in the way he'd learned she loved. But although she gasped and he felt a tremor of desire leap through her body, she only muttered sharply, "Please, my husband, don't!" and pushed his hand away.

"Why not, little dove?" he asked huskily, whispering cajoling words in her little ear, so that his warm breath might have an added, arousing effect on her. "I desire you, my woman!"

To this she answered primly and with, he fancied, the barest hint of glee, "Because it is—it is my time of the moon! And if you lay with me now, while I am yet unclean, White Wolf's warrior medicine will be destroyed."

She sounded smug, to his ears; taunting, almost, that she-witch! He rolled away from her, anger and frustration quickly building within him. It had been many sleeps since they'd last coupled. His hunger for her was a roaring ache in his loins that would not be stilled! The fact that she slept unclothed, and that her bare bottom repeatedly jutted into his midsection each night—reminding his manroot just how delectable and female she was—did little to soothe his fractured pride—nor ease his towering lust!

"If that is so, why then did you not raise your woman's lodge?" he growled sourly. When a Comanche woman was menstruating, it was customary for her to raise a smaller lodge alongside the one she shared with her husband, and to sleep there, secluded, until her bleeding time had ceased. Blue Beads had always done so when her time came around in the five moons they'd been together, so why not this time? he wondered. Was she with child, as he'd suspected? If so, then she was lying to him—deliberating denying him her body out of mulish perverseness, to get even with him for his sharp words that morning! Or—was she merely stating a fact, after all? Perhaps he was wrong, and she wasn't breeding after all? Great Spirit, curse the woman! He didn't know what

193

to believe anymore—and his own male pride forbade that he should argue the matter with her, or humble himself to plead for his husband's rights like a camp cur begging a bone!

That night set the tone for the days following. The hours of daylight grew shorter and colder. The air bore on its current a distinct nip that threatened an early snowfall, but even the wind's chill couldn't compete with the frigid atmosphere between the pair on their sleeping robes each night!

Daylight brought little less antagonism. Tasks were done in silence about their small camp, and done with meticulous attention to detail. Words, when any were exchanged—which was only when conversation was absolutely necessary—were exchanged with exaggerated courtesy.

More nights passed, long and lonely nights spent with Wolf and Blue Beads laying side by side. His rigid back was turned to her rigid back. His eyes were open and staring, hers open and staring. He wanted her, she wanted him—and yet the narrow space between the two now seemed unbreachable!

After two hands of nights spent in this unsatisfying fashion, Wolf could bear it no longer. Her nearness, combined with her distant, unobtainable manner, proved an irresistible combination. He was a young and healthy male of normal appetites, and he loved her. Moreover, he'd grown accustomed to having his body's needs satisfied at regular intervals by any one of several eager, dusky Indian beauties. And yet now, when he'd finally found a woman to his liking and taken a wife, he suddenly found himself lacking in his sleeping robes, spending each night sleepless with unrequited lust beside a cold woman who acted as if he were a stranger—and an unpopular one, at that!

One morning, as Blue Beads gathered up her possessions and headed yet again for the creek—icy now in the early morning hours—he did the very thing he'd told himself he would never swallow his pride to do. He waited until he was certain she had disrobed, and followed her. He intended to make his needs known in no uncertain fashion!

The sight of her standing there, thigh deep in water with drops of it clinging to her curves like the dew on a creamy gold water lily, proved his final undoing. Any last, lingering reluctance to force her vanished like smoke on the wind. By the Great One Above, she was surely a she-demon, a spirit-woman sent from the Spirit World to torment him with her beauty!

Her fragile oval face was hidden by a curtain of wet hair that swept—dark as beaver pelts—to her mid-back. The contrast of long, wet hair against bare flesh was enormously provocative! Her shoulders were pale and rounded as two lovely hills, and coated with frothy bubbles from the yucca root she'd lathered them with, foamy as new-fallen snow. Remembering how he'd loved to nuzzle their moss-smooth roundness, he groaned in torment, but gazed on nonetheless. Although he was torturing himself with his spying, he was unable to look away!

The slender line of her throat flowed down into pert, uptilted breasts, with little pointed berry-crests that were deep rose in color. The peaks had puckered impudently from the water's chilly embrace, he noted and his eyes were drawn to the single, glistening droplet that clung to the very tip of one nipple. Having noticed this, Wolf ached to join her in the water. Ached to sip that droplet from her body like a thirsty bee, sipping nectar from a wildflower!

Silently, he crouched down in the thicket of chapparal where he'd hidden and unlaced his fringed buckskin shirt. Quickly, he drew it over his head. In silence, too, he swiftly unfastened breechclout and leggings and the rawhide sheath that held his knife, and shucked them off. Even more silently, he padded down the shale banks toward her, his raven hair swinging, his eyes gleaming with lusty purpose in the morning sunlight.

Excitement filled his veins. His blood pounded. His heart drummed. *Aieeyiihah!* He was again White Wolf, the hunter, following the hunter's trail; she, the prey he would run to ground, and pierce with his short lance! His grin deepened wickedly as he offered a teasing hunting chant to the Great Spirit—one that would bring his little doe swiftly to her back beneath him!

His arousal was very much in evidence now. His man-root stood erect and proud from his lean, hard hips, and like a stallion parading before a favored mare, he threw back his shoulders, puffed out his chest, and stalked with manly pride and pantherlike grace through the shallows, disturbing hardly a ripple as he went.

A roguish smile lit his arrogant, copper-skinned face, softening its stern lines of moments before as he stood poised for attack, the cold water swirling about his muscular calves. Blue Beads's back was still turned to him. She was completely unaware of his approach! His smile deepened as she raised one slim leg, braced it on a half-submerged boulder, and gracefully leaned down to lather her calf. As she did so, he glimpsed the damp tangle of curls between her thighs, and his groin tightened unbearably despite the chill of the water. He imagined himself firmly lodged between those firm, pale legs; imagined her protests melting into sighs of passion as he rode between them; her tender smiles as she yielded to his loving . . .

Oh, yes, he was certain she would yield with little protest, for she enjoyed their playing upon the bed-robes as much as he did. He was certain she'd missed the pleasures they'd shared! But then, he scowled.

She'd brought no weapons with her to the creek—or at least, none that he could see—and any weapon she planned to use should have been within her easy reach! Furthermore, she seemed totally oblivious to his approach, all her attention devoted to her bathing. Why was she so reckless? Why had she not heeded his warnings, taken them seriously? It was even more apparent to him now that his woman needed to be taught a stern lesson; to realize that he was her husband and her master, and that he would not be refused his rights to her body, nor have his sternest cautions ignored. And perhaps, in the lesson's teaching, she would forget whatever hurt it was she hugged so tightly to her heart and refused to share with him? At the very least, he rationalized, trying to convince himself he was doing the right thing, perhaps his actions would anger her so deeply, she'd forget herself and blurt out what it was that had curdled her sweetness and made her cross as an old she-bear!

He was only three-arrows' lengths from her, ready to spring and catch her about the waist, when she suddenly whirled to face him!

With a whoop, hair flying and storm blue eyes blazing, she drew back an arm and pelted him with first one smooth pebble, then another, and another! Her aim was wicked and deadly, the pile of missiles heaped on the boulder at her feet small but effective. Wherever they struck his exposed body, they stung like scorpion bites! With a yelp, then another, Wolf took first one pebble in the shoulder, then another in the thigh, before he could duck or leap aside.

"Cowardly dog! Did you think to steal me from my husband, then? Take that! And this, too!" she screamed at him with unconcealed glee.

"I *am* your husband!" he roared, twisting to evade the barrage of pebbles that flew like hailstones from her hands. "As well you know! Enough, you she-demon!"

"You, my husband? No, no, I think not! You're the enemy, aiee, yes, you are! My husband would never sneak up on me! No, sly dog, you've lain in wait for Blue Beads—hoping to catch a helpless woman unawares! And what else must a poor woman do but defend herself, eh, stranger? Run for your life!"

More stinging pebbles flew at him, raising bright splashes where they landed in the water after striking his body. He stoically gritted his teeth and ignored them, but the one that struck him squarely on the nose could not be so casually dismissed. It was the final indignity! His eyes watered and his nose throbbed.

With a roar of outrage, he sprang at her like a copper-

197

skinned cougar, thrashing through the shallows to tackle her by the waist and bring her down beneath him in a mighty splash. She howled like a scalded she-wolf, as he shoved her under the water, and tried to wriggle free of his punishing grip. Water sprayed all about them as she resurfaced, squirming like a slippery eel. She clawed for his face, yanked painfully on his hair, hammered her fists against his chest, and kicked out at his groin.

Wolf growled a curse and tightened his grip, scooping her up out of the water and off her feet, the better to control her and punish her for her attack on him. But the feel of her slender, wet body plastered nude against his, the curve of her bottom thumping against his hips as she tried to batter her way free, and the wet, slick mounds of her breasts crushed against his bare chest, were too unbearably tempting! Punishment was forgotten, in lieu of a far more pleasing pastime . . .

"Stranger, you call me, eh, my dove?" he rasped thickly. A new light kindled in his sparkling eyes, so strikingly at odds with his coppery complexion. "Cowardly cur, hmmm? Sly dog, eh?" he snorted in devilish amusement. "Then by the Spirit, I will have me White Wolf's woman—whether she wants me or not!"

She squealed at the top of her lungs, as he turned her slippery body smoothly in his arms. Boldly, he lifted her high in his arms, clear of the water, and raised her breasts to his mouth. Dipping his dark head, he feasted upon them, lifting her to his mouth as if she were a golden ear of corn to be devoured. His busy mouth suckled and nipped at the tempting peaks. Ignoring her furious cries, numb to her attempts to tear out his hair in great handfuls, he lapped greedily at the glistening drops of water that sparkled on the puckered crests with all the gusto and relish of a honey-crazed bee sucking nectar from a flower! And, when he had quenched his thirst for nectar, he removed his arms from beneath her knees and let her fall into the water, leaping after her before she could swim away.

The creek was shallow there, the gritty bottom rough

beneath their thrashing bodies. The water sang all around them, burbling a merry song that was sharply at odds with Blue Beads's muffled roars and shrieks of outrage, as Wolf caught her as she resurfaced, spluttering and gasping, and captured her mouth beneath his own. He kissed her with greedy, reckless ardor, giving free rein to the desires that had been denied him for far too long. And as he kissed her, he fondled her body, thoroughly exploring each curve and hollow as if in truth he was a marauder who would take her by force, and cared not a bit for tenderness. And—though she would sooner have died that confessed as much—his rough, urgent touch, the boldness and closeness of his overtly virile body, was wildly exciting!

Realizing the treacherous nature of her thoughts, she redoubled her efforts to free herself. She tried again and again to escape his steely grip. Yet with one arm curled tightly under her back and around her body to cup the breast farthest from him, virtually helpless to do so—and secretly glad that she was . . .

"Stop!" she ground out, pushing at his chest, flowing water lapping at her chin, filling her mouth and making her gasp for breath.

"Never!" he growled, warming to his role of enemy cur, ravisher of women. "I will have you, captive paleface! There's nothing you can do to stop such a warrior as me! Struggle your hardest, woman! Scream all you wish, for only I and the mountains will hear you!"

His hand slipped lustily between her thighs, seeking and finding the hidden, silky heat of her. In contrast to the creek's chill flow, her body burned like fire beneath his touch, its satin folds all liquid warmth and softness. And, his eager, exploring hands soon discovered, despite her protest, she was little less ready than he for a mating!

Running his hands freely over her sleek wetness, enjoying the glimpses of her bobbing breasts as they crested the surface, then vanished, then crested again in a merry game of hide-and-go-seek, he lifted himself astride her, straddling her hips and pinning her firmly beneath him.

With an anguished groan, she nonethless opened to him, although cursing him with every foul epithet she could summon up as he drove into her fiery sheath. He claimed her with a marauder's wild *yi-yiiing* whoop of victory that thrilled her to the core.

"Savage half-breed dog!" she hissed, biting down hard on her lower lip to staunch her cries of ecstasy as he thrust and thrust again, filling her deeper with each flexing of his hips.

"Paleface enemy bitch!" he growled enthusiastically, grinning as he gazed down into a face transported by honest, earthy lust.

"I hate you!" she whimpered, and wrapped her legs around his hips. She was panting hoarsely as her body arched and fell, arched and fell, bouncing eagerly to match the driving rhythm of his.

"And I, you!" he agreed cheerfully, deepening his plunges, panting himself as he lifted her hips a little higher, parted her thighs a little wider, opening her fully with his hard, intruding flanks.

"Oh, Wolf!" she wailed. His movements grew swifter, deeper, harder, as the raging storm gathered within him.

"Aah, Blue Beads!" he roared, and he felt her arch beneath him, growing suddenly as still as the eye of that storm.

And when the storm finally broke, it unleashed a glorious tempest of sensation within them! It hurtled them far and wide into their own reeling, dizzying world of delight, where none could intrude, and only two could share the bliss that was theirs.

The swift icy flow of the creek rushed all about them as they clung together, crying each others' names. The hush that embraced their cries was the hush of fall, with drifts of colored leaves carpeting the ground like the forgotten feathers of some gaudy bird, and the air redolent of the moldy leaf smell and smoky mists of autumn.

At last, Wolf thought confidently, cradling her to him and showering kisses over her face, *She is in truth my woman once again! Now she will smile and be the woman I remember!*

But in that, he was wrong . . .

Chapter Fifteen

"We must talk," Wolf growled sternly one night after they'd eaten their evening meal in prickly silence once again.

After the lusty interlude they'd shared that afternoon—which now seemed a thousand moons ago—Blue Beads had cast a chilling glance at him, risen to standing and stalked aloofly back to their lodge without a word. To Wolf's dismay, their coupling in the creek, however enjoyable, had solved nothing! The days that followed were exactly like those that had gone before; fraught with stiffly polite exchanges by day, and hostile backs and silence by night.

Wolf was forced to admit that his attempt at lesson teaching had mended nothing. Although he knew that she'd enjoyed their lusty mating as much as he had, clearly she still harbored hurt feelings toward him, and they'd grown like a thicket of thorns between them. Both seemed only to be marking time until moonrise each night, when they could escape their discomfort by pretending to sleep!

Enough was enough, Wolf had finally decided. If she would not unbend and speak to him, then he must be the first to break the ice between them.

"For too long," Wolf continued accordingly, "you have held your tongue, my woman. For too long, your wounded pride has come between us, and you have been cold and distant to me. For two whose hearts beat as one, as ours once did, this icy silence is torture. Speak to me, woman! Tell me what still angers you, and let the healing begin!"

"I am proud?" Blue Beads retorted with a scornful jeer to hide her wounded feelings—and also conceal the fact that she was very close to tears. She gave a little toss of her unbound hair like a spirited wild mare, and her storm blue eyes were brilliant as a cougar's, shining in the ruddy shadows of their lodge as she continued haughtily, "I have held *my* tongue? Ha! Perhaps a harsh word held in wisdom is kinder than a silence which says more than words, my husband!"

She scowled, and her eyes narrowed. "And then again, perhaps *your* silence was an honest one? Perhaps you really would prefer some hussy who freely shared her favors with any man who crawled under the skirts of her lodge, rather than a—a proper wife, whose only sin was to try to please you!"

He frowned, nonplussed as to what she was referring to. A hussy? What hussy! His silence? What silence did she mean? And then—then he remembered the accusations she'd tossed at him one day, and remembered, too, how they'd seemed so foolish, he'd held his tongue, refusing to swallow his pride to argue such a point. So! That was what had caused both her withdrawal and her stony silence! And all this time, she'd thought he regretted making her his woman, but naturally she'd said nothing to him of her fears, oh, no!

She'd jealously hugged them to her bosom, where they'd festered like poisoned wounds. He smothered the sudden urge to take her by the arms and shake her until her teeth rattled. Aiee, that little fool! he thought with fond exasperation.

"Very well. If you would speak of wisdom, then so be it!" Wolf said sternly. "Tell me this; was it wise for you to bathe in the creek that day when I was gone from our lodge?"

There was only silence.

"Answer me!"

"I suppose—no, it was not," she whispered grudgingly.

"And would it have been wiser, more *caring* for me to hold my tongue, and say nothing of your foolishness afterward?"

"Yes!" she insisted mulishly.

"I say not, Blue Beads Woman!" he argued, shaking his head. He took her chin in his fist and tilted her face to the firelight, so that he could look her in the eye. "Your life is precious to me, little dove—more precious than my own. For that reason alone I will guard it jealously!"

"Pah! You lie—!"

"For once let me speak, woman!" he barked, and her mouth snapped shut like a snapping turtle's, becoming as puckered as a pouch opening.

"I would keep you beside me all the winters of our lives, little reckless one," he began, carefully putting his feelings into words she could not possibly misinterpret, "until we are older than the very hills, and have grown gray and toothless. Until the Great Spirit Himself chooses at last to part us, and not one heartbeat sooner!" He smiled, and the smile lit his face, softening its stern planes and hard handsomeness with its glow.

"But if you love me, truly love me, then why did you speak so harshly to me—tell me that?" she cried.

"Why? So that the memory of my harshness would remind you always of the bitter cost of carelessness, my woman. Can you not see? My anger was born of *love*. Love—and the knowledge that I'd come very close to losing you, a fear that made me tremble like the aspen in the breeze! I did not answer you that day because—in my mind—your accusations *needed* no answer. Foolish little one, believe me: I want no woman but you! I have found the one I love, and she is you, my Blue Beads Woman! Her pride is great, her stubbornness greater, her temper very quick, and her manner far from the submissive one most pleasing in a wife, and yet—she is still the one I have chosen! My heart, the heart of White Wolf, will always beat with hers."

Shame filled her then, yet there was also an enormous flood of relief that swelled up from her heart to fill her throat. Truly, she'd been so wrong! She'd misjudged Wolf very badly. He wasn't a womanizing, coyote-trickster who was sorry he'd taken her as his woman, as she'd feared. He didn't regret that they'd run away together, after all, nor blame her for the loss of his friendship with his brother, Broken Claw. Instead, he'd said he loved her above all others, and that his harsh words had been caused by his fear of losing her forever! How could she have doubted him?

"Oh, Wolf! I love you, too!"

With a muffled cry, she flew across their lodge and into his arms, like a weary bird winging homeward to its nest. His strong arms encircled her in a fierce, joyful embrace that lifted her high into the air and threatened to crush ribs, before he bore her down to the buffalo robes beneath them!

Their bodies side by side, they lay facing each other, as nervous and trembling as if this were their first time as lovers. But after a moment's discomfort and hesitation, Wolf made the first move. In the blink of an eye, the beat of a heart, their hesitance vanished.

Their eager mouths touched and tasted and touched again, tenderly devouring the lips they'd hungered for in the white man's fashion of kisses. He gently pressed her over, onto her back. She uttered a breathless giggle that melted into a sigh as his equally eager hands slipped up beneath the fringed hems of her doeskin gown to find the soft curves and planes of her body, and brand them anew with his possession.

"You are so very lovely, my bride!" he whispered. "Lovely as the morning star, lovely as the flowers that bloom on the prairies!"

Her heart soared as he caressed her with loving words and loving hands. Oh, how she'd missed this gentle holding, this soft and tender touching, even more than the joining that followed! She raised her arms above her head and tugged the impeding gown off, tossing it impatiently aside. Quite bare now, she burrowed her fingers deep into his thick, glossy hair, and surrendered herself wholly to the magic of his touch in glorious, wanton abandon.

The slender waist he'd once spanned with his two bare hands was noticeably thicker now, he felt. Her belly was no longer taut and flat as the skin of a drum, but hard with the new life growing within it. *Our child,* he thought exultantly, stroking her stomach with gentle, circular motions, *My son!* His hand skimmed upward over her rib cage to cup her bosom. Beneath it, her heart beat wildly, like a snared bird's beating wings.

Her small breasts had also ripened like persimmons since the last time he'd taken her. There were bluish veins upon them that meandered over her creamy flesh like swollen rivers in the spring thaw. She arched upward to fill the hollows of his palms with the fullness of her breasts, and his groin hardened at these signs of her eagerness to join with him. He growled low in his throat like a hungry bear, seeing how her nipples rode firm and full upon her twin mounds, dark as ripe cherries. The fullness of her breasts betrayed her desire for him! He dipped his raven dark head to each tight nubbin in turn, capturing her flesh between his lips. He gently tugged and suckled at them, until her bones seemed to melt. Silvery tingles of pleasure sang through her body to curl her toes with delight.

Her need for him was near overwhelming, almost frightening in its intensity. Truly she ached with longing! His slow, feathery caresses filled her with eagerness for more ardent touches and fondlings: with the yearning to feel his masculine weight bearing her down, his proud manhood filling the emptiness inside her, joining them inseparably—now, now, and not a heartbeat longer!

Moaning softly, she tugged and rubbed the glossy dark head that was pillowed upon her breasts and implored him to take her, to grant her the rapture she craved.

"Wolf! Oh, Wolf, my husband!" she murmured feverishly. "My beloved, my soul, my dear one, my own!"

His name upon her lips was like a sacred chant, carried upward on the smoke of their fire to the Great One

Above.

Yet Wolf refused to be hurried. His tanned hand travelled slowly downward, exploring every inch of her pale gold body. It lingered over the smooth warmth of her abdomen, flowed lightly as pooling water across her belly and upper thighs, to play over the fleecy thatch of her mons. His touch as delicate as the velvet buds of the pussy willow upon her sensitive flesh, he traced the little cleft of her womanhood to the heated pearl of passion at its heart. When he stroked her delicately there, ragged little whimpers broke from her lips. Her fingers tightened in the shaggy pelts that cushioned them, and she wriggled voluptuously under his touch.

"Now!" she breathed harshly. "Oh, Wolf! Now!"

A moment more, and he was upon her, lodged firmly between her thighs. His huge hands clasped her hips, raising them higher to deepen his entry. He came into her with a deep, delicious thrust that jolted through them like a bolt of lightning, filling them with a heady shock of pleasure. Withdrawing, he plunged deeply again, burying himself to the hilt in her silky heat. Clenching his jaw, he withdrew and slowly, slowly filled her again. She sobbed her pleasure, slender thighs embracing his hips. Her loving arms encircled his chest like mistletoe clinging to an oaken tree. Aiee, yes, he was oak and fire, steel and muscle, love and delight.

Oh, bliss! Such—wondrous—bliss!

Lips parted, eyes closed, fingers biting deep into the steely arms of him, she gasped as rapture swirled her away. She saw the stars wheeling in crazy arcs through the smoke-hole far above them, spinning and pulsing! And, as she watched, the moon suddenly tilted in a lopsided crescent—as if the Old Woman were drunk on the white man's firewater—and Blue Beads laughed aloud in giddy wonder!

Then the stars were plucked from the midnight-meadow skies, and fell showering all around her . . . falling like diamond flowers . . . like silver rain . . .

207

drenching her in white hot star-fire . . . Her spirit soared free of her body on wings of starlight, to climb the heavens with his.

Their cries of rapture commingled as he found his own explosive release with a roar of fulfillment:

"I love you, my woman!"

"And I you, my husband!"

The wall of thorns had been torn down. The gulf was finally breached.

Afterward, they rested sleepily with limbs entwined and warm breaths commingled. When the stars and moon had resumed their rightful tethers in the heavens above, Wolf raised himself on one elbow and looked down at Blue Beads. Contentment filled him as he idly caressed her throat and the shadowy little hollows at its base.

This was how it should be, he thought. His woman curled sweet and drowsy beside him. He'd never tire of gazing at her lovely face in the quiet moments after they'd joined, he knew. Even should the passing winters someday temper the fiery pleasures of their mating, her beauty would endure the trial of time.

Already he had come to know and cherish each delicate line and curve of her face and body, as if it were his own; the slight tilt to the corners of her eyes that reminded him always of a lioness's almond-eyed gaze; the tiny flecks of gold in the depths of those eyes that lit them from within whenever he loved her or made her smile; the lashes, thick and dark as cobwebs, that rested on cheeks dusted lightly with sun-freckles—a legacy of her white blood. So, too, he'd come to know the exact tilt of her narrow little nose. The precise way her mouth curved or tightened, whether in happiness, in sorrow, in rapture, or—of late—in anger! The fluid, graceful line of her throat, the skin smooth, the bared nape so downy and vulnerable, so innocently childlike. The tiny shadowed hollows at its base where he loved to press his lips and watch as her eyes grew darker with desire . . .

"Where is your medicine bundle, beloved?" he asked casually, noticing it was gone as he caressed her throat with splayed brown fingers.

"The white-eyes who escaped you—he stole it from me," she confessed with a heavy sigh, reluctant to dredge up the cause of so many days of conflict between them once again. "Now the magic that protected me since my naming ceremony is gone!" She bit her lip, equally reluctant to give way to the unhappiness the loss had caused her, now that she and Wolf were again lovers and on tender terms.

Wolf shook his head. "No, beloved, such magic can never be lost. It is yours, and yours alone, and becomes powerless when stolen by another. Did the *shaman* not tell you this at the time you received your name?"

She shook her head.

"Only when you choose to give it as a gift to someone does its powers remain strong. Don't be afraid—the white-eyes cannot use its medicine," Wolf promised, his blue eyes glittering fiercely as he remembered the dangerous, pale-eyed one.

For a moment, the uneasy forboding he'd had that night as he spied on the paleface, McHenry, before freeing her, returned. With it, he felt the same, unshakeable certainty that he'd experienced that night; the knowledge that this pale-eyes' part in their lives was not yet ended . . .

"That is good to hear," she responded simply and with obvious relief at his assurances. "The talisman had been with me many winters, and my heart was heavy to think of its power being used against me by that—that evil one." She shuddered, seeing the paleface's icy eyes again in her mind.

Wolf nodded solemnly.

"Did—did you carry another name when you were a boy? Did you have a naming ceremony?" she questioned, curious to know everything about this man she loved, the father of the child she carried.

"I did, yes. For the first six winters that I lived with the Black Hawk band, I was known by the name Blue Jay. Then my adoptive father and his brother, Elk Horns, decided it was time for me to make a vision quest, and learn the new name I'd carry as a warrior—the one whose power would give me the strong medicine of a man."

"How old were you then?" she asked eagerly, fascinated to hear of his past, thinking how good it was to speak freely with him again, without hostility between them!

"Twelve winters. But—although I stood on the threshold of manhood and boasted that I had courage for any challenge—I was as frightened as a woman when darkness fell on the third night of my vision quest!" he recalled with a shamefaced smile.

He sat up cross-legged now in the manner of a storyteller, and she leaned forward to rest her chin on her fist and listen raptly.

"The shadows lengthened, slithering over the rocky ledges like stretching cougars. The moon rose. The stars came out exactly as they had the first two nights. And still, I waited for a vision to come to me in that high, lonely place where our *shaman* had instructed me to wait! My belly was hollow with hunger, growling after three days of fasting and purification in the smoke lodge, and from two long nights already spent on that desolate ledge, where the bite of the wind was sharp and the shadows seemed filled with faceless threats.

"My spirit began to wander from my body, fluttering forth from time to time like a moth to a flame, as if already wanting to dance with the Star People and be free of its earthly life. And, in the part of my mind that remained sharp and clear despite fasting, I began to despair. I feared I would never receive a naming vision from the Great One Above. That all my life, I would carry a boy's name among the People. One with neither meaning nor magic!"

"But you did receive a vision?" she pressed, knowing he must have, but seeking to draw him out.

"I did! Just when all seemed darkest and at its most hopeless, I saw a pack of wolves in the ravine below me, scampering in and out of the boulders like gray shadows. I remember how their amber eyes glinted as they caught the icy starlight, as clearly as if they were here before me now!

"Behind them padded another wolf, this one larger, stronger than they, with a thick pelt as white as the driven snow. Its long fur stood out around its powerful body like a war bonnet of silver feathers, and shone with a ghostly glimmer in the light of the Old Woman shining above."

Hearing his description, Blue Beads shivered, recalling all too vividly the silver wolf she had seen when he'd lain burning up with fever. Truly, it had been his spirit-brother, come to help Wolf's fleeing spirit down the Ghost Path! If she had not challenged it, bidden it go and leave without him, what then—? "Go on!" she urged him shakily.

"This white wolf seemed one of the pack it followed," he continued, "and yet at the same time, strangely apart from it. And somehow, I knew what lay in the wolf's heart; he had never truly belonged among his brother wolves, nor ever would. His differences lay deeper than the color of his fur. They were a thing of the heart and spirit! A great sadness filled me then, for I knew that the lone wolf would never truly be one of his people, but an outsider who walked always alone.

"And as I watched, the knowledge like a stone within me, another, paler pack of wolves swept down the ravine to meet the first in headlong battle! Drooling jaws snapped." He made a snapping motion. "Lolling tongues flailed like quirts as the two packs flew at each other with snarls and yelps. Yellow fangs were bared. Bloodcurdling growls and snarls filled the night air, as the two packs circled and sprang and tore at each others' throats.

211

"The white wolf ran among his brothers, trying to separate the two, to put an end to the fight. He leaped first to one side, then to the other. But the prize over which the packs battled — a freshly killed antelope of enormous size — was too rich and tantalizing for either side to relinquish. And besides, at heart they relished the battle and the taste of each other's warm blood as much as any other reward, for they had long been hated enemies . . .

" 'There is enough meat for all, my brothers!' I sensed the white wolf trying to tell them. 'Why spill each others' blood, when there is so little cause? Come, let's share the gift of Sister Antelope's flesh! Let's fill our hungry bellies, and give thanks for her sacrifice!'

"But the white one's pleas fell on deaf ears. The two packs tore and lunged and snapped at each other until not a single wolf remained standing on either side! Huge drifts of their fur had been torn out and were snarled in the thorn thickets. Their lifeblood pooled in dark gouts on the rocky ground. And the white wolf saw that as the battle raged, the carcass of the antelope doe had vanished, devoured by coyotes and buzzards, ants and beetles, so that only its gleaming bones remained. The two packs had fought over nothing!

"In sorrow at the futility of it all, at the lives of his brothers so needlessly squandered, the white wolf padded away to a high, lonely ridge. There he raised his head to the heavens to howl at Old Woman moon, and give throat to his anguish in a song of mourning. All that long night he howled, until the colors of dawn painted the sky, and Father Sun rose from his lodge in the land of the east wind to ride the heavens.

"And, as Sun rose, the white wolf noticed that in a hollow carved from the rocks below him, a shallow pool of rainwater had collected. The surface was as still as if cupped in a gourd, as reflective as the white-man's looking glass. The white wolf looked down and saw his image glinting there. And, in my vision state, I looked down, too, and saw — the same!"

212

"The same?" she exclaimed breathlessly, caught up in the magic of his spellbinding story.

"It was so! And I was still confused by my vision when I returned to the *shaman* the next morning, puzzled that there had been only one reflection where two should have been—and that one not my own, but the single image of a lone white wolf!

"Old Semanaw, the medicine man, began to explain my vision for me. As I listened, I knew in my heart that what I'd suspected from the first was true. The white wolf and I were *one and the same.* I, like him, would belong to the Comanche pack, and yet never be *of* the Comanche people. My Hopituh blood and my white blood would always set me apart.

"Semanaw explained then that he, too, had been granted a vision concerning me—one of great and far-reaching portent. He said that I, and my children, and my children's children, had a great destiny to fulfill. A destiny that would not be accomplished until many, many winters had come and gone. In a time beyond imagining, when the red men had grown few, and the white men were as countless as the blades of grass and ruled as lords of Mother Earth, Semanaw prophesied that my seed would bring forth a man of great wisdom, one born to bring peace to the world with his eloquence. He foretold also that in my lifetime, I was destined to look beyond old enmities and see the futility of war, and yet be helpless to either end it, or remain untouched by its forces.

"So it was on that night, I became a man," Wolf ended solemnly. "So it was that I took the name White Wolf from my vision. So it was that I came to carry this bundle with the claws of a white wolf as its medicine, and to try always to shun the warpath. Since the time of my naming vision, I have killed only when forced to do so. Here, my woman," he added huskily, "Take this! I give my medicine bundle to you as a gift, to replace your own."

So saying, he lifted the medicine bundle from around his own throat and placed the rawhide cord over her head. "As I told you, when one's medicine bundle is stolen, it powers cease for the thief. But when such a bundle is given as a gift of love, the one who receives it also receives its medicine. Wear it in love and peace, my woman, to protect you—and our child."

"You knew!" she exclaimed softly, her eyes shining.

Wolf smiled. "I suspected, yes, for your beauty has grown these past two moons. It shines out from within you like a candle!" He caressed her cheek, his callused warrior's hand incredibly gentle against its flushed curve. "And then, when you first stopped braiding your hair, as is the custom of our women when they are with child, I was almost sure I was to be a father. But it was only a short while ago, when I touched the warmth of your belly and felt the new hardness there—that I was certain." He tenderly pressed a flattened palm to her stomach and looked down at her with eyes of wonder as he felt the fragile flutter of new life stirring within, as if in response to its father's touch.

"And you are pleased, my husband?" she asked shyly, not meeting his eyes as she ran her fingertip down his muscular arm. When she finally dared to glance up, she saw that his sky blue eyes were twinkling like stars in the fire's glow, and that his teeth flashed white as river pearls as he grinned wickedly.

"Pleased? Is that a question for a man soon to become a father? All men are happy, little one, when they learn that the mare they have chosen as their mate is not barren, but breeding!"

"Mare!" she exclaimed, all fiery indignance again. "I'm no mare, Rude One, but your woman!"

"Hush," he chided teasingly, pressing her back down to the pelts and running his tongue over the sensitive shell-whorls of her ear. "We waste much time in talking, woman! After all, there are far more pleasing things to do, eh? And after I have loved you a second time, we

214

must rest. In the morning, we begin the journey home."

"Home?" she cried in dismay. "You mean, return to Black Hawk's band? To the winter camp of our People?"

He nodded.

"But—what of Broken Claw? He'll kill you if we go back!"

"It is a chance I must take. We can't hide forever, little one. Broken Claw must be faced and dealt with, sooner or later."

"Later, then," she implored him, although his expression was set and closed now. "Please, Wolf, think of your destiny—the great promise Semanaw foretold—and please, please, let it be later?"

"It cannot be. We will leave at sunrise, to find the winter camp of our people," Wolf said firmly. "The mother of White Wolf's child will not endure the harsh moons of winter alone, with no other women to share its hardships and make cold evenings merry with talk, laughter, and friendship. And in the Moon of New Leaves, our son will be born among the lodges of his people, the Comanche, with skilled midwives to bring him safe into the world! I have spoken, woman. In this, you will obey me, for I will not change my mind."

And, although she employed her most seductive wiles to postpone their departure, Wolf would not be dissuaded.

Chapter Sixteen

White Wolf and Blue Beads journeyed steadily eastward in the following moon, each day bringing them closer and closer to the lands of the People.

Although Blue Beads lost none of her fear of a confrontation between Broken Claw and her husband that might end in Wolf's death, she knew she would go mad if she allowed herself to dwell on it day and night. Accordingly, she tried to set her fears aside, and concentrated instead on the child growing within her, its fluttering movements that thrilled her through and through, and on the joy of simply being alone with the man she loved, and being loved in return.

Wolf!

She never tired of being with him. Never tired of riding the wind with him — so handsome, so brave, so cherished, and dear to her — racing across the grasslands at her side, their ponies stretching out in a swift, ground-eating gallop beneath them, and the ride whipping her long hair out behind her and painting her cheeks with vivid color.

Nor would she ever tire of the way his morning glory eyes took on that special radiance whenever he spoke her name, or of seeing him throw back his great, raven dark head and whoop with the sheer joy of being alive in that free and glorious way he had. Nor did she tire of simply talking softly with him in the dark of night when the whippoorwills called and the nighthawks shrieked, exchanging her hopes and fears and dreams with him, and sharing plans for the little ones they would bring into the world. Nor did she ever weary of the frosty, starry nights spent in the warmth of their lodge, when she could lose herself utterly in passion. Then she'd forget her fears of what might come for a few heartbeats, within the shield of his strong arms and body and in the magic of his lovemaking.

Only the Great Spirit knew what lay ahead of them, after all, she reminded herself again and again. He alone could make things happen, or keep them from doing so. It was of no use to fret, for what would be must be. She would enjoy these special times alone with Wolf to the fullest, and remember them always.

When the wind blew even sharper and colder than it had yet done before, she donned the cloak of white wolf-skins trimmed with ermine tails that her parents had given her following the Sun Dance ceremonies, for warmth.

Seeing her, Wolf's heart skipped a beat, and a great knot of love clenched in his throat. He glanced her way often as they rode, certain he'd never seen anything love-lier than his woman, caped in those snowy skins, with streamers of dark hair whipped this way and that about her shoulders by the wind. He would remember her al-ways as she looked in those days, the deep pelts framing her glossy dark hair, and at its heart, the oval of her glowing face. Deep blue eyes shining, full lips red as ber-ries, cheeks windblown and flushed, her face was like the lovely face of a flower; a wildflower blooming amidst the snow. *Great Spirit,* he prayed silently, a catch in his throat, *if it is Your will that I should die, then let my woman's smile be the last thing I see, before my spirit flees my body!*

One day, when they were only a few suns' ride from the winter camp of Chief Black Hawk and his band, they crested some low, forested hills, where the sumac were robed in yellow and red, the aspens a blazing shower of gold, and saw below them the smoking ruins of a little wood-and-adobe homestead. Exchanging glances, they rode slowly down the rise toward it, leaving the pack ponies and the string of captured mustangs among the trees.

Wolf was wary as they approached the smoking farm-

217

house, for the stillness was disquieting. He looked carefully about him, but could see no sign of either horse or man. Whoever had razed the homestead and destroyed the corrals had gone.

When they came closer, they saw a stocky white man sprawled across the dirt yard, a gaping lance wound in his belly. His eyes were wide with the horror of his final agony. A woman—his woman, Wolf guessed—and two little ones, both boys, and an olive-skinned Mexican girl, lay in an untidy heap a few feet away. Their deaths had been neither swift nor clean. Everyone of them had been scalped, and arrows riddled their pitiful bodies. With a heavy heart, Wolf realized that he recognised those arrows only too well!

He quietly signalled Blue Beads with a jerk of his head that they would leave at once, not wanting her to see the slaughtered woman and children. But it was already too late. Her ashen face betrayed her. Without protest, she turned Badger's head to follow him.

"They were like you and I, my husband!" she whispered as they rode back up the hill to their animals. Her voice sounded husky with unshed tears. "They were no different to our People, not in the ways that truly matter! They loved, they mated, the woman bore her little ones in pain and in joy as do our women. The man provided for and defended them, as do our braves. Oh, Wolf, why can't there be peace and understanding between our peoples? Why can't the red man and the white man share the world the Great Spirit has provided for us all, and live together in brotherhood? Truly, there is enough for all!"

Wolf's expression was grave as he nodded agreement. "It is so, my woman."

"The *shaman*, Semanaw, prophesied a great thing for those of your seed, my husband," Blue Beads murmured, recalling Wolf's storytelling and the vision he'd received. "He said that some day, the words spoken by one of your blood would bring peace among all who are enemies, yes?"

"He did," Wolf acknowledged, frowning and wondering what she was leading up to.

"The prophecy is a good thing, a fine thing," she said fervently, "for its promise is one of peace between all tribes, white or red. That the Great Spirit has chosen one of your blood for this purpose should bring you much pride, my husband! When we are once again with the People, I will sew a lodge cover of the finest robes. On its inner walls, I shall paint the story of your vision, and the wonderful prophecy of Semanaw! Truly, this matter is worthy of painting, my husband," she added earnestly, her blue eyes shining. "Far more worthy to my mind than those lodge skins which show the counting of coups and the bloody deeds of a warrior, for peace is a precious thing. It—it is not good for a man to watch his woman and little ones die, no matter the color of their sk—skin!"

He saw then that tears were streaking down her cheeks to dampen the fur of the wolfskins about her. In that moment, Wolf knew that she'd imagined her own grief, his death, their child's death, when she saw the homesteader and his family. Such was the way of women, to see their own grief in the grief of others.

"Do not weep, my beloved," he said huskily, wanting to console her. "We will soon be safe among our people."

"Safe?" she choked out. "Aiee, I fear not, my husband! Broken Claw has the blood rage upon him. He won't have forgiven or forgotten the wrongs he thinks we've done him, I know it!"

"We will smoke the pipe, and I will speak to him as brother to brother. We were friends once, and will settle this peacefully between us," he lied uncomfortably in an effort to reassure her, but she was not convinced.

"No, my love, no! We both know that Broken Claw will never agree to settle this peacefully. You cannot lie to me, my husband, for I am no fool! Did you think I wouldn't know whose arrows those were back there, with

Broken Claw's medicine mark upon their shafts? And did those poor, broken bodies not tell you of the rage that feasts upon his heart, the lust for blood and death that consumes him? No! Broken Claw will never pass the pipe in peace and brotherhood. He will kill you!"

So. She had seen . . .

"Then what would you have me do, woman?" Wolf demanded, his face dark with anger. "Run and hide from him always, like a coward who fears his own shadow? Spend the rest of my days an outcast, afraid to return to my people for fear of him?" He scowled. "I say this is not a life at all—and that I will not live it that way. Hear me! I am White Wolf, and despite my oath, I am yet a man—not a cowardly dog who lives in fear! I will defend the ones dear to me and my own life, and I will not run!"

Gritting his teeth, he slapped his moccasined heels to None Swifter's flanks, and spurred his spotted pony up the rise. With a strangled sob, Blue Beads rode slowly after him.

Although they didn't speak of the matter again, and although both tried to pretend nothing had happened, things were not the same between them after that. Their carefree spirit had gone, replaced by a mounting sense of time and happiness running out for them. Like sand slipping between their fingers, it could not be held back or contained.

It was with mixed feelings that they found Black Hawk's village six suns later, and learned that Broken Claw was not in the camp. He and several other young braves had been gone for many moons, they were told, riding the warpath against the white-eyes. No one knew when he would return.

It was a respite, Blue Beads thought gratefully, anxious to see her mother and Wounded Doe again—but for how long could it last?

* * *

As her mother had promised on the fateful night they became outcasts, her father Many Horses was glad to see his daughter again, though he tried very hard not to let it show.

"Someone defied her father the last time he saw her," he reminded her crossly after she'd entered the lodge and seated herself before him. "Someone should be whipped for her disobedience, and for making her poor father lose face before Elk Horns and his woman."

"Yes, my father," she said dutifully, lowering her head not in shame, but to hide a smile. "But your someone has returned now, and begs your forgiveness and understanding. She brings with her a good husband—one who would offer her father a gift of many ponies, in return for the honor of making her his woman."

"Ponies?" Many Horses echoed, his brown eyes lighting up, his brows lifting. He tried to appear casual as he asked with transparent eagerness, "Exactly how many ponies?"

"Three hands of ponies, my father," she disclosed, opening and closing her fist three times.

"Three hands? Pah! Elk Horns offered *four* hands for my daughter to join with his son," he grumbled, casting a greedy, hopeful eye in her direction.

"It is so," she agreed. "And if the white-eyes' mustangers had not stolen them from my husband, there would have been twice as many horses! However," she added slowly, "there is another gift for the father of Blue Beads—something he will prize more than any number of horses . . ."

"More than horses?" her father repeated doubtfully.

"Yes, my father."

"A fire-stick, perhaps?"

"No. Not that."

"The white man's firewater, then—to keep the cold from his old bones this winter?"

"No. Not firewater."

"Then what can it be?"

She drew back the wolfskin cloak and splayed her fingertips across her swollen belly as she smiled up at him. "Your gift is here, my father," she revealed softly, "within me. In the Moon of New Leaves, your first grandchild will be born!"

"Aah," he said in a low, pleased voice, trying to control the broad, beaming smile that tugged at his lips. "I see! And tell me, daughter, does Black Hawk, your husband's father, know of this little one coming?" he asked craftily.

"Not yet, my father. I wanted you to be the first to hear this happy news!"

Many Horses drew himself up from his willow couch and gathered his robe about his shoulders. Patting her on the head, he said casually, "It seems to me it has been many moons since I smoked the pipe with my woman's brother, Black Hawk, yes? I will go to his lodge at once, and share with him the news that we are both to become grandfathers."

On the bow legs of a born horseman, Many Horses made his way from the lodge at surprising speed.

No sooner had he left than Spotted Pony ducked under the flap opening and came inside.

"Well, my daughter? Did you tell him?"

"I did," Blue Beads confirmed merrily, "and it was just as you said! Already he has forgotten why he was angry at me! He patted me on the head, and said he would go and smoke with my uncle and tell him the news. He was pleased and proud that I told him first, just as you said he'd be. He tried to hide it, but it was there, shining in his eyes! He couldn't wait to tell my uncle!"

"You see? Men! They are easy to outwit, if a woman has just a little cunning—and I have more than enough!" Spotted Pony said with a chuckle.

She seemed to have aged a little in the moons they'd been gone, Blue Beads noticed suddenly. There were a few white strands in her thick black hair now, and the beginning of wrinkles around her eyes and mouth that had not been there before. But other than those few small, unimportant changes, she was her own dear self, and Blue Beads hugged her tightly, happy beyond words to see her again.

"I missed you so, little mother," she murmured. "When I knew that I was with child, I had so many questions to ask, and no little mother to answer them."

Spotted Pony stroked her daughter's unbound hair with a fond touch. "Now you may ask all you wish, and there will be answers, my dearest daughter."

The winter was a hard one that year, and food was scarce, but as Wolf had promised, with the love of her family and the friendship of Wounded Doe surrounding her, Blue Beads was content. If she thought of Broken Claw at all, it was rarely and fleetingly. Her swelling belly and her mounting excitement over the coming child ruled her thoughts. Besides, as her mother wisely pointed out, Broken Claw had grown bloodthirsty and increasingly more reckless over the moons of late summer and fall, by all accounts. In his eagerness to take the lives of as many hated white-eyes as possible, there was every chance he might never return to their camp; that he had been slain on one of the many raids his war party had undertaken, and that his spirit had already joined the Star People. Whether it was right or wrong to pray for another's death, Blue Beads did so often in the moons of snow.

With the help of her mother and Wounded Doe — who'd given birth to a tiny, beautiful baby daughter named Sleek Otter shortly before Blue Beads's and Wolf's return — and with several other willing helpers, Blue Beads made good on the promise she'd given Wolf. With a serene expression, she oversaw the making of a fine lodge cover, mindful as she did so of the old tradition that a lodge-maker must be good-tempered for as long as the work lasted, or else the new lodge would always be smoky. Accordingly, she smiled until her jaws ached!

Spotted Pony cut and fitted the buffalo hides using her own patterns. Wounded Doe and poor, lop-sided Crooked Woman—who was toothless now, thanks to lardy Big Bear's beatings—punched the lacing holes with an awl, while the others lashed the hide sections—twenty-eight in all—together with dried tendons, the ends dampened so that they could be fed through the awl-holes.

They made an efficient team, and when the work was completed to her satisfaction, Blue Beads served her helpers a tasty meal of parched corn and venison stew to thank them for their hard work that day. The next sun, if the weather was dry, they would return to help her raise the new lodge, and then she could begin painting the designs on its inner walls that would show Wolf's vision and Semanaw's great prophecy. Hopefully, she could persuade the old medicine man to advise her on the proper form the design should take. The rest she could do herself. She had several brushes of porous bone and hair, and various pigments; yellow from the humpbacks' gallstones, black from wood that had been burned to make charcoal, green dye distilled from the juices of various leaves, and white from the clay found in the creeks.

"You have done well, my woman!" Wolf approved, gazing in amazement at the pictographs adorning the interior of their new lodge the first time he saw it.

"Semanaw was kind. He helped, and told me what to paint," she said, blushing with pleasure. "You see the white wolf there, and the moon above him? And this—and this here—and here!"

Eagerly, she darted here and there, pointing out to him the various parts of the design, her pride obvious.

"But what is this?" he asked curiously, frowning and stepping closer for a better look. Father Sun had been picked out in red pigment, and below it a white hawk with wings spread wide and mouth agape. Below the hawk was a red falling star trailing a long tail behind it. "This hawk here, painted with white clay—what is its meaning? There were no hawks in my vision that I re-

224

call, nor in that of Semanaw?"

She shrugged. "I do not know, but the *shaman* said that a silver hawk would someday have great meaning in the life of White Wolf, and that I should show it. He is a wise man, yes? I thought it best to follow his instructions in this."

Wolf nodded and grinned, placing a hand on each of her shoulders. Her face glowed. Her eyes shone with pride. Even as big with child as she had become, he found her more beautiful than ever and desired her just as hungrily—maybe more, since the child that had swelled her belly was his own.

"You have done well, and I am proud of you. But, come to *me* now, my woman, and follow instead the instructions of your husband! We will try this new lodge you have made for us, and see if it is good for other things besides painting, eh?"

Taking her hand, he dropped to his knees and stretched out on the buffalo robes, drawing her down across his chest. She giggled with pleasure as he wound her long, dark hair about his throat like a silken tether, binding them together. His hand cupped the full curve of her breast, fondling it lovingly as he nuzzled her throat.

The new lodge, they quickly discovered, was indeed good for many things besides painting!

Chapter Seventeen

Her time was growing near. Blue Beads moved heavily now, making her way between the lodges to draw water from the creek. Her back ached this morning, and she kneaded it as she made her way across the frosty grass and hardened ground to their camp's watering place.

All about her were signs that spring was just around the corner. The water level in the creek was higher, telling her that the thaw had already started melting the snow high in the mountains. The trees, so bare these past few moons, were sending forth new leaves of a delicate green. The sun shone warmer than before, and the wind was milder. Red-winged cardinals were hopping and fluttering in the silver-trunked cottonwoods, their vivid plumage a welcome splash of brightness after the long, white winter. And as she glanced up, squinting against Sun's wan yet bright light, she saw an arrowhead flight of geese in the sky above her, heard their honking, and smiled with delight, her sore back forgotten. The geese had returned at last—a sure sign that warm weather was coming!

In another moon, her child would be born, and her mother and the midwives would be there to help it safely into the world, she thought with relief. Although she'd implored Wolf to stay in the mountains of New Mexico out of fear of Broken Claw, she was glad now that he'd refused and insisted they find Black Hawk's band. Now that her time was drawing nearer, she'd begun to have the same doubts that plague all women who're soon to become mothers for the very first time. Would she be strong enough to bring her child into the world? Would the birth be swift and easy, or long and difficult? And would she survive it? Would the child be born perfect, strong and healthy, or tiny and weak, too weak to survive? But on the other hand, casting all dark doubts and shadowy fears to the winds, she looked forward to the birth and the joy that would—with the Great Spirit's help—come after the birthing. Oh, how she longed to hold her baby in her arms, to feel its eager little mouth tugging at her breast!

Wolf, she knew, was little less eager to become a father than she was to become a mother! A frown, a sigh, the least little sign of anything amiss on her part, and he'd ask anxiously if her time had come, and if he should fetch the old women to attend her? He'd become so agitated at such times that she'd finally implored him to cease his worrying, promising, "When the time is here, my husband, be assured that I will know it, and will tell you before all others. For now, be calm! Everything will go well, I promise you. After all, your child is not the first to be born!"

"That's true—but he *will* be the first child of White Wolf, and of his woman, Blue Beads. My—my—heart would be on the ground, should anything happen to you, beloved one," he'd confessed huskily.

Her smile had been tender as she ruffled his hair and looked deep into his morning glory eyes, so filled with love and concern for her. Her words had, she hoped, reassured him, stilled some of his doubts. "I know, my husband, but please, don't fear for me. My mother—my paleface mother—brought seven babes safe into this world! And I—why, I shall be just like her in this matter!"

Wolf had busied his hands by fashioning a beautiful cradleboard for their little one in the long days of winter. When it was done, he'd hung it with great pride on the walls of their lodge in readiness for their child's arrival. Its covering was of fine white buckskin, laced with the utmost care. It was decorated with beads worked in triangles, and hung with amulets to bring good fortune to the babe. There was a loop by which it could be hung from Blue Beads's saddle horn when they moved camp, and the two sharp stakes that extended from its back support would protect the infant's head in case the cradleboard should accidentally tumble to the ground headfirst. The stakes would stick into the ground, and bear the impact. Truly, it was the most beautiful cradleboard she had ever seen, and her husband had grinned self-consciously at her lavish praise of it, she remembered fondly.

Wounded Doe had been busy, too, and had fashioned two small, flat pouches, sewn with colored beads in the shape of pretty yellow-and-blue turtles, as gifts for her friend's baby. The turtle was a good-luck talisman to ensure longevity, as well as fertility. One pouch would safely contain the newborn baby's navel-cord, and would be tucked amongst the fur wrappings of the cradleboard to bring good fortune to the child. The other pouch, although exactly the same, would hold nothing! It would serve as a decoy to draw away any evil spirits that might seek to harm the baby. This pouch would be placed elsewhere, perhaps in the fork of a tree.

For her part, Blue Beads had prepared soft, warm rabbit skins in which to swaddle the baby once it was born. She'd left her hair unbound at all times from the moment she'd first suspected she was with child, so that nothing would entangle the infant at birth and prevent it from being easily and safely born. All that was left now was the waiting—and these past few suns, the waiting had been difficult indeed, she considered ruefully!

After filling her water bladders, she stopped to talk with some of the other women who were drawing water, and smiled and paused to watch as the bravest among the camp's children shrieked and shivered as they took the first swim of the season in the icy creek, before starting back toward their camp.

When she was still some distance from her lodge, a shout rang out from the camp lookout, who kept watch from a high vantage-point above the camp and could see for some distance about it.

"Aiee! Our war chiefs and warriors return!" Kansaleumko whooped. "See! They ride the zigzag path of victory!"

The blood blanched from Blue Beads's face. A sharp pain stabbed through her back, leaving her momentarily breathless and gasping with pain. When it had eased a little, she cast a wild look about her and began hurrying back to their lodge, clumsy and awkward with the additional weight she now carried and the gnawing discomfort in her back. The war party had finally returned, and with them would come Broken Claw!

But before she'd gone more than a few paces, the victorious war party had swept through the village, whooping and kneeing their painted ponies—laden with booty and many scalps—recklessly into the very center of the lodges, scattering little children, dogs, and old ones in all directions before their ponies' wicked hooves. Blue Beads, too, was forced to hurriedly stumble aside, crying out as one coal black pony only narrowly missed trampling her under hoof.

Smothering an angry retort, she flung her head about and glanced up, her storm blue eyes flashing, a stern scolding on her lips. But instead her heart thudded sickeningly to the pit of her belly, as she looked up into the eyes of the black pony's rider and saw Broken Claw towering above her.

His long, hawklike face was painted in the red and black of war as he leered malevolently down at her. Clinging to his waist was a young paleface, a female captive of perhaps twelve or thirteen winters. Her long hair was a dull yellow, snarled with twigs and leaves. She was dirty, naked, dishevelled, bloodied, and bruised. Her gray eyes were huge and dilated, wild and vacant with shock and terror at her capture.

With a contemptuous sneer, Broken Claw looked Blue Beads over. His black eyes kindled with hatred as they travelled over her, finally coming to rest on her hugely swollen belly. If he'd had any lingering doubts, her condition was all the proof he needed that White Wolf had indeed made her his woman!

"This one will amuse me in my robes, for a while," he boasted, jerking his head at his terrified captive, who cowered behind him, fearing a blow. "But when I tire of using her, you will be mine, Blue Beads Woman," he threatened menacingly, his black eyes aglitter like the eyes of a snake, his upper lip curled with scorn. "And when that day comes, I will carve that weasel's whelp from your belly, and feed its bloody carcass to the ravens! After all, is it not said that little vermin grow to become big vermin?"

Her heart almost stopped beating within her breast. Her eyes slid closed as faintness swept over her. She wanted to run, but fear and shock at his terrible threat rooted her to the spot!

With a harsh burst of laughter at her obvious upset, Broken Claw cruelly shoved his captive from his horse, and sprang down to the ground to loom over the pregnant young woman.

"Ask this yellow-haired one if she enjoys the mating of Broken Claw!" he jeered, nodding at the terrified white girl who was cringing in the dirt at his feet, "and she will tell you that he is a man among men! That his manroot is always hard and ready to enter a woman. Ask this one if she prefers such a man, or would mate with a weasel instead—one who'd betray his brother and steal the woman he'd chosen for his own!" he taunted.

"The choice was mine, Broken Claw," Blue Beads said in a low yet controlled voice, despite the fierce trembling inside her. "If you would be angry at someone, then be angry at me, not him! I would also remind you that White Wolf is a man, Evil One. He enjoys his *woman*, and would find no pleasure in mating with children, as do you!" she tossed at him with unconcealed disgust.

"Brave words, little one," he hissed, furious at her defense of White Wolf, "but hear this! Before this moon is old, you will lie beneath me as my woman!" he threatened her, pounding his chest to give his words emphasis. "Hiyeeah, you will lie naked beneath *me*—while your Wolf's corpse feeds the vultures!"

Seeing his contorted face, she knew it would do her no good to say more. Swallowing the hot denial that sprang to her lips, she summoned all her dignity and strength. Giving him a last, icy stare, she turned and walked away.

When Wolf came to their lodge later that day, she knew with a single glance at his face that something was badly wrong. After he'd ducked under the flap, he stood looking down at her for a long moment without speaking.

"Broken Claw has returned," he said at length.

Biting her lip, she nodded. "Yes. I saw him."

"He yet has great anger in his heart toward me."

"Yes. His—words—to me—were—angry ones," she admitted carefully, reluctant to look into Wolf's piercing blue eyes. The quiet, controlled manner he had about him now was a deceptive one she'd come to recognize in the moons since she'd become his woman. It was the way of him to become quiet and stern-looking like this only when he was very, very angry, and she had no wish to enflame his anger further by repeating Broken Claw's threats against him, herself, and their unborn child.

"He spoke with you?" Wolf snapped, his head jerking up, his eyes twin blue flames in his savage face.

"A word or two, yes."

"When?"

"This morning, when he rode into the village."

"Did he come here? Did he dare to enter my lodge?" Wolf barked, his eyes blazing. "Did he touch you?"

"No! He was not here, I swear it! He—he frightened me, though. It was when I was returning from drawing

231

water that we spoke." She looked away, unable to meet his eyes.

"To frighten you so must have taken more than a word, it strikes me," Wolf said sternly. "What did he say? Tell me?"

"Nothing important, my husband—just what could be expected of one such as him!"

Wolf's expression softened. He stepped toward her and took her in his arms, tilting her face up to his by her chin. "My woman is clever. She tries to soften the anger of White Wolf by keeping the words of Broken Claw from him, eh?"

"Yes!" she confessed.

"I thank you, beloved, but—it is already too late to prevent what must be," he told her with a heavy sigh.

"Too late! Why? What do you mean?" she cried, turning his sternly handsome, copper-skinned face to hers now. Her eyes searched his blue ones, and found in their depths the answer she dreaded.

"A duel!" she exclaimed. "You are to fight to the death with cord and knives! Aiee, it is so—I can read it in your eyes! Please, Wolf, I beg you, no! If we hurry, we can run away together again—find another band where Broken Claw cannot harm you—be happy together again, just the two of us. I beg you, my husband—for my sake—for the sake of our unborn child—listen to me!"

"But can you not see—it is for your sakes that I do this!" he insisted firmly, gripping her by the upper arms. "My father called a council of elders at Broken Claw's urging, soon after the war party returned. They agreed that Broken Claw had been wronged, and permitted him to make the decision of what action should be taken. He sneered and demanded that I give you into his hands— or fight him. So you see, Broken Claw's choice was no choice, not for me! Since I could never relinquish you, beloved, as long as I draw breath, my choice was to fight!"

232

"But the duel of cord and blade is a fight to the death—!" she wailed brokenly, clinging to him. "There can be no survivor, not in this! If you should kill him, your second is then honor-bound to slay you! It is the way!"

Wolf nodded soberly. "It is. But whoever wins, the end will be the same, don't you see? With Broken Claw dead, he can never take you as his woman, and you will be safe from him. Knowing this, little dove, my spirit will happily walk the Ghost Path!"

"Aiee, yes—while I walk the path of life—alone!" she sobbed bitterly. "You don't have to do this, my husband! There must be another way?"

"There is no other way, not one with honor. Come, I have spoken. I am your husband, and it will be as I say," he reminded her in a firm, gentle voice.

"Nooo! I cannot bear to lose you! Nooo!"

She let out a great cry, her white face, her frantically working lips, beseeching him to reconsider. But even as she screamed her denial, a white hot pain knifed through her, robbing her of speech. With a gasp, her hands flew to clasp her swollen belly, then there was a splash as her waters broke on the ground beneath her. She doubled over in agony.

Wolf was at her side in a heartbeat, taking her by the shoulders and easing her down onto a low couch of willow boughs.

"Wait here and rest, my heart," he commanded gently, pressing her down when she would have risen. "Our child is impatient to be born! I will go and bring your mother to tend to your needs."

He started to leave the lodge, but her cry halted him.

"Wait!" she panted, pushing herself up onto her elbows.

"What is it, my woman?"

"When?" she demanded, breathing harshly. "Wh—when will it be?"

"The duel?" She nodded, closing her eyes. "At the

233

next sunrise," he disclosed reluctantly.

"So soon?" Her voice was an anguished whisper.

He nodded soberly and ducked through the opening.

Chapter Eighteen

The throbbing heartbeat of drums filled the torch-lit darkness with a compelling, blood-stirring beat, as Black Hawk's warriors celebrated the war party's victorious return to camp that same night. Firelight stained the faces of the Comanche braves with ruddy warpaint. The shifting light and shadow made them appear no longer human, but otherworldly, copper-skinned demons, with features carved from stone!

A tall stripped pole, raised in the place of honor, had been triumphantly hung with the three dozen fresh scalps Broken Claw and his raiding party had taken since the last Sun Dance ceremony in the summer moons. There were long and short ones, curling yellow and brown ones, red and gray and even white ones, as well as many black ones, each dressed and stretched over a hoop of willow and decorated with beads and feathers.

At the pole's base huddled the pitiful captives. Only seven had survived the terrors of the long, gruelling warpath the Comanche had ridden, and the privations and tortures their captors had subjected them to. Among them was the girl with the dirty yellow hair and glazed gray eyes whom the war chief, Broken Claw, had claimed as his prize; three young Mexican women, a Mexican youth, and two white mountain men. The stink of rank terror hung about them all like the musk of the skunk.

Before each warrior was heaped the loot he'd laid claim to following the raids; several much-prized shooting-sticks and cases of ammunition, spectacles, silver-backed looking glasses, lace *mantillas* and shawls, ornate Spanish saddles and saddle ornaments of chased silver, blankets and sturdy soup kettles of both copper and serviceable black metal. Beyond the gathering, each one securely hobbled, were over two score fine horses, pure Andalusian stock many of them, taken from the wedding party of a young Spanish *hidalgo* en route to his bride's *hacienda* across the Rio Grande. The animals were finely boned in comparison to the shaggier, sturdier Indian mounts, and would be used for breeding and improving the Indian stock.

The braves of the camp sat cross-legged in a crescent about the open clearing before Black Hawk's lodge. The camp's *shamans* flanked Black Hawk, who was resplendent this night in his war bonnet of eagle feathers, one feather signifying each of the coup he had counted in his youth. Old Semanaw, The Wise One, leader of all his medicine men, sat at his right hand, ready to offer sage counsel. He wore a gray wolf's head with the pelt, paws, and tail still attached, hanging down over his bony old back, its edges hung with the claws, feathers, and teeth of many birds and animals.

Beside Semanaw sat White Wolf, and the one the young warrior had chosen to act as his second in the duel that would be fought at sunrise; his friend of many winters, Hawakakeno, Wide River. Across the semicircle from them sat a brooding Broken Claw, with his father, scowling Elk Horns, seated next to him on one side, and his second, Nistiuna, Wild Horse, on the other. The darkling looks they gave White Wolf and his second were murderous ones.

Nistiuna! thought White Wolf with a grim half-smile, *Now there was a dog well named!*

The wild-eyed, ugly one had a reputation for stirring up trouble; a bad name for keeping fierce hatreds alive and virulent far beyond the point when time would normally have dulled them. Some even said that Wild Horse carried in his blood more than a hint of craziness, coupled with a great craving for the palefaces' firewater that sometimes led him to reckless lengths in order

236

to obtain it. Consequently, Nistiuna was neither respected nor liked among the people, and before this past winter, Broken Claw would also have given him wide berth. In Wolf's mind, this new brotherhood between the pair was proof of the enormous changes Broken Claw had undergone since the friendship bond had been severed between them. After all, was it not said by the People that a man was known by the friends he kept?

The warriors began to dance then. One by one, they leaped into the circle to dance the story of the many coups they had counted, the victories they had numbered. From one, the gathering learned of the war party's daring ambush on two paleface wagon trains at the height of last summer; from another, of the raiders' unexpected attack on many paleface ranches in the cold Moons Of Deep Snow, and at last of the final victory, a daring, all-out assault on a company of long-knives, who'd been slain to the last hated bluecoat among them!

Broken Claw himself swaggered to his feet to dance this great triumph, his braids whirling, his black eyes fierce and shiny as wet stones as he acted out the thrilling story.

Watch me, my brothers! This is how it was! He motioned boastfully, and with his dance, with movements as strong and graceful as a male antelope's, he told the gathering of how some of the female captives stolen in earlier raids had been used to bait his cunning trap in this one.

Now we bind the women, he motioned slyly, his moccasined feet lightly stamping out the rhythmn as he circled the gathering, his hand motions vividly describing their binding. *We bind them fast. They cannot escape! We hide among the rocks, and we watch, we wait!* he gestured *Soon, we see them! Soon the long-knives come! We know that foolish ones have swallowed our bait! Like little children, they come, riding their ponies deep into the ravine! Like trusting children, they look neither left nor right as they ride among us! Their*

237

thoughts, their ears, their eyes, they are all for their screaming women! Riding, riding, they come closer, closer! They do not see where Broken Claw and his warriors are hiding! They do not see where we, like shadows, lay in wait for them!

Then comes a panther, stalking, stalking, his bow in hand! he danced, and to the watchers, he *was* that panther, stalking its unsuspecting prey. *Hiyeeaah, then comes a clever panther, a cunning panther—someone who sees the enemy on the trail below, and lets fly his arrows! His medicine is powerful! His war chants are heard by the Great One! A white-eyes falls. Another—still another! The panther vaults astride his brave pony. He rides after the long-knives. His brother panthers follow! Soon, all the hated ones lie dead upon the ground. Soon, their blood waters Earth Mother. Soon, their bodies are fit only for the corpse-eaters, the carrion-eaters of the earth and air! This, my brothers, this is how it was! This is the glorious tale of our cunning, the song-story of our victory against the white-eyes!*

His story told, Broken Claw threw back his copper head and gave an ululating, yi-yiiing howl of triumph. His fist swooped out. His brown fingers curled, and he hauled his feathered battle standard from where it had been planted in the hard ground before his seat, and brandished it above him. His dance grew wilder now, more impassioned, his stamping harder, more stirring, setting the blood to racing in the veins of the watchers. He whirled fiercely, the feathers in his scalp-lock spraying about him, his torso gleaming with sweat as if it had been greased with bear fat, his long, painted face contorted in an unholy, savage grin.

Faster he whirled. Higher he leaped. The tempo of the drums increased their pounding heartbeat to match his frenzied dancing until, with a last, ear-splitting whoop, he rammed the point of the war standard into the ground scant inches before Wolf. It shuddered with the impact as he threw out his chest and looked down on his rival with a scornful smile.

"As I have taken the lives of our enemies, former brother, so shall I carve your weasel's heart from your living body, and feed it to the ravens! Sunrise, White Wolf, my *brother*," he sneered, breathing heavily. "Sunrise! Then we will settle this matter, man to man—unless White Wolf hides behind his woman's skirts as he did the last time, and tries to flee me?" he jeered, before contemptuously turning his back on Wolf and stalking arrogantly away.

White anger blistered through White Wolf, tightening his jaw, tensing his sinews. By the Spirit, he would avenge these insults to his courage, his manhood! He would redeem himself by bathing in Broken Claw's blood! he seethed. His face like thunder, his eyes—so striking against his dark copper complexion—as pale and glacial as ice, he clenched his fists and strained forward, about to leap to his feet and answer Broken Claw's insults with violence.

But his friend, steady, reliable Hawakakeno, gripped his arm and forced him back down.

"No, my brother, ignore him!" Wide River counciled, maintaining his fierce grip on Wolf's arm. "That one deliberately seeks to goad you into anger, and by so doing, throw you off your guard. He knows that in a fair fight, he's a poor match for you, my friend! The morning will be soon enough to decide who speaks truly, and who lies!"

"Your friend speaks with wisdom, my son," old Semanaw observed, nodding his white head sagely. "Hear him, and do nothing in anger for the time being. The evil that flourishes in your enemy's heart will yet prove his undoing! Believe me, White Wolf, for it is I, Semanaw, He Who Is Wise, who speaks. It will be so!"

"But it is knives we will duel with at sunrise—and to the death, old Grandfather," Wolf reminded the old *shaman* softly and with a heaviness to his voice. "There can be no survivor, no victor, not in this battle of cord-and-blade. When the sun next sets, even if I should kill Broken Claw, I will not be alive to see its beauty, surely you know this? As my second, Hawakakeno is honor-bound to slay me, even if I triumph. Or Nistiuna to kill Broken Claw, if he should best me. Whatever the outcome, my woman and unborn child will be left alone, without husband or father to provide for them. You have always given me wise council in the past, great Semanaw. You've proven yourself a true friend to White Wolf many times. And so, I have one last thing to ask of you."

"To see that they are cared for, yes?"

Wolf nodded.

"Then have no fear. If there should be a need, it will be done," Semanaw agreed solemnly. "But—remember your manhood vision, my son! The great prophecy that was foretold you then! And remember also that all things are in the hands of the Great One Above, however certain the outcome may seem."

"I will remember, Grandfather," Wolf promised. "I must go now, to purify myself. When I am done, I will climb to a high place, and there ask the Great Spirit to watch over my woman, and to see my child brought safely into the world. I will also ask Him for courage. Hawakakeno, my friend, I return at Sun's first light. You will be here?"

Hawakakeno's broad, pleasant face tensed. "I will be here. Have no fear of that, my brother. Here, and with your knife-friend sharpened to its keenest edge!" Hawakakeno promised.

With that, Wolf seemed satisfied, and rose to standing. With deliberation, he reached out and tugged the war standard from the dirt. His lip curled in derision as, in one powerful twist of his wrists, he broke it over his thigh, tossing the broken pieces contemptuously aside. A moment more, and he'd left the victorious celebration of the warriors, the pounding drums, the leaping firelight, far behind him.

Broken Claw noted how Wolf had calmly, deliberately broken his proud war standard to insult him, and bitter hatred twisted and clawed even deeper into his heart,

The Publishers of Zebra Books Make This Special Offer to Zebra Romance Readers...

AFTER YOU HAVE READ THIS BOOK WE'D LIKE TO SEND YOU **4 MORE FOR** *FREE* AN $18.00 VALUE

NO OBLIGATION!

4 FREE BOOKS

TO GET YOUR 4 FREE BOOKS WORTH $18.00 —MAIL IN THE FREE BOOK CERTIFICATE T O D A Y

Fill in the Free Book Certificate below, and we'll send your FREE BOOKS to you as soon as we receive it.

If the certificate is missing below, write to: Zebra Home Subscription Service, Inc., P.O. Box 5214, 120 Brighton Road, Clifton, New Jersey 07015-5214.

FREE BOOK CERTIFICATE
4 FREE BOOKS

ZEBRA HOME SUBSCRIPTION SERVICE, INC.

YES! Please start my subscription to Zebra Historical Romances and send me my first 4 books absolutely FREE. I understand that each month I may preview four new Zebra Historical Romances free for 10 days. If I'm not satisfied with them, I may return the four books within 10 days and owe nothing. Otherwise, I will pay the low preferred subscriber's price of just $3.75 each; a total of $15.00, *a savings off the publisher's price of $3.00.* I may return any shipment and I may cancel this subscription at any time. There is no obligation to buy any shipment and there are no shipping, handling or other hidden charges. Regardless of what I decide, the four free books are mine to keep.

NAME _____

ADDRESS _____ APT _____

CITY _____ STATE _____ ZIP _____

TELEPHONE ( ) _____

SIGNATURE _____
(if under 18, parent or guardian must sign)

Terms, offer and prices subject to change without notice. Subscription subject to acceptance by Zebra Books. Zebra Books reserves the right to reject any order or cancel any subscription.   099002

GET
FOUR
FREE
BOOKS
(AN $18.00 VALUE)

AFFIX
STAMP
HERE

like the turning of a lance point.

"See how he runs from me!" he jeered in a loud voice that none could fail to hear as he nudged Nistiuna in the ribs. "The coward leaves us! He goes to his lodge, to hide his face in shame!"

"Truly, it is so! Osolo is no longer a wolf, but a man-woman!" scoffed Nistiuna in high glee. "The paleface woman has softened his manroot! He is fit only to wear skirts and the painted moons of a virgin now! He has no place among warriors!"

Broken Claw sprang to standing. He leaped into the torch-lit circle once again. Imperiously, he gestured to two of his men.

"You, Long Nose, and you, Sahonkeno, bring two of our captives! We will see if those who share Osolo's white blood are as cowardly as our half-breed brother!" he spat with contempt.

As his braves sprang eagerly to do his bidding and dragged the sobbing captives by their hair before him, Broken Claw drew his long-bladed hunting knife from the sheath at his waist. His fathomless black eyes glittered as the honed metal winked back at him with a sly, silver glitter all its own. The narrow channel that ran the length of the wicked blade seemed like the slash of a narrow mouth to his eyes; one thirsty for white blood . . .

"You must try!" Spotted Pony remonstrated, taking her daughter by the shoulders and shaking her. Blue Beads's face was deathly white, bluish about the lips. An unhealthy sheen of sweat filmed her brow and upper lip, and exhaustion ringed her eyes with dark shadows. But the exhaustion came from fighting the birth of the child, rather than laboring to bring it into the world, and Spotted Pony was at her wits' end with fear for both her daughter and the unborn child. "Unless you will the babe to be born, the child will die within you!"

241

"Better we both die!" Blue Beads said dully, throwing off her mother's hands. "Better we both die, with no husband or father to care for us. I love him! I love Wolf so, little mother!" she sobbed, tears sparkling in her eyes. "How can I bring my child into this world, knowing he'll never have a father! Knowing the one who holds my heart is gone? Leave me . . . leave me alone . . . just go away!"

Spotted Pony muttered worriedly under her breath. Truly, she had never dreamed that such sorrow lay ahead for them when she'd helped her daughter to run away with her nephew and become his woman! If she had, she'd never have helped them, never! Now her first grandchild would perish in its mother's belly, and with its death, her beloved daughter would die, too! Aiiee, by the Spirit, it was too much to bear!

Wringing her hands, Spotted Pony ducked out of the birthing lodge and staggered outside to where a trio of toothless old crones—the village midwives—sat huddled in their blankets, gummily sucking on their pipes and exchanging disgruntled glances as they waited.

Earlier, Blue Beads Woman had sent them from the lodge into the cold spring night. Yes! Spotted Pony's defiant, disobedient paleface daughter had rudely screamed at them to be gone—to get out of her lodge and leave her alone—they, the honored ones!

Their old feathers were thoroughly ruffled, their pride wounded. One glance at their wrinkled, leathery old faces, and Spotted Pony knew it would be no easy task to persuade them to return to help her daughter.

"My child is heartsick, old Grandmothers," she began cautiously, choosing her words with the utmost care. "Forgive her her outbursts, if you can be so forgiving, for she means nothing by them, truly she doesn't. You—you have heard that her husband is to fight Broken Claw at first light tomorrow morning, a duel with cord-and-blade? Then you know that he must die, one way or the other?"

242

"We had heard, yes. But such is the way of things, when a young woman defies her father's wishes and runs off with an unacceptable one!" one of the crones said, with a shrug and a pious sniff that made Spotted Pony want to wring her scrawny neck like that of a wild turkey.

"It is true. No good ever comes of such disobedience, such wilfulness—and here's the living proof! Aiee, the young women of today! How strange they all are! Why, when I was a young girl, things were very different! We listened to our parents then!" cackled a second one. "We didn't dare to defy them."

"Nor I," agreed the third. "Children today—pah! They think they know everything, and will not listen to the wisdom of their elders!"

"You're quite right," Spotted Pony agreed demurely. "My daughter is impudent and disobedient—but for all that, my aunts, I love her, and long to hold my grandchild in my arms!"

"Yes, it is a good thing to be a grandmother," agreed the first midwife. "Even when the child's mother is impudent and disobedient . . ."

"Yes!" Spotted Pony agreed, encouraged. "A very good thing! But alas, for me that day will never come! My womb was cursed and I am barren, and now my adopted daughter will die in childbirth! Aiee, aieee, if only Yellow Beak of Iron Kettle's band were here with us! He'd know how to help her, make her deliver the child! He'd know what to do!" she sighed, casting a crafty eye at the trio of crones.

"That old fool? Paggh! What can *he* know of the birthing of babes, that one with his withered manroot hanging between his legs! This is women's business!"

"Well, yes, that's true, but he—he *is* very wise, no . . . ? Spotted Pony insisted with an expression of innocence. "Perhaps he would know of some herb to make my daughter's body give up the babe?"

"Him? That fusty, toothless old tortoise? I doubt it,

243

eh, my sisters? All that old coyote knows is potions of buffalo piss and lizards' eggs! He's a quack, and his medicine is weak! What the girl needs is a good strong dose of squaw root. That'll make her pains stronger! She'll not be able to keep the child from being born once they start, not after that, try as she might!"

"Squaw root? Rubbish!" insisted the third old woman scornfully. "You don't know what you're talking about! The only way is to grease her passage with bear fat— that'll bring the babe in a hurry. I've seen it work many times!"

"I still say my idea's better," whined the first crone in a petulant tone.

"Mine is," insisted the proponent of the bear grease.

"You're both wrong," the third woman declared smugly. "We must make her walk about, and then . . ."

Still arguing, they clambered stiffly to their feet and hobbled back inside the birthing lodge, one after the other, with Spotted Pony offering a silent prayer of relief as they did so.

White Wolf returned from the high ridge where he'd gone to ask the Great One for strength, just as Father Sun was sending up fingers of saffron gold behind the dark mountains.

Calm in heart, his mind renewed and steady of purpose now, he strode between the conical lodges of his people, offering each tepee he passed and its sleeping inhabitants a silent farewell.

The birds had already wakened. Their song rose sweet and warbling to welcome the dawn. He saw the flirting of the red-winged cardinals among the new leaves of the cottonwoods, and smiled at this small pleasure, this farewell gift from Earth Mother's little creatures. Truly, his vision was sharper than ever before, this final morning! He could see the dew clinging like a sparkling trade bead to each blade of grass. See how each new leaf was

244

furled upon its twig, each flower bud tightly clasped, only awaiting the sun's golden warmth to unfold. Never had the world seemed more beautiful than now, when he was soon to leave it . . .

And then, when he was yet several paces from the birthing lodge, he heard a sound that was sweeter, more welcome to him than any other. It was the squalling cry of a newborn babe! The loud, lusty cry was one of indignation at being thrust from the dark warmth of the womb into the brightness of the shining world. It was the first cry of his child, the seed of his loins, and his heart leaped with joy within his breast. His footsteps quickened.

Just as Wolf reached the birthing lodge, Spotted Pony exited, carrying the infant wrapped snugly in rabbit skins. She saw him, and smiled sadly as she came toward him, thinking, *Aiee, what a burden, to see his child for the very first time, and know he must soon die, and would not be there to watch it grow!*

Although it was the accepted custom among the People for a girl's mother to exchange no words directly with her son-in-law, today would be an exception, she decided. Such sad circumstances warranted it, and besides, she'd never been much of a one for following conventions . . .

"Behold, White Wolf, my son! You have a new friend!" she announced, holding the swaddled child out to him. It was the accepted announcement following the birth of a boy-child.

"By the Great Spirit, a son!" he breathed, looking down with awe and wonder into the tiny red face, screwed up now as the babe gathered its strength and prepared to bawl again. "Truly, he has a loud voice, and looks strong and healthy, too!"

"He is, he is—and perfect in all his parts, too!" Spotted Pony declared proudly, a beaming grandmother. "Has he a boy name?"

"He has," Wolf said softly, pressing his lips to the

babe's brow in blessing, and gently stroking the soft black hair that capped his tiny head, as he remembered the warbling cardinals in the trees as they greeted the rising Sun. "He is to be known as Red Wing, son of White Wolf, pride of his father."

"Red Wing. It is a fine name," his mother-in-law approved. "Would you—would you see my daughter now?"

"She is well?" Wolf asked, looking up sharply, his anxiety transparent.

"She is well, but exhausted. The midwives gave her a draught, and she is sleeping now. It was a long, hard birth you see, and she fought against it. But after she rests a little, she will be well again in body, if not in spirit. Oh, my son, her heart lies on the ground! She is desolate, and will not accept that she must—that she must lose you!" Her voice trailed away, became a whisper. Her eyes filled with tears. "Will you go now, and speak with her?"

Wolf hesitated, then shook his head. "No, little mother. Our good-byes have already been said. To say them again would only cause her further pain. When it is over, tell her not to grieve, nor to cut herself or her hair in her sorrow, as is the way of our women. Say that since we met, my heart has beaten only for her, and that I could not bear to think of her beauty marred by grief wounds for me. Tell her that she has given me a fine son, and that I am proud and grateful. Tell her also that I loved only her among women, and that someday, we will ride the wind together again, in the After World."

"I will tell her," Spotted Pony promised, and Wolf nodded.

"Farewell, little mother," he murmured, and walked away from her, toward the open clearing by his father's lodge, where Hawakakeno already awaited him.

At Black Hawk's nod, the two warriors' left arms were

lashed together from wrists to elbows with strong cords of buffalo hide. In Wolf's right hand, Hawakakeno placed his friend's hunting knife, the blade he'd spent the whole night honing along both its edges until it was razor sharp. The wicked blade was long, almost the length of two men's hands, anchored firmly in a handle of buckhorn. Nistiuna placed a similar weapon in Broken Claw's fist, then the two seconds retired to a spot some distance across the clearing to watch the outcome, their own knives in hand and ready for their final part in the duel.

Such battles rarely lasted more than a few moments. This they knew from bitter experience. Lashed together as they were, armed with such wickedly sharpened, long blades, death claimed one combatant or the other very swiftly.

Wolf could feel his heart throbbing like a drum in his chest as he waited for the duel to begin. Each beat left to it was for Blue Beads, and his tiny son! Each breath remaining, he spent to keep them safe from Broken Claw's madness. *Great Spirit, I am ready!* he prayed silently. *What must be, will be. Hiyeeaah! It is a good day to die!*

He drew a deep, steadying breath and tightened his grip on the buckhorn handle in his fist, curling his fingers about it. It was a good knife, a fine knife, more than a weapon. It had become a friend, of sorts; his companion of the hunt, his defender in battle, and helpful in a thousand other ways. It felt right in his grip, the handle worn smooth from many winters of usage, the ridges where his fingers curled familiar, comforting ones. *My Keen One, My Old Friend, do not fail me now!*

His brilliant blue eyes blazing in his dark-skinned face, he looked toward his grim-faced father, standing between the seconds. Black Hawk would give the signal for them to start, and then would come the beginning of the end. Their eyes met, and Wolf saw the love and

247

dawning of imminent loss in his father's.

Farewell, beloved son, Black Hawk's sorrowful brown eyes told his. *My pride in you is great! Die swiftly, and well!*

Then Black Hawk nodded.

Chapter Nineteen

No sooner had Black Hawk's chin lowered than Broken Claw twisted sideways, his knife arm raised, the wickedly pointed blade angled to one side. With his left arm lashed to Wolf's, he viciously slashed downward through the air, eager and thirsty to draw first blood.

"You die, woman-stealer!" Broken Claw spat, his eyes twin pools of venom.

Golden sunbursts flashed off his blade as it swooped downward in a streaming silver arc. Broken Claw's yip of triumph rent the air, but it ended hollowly. The onlookers gave a collective gasp as the edge of the wicked blade missed Wolf's abdomen by a hair's breadth!

Aiee, they muttered, if White Wolf had not sucked in his breath, he'd have been laid open to the ribs!

Broken Claw roared with thwarted rage.

"The woman didn't want you, dreamer!" Wolf taunted. "I stole nothing that was not mine! And what is more, I won't die easily, old friend!" His eyes glinted frostily, like chips of broken blue glass, as he jerked the knife in his grip and goaded, "Come on, rejected one, try again! Maybe you'll have better luck with me than with women, eh?"

Livid with rage, Broken Claw snarled like a wild animal. He drew back his blade again and slashed wildly, drawing a silver rainbow around his body in the light.

At once Wolf sidestepped, then twisted abruptly to one side. He felt the wind stirred by Broken Claw's knife fan his back as the unexpected move jerked his opponent clear off his feet and brought him down onto his knees. Wolf pitched after him.

Left arms still bound together, the two slammed to the dirt, landing with Wolf on top, straddling Broken Claw's belly. Their bared torsos dripped sweat in the morning sunlight. Their blades flashed and stabbed and slashed again and again; two heads of raven hair, two lean, muscled chests, two sets of wiry flanks, twisting and writhing to escape each other's deadly knives.

Suddenly, blood erupted from a wound in a scarlet storm—from whom, it was impossible to tell!—then from another . . . still another . . . as both men grappled for position to mortally wound the other. Sinewy arms strained. Legs encased in buckskin scrabbled furiously for purchase. Breechclouts and fringes slapped to and fro, sodden with blood and mud. Necklaces of bear claws, fur and feather scalp ornaments were lost in the foray; ground into the churned dirt beneath the two as the fight to the death built in ferocity. Both braves now had their lips drawn back from their teeth in a terrible, grinning rictus of hatred. Their eyes blazed, startling blue into pitchy black, while the reek of blood and sweat and animal hatred hung like the stink of sulphur on the dewy cool of the morning air.

"Sing your death chant, my brother!" Wolf taunted in a harsh rasp. "Your time has come to die!"

He raised his fist aloft, using his weight to pin Broken Claw beneath him, his blade angled to mortally wound his foe.

But Broken Claw's eyes flickered to something over Wolf's shoulder. His face contorted in a malevolent grin of triumph.

"Son of a Hopi whore, I spit on your threats!" he threw back. "It is you the Corpse Carrier comes for, not I!"

In the same moment, Wolf heard a woman—Wounded Doe?—scream: *"Behind you! Behind you, my brother!"*

With superhuman effort and an agonized grunt, Wolf at once rolled sideways, using all his strength and impetus to haul Broken Claw over, atop of him, and by so doing reverse their positions. It was then, in the very same instant that a *third* man's blade swooped down, that he saw Nistiuna, crazy Nistiuna, Broken Claw's second, looming over them, his expression a gleeful one as he stabbed downward! Broken Claw took the blade meant for Wolf deep in the back of his shoulder, spraying fresh blood over them both!

"Son of a scorpion!" Wolf derided Broken Claw, his jeering tone like the lash of a whip. "Are you too womanish to fight your battles alone, then? Must your 'sister' run to aid you? Come, 'sister' to Broken Claw," Wolf taunted Nistiuna, "I can take you with us down the Ghost Path, if such is your choice!"

"Enough!" thundered Chief Black Hawk's booming voice as he sprang to his feet. "Hawakakeno, free them!"

Wide River, Wolf's second, hurried to cut the buffalo-hide bonds that joined the two warriors' left wrists in answer to his chief's commands. The braves, still grimacing ferociously at each other, both staggered to standing. They stood there, swaying like drunkards on their feet and dripping rivers of blood from several slice wounds, while Chief Black Hawk strode slowly across the open ground to stand before them, his nostrils flared with disgust.

Meanwhile Nistiuna, Wild Horse, hung back, grinning foolishly. There was about him, Wolf realized groggily now, the reek of white man's firewater.

"The duel is ended! You have brought dishonor upon your father Elk Horns's lodge, and shame upon both your proud names in this soiled moment, my nephew!" Black Hawk gritted at Broken Claw. His long, sad, hatchet-featured face was grave indeed. "You," he continued scornfully, "you who were raised in my own lodge, and called me second-father—have you forgotten my teachings so soon? Have you no honor in you, that you'd betray our sacred customs in this manner?"

Broken Claw, still breathing heavily, remained impassive and said nothing, his expression dark and unreada-

251

ble, though his eyes were roiling snakes, coiled to strike.

"And what of you, Nistiuna? This was not your quarrel—and yet you drink the white-man's crazy water and make yourself a part of it! Semanaw, Wise One, hear me, for what I am to say shall stand for all the suns yet remaining of my life!" Black Hawk continued.

"The taste of vomit will always burn my tongue when I see this worthless pair henceforth! Their foul stink is that of cowards—the stink of dung heaps! Say now the words that will banish forever such cringing cowards—the words that will rid our village of these lice! Send these crawling ones forth! Let them find another band, one where such maggots are welcomed! And let it be known hereafter among our people that in the camp of Black Hawk, *all* warriors are their own men! All will fight their own battles, and do so alone—even should such a warrior be the son of a chief!"

There was a ringing hush following his terrible words, but it lasted only a second before Broken Claw's poisonous rebuttal dripped into the void.

"Your words are the words of an old humpback, my uncle, all piss and gall, but without substance! Too long you have kept to your lodge like a woman. Too long you have shunned the path of war. You have grown weak! You lack a true man's fire! Fear not, my uncle," Broken Claw jeered softly. "Nistiuna and I will go from this camp of scared women and old ones—aiee, we will go gladly! We will find another band, one where the true ways of our People are not warped by ties of kindred. One where justice flies true and straight like a perfect arrow, instead of following a crooked path. Here there can be no justice, not for one who has been wronged by *your* son! Your words are empty ones, mighty Black Hawk—as empty as hollow logs!" His lips twisted in a contemptuous sneer, one so mocking it took all of Chief Black Hawk's forbearance to keep from striking his face with a knotted fist.

"Your bitterness stems from a twisted heart, my nephew!" the chieftain said with deadly softness, "and so, we will ignore your insults—this time. You know full well that I was willing to watch my son die, for the sake of your petty cries for justice!"

Turning regally, Black Hawk regarded the circle of hushed onlookers and said in a louder voice, "Let it be known by all who stand here today, witness to these matters, that justice has forever been served! Broken Claw forfeits all claims to the woman, by virtue of his treachery! She belongs now to the warrior White Wolf, by right of blood and of battle. Let no man say otherwise!"

To Broken Claw and Nistiuna, the chieftain rasped, "Go, dogs! If you yet linger here when Sun seeks his lodge in the west, you will die!"

Broken Claw flung about, his injured arm hanging loose at his side. As he thrust his way past Wolf, he hissed, "Perhaps you have won this sun's battle, but you've not seen the last of me—this I swear! One day, your woman will be mine, and I will have my revenge on you! One day, my friend—even should it take 'til the end of time!"

Then he was gone, with Nistiuna slinking at his heels like a greasy shadow.

Semanaw came to Wolf then, and from rheumy eyes peered at the long, slender wound that ran from under his jaw down the side of his throat to his collarbone.

"So, my son! Did I not speak truly?" the old *shaman* demanded with a self-satisfied, wheezy chuckle that set his bear claws and ornaments to clattering. "Did I not say that nothing can be, unless the Great Spirit wills it? Today was not your day to die! Your destiny is not yet fulfilled as the prophecy foretold it. And so, Broken Claw is gone from your life, the woman yours, and all is well!"

"Well?" Wolf growled, scowling. "No, wise Grandfather, all is far from well! So long as Broken Claw lives, my woman will never be safe! Better I'd taken the Ghost

Path—and that evil one with me—than live to see him cast out of our camp, left to stew in his broth of anger once more. He is not done with us yet, wise Grandfather!" Wolf said, and his words had the eerie ring of prophecy, to the medicine man's thinking. "No, never! He swore as much, but even if he'd said nothing, my *bones* tell me that there is more to come. Far better I'd slain him, and cut out his heart . . ."

And with that, he strode off to his lodge, brusquely shrugging off Semanaw's offer to see to his wound.

Life's season is short
For the children of
Earth Mother,
Soon it is finished.

came a woman's choked voice from within his lodge.

Now he is gone,
Gone like a leaf in the winds . . .
My heart has fled with him,
Fled with the spirit of my beloved!
My soul is shriveled
As a burned leaf . . .

Wolf hesitated, his hand poised to raise the tepee flap. Instead, he waited, listening as Blue Beads mourned him within their lodge.

Her usually sweet singing voice was husky with sorrow, hoarse from too many tears and grieving. A knot rising up his throat, he quickly ducked under the flap of his lodge—the home he'd thought never to see again—and went inside.

Blue Beads was seated cross-legged before the fire, her head bowed, her long dark hair shielding him from her view. She'd unlaced and pulled down one side of her deerskin shift to bare her breast and nurse their child.

Tears streamed down her cheeks as she looked down at the baby.

The infant was suckling, his little smacking, grunting sounds of contentment incongruous against the mournful lullaby sung by his mother. A sturdy little clenched fist pressed rhythmically against her swollen breast, kneading its blue-veined whiteness, and a dark, tear-dampened little head shifted as the baby paused to draw breath, before burrowing snugly against his mother's warmth again.

"—he has gone, my little one," she whispered brokenly. "Gone like a leaf on the wind . . ."

"No, not gone!" Wolf said suddenly, the knot strangling his tongue suddenly loosened. "Your husband is not gone, but here and unharmed. Broken Claw—he is the one who is gone, cast out from our people! I am here with you, and with our son."

Her eyes—so haunted, so tragic moments before—suddenly leaped back to life. Joy blazed from their deep blue depths, dispelling tears. Her hand flew to her mouth to stanch the cry that welled up from inside her, but it was too glad, too heartfelt, and would not be stanched.

"Alive! Great Spirit be praised, you're alive!" she cried. "Come, my husband! Come to me!"

Wolf needed no further invitation. He crossed the lodge in three strides, and dropped down to his knees behind her, pulling her back to lean against his broad chest. He encircled both beloved woman and cherished child in powerful, loving arms, his embrace fierce and tight with relief. They both laughed giddily as tiny Red Wing squealed in protest at being so snugly held.

"Truly," she murmured, tears of joy filling her eyes, laughter bubbling on her lips, "your son is a complainer, much like his father!"

She raised her free arm, reached back behind her, and caught him about the neck, pulling his raven head down to her raised face. Her fingertips touched the stickiness of

255

congealed blood there. "No! You are hurt!" she exclaimed.

"A scratch, less than nothing," he disclaimed. "Come, kiss me, and it will be healed, paleface woman, for there is strong medicine in the warmth of your lips!"

Their mouths met, and then, after a long, lingering kiss, he shuddered with the force of his tumultuous emotions. He buried his face in the glossy wealth of her hair, his lips travelling over her throat and down to the same breast at which the child suckled. He kissed the warm swell of her bosom very gently, then the infant's flushed cheek. "Enjoy, my little one, for when your mother's birth-time is ended, you must share those treasures with your father!" he threatened, stroking a downy cheek with his calloused fingertip and eying her wickedly for a reaction.

"Wolf!" Blue Beads scolded, and Wolf chuckled in amusement.

"Perhaps I should be grateful Broken Claw is as he is, and Nistiuna his sworn brother, after all," he reflected softly, caressing his son's tiny arm. "Because of his evil heart, his treachery, I've been given back my life with you and our babe. If the fight had been fair—! Hiyeeah, truly, it would not be so! My spirit would even now walk the Star Path that hangs in the sky!"

Blue Beads shivered and pressed a finger across his lips. "Please, enough of such dismal thoughts! I'm just so glad you're alive and here with us! Now, will you hold your son, my husband?"

He grinned. "I will—if he is done filling his belly! And with the next rising of the sun, I will go forth from our lodge and sing his birthing song about the village, as a new father should!"

He took Red Wing from her, and carefully held the wobbly-headed infant, swaddled in soft rabbit furs, aloft. "A son! My son! And what a son!" he boasted, pride shining in his eyes as he looked upon the drowsy, red-faced infant. "You are our hope for the future, little war-rior, and the pride of your father!"

A blue-and-yellow-beaded pouch, prettily shaped like a turtle, fell from the infant's swaddling onto his lap.

"Ah. His navel cord?"

"Yes," Red Wing's mother confirmed with a smile. "Wounded Doe made it for his birth."

"And there is another?"

"Of course—a second one just like it. Is that not the way?"

He nodded. "Where is the other one?"

"In the fork of the cottonwood tree just outside our lodge, my husband." She smiled. "My little mother put it there herself. She said that there, even the most blind and foolish of evil spirits couldn't fail to find it! So you see, you have nothing to worry about. Our son's real navel cord is safely hidden in his blankets, and he'll have good fortune always!"

"Always," Wolf echoed. His morning glory eyes were warm and tender with love as he looked over Red Wing's tiny dark head and into his woman's smiling face.

Chapter Twenty

"Devin, do you believe in reincarnation?"

Devin Colter grinned over the brown cardboard box he was carrying, his brown eyes twinkling.

"Reincarnation, mmm? Well, certainly not before the fourth date, or possibly even the fifth—and even then, not before breakfast! I'm an old-fashioned guy, pretty lady. Never let it be said that I'm easy," he warned, his lips twitching with the urge to laugh.

"Oh, you! You know very well what I meant! Be serious for once, and answer me!" Kelly retorted, laughing herself nonetheless. She did so partly in embarrassment that she'd finally managed to broach the subject she'd been dying to discuss with him for weeks, and partly because he could always make her laugh so easily.

Devin set the box down, and promptly flopped onto the sofa, regarding her solemnly.

"Serious, mmm? We—ell, then I guess my answer would have to be an unqualified I don't know! I've never really given it much thought, to be honest. Why the sudden interest in reincarnation, anyway? That's kind of a heavy subject for—" There was a pause while he peered at his watch, "Four in the afternoon. Unless—oh, my God, I think I've got it!" he exclaimed, slapping his forehead.

She grimaced. "All right, I'll bite. Got what?"

"You're convinced you're the reincarnation of a slave driver from a southern plantation—a gen-u-ine throwback from the eighteen hundreds! That's why you've been working me so damned hard, cracking the proverbial whip!" He groaned and went limp, his long, muscular arms flopping over the back of the sofa, his tongue lolling out like a thirsty bloodhound. "No more work, please, Miz Scarlett? A beer! A beer!" he croaked. "My kingdom for a beer!"

She snorted in disgust, but was still laughing as she lobbed a velvet pillow at him. "No, you crazy idiot! These *are* the eighties! Get it yourself! I'm beat, too—and besides, you're soooo much closer!" she wheedled, and stuck out her tongue.

"Arr, but you're a haard woman, Kelly Michaels—a teerruble haaard woman!"

He uncoiled to standing and started toward the apartment's tiny kitchenette, his blue-jeaned hips easily weaving their way between the boxes of household goods, which had arrived at Barbara's from England three days earlier.

One of Bill's patients, a Mrs. Iverson, had mentioned that she had an apartment for rent in the Scottsdale area—the same building, in fact, in which Margot, Barb's mother, had her apartment—and Bill had passed on the information to Kelly, who'd promptly called the woman and arranged to view the studio. Tiny but well-maintained, it had come partially furnished. The color scheme was light and airy with lots of white paint and picture windows, and she'd decided within minutes that the place was perfect for her needs. She'd promptly paid a deposit and signed a six-months' lease, much to Barbara's disappointment.

"I don't know why you're in such a darned hurry to leave us," she'd grumbled when Kelly'd announced her decision over dinner preparations that evening. "It's not as if we're anxious to get rid of you, after all!"

"Of course you're not," Kelly'd tried to placate her. "You've been just wonderful, both of you—more than wonderful! And I'll really miss seeing you and Bill and this gorgeous nephew of mine every day, right, sweetie-

259

pie?" she'd cooed at the adorable baby squirming on her lap, trying to roll over. "But, Barb, I can't stay here, living off you two indefinitely, now can I?" she reasoned.

"Why not?" Barb had persisted in her mulish way. "We love having you, you know that, Kell."

"I know, I know—but this isn't college any more. You have your own family now, Barb, and lovable as I am, I'm still a third wheel—playing gooseberry, they call it back in England! Besides, I've gained so much weight from your wonderful cooking—my body'll thank me for the move!" Kelly teased her lightly, patting her full stomach with a rueful smile. She hadn't been gilding the lily about that, not really. She had gained a little weight since July, but both she and Barbara knew that on her, those added few pounds were an improvement. The hollow-cheeked look had gone, and she looked and felt better than she had in months—years!

Barbara had sighed. "Your mind's made up, isn't it?"

"Yes, Barb."

"And wanting to have that hunk, Devin, all to yourself wouldn't have a thing to do with you moving out, I suppose?" Barbara asked archly, but with a smug smile that she'd been the one responsible for bringing the two of them together.

After six weeks of steady dating, Barbara and Bill had come to consider Kelly and Devin something of an item. Barbara in particular was clearly delighted with the results of her matchmaking so far! Kelly and Devin had wined, dined, and danced several nights away together at local restaurants and nightclubs. They'd played tennis, gone swimming, and discovered a mutual enjoyment of horseback riding and hiking. Their rides had covered some of the rugged sightseeing trails which encompassed various historical and scenic spots beyond the city, ones equally popular with the flocks of tourists visiting the beautiful state; Apache Trail, Lost Dutchman State Park in the Superstition Range, and so on. They really seemed to enjoy each other's company—so much so that it had showed!—and had so many things in common, that Kelly knew Barb had high hopes that something permanent would come of the budding romance.

In answer to her unsubtle comment, Kelly—to her friend's delight—had actually blushed, she recalled. "That might have a little something to do with it, yes," she'd admitted, and promptly changed the subject. "Now, what time do I start work on Monday?"

"Nine. We open the boutique at ten," Barbara had supplied sweetly, looking even more plumply elfin than usual. "Oh, and Kelly, dear—?"

"Mmm?"

"You're not fooling me one bit! You *do* like him. You like him a lot, don't you? Come on—'fess up, kid!"

"Devin?"

"Of course, Devin!"

"That would be Devin Colter, I presume?" Kelly'd asked, all frowns and innocence. "Dr. Devin Colter?"

"Darn it, Kelly, come on—!" Barb had threatened, brandishing a serving spoon in her direction.

"Oh, I guess he's okay," she'd confessed with a shrug that was a shade too nonchalant to be genuine, and quickly pretended to be engrossed in little William's antics rather than meet Barbara's eye. "Now, getting back to the Great Move! You wouldn't happen to have an old can opener you don't need around here, would you?"

Barbara had rolled her eyes in disgust and gone to ferret one out, Kelly recalled with a grin, claiming as she did so that she was only loved for her kitchen utensils, and not for herself.

"Here, catch!" Devin ordered, tossing her an ice-cold can of beer.

She caught it, and flipped the tab with a pop and a hiss as he wove his way back between the stack of cardboard boxes and dropped down onto the sofa beside her. He promptly propped his long legs on the glass-topped

261

brass coffee table. His tanned right arm, the blue-plaid sleeve rolled up to the elbow, slid companionably along the back of the sofa behind her. He took a frosty gulp of beer, while she sipped thirstily at hers.

"God, that tastes good! I can feel it trickling all the way down!" she approved with a sigh, and pressed the icy, sweating can to her hot cheek.

"Hmm," he agreed, setting his beer aside. His dangling hand toyed with her hair, which was caught up in a perky ponytail today. Little dark wisps had escaped its confines, and perspiration from her exertions had made them curl. Tendrils framed her oval face. Damn, she looked so fragile, so lovely and delicate, yet even slender as she was, she was no shirker when it came to hard work, Devin thought approvingly. She'd lugged more than her share of heavy boxes from the rented U-Haul to the elevator without even a squeak of complaint.

"And now for my well-deserved reward after a hard day's work, Madame Simone LeGree!" he growled. "Let me kiss *you*, purty lady—see if you taste anywhere near 's cool and deelicious as this here Coors . . ."

His eyes darkened as his large hand cradled her head and tipped it ever so slightly around so that he could kiss her full on the mouth. At once, her eyes slid closed, the dark lashes curving against her cheeks as she leaned back with a contented sigh. She gave herself up to the delicious sensation of his lips moving on hers, her earlier question forgotten.

The first time he'd kissed her had been when they'd rested the horses above Apache Lake on the Apache Trail, the first weekend after they'd met, she remembered dreamily. He'd asked her if she'd like to do some sightseeing on one of his rare weekends off, and she'd agreed.

She'd sensed he meant to kiss her all that day by the way he'd kept staring at her, even when he'd thought she wasn't aware he was watching her. The knowledge had made her nervous and unusually quiet as their rented horses picked their way along the hikers' trail behind Horse Mesa Dam; so nervous she'd hardly noticed the beautiful, unspoiled scenery or the wildlife.

But when they'd sat side by side, looking down at the lake winking like a mirror in the dazzling afternoon sunlight, and the lovely vista of the Four Peaks of the Mazatzal Mountains soaring skyward to the north behind them, it had seemed so natural and right that he should kiss her, her nervousness had evaporated. She'd gone into his arms willingly, yielding her mouth completely to his, intoxicated by his nearness and the serenity of the wilderness beauty all about them.

Today his lips felt icy from the beer, yet his kisses grew increasingly warmer as his mouth moved against hers—gentle, but arousing, too. She relaxed completely and let her head go way back, cradled heavily against his arm behind her as his tongue traced the margin of her lips. She parted them and pressed her long fingers against his face, cupping his jaw and cheek in a gentle caress that brought him closer and deepened the kiss.

He felt so deliciously strong and masculine! The slight roughness of his beard shadow was a distinctly pleasant sensation she thought she'd never tire of. He smelled wonderful, too; all clean, male sweat and soap mixed with aftershave—something cool and lime-scented and fresh-smelling—and she sighed with pleasure, murmuring, "Mmm, Devin, that's so nice . . . really, really nice . . . !" when he broke the kiss to nibble on her ears. When he finally came up for air, she murmured a little ohh! of disappointment.

Smiling at her expression, he leaned back a little, and traced the contours of her face with his fingertips, following the curve of her lovely, high cheekbones down to her pointed little chin, then grazing his knuckles over her slender throat to caress her collarbone, exposed by the open collar of her cambray shirt. As always, the gentle yet enflaming way he touched her, kissed her—his very nearness—made her heart flutter wildly in response. Her breathing seemed suddenly shallow and constricted.

"Oh, Kelly," he said softly, reprovingly, his tone huskier than moments before. "Oh, purty, purty little Kelly, you heartless wench! You haven't a clue what that ponytail and those sassy blue jeans do to me, or y'all'd have mercy on a poor sinner!"

"Ponytails and blue jeans turn you on, hmm, Dr. Colter?" she came back swiftly, her deep blue eyes sparkling with amusement, although her voice was trembly-sounding to her ears, rather than stern. "Why, I'm frankly shocked that they'd let you practice medicine! You sound like a class-A dirty old man, to me! Pediatrician, indeed!"

Laughing, she tried to spring up off the sofa, with a cry of "Back to work, Doc!" to dispel the sudden, electric sexual tension crackling in the air between them, but Devin had other ideas.

"No way my interest in you is in any way professional, pretty lady. Ponytail or not, you are definitely—but def-in-it-ely—no kid," he breathed in her ear after succeeding in pulling her back down across his lap and into his arms. "You're all woman, Kelly—and right now, one that's driving me wild! Let's leave this damned unpacking for now, hmmm? I'll carry you off to the bedroom and we'll play doctor for a while instead, what do you say to that—?"

" 'And we'll' nothing!" she insisted hotly, squirming away from him. "Besides, on a purely practical note, the bed's still in pieces, remember? Not that that makes any difference—the answer's still no!" she added hurriedly.

"Ah, but the carpet's a mile high, and just as soft as all get-up," he wheedled, grinning lecherously and making another grab for her. "We don't need a bed for what I have in mind . . ."

He caught her about the waist and wrestled her down to the off-white carpet, trapping her beneath his hard hips amidst towering walls of packing boxes—hardly a romantic setting for seduction!

"Gotcha!" he threatened huskily, his weight balanced on his palms planted on either side of her body as he laughed down into her face. His eyes were dark with passion. "Christ! The damned unpacking can go to the devil . . ."

Romantic setting or not, she was shaking with silent laughter and lay quiescent beneath him as he kissed her throat, her ears, her eyelids, the smudge of dust across her nose and cheekbones, until her laughter abruptly vanished. It melted, faded to a deep, purring groan as his mouth captured hers yet again. His kisses were more ardent, more intense now—and far, far too arousing to be amusing.

He slanted his lips across hers, parting her mouth with his tongue as he delved into the soft recesses beyond. His eyes were even darker with desire when she opened hers to look up at him. Something deep in her belly stirred. A response she'd never expected to feel for any man, ever again, flickered through her like summer lightning. She shivered in expectation as she felt his hand tug her shirt-tails free of her jean's waistband, and then gasped at the thrilling shock of his bare palm gliding beneath her blouse and over her skin, grazing across her rib cage, then skimming higher to cup her breast in delicious heat. As his gentle fingers closed around her full curves, he teased the nipple with the ball of his thumb until it tightened. Little shock waves ricochetted through her. She shuddered and stilled his hand with her own clamped over it, frightened by the immediacy of her response as her fingers dug into his wrist.

"Oh, lord, Devin, please, please don't do that!" she whispered.

"Kelly, honey, c'mon, you don't mean that," he countered softly, his voice husky. "You love it when I touch you like this—you think I can't tell? C'mon, let me love you, sweetheart? Let me take the bad memories away . . ."

He leaned up, and in a sort of hazy dream state she sensed him freeing the buttons of her shirt while he showered kisses over her face, parting the pale blue fabric to bare her breasts. Another moment, a second shaky intake of breath, and then his dark head was pillowed between them. His lips tenderly nipped and suckled at each sensitive peak in a way that made her toes curl, and her fingers tighten uncontrollably in his crisp black hair.

As he continued to gently caress her breasts, she heard the rasp of the zipper as he unzipped her jeans with his free hand, and then his mouth moved lower and lower, nuzzling her navel, moving down, until his warm lips were branding the vee of lacy peach cloth she wore beneath. A moment more, and she felt denim sliding down her hips, her legs, and then off, and the cool, air-conditioned draft contrasted sharply with the heat of his hands, lazily caressing her thighs in silky, circular motions.

Bare now except for her wispy panties, she lay beneath him, dizzied and dazzled by the way his caresses were making her feel. With Devin, it didn't feel embarrassing that she was lying there half-naked. Nor did it feel in any way wrong. On the contrary, it felt damnably, dangerously *right!* Her body had grown flushed all over, warm and rosy with desire. Her limbs felt loose and languorous. The carpet beneath them was as soft as a bed of moss, the plush pile easily a mile high, as Devin had teasingly promised. The urge to simply lay back and sink into that velvety softenness, to let him make love to her as he wanted, was enormously tempting. Devin was gentle and handsome. He was also sensitive and funny, not to mention intelligent. His athletic body was beautiful, tanned and hard over hers, and she knew that he'd be a wonderful lover. Even more importantly, he *cared* for her, she knew that instinctively. He cared more than she wanted to admit—or more accurately, than she was ready to acknowledge.

It frightened her, if the truth was known, having a man care for her again, after Tony's cruel brand of love. Intimacy on any level, physical or emotional, terrified her. Tony, damn him, had taught her that love and jealous possessiveness went hand in hand, and that love could wear two frighteningly different faces; a hurting face just as often as a gentle one. And yet—oh, lord, she wanted Devin! Wanted him more than she'd thought she could ever want a man again! And maybe, just maybe, he was right? Maybe he could take the bad memories away, and replace them with good ones that weren't painful to recall?

Shyly, she reached up and slipped the buttons of his shirt free, tugging the blue-checkered cloth down off his wiry shoulders. A broad chest appeared, bronzed and well-muscled and furred lightly with a T of crisp, curling dark hair. The narrow column of the T disappeared into a leather belt with an ornate silver cowboy buckle at his lean waist. She caressed his broad shoulders, traced that fascinating trail of masculine hair down to the glint of silver, but found she couldn't bring herself to undress him further, as he'd undressed her.

She wetted her lips, her heart pounding like a crazy thing. At any moment, she was half-convinced he'd change from the gentle man she was falling in love with! Afraid that, like Tony often had at such times, or like Doctor Jekyll and Mister Hyde, he'd become different; would lose control and grow rough and uncaring, would turn something beautiful and meaningful into something abhorrent and degrading. An act of punishment, rather than an act of love and passion . . .

"Oh, lord, Devin, I'm sorry, but—I can't. I really don't think I can—!" she cried, beginning to tremble uncontrollably in his arms. "Maybe—? Yes, please, Devin—oh, God, maybe you should just—just go now? Please go!"

267

"Hush, baby. Hush, sweetheart . . ." he crooned, stroking her hair away from her face. " 'Mmmm, you see? You can trust me. I won't hurt you, baby, ever. I won't do anything that isn't okay with you, alright?"

Little by little, he silenced her with soft murmurs and a shower of little kisses that dusted her nose, her eyelids, the tops of her breasts. "You don't have to do a thing, but let me hold you, kiss you. Just relax, honey. Relax and enjoy. Just let it happen, and I'll love you like you deserve to be loved, baby . . ."

She clung to him, only too willing to let him take the lead, wanting to believe he was right, and that everything would be fine.

Beyond, through the studio picture windows, the brilliant blue sky was ablaze with a crimson sunset, streaked with flame and rose.

"I'm sorry. Oh, Devin, I'm so damned sorry. I warned you—I told you you should leave, remember? Staying was a mistake! You see how I am? I just—I just can't anymore!" she whispered later, sitting up and gathering her discarded clothes over her breasts to cover her nudity. She turned her back to him and her shoulders shook.

"Hey, c'mon, I told you, sweetheart, it doesn't matter, not to me. I understand, Kelly, I really understand how you must feel," he murmured, sitting up and stroking her lovely long dark hair in an effort to soothe her. "There's no hurry, nothing to prove, not with me. There'll be other times, honey, and one day, when you've come to trust me, it'll be beautiful for you as well as for me. You know how I know that, babe? Because I love you, Kelly! You hear me? I love you!"

She nodded dolefully, her deep blue eyes shining with tears in the fading amethyst light that filled the studio now, in the aftermath of that glorious, gaudy sunset. The glint of stars showed between the amethyst, as if tiny silver spurs had been strewn across it.

Oh, lord, what must he be thinking? she wondered, feeling sick to her stomach. She bit her lip. That she was a tease, of course, what else *could* he think! Despite his reassurances, he was still a man, and probably had her pegged for the kind of woman who delighted in leading men on, in beckoning them down a sexual garden path, promising everything, but—once the poor guy was hot under the collar—backed down at the last minute and cried wolf. Cried wolf? Oh, lord, that was a good one! She hadn't been able to think of anyone but that damn Indian fantasy-man she'd conjured up the entire time he was kissing her, caressing her—! But how could that be, when she enjoyed being with Devin so very much? Was as attracted to him as strongly as she knew she was? It didn't make any sense, loving someone who wasn't even real, who didn't exist except in her mind!

"I think you're beginning to love me a little, too, honey. But you've been hurt in the past, badly hurt," he continued when she made no comment, but simply sat there with her head bowed, thinking God-only-knew-what. "It's hard to trust someone again afterward, isn't it, honey? Kind of like falling off a horse! It's a bitch to have to scrape up the guts to climb back on again, take another chance, right? But there's no hurry, baby, no hurry at all. We've got all the time in the world! Forget this afternoon! Sooner or later, it'll come out right for us, Kell. You have to believe that. Now, c'mon, come back over here beside me. Let me hold you, sweetheart."

Gratefully, she lay back down beside him, letting his strong arms cradle her against his chest. The thud of his heartbeat was measured and even beneath her ear, his body warm and vital as it cradled hers. Tears she'd thought buried and done with months ago, following her divorce, welled up from nowhere, a result of his gentleness and understanding. They splashed down her cheeks to dampen his chest.

Soothing her hair and muttering silly little clucking sounds that were wonderfully reassuring despite their inanity, Devin let her cry herself out.

"Better?" he asked much later, when her shoulders had left off shaking and she lay quiet and still again in his arms.

"I think so," she agreed with a noisy sniff.

"Hmm. I sure hope you're right! If not, we've got all the makings of a three-alarm flood right here. Hold on, babe, while I wring the carpet out—!"

"Oh, you idiot! You never quit, do you?" she managed to come back, smiling through teary, red-rimmed eyes and a red-and-white blotched face.

"Make that *hungry* idiot," he amended, "because right now, I'm starving! Got anything to eat in that dinky little refrigerator back there?"

"Not a thing, unless you count baking soda."

"I'll pass, thanks anyway! Feel like going out for a bite to eat, then—a big bite, mind?"

"Okay—but tonight's my treat, understand?" She sat up, turning away so that he couldn't see her swollen, bleary eyes and reddened nose. She'd never been one to cry beautifully and end up looking forlorn and tragic, like a movie heroine. When she cried, she only ended up looking awful, more like a squashed strawberry, Barb had once candidly described her! "Buying you dinner is the least I can do, after all your help today. I'd never have gotten everything moved in so fast without you. Thanks, Devin—for—for everything."

He turned her face up to his by the tip of his finger. "Hey, it was my pleasure, Kelly. I wanted to help, and I had a day off coming, so what the hell? You don't owe me a thing, sweetheart—and I mean that. Not a darned thing, okay?"

She knew by the seriousness of his expression that he was referring to more than her offer to buy him a meal, and nodded. "I understand, Doc. In fact, I had a rather modest restaurant planned for supper this evening." She smiled, and it was like the sun shining through after a rain shower, he thought, the brave little gesture tugging at his heartstrings.

"Ah, the ever-popular, ever indigestible Romeo's that Barb raves about, no doubt? All you can eat plus the salad bar for a buck-fifty, right?"

"Uh-uh. I was thinking more on the lines of—Chez McDonald's!" she confessed, wincing as she anticipated his reaction. She wasn't disappointed.

"Oh, lord, no! Anything but that, anything—! Not—not the—not the Golden Arches—please, Miz Kelly, anywhere but there!" he groaned, clutching his stomach.

"It's that or nothing, pal!" she played along in a tough voice.

"Aw, shucks! Get dressed and lead the way then, pretty lady," he said with a resigned expression. "Beggars can't be choosers, can they? And besides, I was lying through my teeth. I'm a Big Mac addict—a paid up member of B.M.A!"

He swatted her playfully across her bare bottom as she scrambled to her feet. "Better move on out, pretty lady, before I decide to put *you* back on the menu!"

Incongruous as it seemed later, it was over Big Macs and French fries and salads that their conversation turned to the subject of reincarnation again, but it was Devin who initiated the subject, not her, albeit indirectly.

"You know, Kelly, I don't mean to pry, and if you want to tell me to take a hike and mind my own business, well that's fine, just go right ahead," he urged, squeezing ketchup over his fries with as much enthusiasm as one of his own small patients. "But—who's this Wolf character, anyway?"

"Wolf?" she echoed, startled. The color had returned to her cheeks, but now she paled again, looking—he

271

thought—a little guilty as she put her hamburger down. "How—how did you know about Wolf?"

He grimaced and seemed uncomfortable, as if on second thoughts he regretted asking her, now that he'd done so. "You—er—mentioned his name a time or two this afternoon." He shrugged. "It's no big deal."

Realizing just *when* that afternoon he must be referring to, she blushed and looked embarrassed and said in a small voice, "Oh, God. I did, did I?"

He nodded uncomfortably. "Er, 'fraid so."

"Devin, I'm so sorry. Really, I am." God, what she must have done to the poor man's ego, calling him by Wolf's name at a moment like that!

"Hey, I told you, remember—no apologies needed. I was just—oh, curious, I guess. Your ex—his name was Tony, right?"

"That's right."

"Then who's this Wolf character? Someone you knew after Tony? Or before?"

She heaved a sigh and put her hamburger down again, still untouched, staring unseeing at a hoard of squealing children in the throes of a lively birthday party, complete with balloons and noise-makers, across from them. "Wolf is—well, let's just say he's kind of difficult to explain!"

"Aah."

"Don't say aah like that, as if you know exactly what I'm talking about!" she flared with mercurial suddeness, her eyes crackling with irritation. "You couldn't possibly understand, so stop sounding so goddamned wise!"

"Hey, hey, calm down, I didn't mean anything by it! I just figured he must be an old boyfriend or something, right? And since he's clearly someone you'd rather not talk about, that's an end to it. Forget I asked, subject closed, okay?"

"Oh, lord, I'm sor—Oh, damn it, Devin! There I go, apologizing again! Really, I didn't mean to jump all over you. It's just that—well, it was Wolf I wanted to ask

272

your—your opinion about this afternoon, remember? When I—when I asked if you believed in reincarnation?"

"Sure, I remember, vaguely. But I thought you were joking?"

"Well, I wasn't. I—I wanted to talk to you, to ask you something. You see, there's something weird going on—with me. And I can't—I just can't seem to be able to find a rational explanation for any of it! I'm afraid, Devin, really afraid! I think—" she shuddered and bit her lip, forcing herself to look at him, "I really and truly think I might be starting to lose my—my mind!"

Her expression was so earnest, so serious, that for once he forgot the teasing comeback that sprang to his lips and simply nodded gravely. Reaching across the table, he took her hand in both of his and squeezed it. "That does sound serious. So. Why don't you tell me about it, Kelly? All of it. Right from the start."

Slowly at first, and then with more confidence when he remained silent and his expression grew interested, but neither judgemental nor amused, she told him everything about that first day; about going to the Paloverde boutique with Barbara and meeting Sam Cloud for the first time.

"He's the most peculiar old man I've ever met—a Hopi medicine man, according to Barbara. Have you met him?" she asked hopefully.

"Heard of him, yes, quite a bit. But I haven't had the pleasure of meeting him myself yet."

"Well, anyway, everything happened so fast! When Barbara slipped in back of the store to find some papers she'd misplaced or something that morning, this Sam insisted that I let him tell me my future. Well, I'm a confirmed skeptic—I don't believe in that fortune-telling garbage at all—but I went along with it anyway—mostly to please Barb. You know how insistent she can be when she's into something? And besides, I didn't want to be rude to the old man. He seemed nice enough at first—

just a little eccentric."

"Hmm. I'd be unkind and call our Barbara downright pushy at times, bless her!" Devin said wryly. "But anyway, go on."

As calmly and briefly as possible, she told him what had happened, leaving out none of the details of the story as she remembered it.

"It was so strange," she added afterward. "I could remember everything I'd said, as if it'd really happened to me—as if I'd *been* that poor little girl, Mary Margaret Kelly! And when I got to the part about describing how the fort had been attacked by Apaches, and the massacre of those poor, helpless people, I could *feel* her terror, Devin—as strongly as if I'd really been there. My heart was thumping so loud, I thought I'd have a stroke or something! And the details—God, they were so sharp and clear, Devin! But I don't know how that could be! Or how, if it's my imagination, I could have made any of it up!"

"And that was it? All of it?"

"I wish it had been all," she said with quiet conviction, grimacing. "When I came around, or woke up, or whatever you want to call it, I was furious at Sam and snapped at him before I left the store. But Barb had overheard some of the things I'd told him, apparently, and she was burning with curiosity. Later that same day, she asked me if I remembered any of what I'd said. I was frightened—confused—and so I lied. I hated doing it, but I did anyway! I told Barb I didn't remember a thing, that nothing had happened, but I *could,* Devin. I could remember all of it, crystal clear! Something weird had happened to me! And then—" she bit her lip, "there was that night, the one when you came to dinner for the first time, remember?"

"I remember. It was the first night we met." He smiled.

"Right. Well, after you'd left, I went to bed and—I had a dream, or *something.* Only—only it wasn't like

274

dreaming. It was as if I was reliving the past again—*my* past, only it was a past I know I haven't lived! And there was none of that—that—? Oh, what would you call it—expanded sense of reality? That *craziness*, that fantasy quality, that real dreams have, where times and places are all off kilter, and everything's larger than life? No! This—this was all quite logical and straightforward and—and oh, Devin, I didn't want to wake up!

"You see, by then, I was beginning to believe I'd fallen in love with the Comanche warrior, White Wolf, who'd rescued me from the Apaches, and he—I know it sounds crazy—but I know he loved me, too! My parents had arranged for me to marry another warrior, a war chief called Broken Claw, but I couldn't go through with it, not loving Wolf as I did. So White Wolf and I ran off together to escape Broken Claw and my father's anger. It was the only way we could be together, because you see, back then, the Comanches accepted marriage between a man and a woman who'd eloped once the marriage had been—had been fully consummated before they were overtaken and brought back."

She blushed as she told him the rest of the story, about her kidnapping at the hands of the white men, and Wolf's rescue of her, their return to Black Hawk's band and the knife duel, ending, "So you see, Wolf and I had a child and everything when the—er—the dream or whatever it was ended, and I woke up!"

Her face flamed. She couldn't bring herself to look into his eyes, certain she'd see amusement there, or disbelief and incredulity—or still worse, pity.

He hesitated for a moment or two after she'd finished, choosing his words carefully before commenting. To his eyes, she was obviously squirming with embarrassment at what she'd told him, and her defensive tone further warned him that he'd have to tread very carefully or run the risk of either making her angry, or alienating her. Either way, emotionally she was skating on thin ice, in his opinion, and he'd lose her confidence and trust. He didn't want either to happen.

"Kelly," he began slowly, feeling his way like a blind man on an unfamiliar staircase, "I don't think what you've experienced is anything serious to worry about. You haven't said much about your marriage or Tony, but what you haven't said has told me quite a bit. You were terribly unhappy with him, right?"

"Yes, but—"

"Wait, babe, let me finish, okay?" She nodded. "You were terribly unhappy, and when it ended, there was a lot of guilt and self-blame and grief on your part. That's only normal, honey. A divorce—any divorce, however amicable and civilized—is the death of something important to us. Grieving's a normal, healthy part of dealing with that loss. And whether it's the death of a loved one or the ending of a relationship, the stages we go through are all pretty much the same! Denial. Rage. Sorrow. Loss. Depression. And then finally, acceptance, and a readiness to move on, to get on with our lives. On one level, I'd say you want desperately to be happy again. But you're afraid what happened with Tony has made you unable to have a successful relationship with a man, a real relationship, built on trust, and so your subconscious has gone ahead and inven—"

"*No!*" she cut him off, her tone adamant, her expression furious. "Devin, I'm sorry, really. I am, but I've already thought it through from that angle, and I just don't buy that pat little explanation! Even granted it were true, I couldn't possibly have come up with all the details and descriptions I've told you to make up such a pretty little fantasy! Believe me, I simply don't possess the raw knowledge it would take, let alone the imagination! I could see it if I'd majored in history or anthropology or something in college, but I didn't. My major was strictly business college stuff. And what I've read about Indians—American or otherwise—could fit on a postage stamp and still leave room for more! I don't know *how* I could possibly know what I know, unless—" She hesitated, reluctant to finish the thought.

"Unless what?"

"Unless Sam Cloud flipped some kind of a switch in my memory," she said lamely, the words spilling out of her in a rush. "Unless he was right, and I *am* reliving a past life—one that I lived over a hundred years ago. But if that's true, then the other things he said must be true as well, and I don't want to . . . I'm afraid to even think about those!" She shivered, and hugged herself about the arms.

"What other things?"

"He told me that I have no destiny, Devin, or at least, none that would bring me happiness in this life! He said the strangest thing; that my destiny still lay in the past, and that I'd have to go back there, to complete it, if I ever wanted to be happy again. That I *must* go back, for the future to work out as it was intended."

"That crazy old fool!" Devin exploded, furious that this unknown and probably senile old relic from the reservation had filled her impressionable head with such nonsense at a time when she was still so fragile emotionally.

The teenagers in the booth across from them stopped necking and turned to stare at them curiously.

In a lower voice Kelly asked, "But is he crazy, Devin? Is he really? Oh, lord, I wish I could believe that! But you see, I'm beginning to wonder if he—if he isn't right!"

"Oh, come on, Kelly!" he argued, exasperated. "Unfulfilled destinies? A past life as an Indian's woman? Be reasonable!"

"I'm really trying to be just that, Devin. But it isn't easy! You see, there's—this—too!"

She pulled aside the collar of her shirt and he saw a small half-moon of white scars on the side of her throat where it met her collarbone.

"Teeth marks? Ah! I get the connection. A legacy of

277

your unwholesome friend, Whiskered One, right?"

"Go ahead and laugh, if that's how you feel, Devin, but I swear, I didn't have this scar before! It was just—there—the morning after my dream!"

"Okay, I believe you. But maybe there's a logical explanation for it, hmm? Maybe you just didn't notice it before? Maybe it happened when you and Tony—"

"*No!*" She shook her head emphatically a second time. "It's up to you whether you want to believe me or not, but I *know* it wasn't there before!"

The sudden, urgent pipping of the pager he wore clipped to his belt effectively sidetracked any reply—disastrous or otherwise—that he could have made. For once, he was glad of the interruption. Saved by the bell!

"Uh-oh. Emergency, honey. Gotta go!" he told her when he came back from the pay phone. "I'll drop you off first. It's on my way."

They drove back to the Scottsdale Gardens in minutes, and he insisted on seeing her safely inside her apartment.

"I'll call you later, honey," he promised, brushing a kiss to her forehead, and then he'd gone.

Chapter Twenty-one

"Four days off? But didn't you say you were on call this weekend?"

As he'd promised, Devin called her later that evening from the hospital lounge.

"Right, I was, but I switched shifts with another pediatrician who owes me a favor. Pete's handling my well-baby clinic on Saturday morning, and my hospital rounds on Saturday and Sunday. Monday and Tuesday I'm off anyway, so no problem there. So? How about it?"

"I'd love to go with you, but . . . I start work at the boutique on Monday, remember? I'm sorry, Devin, but I really can't let Barbara down, not after everything she's done for me." Kelly absently wound the spiral phone cord around and around her finger, and gazed out at an unobstructed view of the mountains, looming dark against the lighter horizon. *The land of the Peaceful Ones,* an inner voice reminded her. *Those who dwell where the south and west winds raise their lodges . . .*

"You won't be," came Devin's voice, bringing her sharply back to the present. He sounded even more Texan and ruggedly male over the phone, which had been connected the day before. "I knew you'd be worried about that, so I've already cleared it with Barbara and Bill. I called them before I called you, and Barb says not to worry about a thing. She can handle the boutique on her own. And besides, Momma Margot's due back Friday night from Illinois, so if she needs someone to watch little Billy, her mom'll be there. So you see, it's all taken care of. No excuses! We're going, okay? Seriously, honey, the best thing you can do is find this Sam Cloud and confront him. Talk to him face to face. I've a hunch he's the key to all this, somehow. Maybe the old coot slipped you a peyote button in your coffee, or something?" he suggested, and she knew by his tone he was only half-joking.

"All right. I guess it can't hurt to talk to him. But why do we have to go all the way out to the reservation? Why can't we—I—just have it out with him at the store Monday morning? Wouldn't that be the easiest way?"

There was a pause. "Kelly, Barbara told me Sam up and quit the day after you met him."

"Quit?" she exclaimed, genuinely startled. Barb had said nothing about that! "But why on earth would he do that?"

"Damned if I know! Maybe he was more upset when you freaked out than he let on? Or just maybe your reaction to his mumjo jumbo scared the pants off him, and he decided to cool it with the Indian mystic number, in case you called the law on him? Anyway, whatever triggered it, Barb said when she asked him where to send his final paycheck, he told her he was going home to the reservation lands at Walpi and gave her a post office box number to mail the check to. That's where we'll find your Sam, honey! The Hopi are a reserved people—they prefer keeping themselves to themselves, from what I know of them, and haven't gone into tourism in a big way like their neighbors, the Navajo Nation. But their Snake Dances will be held the day after tomorrow, and the Hopi allow a few tourists onto their mesas to view the ceremonies, so our timing couldn't be better. Come on, Kelly. What have you got to lose? Bill swears the dances are really something to see—they dance with live rattlers in their mouths, according to him! We can kill two birds with one stone. Play tourist for a day or two, then go and see this Sam character, talk to him. It might be all you need to lay these—"

"Fantasies?" she supplied in a strained voice that was quite unlike her. "To lay my fantasies to rest? That is what you were going to say, isn't it?"

"No, honey," Devin said patiently, his voice oozing calming-bedside-manner over the phone, in a way that she suddenly found infuriating, rather than appealing. "I was going to say nightmares, but I guess fantasies is as good a name for them as any, failing a more accurate one, right?"

"I suppose so. I guess I'm just tired and on edge."

"Well, then? What's it to be? Are you coming with me, or chickening out?" There was a challenge in his voice.

"All right, I'll come," she capitulated with a heavy sigh after a lengthy pause, though her tone was still reluctant. "What time do you plan on leaving?"

"I'll pick you up early in the morning—around seven, okay? We'll have breakfast, then hit the road by eight-thirty or so. Oh, and before I forget, plan on bringing some cool, comfortable clothes to wear. See, I thought while we were up north anyway, I'd show you the Grand Canyon, too? It's not that far by car. And since I used to play medic at the emergency clinic at South Rim tourist station when I was on vacation from med school, I can guarantee you the full on, guided tour! Interested?"

"Fascinated," she said with some genuine warmth in her tone, to his relief. "Who wouldn't be? I've never seen the canyon, but I've always wanted to. It—it sounds like it's going to be quite a weekend, Devin. Thanks for changing your plans for me," she added, willing more enthusiasm into her voice than she felt. Somehow, Devin's plans filled her with unease—not unlike a dreaded visit to the dentist's—rather than with anticipation over a fun-filled, exciting weekend in the company of a man she found very attractive!

"Hey, it'll be great, I promise. See you at seven. In the meantime, good night, babe. Sleep tight. Oh, and by the way, pretty lady—?"

"Yes?"

"I meant what I said earlier. I love you, Kelly."

She paused, feeling compelled to say something similar in return, but then heard the click as Devin hung up, and the humming of the empty line in place of his husky voice.

Perhaps it was better that way, she decided as she turned off the lights and headed for bed.

A red-and-silver semi, bearing the legend Tomkins Produce — Best in the West!, pulled into the truck stop that appeared like a lighted pink oasis just off the empty road outside of Flagstaff the following morning.

With a hiss and a protesting squeal of its air brakes, the trucker, Joe Lorenzo, brought the eighteen-wheeler to a noisy halt, nose and tail perfectly aligned alongside several of its fellows.

A lively trumpet rendition of *La Bamba* blared out into the chilly morning air as the trucker swung open his cab door and clambered to the ground. The catchy Latin number mingled with the melancholy sounds of a tinny country and western ballad played at top volume on the jukebox in the truckers' cafe. The smell of frying eggs and bacon, toast, and grease wafted on the morning air, which was cool at this elevation, around forty-five degrees.

As the trucker came around the front of his rig, the passenger door opened and a second man jumped down from the cab. Tall and lean, he was black-haired and bearded, dressed in a ripped and stained blue T-shirt and threadbare blue jeans that fell just an inch or two short of both his ankles and the filthy white sneakers that covered his bare feet. In his arms, he carried a battered grocery sack. It was still hugged against his chest, as he'd held it since he climbed into the semi's cab the evening before.

The trucker still hadn't discovered what the hitchhiker

had inside that rumpled sack that was so darned important to him. From the wild-eyed and shabby look about him and the way he hugged that baby to his chest, Joe'd had him figured for a wino—or at the very least, a bag man, street person, or whatever the polite word was for his kind this month. Being of a soft-hearted nature, the trucker'd taken pity on him.

Poor friggin' son of a bitch, he'd thought when he'd spotted him thumbing a ride just outside of Orange County, and despite his disreputable appearance, Joe'd pulled over and picked the guy up. The miles got lonely sometimes, especially at nights, when the long, dark road seemed to stretch forever ahead, roiling away from him like a black sidewinder just out of reach of the white arcs of the highlights. So friggin' lonely that Joe—who was a talkative type by nature—sometimes found himself talking to his friggin' load, and even imagining, on occasion, that the crates of vegetables and produce talked back! Figuring a silent companion was an improvement over a friggin' talking tomato, Joe had offered him a ride.

"Climb on up, *hombre!*" he'd urged, and when the man had done so and settled himself comfortably, Joe'd started his eighteen-wheeler rolling again and asked, "So, where you headed, man?"

He hadn't expected a definite answer. Hitchhikers with the down at the heels look about them this guy had more often than not didn't give a damn where they were going, so long as it was someplace else! But Joe had been surprised when the Anglo had answered in an educated tone, "Phoenix, my friend. I'm headed for Phoenix, or as close to it as you're going?"

"Phoenix? No sweat! Me and my baby, Dolores, here'll take you right there, *amigo,*" Joe'd said with a grin, patting the dash of his cab affectionately.

He'd settled back into the long drive ahead, anticipating that, for the next few hundred miles at least, he'd have someone to talk to.

On that score, however, Joe'd been wrong. His passenger had said little after his initial comment, and his silence had been worse, in some ways, than driving alone. It had made Joe feel uncomfortable, though why it should have, he couldn't put his finger on. He'd secretly felt relieved when the truck stop had hoved into view soon after daybreak, and his taciturn passenger had decided he wanted off Joe's rig.

"The valley of the Sun, eh, *amigo*," Joe declared with a grin, coming around to meet the man. "You got friends waiting for you there? A woman, perhaps?" He winked.

"Better than that," the man had said, smiling slightly as he said it. "A wife."

"Aah! No wonder you're in a hurry to get back there, *amigo!* Say, you hungry? This place has the best egg burritos this side of my mama's kitchen, and a salsa that'll fry the roof right off o' your mouth! Breakfast's on me if you're hungry, man, then I'll take you the rest of the way. How about it?" he offered, feeling guilty now for thinking the Anglo's silence was somehow weird. Maybe he'd just been too tired to talk?

Again, the man gave that slow, secretive smile. "Thanks, but no thanks, friend. See, I'm real anxious to get on home—you understand how it is, when a man's been gone for a while?" He winked, and Joe grinned and nodded as the man clapped him companionably across the back as he stepped past him, murmuring, *"Adios!"*

"Adios!" Joe rejoined with a wave, and watched the man shuffle across the sandy parking lot to the shoulder of the road. He walked, Joe noticed with a frown now, as he'd sometimes noticed men who'd done hard time inside walked when they were first paroled; eyes to the ground, shoulders bowed, feet barely moving, as if they still wore shackles.

Joe fully expected him to stick out his thumb and try

to catch a ride the remainder of the way to Phoenix, for even at this early hour there was plenty of traffic headed down Interstate 17 for the city. But to Joe's surprise, he kept on walking without looking back, and in minutes he was only a tall, gray blue blur against the rust and sand or pine forest colors of his surroundings.

With a shrug, Joe turned and went into the truck stop, the hitchhiker forgotten as his belly rumbled in anticipation of Rosa's egg burritos and red hot salsa, warm tortillas, and chorizo.

The strident ringing of the phone waked Barbara that same morning. She muttered a curse, groaned and rolled over, opening one bleary eye to glance at the clock radio as she did so. It read SAT: AUG 23 : 6:45 A.M. in glaring red digital numbers. A quarter of seven! Who on earth'd be calling at that hour? But then, as a doctor's wife she'd almost—if not quite—grown accustomed to patients calling any old time they felt like it, even if there was no emergency, and switched into what she laughingly termed her professional mode!

"Dr. Douglas's residence. May I help you?" she managed to say in an efficient, pleasant tone.

"Would that be Dr. Bill Douglas? The William Douglas from Colorado?" a pleasantly masculine voice asked.

"Yes, that's right. Are you a patient of his? If so, you're welc—"

There was a loud click as the caller abruptly hung up on her.

"Well! Thanks a lot to you, too, buddy!" Barbara fumed, slamming the receiver down and swinging her legs off the bed. "There's a name for people like you, pal, and it ain't pretty!"

She stood, yawned hugely, and stretched, smoothing down her sleep rumpled brown hair as she staggered toward the bathroom. A hot shower would wake her up, she decided, and then thought ruefully, *And if that doesn't work, William Jr. will!*

At three months, her little rug-rat had the appetite of a linebacker! *My son, William "The Fridge" Douglas,* she thought, smiling to herself as she peeled off her night-shirt and stepped under the hot jets of the shower. As she did so, she remembered Devin's call late the night before, and the love and concern in his voice as he talked about Kelly and his conviction that she was suffer-ing from a delayed reaction to her stressful divorce.

"She's got it into her pretty little head that these wild dreams she's been having are something more, Barb, and that they're somehow tied up with that old Hopi *shaman* you've got working at the boutique. The best thing for her would be to confront him, see how harmless he re-ally is, and find out she's got nothing to worry about."

"I see your point, Devin. And personally I think you're probably right, but Sam doesn't work for me any-more. He quit—the day after I took Kelly to the Palo-verde."

She'd told him then about Sam asking her to mail his final paycheck, and Devin had suggested he take a long weekend off and drive Kelly to the reservation to talk with him, in the hope that he'd be able to set her fears to rest. The rest was history. Right about now, he and Kelly should be headed north for the weekend, she thought, smiling a satisfied little smile as she reached for the washcloth. Four idyllic days alone together—the awe-inspiring beauty of the Grand Canyon—just the two of them! She couldn't have engineered it any better if she was Cupid himself, she thought smugly!

Unheard by Barbara, who was soaping and singing blithely under the stinging spray, the clock radio alarm came on punctually at seven. She'd set it on "wake to music," but the news was on right now, as it was on the hour, every hour.

286

" . . . Los Angeles' authorities have today broadened their search for the missing patient San Francisco Veterans' Hospital attendants once called Indian Joe," the newscaster announced, "after reported sightings of a man matching his general description in the Anaheim area. Anthony Michaels, a former major and pilot with the Air Force, walked away from the San Francisco hospital where he'd been receiving psychiatric treatment in early July of this year.

A spokesman said that, while Michaels is not considered a risk to the community at large, he could prove dangerous to himself. Anthony Michaels is described as six-feet-two-inches tall, of slim build, with straight black hair, and brown eyes. The top two joints on the ring finger of his left hand are missing. If you've seen this man or have any information regarding his whereabouts, please conta—"

Barbara came out of the bathroom, humming. She had a fluffy pink towel wound around her, fastened under her armpits, and her short hair was damp and curly. She reached over and changed the radio station, singing along with Willie Nelson as country and western music replaced the newscaster's voice.

The bedroom door opened and Bill barrelled in. He was wearing a sweat-sodden Nike tank top, shorts, and running shoes. His hair, face, arms, and legs dripped sweat.

Barbara wrinkled her nose as she came toward him, unable to comprehend how people could actually *enjoy* getting themselves into such a state, let alone do so willingly.

" 'Morning, hon," she greeted him.

"Mornin', babe. Oh, damnit, I'll be late for rounds again!" Bill grumbled, hopping on one foot to tear off a shoe, then flinging it down and switching legs to tear off the other. "That Great Dane on the corner—that black brute that does its thing on our lawn and rips up our trash?—it chased me two blocks past our house before I outran it! Believe me, babe, one day, *one fine day*, I'm

287

going to shoot that damned dog—and its owner!"

His handsome, broad-featured face was red with indignation and exertion.

Hiding a smile, Barbara went up on tiptoe and kissed him good morning on the tip of his nose—the only part of him that didn't look conspicuously sweaty.

"Yes, hon," she sympathized. "I know you will. Now, hurry up and shower, while I fix breakfast."

Chapter Twenty-two

It was mid-afternoon before Devin and Kelly reached Hopiland, and the light was already beginning to fade over the rose-and-pink, rocky reservation lands, tinting them purple and transforming strange stone formations into even stranger new shapes.

Old Oraibi at the edge of Third Mesa, was—Devin said—the eldest continually inhabited town in the country. He wanted to make Oraibi their first stop of the weekend, if visitors were being allowed to visit the ruins that day.

Some of the older, terraced portions of the pueblo that had once boasted two- or even three-story dwellings were beginning to deteriorate, Devin said, and tourists were sometimes turned away.

Today was one of those days, and so they continued on to Second Mesa, stopping en route at a Hopi silver-smith's workshop to admire the fine pieces of turquoise and silver jewelry for sale there, fashioned by local Indian artisans, and several pieces that showcased the newly revived lost art of silver overlay.

One piece in particular caught Kelly's eye, and she asked to see it, while Devin browsed, admiring ferocious-looking *kachina* dolls made with exquisite attention to detail, beautiful brown-pattered Hopi pottery, and leather goods.

The piece that had attracted her was a flat, crescent bracelet of silver. Instead of being set with turquoise stones, as were many of the other fine pieces, this one boasted two deep blue glass beads, mounted one above the other. Vertical zigzag lines flanked the stones, and the remaining surface was patterned with delicately drawn designs of flowers, alternated with stylized suns or flying

289

bird shapes.

"How much is this?" Kelly asked, slipping it onto her wrist and holding out her arm to admire the way it looked.

The Hopi artist-salesman named a price that made her eyes widen. She hastily removed the bracelet and returned it to him with a wry grimace. "Whoops! It's just a little out of my price range. I'll pass, thank you!"

"It's expensive mainly because it's quite old," the man explained, "We estimate mid-eighteen hundreds. The design is real unusual, too."

"Because of the use of glass beads, rather than turquoise?"

"Partly," he agreed, nodding. "And by the way, the stones are genuine sapphires, not trade glass, which adds substantially to the price. Not very good sapphires, admittedly, and they're poorly cut, but still, that only makes the piece especially unique, don't you think? Of course, we can only speculate on how sapphires—however poor their quality—came into the hands of the Hopi silversmith of the period who used them!"

He grinned, his broad, brown-skinned face amiable and attractive under a shock of straight blue black hair. "Seriously though, it's far more likely the smith got them from trading with other tribes, than from any other way—such as booty from a raid on the palefaces, for example! The Hopituh have always been relatively peaceful folk. We mind our own business and keep pretty much to ourselves. The old way and our ancient traditions and values are still important here, you see? We strive for harmony in our lives, and material things— well, they're not what's important, not really.

"You know, a few years back, my people used to pawn their best jewelry at the trading posts in hard times. Old family heirlooms handed down from grandmother to mother to daughter often went unredeemed and eventually became the property of the trader. Some of the finest pieces that the collectors could get their hands on came to be called pawn pieces. Nowadays, though, my People are a lot smarter—we pawn our radios and keep the family heirlooms like this one!"

She smiled. "The jagged lines—here, and here—they represent lightning, don't they?"

The Hopi artist nodded, pleased by her interest and apparent knowledge of his people's culture. "That's it exactly! Lightning—and snakes. My people believe the snakes speak for them to the gods who live in the Underworld, and ask them to bring plentiful rains for the crops, once they're released after the Snake Dances."

"And this one, here? Is it Tawa, the Sun God?" she pointed.

"Hey, you're right again! My people offer Tawa prayers of thanks for each new day, along with a pinch of sacred cornmeal. The Moon, on the other hand—you see his symbol, right here?—is imagined as a wrinkled old man. But we also have a pretty legend that tells a different story. It is said the moon was made by another of our goddesses—a very important one named Spider Woman. She wove a white cotton robe on her loom, and hung it in the sky to give the People light in the dark of night."

"Ahha! I have a hunch someone did some late-night reading for the weekend, hmm, hon?" Devin asked, coming to stand alongside her and grinning. With his thumbs tucked into his jeans belt and his tooled leather boots, he looked more rodeo cowboy than up-and-coming, successful pediatrician!

"Not guilty," she denied. She smiled at the salesman and shrugged, adding by way of explanation, "Just a lucky guess!"

"Good ones, too! My name's Mike Dallas, by the way," he introduced himself, extending his hand.

"I'm Kelly Michaels, and this is Devin Colter."

They shook hands.

"Nice to meet you. You folks planning on going to

291

Walpi for the Snake Dances?"

"That's the plan," Devin admitted. "We drove up from Phoenix early this morning, and . . ."

Kelly drifted away to look at some woven baskets while the two men exchanged pleasantries. Although the baskets and coiled basketry plaques with their bright geometric designs were attractive and unusual, her thoughts were still on the silver bracelet, which had seemed uncannily familiar. Slipping it on her wrist, feeling the silver take on the warmth of her body, running her hands over the intricate design, it'd felt as if she'd touched the bauble in just such a loving way hundreds of times before. *Déjà vu?* she wondered, then scolded herself and drove such a notion from her mind. *Good God, girl, let it rest, before they cart you off to the funny farm in a straitjacket!* she scolded herself sternly.

They drove on in Devin's white Chevy pickup, stopping off at the Hopi Cultural Center before enjoying a tasty yet simple meal of mutton stew and *piki* bread at the coffee shop nearby. It was already dark when they left, and Devin suggested that they check into the nearby, surprisingly modern motel for the night. Kelly agreed, although with some reservations.

After what had happened the afternoon before, she was apprehensive, wondering if Devin expected them to share a room for the night, and if so, if she could bring herself to refuse him a second time.

But to her relief, Devin came back with two room keys, and tossed one to her before grabbing her bag from the back of the truck. "Better get a good night's sleep tonight, pretty lady," he suggested with a rueful grin. "We've a full day ahead of us tomorrow."

So saying, he tugged her into his arms, pressed her back against the pickup's cab and kissed her full on the lips, stroking her dark hair away from her face in that cherishing way he had. When he released her, he couldn't resist adding hopefully, "Unless, that is, you've got other ideas . . . ?"

"Mind if I take a rain check on that unless, Mr. Colter?" she asked softly, smiling up at him self-consciously.
"Right now . . . well, feeling confused the way I do, it
wouldn't be fair, not to either of us."

"I guess you're right," he agreed, without any hypocriti-
cal pretence at sincerity. He wanted her, damn it, and
while he was willing to wait until she felt the same about
him, he had no intention of pretending otherwise!
"Here," he added, fishing into his jeans' pocket. "Just a
little something to remind you of me in the long, lonely
dark hours," he teased, pressing something bulky wrapped
in tissue paper into her hand.

She knew what it was by feel alone the minute her
fingers closed over it, and immediately protested. "Oh,
Devin, you didn't? Really, you shouldn't have done this —
it was way too expensive!"

"Not the way I figure it. See, it's all part of my evil
plan to seduce you, ma'am. Just call it an out-and-out
bribe," he teased in a wicked, lecherous tone. "And kick
yourself for turning me down tonight . . ."

Taking her elbow, he gently propelled her to the door
of her room, unlocked it, and set her bag on the floor
just inside, murmuring, "Good night, babe. Sweet
dreams," before he drew it shut behind him.

He didn't dare linger to kiss her again. Her warmth,
her loveliness, his desire, and his need to protect and
take care of her in her vulnerable state, were just too
damned strong to take that chance! If he touched her
again, smelled the fragrance of her hair, felt the warmth
of her slender female body pressing against him, well,
hell, he'd regret it in the morning — maybe!

She heard his footsteps moving away from the door,
and stood in the silent darkness for a moment or two,
before turning on the light.

The bracelet gleamed within its nest of tissue with the
gentle lustre of old silver, the two blue stones throwing

back a dark blue, lambent fire. The jagged lightning lines that flanked them seemed even more deeply etched into the soft metal than they had earlier. "Blue Beads?" she whispered on the silence. "Is that who you belonged to? Oh, God, *is* this all just a fantasy—or am I really going crazy?"

A shiver ran through her as she looked for the first time inside the crescent-shaped bangle, for she saw there a repeating pattern of paw prints encircling the inside surface, as beautifully, lovingly worked by the native artisan as the exterior design.

Crazy or not, she knew without needing to ask any wildlife expert that the paw prints were those of a wolf. Nor was it any real surprise to her that she dreamed of him again that night . . .

Chapter Twenty-three

Three winters passed. Three changings of the seasons that the white men called years and which they numbered 1863, '64, '65 with strange squiggles in their talking-leaves came and went for Blue Beads, White Wolf, and little Red Wing. And they were, for the greater part, happy years.

Food was always in short supply during the Hungry Moons-of-Deep-Snow, of course, now that the whites had begun to cross the plains in great numbers and had killed or frightened away many of the vast herds of buffalo that had once roamed there. Yet they shared what they had with others, and had endured. Some of their band had not fared as well, however.

Wounded Doe's mother-in-law, Little Dove, had taken lung fever in the snow moons of the first winter. She'd been found frozen to death one morning, chest-deep in the ice-bound creek where she'd gone in desperation to cool the fever-spirits raging through her body. Crooked Woman's husband, Big Bear, had also fallen sick, and for several moons had lingered with a gnawing pain in his belly. They'd watched as he'd grown thinner and thinner, unable to keep down the food prepared for him. At length, his skin had taken on a marked yellowish tinge, and finally a bloody flux had emptied from his bowels and he had also died.

Following the ritual slaying of Big Bear's ponies so that he might ride them in the After World, and the raising of his body in the forks of a towering cottonwood so that his spirit might easily return to the Great One Above in the way of their people, Wolf had instructed Blue Beads to ask Big Bear's desolate widow to share their lodge. He'd added that it would be a good thing to have one of the respected old ones always nearby, to share the wisdom of her years with them while enjoying the warmth of their fire and the meat he could provide for her.

Both pleased and touched by his compassion and kindness, Blue Beads had happily done so. And, after a few moons of being treated with respect and consideration and affection by the young couple, Crooked Woman's former downtrodden demeanor and timid silence—a result of her husband's cruelty in his lifetime—had vanished. Simply put, she'd blossomed! Now she helped Blue Beads with the unending chores of fleshing hides, cooking, cutting and sewing garments, raising or lowering the lodge, gathering berries and herbs, and so on. She was always eager and ready to lend a hand with anything that needed doing, even singing happily as she worked, and dropping fond, if gummy, smiles upon them all, for she considered them the family that life had denied her.

Having lost two babes herself in her younger years, she doted on little Red Wing especially, and was as much a grandmother to him as Spotted Pony. Truly, it was good to have an old one in their lodge! At last, their little family felt complete, and although Blue Beads sometimes yearned to conceive a second child, she was content.

Their band had peacefully roamed from encampment to encampment those three winters, sharing the summer Sun Dance circles and the spring horse fairs on the plains each year with other bands of the People, for, unperturbed by Broken Claw's accusations of cowardice, Wolf's adoptive father, Chief Black Hawk, had continued his policy of avoiding war with the white-eyes wherever possible. He had seen their numbers, marvelled at the wonders they had invented, and—being an intelligent man—he knew in his heart of hearts that the whites were an unstoppable force. Better to make friends with those whose medicine was so very great, he reasoned, than bitter enemies. And so, he made it known to one and all that he would pass the sacred pipe and parlay for peace with all men who proved themselves willing to become friends, be they white or red.

Accordingly, he gave orders to strike camp and moved his people safely out of harm's way whenever it was heard that other bands had raided ranches or Black Robe missions or forts and taken white captives, for at such times bloody reprisals for these attacks might be expected from the long-knives, who did not seem to care which band of Indians had been responsible, but took their revenge on any and all unfortunate red men who happened their way.

"Peace," he had been heard to say on several occasions, "is a great blessing. But alas, that blessing is never fully appreciated except by the Old Ones, whose days remaining on Mother Earth are few, while the young—with many suns yet to live—rush to squander their precious lives in battle!"

Still, the hot-headed young braves of the tribe grumbled at his decision. Their blood ran hot and swift with the fiery elixir of youth. They craved the danger and excitement of battle, the thrill of pitting their warriors' skills and their peerless horsemanship against the hated enemy! They argued hotly to paint for war, but in this matter, Black Hawk remained adamant. He urged his battle-hungry young warriors to join their allies, the ferocious Kiowa, if it was raiding they craved. There were many Kiowa bands who roamed the Plains, ready and eager to take the path of war against the whites, and to measure their bravery and glory by the number of scalps they'd taken, the coups they'd counted. This some of Black Hawk's band had finally done.

In those peaceful years, White Wolf and Blue Beads's love deepened, rather than lessened: their desire for each other grew stronger with every passing moon. They came to know each other's thoughts and feelings almost as well as they'd come to know each other's bodies. There were many times when only a look needed to be exchanged between them for one to know intuitively what the other was thinking. Spotted Pony saw the unspoken messages that passed between them, their glowing eyes and affectionate little touchings, and felt enormous satisfaction that all had turned out so well for them. Truly, theirs was a joining smiled upon by the Great One!

As for their son, Red Wing, he was no longer a red-faced, squalling infant, but a sturdy little toddler now, with thick, glossy, dark brown hair that swept untamed to his little shoulders like his father's, and wide, intelligent eyes the color of a blue lake in the shadow of the pines. Although, like the other children of their band, he ran about naked in the warmer moons, his complexion was still fairer than Wolf's, but darker than Blue Bead's, and his features plainly showed the influence of his mixed bloods. The combination was a pleasing one. His doting foster grandparents agreed that there was no child among the Black Hawk band either as handsome or as clever as little Red Wing. His mother and father could find no fault with their elders' opinions, for they were also their own!

Indulged as were all the children of the People, and left undisciplined by either harsh words or whippings, Red Wing and his playmates learned what was and what was not wise largely by experiencing the consequences of their actions for themselves. A toe poked carelessly into the pretty, glowing embers of the fire resulted in a painful burn, for example, and this and other similar lessons were ones that rarely needed a second learning. Bitter experience proved a harsh but thorough teacher of itself for little Red Wing!

One morning, in the Moon of New Leaves of 1866, Wolf wakened just as the long, pale fingers of dawn were lightening the ashy sky framed by the smoke-hole.

Leaning on one elbow, he tenderly watched his woman as she slept beside him. She was unclothed, and one of her shapely legs was thrown comfortably across his flanks, her body turned and snuggled heavily into his.

Her breasts—fuller since the birth and weaning of their son—were crushed against his chest. The curve of her bottom rounded out the buffalo robe that had slipped half off her body. Both caused a hot rush of desire to harden his manroot!

He glanced over his shoulder, and saw that Crooked Woman was still sleeping, snoring noisily. Red Wing was curled beneath a pile of soft pelts with his yellow pup cuddled beside him, whimpering in its sleep as it chased dream rabbits. Wolf smiled fondly as he noticed that his son's little hand was still gripping the new hide drum his Grandfather Many Horses had fashioned for him the sun before.

But the smile slowly dwindled from his lips. It became a rueful sigh as his gaze returned to his sleeping woman. Hiyeeah, how he longed to be alone with her, just for a little while; completely alone, and able to give full rein to his driving passion in both actions and words that no other eyes could see or other ears could hear!

After the long winter, spent for the greater part in the close confines of his lodge with others always nearby, they had enjoyed only brief, furtive matings, altogether too hurried and restricted for his liking. Now, with the spring, he could feel the sap rising through him like a strong young tree! He pulsed with desire, throbbed with need, craved the release of a long and lusty mating—and therein lay the problem this morning; the reason for his rueful sigh!

For as much as he genuinely welcomed Crooked Woman's presence in his lodge, and as much as he was still more than willing to provide for her needs as a son might do, and had even grown fond of her over the past moons, he was still a man who preferred privacy when he mated with his woman, unlike some. An old one and a small and very curious child nearby could hardly be forgotten, even in the lusty heat of joining when bloods ran hot and swift. No, not even when they seemed to be asleep!

"My husband has a great man-hunger this sun rising, yes?" came a seductive, sleep-husky voice that quavered with laughter.

He looked down into his woman's smiling eyes and grinned without embarrassment. "A great man-hunger indeed! The greatest man-hunger ever endured—and all for a certain someone whose name I've forgotten!"

She giggled, and pulled the buffalo robe up over them. Under the covering, she sought out the cause of his discomfort, running her hand down over his rock-hard stomach to sensually palm his rigid manhood. "What a pity you've forgotten my name, Absentminded One, for I have the very thing to feed this great man-hunger of yours!" she teased, rubbing her body seductively against his as she caressed his hardness. "Come, beloved, let me show you . . ."

"Pale face witch! I'm sure you could show me very well," Wolf whispered softly, nuzzling her cloud of dark hair and the soft flesh at the angle where her jaw flowed into the line of her throat. He inhaled deeply, drinking her fragrance within the close confines of the buffalo robe and thinking, *By the Spirit, her woman scent is like a love potion!* Her perfume was stirring in his nostrils; a delicate, inflaming musk that caused his groin to tighten. He added vehemently, "But—I have no great eagerness to have you show Crooked Woman, and our son, too!"

"But it's still too early and far too cold to send them from our lodge on some pretext or other," she pointed out in a low voice, muffled by the heavy robe. "I'm afraid my poor, hungry Wolf must go hungry awhile longer, and howl at the Morning Star for what he cannot have . . ."

She pouted and looked under her thick lashes at him, in the way she knew only served to quicken the pounding in his heart and loins.

"Enough of your torture!" he growled. "I have an idea! Do you remember last summer circle?" he queried craftily.

"That time in the tall grasses after the Sun Dance?" She smiled, a slow, pleasurable blush and warmth filling her. "Aiee, how could I forget?"

They'd lain in the tall scented grasses, starred with brilliant prairie wildflowers, and mated several times in succession under the blazing summer Sun. With such fierce urgency and raging passion firing their blood, it had seemed that a sweet, wild madness possessed them! His manroot had never tired, her ardor had never slackened, until—exhausted and sated—they had finally plunged into the creek to refresh themselves, and dried off lazing once again in the tall golden grass under the warmth of the sun.

What had added an extra fillip of excitement to their coupling had been its clandestine nature, its sense of danger and excitement and imminent discovery, for Wolf had left their encampment, pretending to go hunting, only to return shortly after and surprise her as she gathered herbs and healing grasses to replenish her supplies. The spot they'd chosen was so perilously close to camp, they'd risked being surprised at any moment . . . and it had been wonderful!

She smiled again as she remembered. Her nipples tightened, prodding against the smooth, warm flesh of his chest like little pebbles. In response to her obvious arousal, his sleek hardness throbbed and stirred in her hand.

"But—it was warm in the summer moons," she pointed out, though a smile began, curving her lips and reaching her eyes, here to sparkle like dancing stars. "And the grasses were tall and concealing, and so very soft . . . This is the Moon of New Leaves. The grass is yet short—and the morning dew is cold!"

"Huh!" he snorted. "Not for long will the woman of White Wolf complain of the cold," he promised wickedly, trailing the tip of his tongue down over her shoulder and along the sensitive flesh inside her arm, before gently rolling her over to fasten his hot mouth over the taut coral peak of her breast.

A wave of passion swamped through her. Heat licked and curled through her loins, spreading fiery little tentacles everywhere through her body. Her scalp tingled, and even her toes curled with yearning. Meanwhile, his free hand trailed lazily across her belly, working down to the triangle of soft dark hair that modestly hid her woman-flower. Delicately, he invaded her velvet petals, a marauder whose trespass she welcomed with a gasp of pleasure as Wolf added huskily, "For like so . . . and like, so . . . I shall set my woman afire with longing—such longing, she'll forget to shiver!"

"Aiieee, already she smolders!" Blue Beads moaned, throwing back her head in rapturous abandon as she pressed her hips against him. Her eyes had taken on the liquid, languid look of a woman fully aroused and eager to satisfy her desires. "But, aiee, stop what you're doing, my husband, or there'll be no kindling gathered for the fire this morning, and no warm meal ready for your son when he wakes . . ." She raised her brows questioningly.

The double-meaning to her words was not lost on Wolf. Neither was her arch expression. His grin deepened roguishly. "Ah! Then you must go, woman, at once, and see to your tasks, while I—er, I will sleep a little longer!"

Giggling, she sprang up and snatched her shift from its peg, slipping it on over her head and smoothing its fringed hems modestly down over her hips to her knees. Her seductive body, its lissome curves moving enticingly beneath the supple yellow garment, wrenched a clench-jawed groan from Wolf. "By the Spirit, hurry, my woman," he gritted. "A man can take only so much, and no more, when he is—hungry!"

She took up a light cloak of deerskin and threw it about her shoulders. Tossing her heavy, sleep-tousled hair back from her eyes, she shot him a farewell glance from beneath her lashes that was beckoning and seductive all at once. Then she ducked under the tepee flap with a little wriggle of her hips, and sped gracefully away between the lodges.

Despite the chill and the fact that her feet were bare and she'd worn no leggings—knowing she'd only have to remove them in a few heartbeats anyway!—she was warm all over, smiling to herself as she quickly left the camp proper, and started down the rocky path that bordered the creek.

Three winters, and Wolf still held the power to arouse her in a single glance, a touch! Three winters, and she desired him even more than the sun they'd joined! And she knew just the place for their tryst, she thought with a pleased little giggle as she went, swinging the folds of the deerskin cape about her bare legs: a cozy bower just off the well-worn path to water!

The spot she'd chosen was concealed between dense bushes covered in tiny yellow green leaves. There, tussocks of lush grass already softened the winter-hardened ground, and the first pastel wildflowers had begun to show their shy faces, as if peeping out from the earth to see if the frost had really vanished. There was a little waterfall further down the trail, too, dropping over a low rocky shelf before tumbling into the icy pool below where the wild things came to drink. At dusk, she'd spotted raccoons, mule deer, and coyotes there, and, once, a tawny cougar dipping its golden head to water. With the spring thaw that had started several suns before, the volume of water made a pleasant, chuckling sound which, combined with the chirruping of nesting birds in the boughs nearby, would sing them a perfect love song!

Her eyes sparkled with anticipation as she sped along the narrow path. Her cheeks were pink. Her lips were moist, her heart racing. Like a young girl slipping secretly away to meet with her sweetheart for the very first time, she trembled with excitement . . .

A party of fifteen renegade Kiowa wove their way silently through the woods that had sheltered the camp of

Black Hawk from the harsh blizzards of winter.

Slipping from his pony, one of their number ran ahead to scout the camp that, for the greater part, was still sleeping at this early hour. The scout would learn the position of the lookouts, and gauge by the number of war ponies tethered before the lodges, how many warriors were in the village to repel their attack.

He returned several moments later, wearing a broad grin. The others — all painted for war — exchanged evil smiles when they saw his gloating expression.

Without uttering a word aloud, the scout signalled with sign language that they should ride up the sloping, rocky bank that followed the course of the creek. With a contemptuous grimace and an obscene gesture, he motioned that from there, they could easily swoop down on the unsuspecting village below, slay the sleeping warriors, and steal the best and youngest of the women away to warm their own robes! The others grunted with pleasure and agreement. They'd missed the comfort of a woman's warm body on cold nights since they'd broken away from their band, and there were women aplenty in the encampment up ahead. What did it matter if the people of cowardly Black Hawk considered them allies? They were outcasts, to the last brave, and outcasts called no man brother!

Nistiuna gave a drunken giggle as he glanced across at Broken Claw, whose dark eyes glittered with excitement.

"Revenge will taste sweet this sun, eh, my brother?" he slurred, swaying a little as he sat his pony. "Many moons have passed since White Wolf shamed you and stole your woman. It is time for him to pay! Will you share the paleface woman with me, as we once shared the yellow-hair captive three winters past, and the Mexican virgin that came after her?"

"Share? Ha! When I am done with her, I will share her with *all* my true brothers," Broken Claw swore harshly, his jaw clenched as hatred rose like bile to sting the back of his throat. "She'll regret choosing that weasel over me 'til her dying breath! Hear me, mighty warriors! We ride!" he commanded, quirting his coal black gelding ahead of the rest.

In single file, the ponies strained up the rocky slope that led to a rise above the sleeping village, halting only when they saw a slender, pretty captive white woman hurrying down the path. The renegades exchanged leers, while Broken Claw sucked in a breath as he fell back behind some boulders, and watched and waited. *Truly, the Great One had answered his prayers for vengeance! He had sent her to him—and she was alone!*

While Blue Beads waited for Wolf to join her, she spread her deerskin cloak over the dew-wet grass and sat down upon it. Idly picking dozens of pale blue spring flowers, she wove them through her hair, humming as she did so to still the wild excitement coursing through her veins.

A furtive rustling came from the bushes close by, and at once her head jerked around in the direction of the sound. A smile lit her face and played about her lips. So soon? she thought. *Truly, he must be very impatient to join with her!*

"Who is there?" she asked innocently.

There was no answer, but the rustling sounds came again.

"Who is it who spies on me?" she demanded, rising to her feet and making a determined effort to appear stern and not smile. "Show your face, roguish one!"

More rustling, but there was still no answer. She giggled under her breath. Aiee, that Wolf! What a trickster he was!

Breathing shallowly, she padded barefoot across the grass in the direction she'd last heard the furtive movements. Grasping two fistfuls of the bushes in her fists, she yanked them apart.

Laughing, she threw back her head and declared, "Ah

305

ha! I have found you, my hus—!"

But her laughter abruptly died on her lips as she found herself looking—not into Wolf's beloved face—but into a leering mask of red and black—a terrifyingly familiar face that had haunted her dreams, painted garishly for war!

"You!" she choked out, backing away.

Her heart faltered. Her knees quivered. Dread churned in her belly as she gaped at him.

Broken Claw stepped out from between the bushes and entered the little bower that had promised delight, and had now become her cage. He laughed scornfully at her shocked expression as he stalked her.

A fan of wild turkey feathers adorned his scalp. A silver bauble dangled from the lobe of one ear. His chest, bare except for his war paint, medicine bundle, and a necklace of teeth, bore the scars of the duel he and Wolf had fought all those winters ago. She would have known him anywhere!

"Yes!" he seethed, "It is I! Did you think I'd forgotten your betrayal? Did you think I'd forget the ridicule you brought me? Never! Now, pretty doe, you will pay . . ."

Before she could whirl away and flee him, his left hand came out like a striking snake to grip her shoulder. His right coiled about her waist to slam her hard against him. He lowered his head to her throat, holding her fast against him while his other hand grasped the hem of her shift, shoving it up about her thighs. His intent was obvious. He meant to take her! She twisted sideways, panting heavily, thrusting at his chest, hammering at it with her clenched fists—and to her surprise, managed to escape his arms!

She darted toward the narrow opening in the bushes, but—it was only a game he played; the game a cougar sometimes plays with its prey, toying with a terrified little animal before the bloody kill! Even as she reached the opening, she heard his cruel laughter as he leaped after her. Fire seared her scalp as his fingers knotted in her flying hair. Viciously, he yanked her backward. And, still gripping her hair, he swung her around by it to face him. With a brutal grip on her throat instead now, he forced her to her knees, then down, shoving her over onto her back before following her down.

"*Wolf!*" she screamed. "*Wolf! Oh, help me!*"

Yet even from there, some distance from camp, she could now hear the screams rising from the village on the chill morning air; the curdling whoops of the renegade warriors, the wailing of babes . . . The blood ran cold in her veins with dread. Aiee! Their encampment was under attack! What of her baby? What of Wolf? Their families? Were they dead? Wounded?

"Your Wolf will not come!" he spat at her. "Scream all you will! By now, that weasel dances on the point of Nistiuna's lance—as soon you shall dance on mine!"

So saying, he thrust up her skirts and gripped her thighs, one in each of his punishing hands. His fingers sank deep into her flesh, each one bruising, painful, like the bite of a cruel fang. She flailed at his face, but he gripped both her wrists in one huge hand and forced them up and over her head, pinning her to the grass. Then he wedged his knee between her thighs, and reached beneath her shift to fondle her breasts at will. She saw the triumph that leapt into his eyes when he knew she couldn't escape him, and a little of her former spirit returned. She screamed wildly again; screamed until her throat was hoarse; screamed until no sound would come from her mouth.

But although she managed to free her hands, and although she threshed and fought him, beating at his head, his shoulders, his chest, tearing out great hanks of his hair, jabbing her fingers at his eyes, and cursing him with every vile name she could summon, he was too strong, too determined. She too weak, too weak by far, she realized, exhausted by her struggles . . .

With a wild whoop, he pulled his breechclout aside and thrust into her. A burst of tearing pain blazed through her belly, then another and another, each thrust building on the last agony. His fingers gripped her waist. His hips slammed against her. His hot, wet mouth seemed everywhere at once, his lust a foul reek that filled her nostrils.

Nausea dizzied her. Her gorge rose up from her belly to scald her throat. Then blackness, merciful blackness, threatened to crowd out all feeling, all caring, all shame, all hurt. *Wolf!* she wept silently, *Wolf!* and rushed head-long to meet the darkness with open arms . . .

A stinging blow to her cheek jolted her back to consciousness. Another fist slammed against the opposite side, flinging her head sharply to left, then right, in bruising succession.

"No, you don't! Wake up and fight me, woman! Fight me! You won't escape me that way, never!" he snarled, renewing his assault.

She gasped. She whimpered, mewling like a hurt kitten. Her eyes flew open to horror once again, and the nightmare of Broken Claw looming over her, grunting as he rutted between her thighs. There was an expression of savage triumph on his face as he raped her. As she saw it, knew it for what it was, she suddenly also knew what she could do to get him off her. He would either kill her, or not. Either way, she had nothing to lose . . . not now. Wolf would never want her back, not after this.

"Fight you? For what purpose, cowardly dog? You are less than a man!" she whispered, forcing her face to register contempt, her tone scorn, rather than the pain of his blows. "My husband is worth ten of you—a hundred! You rut like a puny jack-rabbit, while Wolf—he is a stallion!"

"Silence!" he raged, his fingers splaying across her throat, squeezing, squeezing, as he shook her. "Speak his name again, I kill you!"

"Go ahead!" she urged hoarsely. "I have known the love of a true man, and I will go to the After World singing his praises—!"

308

"*No!*" His fingers tightened, pressing against her windpipe, gagging her. "You will sing in praise of me, not him!" he spat. "You will call me man, *your* man—or I will choke the life from your body!"

"Not man, *never* man—and never, ever *my* man!" she managed to gasp. "You carrion-eater! You rotting carcass! You filthy mad dog!"

The stranglehold he had about her throat grew tighter, tighter, until speech was impossible. The blood pounded in her ears; a singing, crimson whirlwind that roared and rushed and thundered. Light dwindled from her vision, leaving only a tiny star of brightness at its heart. She fought for breath, choking, drowning for lack of air, and dimly, as if from a great way off, heard him screaming at her:

"Say it, curse you, woman! Say instead that Broken Claw is your chosen one . . . say that you'll never leave him . . . swear that you'll be his woman always from this sun forth! Say it . . . say it . . . curse you!"

"Wolf!" she mouthed silently. "Beloved—" Then her head lolled slackly to one side. Her eyes slid closed and stayed that way.

Broken Claw relaxed his stranglehold. With an anguished sob, he drew his fingers away, uncurled them, and looked down at his hand, aghast. For once, he was oblivious to the maimed finger that had given him his man-name, for it was as if—as if those powerful fingers were separate from him! No longer a part of his body. As if the evil they had done belonged to another!

Shuddering, his eyes bulging in horror, he looked down then at the woman lying so still in the grass, with crushed blue wildflowers still woven in her hair and the marks of his fingers already purpling about her pale throat. A great knot of agony swelled in his breast, rose up his throat. Then the great, keening wail of grief tore up from inside him. Opening his mouth, he threw back his head and let it rip free, curdling upward to the scudding clouds.

"Whyyyy, curse you!" he howled. *"Why did you make me do this thing? Why, Blue Beads Woman? I loved you! I loved you above all others!"*

But there was no answer. Only an eerie silence all about him, and the sound of his own labored breathing.

The blowing of a pony and the sounds of its hooves thrashing away through the undergrowth nearby brought him around from his stupor. He flicked his head as if to clear it, and looked up to see Nistiuna appear between the bushes, astride his buckskin mare. He was leading Black Arrow behind him, and his eyes were dilated with excitement.

"The fight went against us!" he jabbered. "They were too many, too strong! Six of our brothers lie dead at their hands! Come, let's flee, my brother!"

He had, Broken Claw noticed, an arrow wound in his thigh, which was bleeding heavily, spilling blood down the glossy coat of his pony. Still dazed by what he'd done, he rose slowly to standing, took the rein from Nistiuna in silence and swung astride his pony.

"Well?" Nistiuna asked as they kicked their ponies into a gallop, weaving their way expertly down the sloping creek banks and back toward the woods.

"Well what?" Broken Claw asked sharply, his expression a strange and brooding one.

"Was she any good, before you killed her?" Wild Horse demanded slyly, licking his lips. "Was she worth all this? And did you lift her hair, after?" Broken Claw turned his head and stared at him as if Nistiuna were speaking words of madness. "Well, did you?" he repeated. "Where is it?"

"I will warn you but once," Broken Claw menaced softly, gritting the words. "Speak of this sun ever again, and I will cut out your heart!"

With that threat, he lashed his pony into a thundering gallop, widening the distance between the gold and the black in a matter of heartbeats.

Riding swiftly, the renegades fled the camp of Black

Hawk, headed for the open plains.

It was Crooked Woman who found her, lying still as death in the little bower, with her deerskin shift rucked up about her belly.

With a cry, the old woman fell on her knees beside the young woman, and held her palm before her mouth to see if she was still breathing. Relief at finding she was brought tears to Crooked Woman's faded brown eyes. As she knelt there, weeping silently as she pulled the shift down to cover her body and gently caressed her bruised face and throat, Blue Beads stirred. A low whimper of pain escaped her.

"Tush, tush, my little bird, you are safe now," Crooked Woman crooned, sliding one arm beneath the girl's shoulder and raising her up to cradle her against her withered chest. Stroking her hair, she added, "They're all gone, never fear! Those renegade devils have fled, save for those our warriors cut down before they could run!"

"And Wolf?" Blue Beads queried in a cracked voice.

"Even now, he searches for you, his woman, of course" the old one told her gently. "But it is I who have found you, thank the Great Spirit! Tell me, little daughter, are you hurt badly anywhere? Bleeding?"

Blue Beads shook her head, struggling to sit up. In all honesty, she hurt everywhere, but apart from her bruises, she'd escaped serious injury. The bruises would fade, with time. "My son?" she demanded, dreading the woman's answer.

To her surprise, Crooked Woman actually chuckled. "When the lookout sounded the alarm, your husband took up his weapons and ran from the lodge. He charged me to watch over his son, and so I ran with him and we hid—by the dung heap!" she revealed proudly. "I knew no renegade offal would think of looking there for captives! Never fear, he smells far from flower-sweet, but he is unharmed!"

311

Blue Beads managed a little smile at this, though her face pained her. Thanks to the Great Spirit, two of her loved ones were unharmed; three counting Crooked Woman!

"In fact, none of our number was killed," Crooked Woman disclosed then. "Though a few suffered small wounds. Our braves were too well prepared, their medicine too powerful! When those coyotes saw that their arrows were returned tenfold, they ran like the cowardly rabbits they are! Come, my poor, dear one, lean on me. If you think you can walk, we'll go back to your lodge? I'll see to your hurts, while I send someone to find your husband and tell him that you're safe . . ."

There was misery on Blue Beads's face as she nodded and struggled awkwardly to standing, holding on to the old woman for support when her aching limbs threatened to buckle. Safe! she thought miserably, Aiee, safe indeed, but at what cost? Would her husband want her back, after what Broken Claw had done to her? Would he still want a wife who'd been used by his enemy? Better she'd died!

Crooked Woman had bathed her bruises with cold water from the creek and applied a soothing ointment to them and the vicious marks about her throat when Wolf returned from his search for her. Thankfully, Crooked Woman had taken Red Wing to the creek to wash the odor of the dung heap from him, and they could be alone for a short while.

Her expression was bleak as he entered their lodge and came to sit cross-legged before the fire, across from where she lay. But as for his expression—she couldn't tell what he was thinking, it was so stern, so dark, so unreadable! His eyes, though—their expression needed no explanation, for they were as hard and cold as the sky reflected on the icy surface of a lake!

Would he send her from him, she wondered, tears

312

smarting behind her eyelids? Cast her out of his lodge? Take another, unsoiled woman to replace her in his heart and on his robes? She swallowed painfully, but the bruises encircling her throat hurt far less than the thought of such a possibility . . .

He spoke suddenly, and his tone was harsh and frightening to her ears.

"I am to blame for this!" he said in a tight, controlled voice of enormous bitterness. "Your hurt is my doing! I should never have let you wander off alone! I should have gone with you! What true man lets lust rule over wisdom?"

"But I should have taken my knife," she whispered hoarsely, "as you always insisted I do. The blame is not yours, but mine! Forgive me?" she wept, her fears brimming over. "Please don't send me away!"

"Send you away?" he echoed, uncertain he'd really heard her correctly. "For what reason?"

He saw her eyes then, the dread in their deep blue depths, and understood her fears. His expression softening, he went to her, taking her gently in his arms, wrapping her in the safe haven of his embrace. "To send you away would be to cast out my very heart, my soul! What happened has nothing to with you and I, my little one, nor any part of love or mating. You were wounded, as our warriors were wounded. Could they help the swifter arrows that pierced them before they could string their own? Do we blame them for their slowness—or you, for being weaker than your attacker, unable to overpower him? No, my foolish little one! Speak of it no more."

"But—I could have a child!"

"Perhaps," he acknowledged. "But we will deal with that chance together, if it should come to be. There's no means to tell, after all, whether the child would be mine, or that other one's seed." Scowling nonetheless, he paused, and in the silence she knew that he was trying to find his next words, and doing so with difficulty. "Your—attacker—can you describe him to me?"

"Better than that," she whispered, burying her face against his chest to blot out the memory of that garishly painted, terrifying face; the night dark eyes aglitter with triumph. "I—I know his name!"

"His name? Who is he then?" Wolf demanded, holding her at arm's length now, his eyes searching her face. His lips thinned. His jaw tightened. A nerve at his temple danced under the taut copper skin there. "Tell me his name!"

She told him, and saw the terrible rage that suffused his face; the fury that filled his eyes.

"What will you do? Please, Wolf, don't go! Don't leave me!"

But with quick, angry movements, he released her and sprang to his feet, striding across their lodge to the farthest wall. From the pegs there, he took down the rawhide parfleche that contained his paints, and began lining his face with the red stripes of war . . .

When he was done, he turned to face her. He held his battle shield in one fist, his huge feathered lance in the other, and Blue Beads shivered at the frightening picture he made.

"I must go, my woman, you know that! I can no longer uphold my oath, and yet be a man. He has harmed my woman in his thirst to dishonor me. His renegade brothers have attacked our people. For these things, he must pay! The time for reckoning has come!" he seethed.

A frisson of fear shimmied down her spine . . .

Chapter Twenty-four

Wolf had been gone from their lodge for six suns when white men came to the village of Black Hawk's people.

In her own lodge, moving stiffly still from her bruises as she prepared a morning meal of boiled corn mush, roasted venison, and boiled sausage for Crooked Woman, herself, and little Red Wing, Blue Beads heard the cry that rippled through the lodges of the Comanche like a breeze rustling through a maize field.

"Palefaces are coming! Their mules are laden!" it said, growing in volume like the drone of many bees.

The lookout above the camp had started the cry, and now the people took it up. The same words were on every tongue as women and children, old crones, *shamans,* storytellers, and arrow-makers came tumbling from their lodges to gape at the newcomers with their strange pale skin; skin so white, it resembled nothing so closely as the white bellies of the fish that swam in the rivers, lakes, and streams.

Blue Beads was curious to see the new arrivals, too, for what could the paleface enemy want with Black Hawk's people this time, she wondered scornfully? Did they come to treat for their false peace? To make promises that would be broken by their weak and lying chiefs, before the pigment was dried on the "talking-leaves" they painted such promises upon? Or did they instead come to count the young warriors in the camp of the People? To reckon the number and strength of their men and weapons, the swiftness of their ponies, and so prepare for an attack on their camp under the guise of friendship, as the renegades had attempted to do seven suns ago? On the other hand, maybe they really did come with peaceful thoughts and true hearts, wanting simply to trade? To barter beads and iron kettles, red blankets and looking glasses, bullets and shooting-sticks, for the pelts of the beaver and otter they so prized? Whatever the reason, the arrival of palefaces other than as terrified captives of war or as long-knife pony soldiers wielding fire-sticks was rare enough to thoroughly fire her curiosity!

"Eat quickly, my son," Blue Beads urged Red Wing. Love and maternal pride filled her as he obediently did as she'd told him. He scooped up the mush with his little fingers and gulped it down. He sank his strong white teeth into the succulent meat and gnawed it from the bone like a hungry wolf-cub, which was exactly how she thought of him — as Wolf's Cub!

Next moon, their son would be three winters old, yet already he was stronger and smarter than any of the other little ones he played with in and out of the lodges. Grandmother Spotted Pony had remarked on his keen mind and strong, sturdy little body many times. Grandfather Many Horses had been no less generous with his praises. So, too, had his paternal grandfather Chief Black Hawk showered him with affectionate pats, hugs, and little gifts from the hour of his birth; a tiny bow and blunted arrows, a yellow mongrel pup he'd named Growler that now followed him everywhere, a little gourd drum, and a whistle of eagle bone, among other things. They all doted on the boy, and he on them! If ever she was unable to find him, it would always be in Many Horses's or Black Hawk's lodge that she eventually did so, sitting on either of his grandfathers' laps, and listening wide-eyed to Many Horses's tales of the Thunderbird that brought the rain and lightning with its terrible flashing eyes and beating wings, or to Black Hawk's recounting of the coups he had counted against his enemies in battle.

"Papa coming home soon?" Red Wing asked, looking up at her inquiringly from eyes so bright and blue, the spring sky paled by comparison. With his fair skin and hair as dark as the raven's glossy plumage, and those big, black-lashed eyes as vivid as the cheeky jay's wings, he was an extraordinarily beautiful child among a camp of beautiful children. He would someday become a handsome brave, too; the focus of the village maidens' flirtatious glances in winters to come—as his roguish father had once been, she thought with a fond little smile. Hot on the heels of that thought, she offered up a silent prayer for Wolf's safe return. *Oh, Great Spirit, let him triumph over our enemy, Broken Claw!* she asked. *Let him return safely to his loved ones, who need him so!*

"I do not know when your father will return, little one," she told the toddler truthfully, taking him by a pudgy hand that was sticky with mush and grease. She paused to wipe both his hands and face clean and smooth down his hair, before adding, "But I do hope it's soon, don't you? Meanwhile, we'll go and see these palefaces who've come to our village, yes?" She smiled at Crooked Woman. "Won't you come with us, my aunt?"

Crooked Woman shook her head and grimaced gummily. "Once you have seen one pale face, you have seen them all! Besides, their unwashed bodies stink of their sweat, and I have a delicate nose! You run along and enjoy yourself for a while. I'll watch the fire and finish the moccasins I'm working on for the little cub."

"Am I a paleface, Mama?" Red Wing asked as he and his mother left the lodge to join the tide of people heading for the open area before Chief Black Hawk's tepee.

"Why would you ask such a question, dear one?" she said, stopping and looking down at Red Wing curiously.

"Because Sleek Otter and Small Cloud teased me! They said that you and papa were more paleface than Comanche!" he repeated indignantly. "That's not true, is it, Mama? Grandfather Black Hawk says I'm the grandson of a Comanche chief, and will some day become a proud warrior of the People!"

"And so you will," Blue Beads agreed solemnly, tears in her eyes.

"Then Sleek Otter and Small Cloud lied!" Red Wing

declared, looking terribly small and fierce with his lower lip pugnaciously stuck out and his little fists clenched on his hips. "And lying is wicked—Grandmother Spotted Pony and Aunt Crooked Woman both said so!"

"Hmm, they weren't exactly lying," his mother began slowly, wondering how best to explain to the small child in words he would understand. "But they were trying to make you unhappy, and that was very mean of them! You see, I was born to a paleface mother and father, but when I was eight winters old, the same age as Small Cloud, the Apaches killed them and carried me away."

"Our enemy, the Apache!" His eyes were round as small moons now, his little mouth an *O* of shock.

"Aiee, yes! But your father saw me while he and other braves were hunting wild horses. He knew the Apache would not treat me kindly, and so he stole me from my captors and carried me away to his aunt, Spotted Pony! He asked her to raise me as her daughter, and she did. That was many winters ago, and now my heart belongs to the People and to your father." She gracefully touched her fingertips to her breast. "My tongue speaks only the Comanche tongue, and has forgotten the strange language of the palefaces. I would give my life for the People, if need be, and so they are my people in *spirit* now, even if my blood is the blood of the palefaces. Do you understand, my son?"

"I think so," Red Wing acknowledged, although he wrinkled his nose and frowned a little. "And papa? Were his mother and father palefaces, too?"

"Not both of them. Your father's mother belonged to the Hopi people. The Hopituh, the Peaceful Ones, live in stone lodges built among the cliffs and mesas south of the setting sun. They never leave them to follow the sacred humpback and the pronghorn herds, as do we, but dig in Mother Earth and plant corn and squash to fill their bellies. Your father's father was a Black Robe, though."

"A Black Robe? What is that?" the child asked.

"A *shaman* of the paleface people, one who teaches the word of their one God, his son, Jesus, and the goddess Mary. This Black Robe, your father told me once, had eyes as blue as the sky, and hair the color of summer grasses. He wanted to teach the Hopi of Walpi, his religion," his mother explained, "for all white men believe that their God is the only god.

"Now, in the way of the palefaces, it is forbidden the Black Robe *shamans* to take a wife or to father children, and yet this Black Robe paleface loved your grandmother very dearly. He forsook his vows for Yoyokee Hama, Rain Girl, and left his *shaman* society. Together, they loved. And together, they made a child, a little boy-child with eyes as blue as his father's and hair as black as his mother's. When this boy child was just twelve winters old, his people were attacked by their enemies. Many were killed, others carried off to a faraway place to be traded as slaves to other tribes, or sold to the Spanish *hacenderos* to work on their *ranchos,* in exchange for silver, weapons, horses, and such. The boy was one of them. And a Comanche chieftain who had no sons of his own paid many humpback robes and many fine ponies to free him from his captors. He loved him and raised him as his own son. The chief's name was Black Hawk, your grandfather, and do you know what the boy's name was — ?"

"White Wolf, my father!" Red Wing supplied, astonishing her with his keen grasp of all she had told him.

"Yes! It was so! And so you see, my son, you are as much one of the People as that silly little Sleek Otter or Small Cloud — and very much loved!"

Red Wing beamed, and the smile reminded her so painfully of Wolf, it tugged at her heartstrings. "Come," she said huskily, "enough talking for now. Let's go and see what all the excitement is about, shall we?"

The central gathering place was ringed by onlookers, all craning their necks and jostling each other to see what was going on. Holding Red Wing firmly by the

319

hand, Blue Beads squirmed her way between the people to get a closer look.

Three white men sat their huge chestnut horses in the center of the gathering place. They had two heavily laden pack mules on leading reins behind them, and appeared decidedly ill at ease, but determined, to Blue Beads's eyes. Several armed Comanche braves sat their smaller spotted ponies on either side of the white-eyes. They were obviously the escort who'd ridden out to see if the strangers came in peace, or with thoughts of attacking the camp!

The oldest of the pale faces, a tall, burly man with dark whiskers on his chin, wore a coonskin cap with a striped tail hanging down behind it; a fringed buckskin shirt, breeches and tall moccasins. The other two, one a young brave, she guessed by the erect yet easy way he sat his horse, and the other much older, were similarly dressed, though they wore the big hats with the curled-up brims so favored by the white-eyes. These last two had their backs to her side of the crowd, so she couldn't see their faces. Neither could she hear what they were saying, or Semanaw's translation of their strange tongue for Chief Black Hawk's benefit.

In the end, Blue Beads gave up straining her ears to catch a word or two of their conversation. Instead, she shifted her attention to the pack mules, and her eyes shone. Of course, the palefaces had come to trade! What treasures the canvas covers lashed over the mules' bulging loads must conceal! Would they have the pretty blue trade beads she wanted, the ones whose color matched Wolf's eyes so perfectly? Oh, she hoped so! They'd be the very thing to decorate the front of the fine new shirt she was making for him . . .

Feeling eyes boring into her, she slowly turned her head. The burly, bearded white man was staring at her, and inevitably, their gazes met. She saw excitement leap into his dark blue eyes as his glance fell upon her face, and quickly averted her eyes and looked down at her moccasins. Heat filled her cheeks. Aiee, no! The very last thing she needed was to attract the lusty notice of one of the hated enemy yet again!

Her capture by Whiskered One and Pale Eyes over three winters ago was as sharp in her mind as if it had happened just last sun. So was her memory of Wolf's anger at her carelessness! She'd taken precautions never to leave the safety of the lodges unarmed since then, until the attack of the renegade Kiowa and her assault at Broken Claw's hands. The incident had further impressed upon her the need to be vigilant and prepared at all times for attack, even when close to their camp. She'd not be caught off guard again, she vowed!

But when she risked another glance back at the white eyes, she saw with relief that his attention had shifted. He'd obviously forgotten her, for he was now leaning forward over his saddle horn, his head cocked to one side to consider something Black Hawk was saying.

Moments later, the crowd fell back to make room as the three white men dismounted their horses and handed the reins to the Comanche braves, though they would not similarly relinquish their long fire-sticks, much to the obvious displeasure of Kansaleumko, Rolling Thunder.

Chief Black Hawk, bearing himself proudly and with dignity in his eagle-feathered war bonnet and finest garments, led the way into the ceremonial lodge. He carried reverently in his arms a quilled and painted rawhide case of superb workmanship, in which he knew reposed his ceremonial pipe of carved red sandstone, hung with fluffy white eagle feathers. The council lodge was the largest of all the lodges in the village, used only for councils of war and the making of important decisions. Its walls were left unpainted so that all men might concentrate on serious matters without distraction.

Semanaw and the chief's closest advisors followed him inside, and then came the three white men, ducking their tall bodies low to go under the flap opening in the wake of the chief. Rolling Thunder and two other war chiefs who'd made up their escort brought up in the rear, while three small boys—puffed up with pride at being given such an important task—took the reins of the palefaces' towering mounts—animals far bigger than the mustang ponies tethered outside the lodges. They led them away to be watered and hobbled while their masters discussed their business.

"Now they'll pass the peace pipe, and talk and smoke for hours!" grumbled a familiar voice at Blue Beads's elbow, "and it will be two full suns, maybe more, before we get so much as a *peek* into those packs!"

"My friend is impatient!" Blue Beads smilingly accused her friend Wounded Doe. "And impatience is unhealthy for one so heavy with child, she looks as if she's swallowed a buffalo hump or a summer squash!"

"Aiee! I feel as if I've carried this second babe for two winters already!" Wounded Doe complained, rubbing her aching lower back and enormous belly in turn. Her time would come any day now. She had the drawn look and cranky, weary sound of one whose time was very near. "Sleek Otter!" she chided her daughter, "Stop pinching little Red Wing! And if you won't stop, and he pinches you back or pulls your hair, don't come running to me! Aagh! I'll be blind to your tears!"

Blue Beads laughed. "Oh, don't scold her! Red Wing is quite capable of holding his own against Sleek Otter— aren't you, my son? Tell me, has Little Cougar gone to smoke the pipe and discover why the palefaces have come here?"

"He has," Wounded Doe said with a tight-lipped grimace. "Didn't you see him among the others? And what of your man? Has your Wolf not yet returned?"

"He has not," Blue Beads disclosed in a small, telltale voice that revealed the true extent of her fears to one who knew her as well and for as long as Wounded Doe had.

"Then since we've been deserted by our men, let's go to your lodge and ask your mother and some of the

322

other women to join us until our menfolk return, shall we?" Doe suggested brightly. "We could put the children to bed early and play find-the-button or something to pass the time—if you are feeling strong enough, that is?" Her round eyes were gentle with concern as she touched Blue Beads's hand in a gesture of affection. True, her bruises from Broken Claw's attack were almost gone, had faded to a yellowish green now, rather than the livid purple of before, but what about the bruises to her spirit?

Blue Beads smiled. "I am feeling quite well, and would enjoy some company. I have a sack of coffee that Wolf found a few suns before the Kiowa attacked, left behind in the ruts from a white-eyes' wagon train after it'd passed by. Would you like to try some with the sweet powder in it? It's very good!"

"Oh, yes, I'd love to." Doe agreed, beaming. "Oh, you're so lucky, my cousin, to have such a man as Wolf!" She pouted. "He always brings you the most wonderful presents, while Little Cougar gives me nothing but—"

"Babies!" Blue Beads cut her off with a grin. "But count yourself lucky, my ungrateful friend, and instead consider poor Kianceta, Weasel. Three winters married, and not a babe in sight for her, poor thing . . ."

Arm in arm, the two young women gossiped as they wove their way between the people and the conical yellow lodges, heading for the tepee of White Wolf and Blue Beads. Little Red Wing and Sleek Otter—still rudely teasing each other—gambolled after their mothers like puppies.

As Blue Beads had shrewdly guessed, Wounded Doe was very close to her time. Her birthing pains began that same evening, while she and the other women played at find-the-button, gambling using their precious stores of dyed porcupine quills for stakes.

But when it became apparent that Doe could no longer concentrate on the game, Blue Beads shooed the other laughing, excited women from her lodge, asking only her mother to remain behind with Crooked Woman and herself.

Spotted Pony, who'd helped with the births of many other babes before she'd assisted in her grandson's safe entry into the world, ran knowledgeable hands over Wounded Doe's belly.

"This little one won't be long coming into the world!" she decided, smiling down into Wounded Doe's shiny, sweaty face as another strong contraction squeezed her belly. "Your child is ready and eager to be born! Blue Beads, my daughter, run and fetch the midwives, while old Aunt and I see Doe back to her lodge."

In short order, Doe was settled in her own tepee, surrounded by the cackling gaggle of old crones who were the midwives of the tribe. They, too, examined her, and also declared that the birth would be easy and swift, much to Spotted Pony's satisfaction. The pains were coming at regular intervals now, and doing so only a few heartbeats apart. They were strong while they lasted, making Doe's belly rise in a great peak, before subsiding as the pain ended. In the light of the bear-tallow lanterns, the laboring woman's face contorted and turned bright red with effort and pain with each pang. Then her body would relax, and she'd be weary but smiling in between.

"Soon you'll hold your little one in your arms, my friend!" Blue Beads encouraged her, bathing her friend's face with a square of hide, "and a proud father will go singing his child's praises among the lodges of the people! Look! Already White Feather is driving the birthing stick into the ground for you to hold on to. Be strong, my cousin, it won't be long now! You can do it!" she urged reassuringly.

Yet Old Woman moon had set above the mountains and coyotes were yipping before the compelling urge to bear down gripped Doe. Blue Beads drew back and watched with bated breath as Doe knelt upon a clean hide, her knees spread wide for purchase, and held on hard to the stick driven into the earthen floor before her. When the next pain came, she clenched her jaw, braced herself against it and bore down, squeezing her eyes tightly shut and holding her breath.

"A head! I see the head!" White Feather crowed, her scrawny old arms outstretched to catch the babe that would soon make its appearance into the world.

Doe pushed a second, then a third time, her straining grunts and bellows filling the tepee, while her friend and helpers watched and offered silent prayers and loud, encouraging murmurs for her safe delivery of a healthy, perfect child. A fourth, monumental push — a groaning gasp — a drawn-out, wailing moan of relief — and then the infant's bloody shoulders emerged. The rest of the babe slipped from its mother's straining body into White Feather's arms, like a salmon sliding into a stream!

Spotted Pony cut the cord with a sharp knife after the last strong pulse of blood had passed to the babe's body from that of its mother. She tied it with a thin length of rawhide, and dusted the wet stump with puffball powder, taken from her parfleche of herbs, remembering uncomfortably what had happened to another navel cord soon after her grandson's birth; one tucked among the swaddling of Red Wing's cradleboard.

The navel cord in its yellow and blue pouch shaped like a turtle had disappeared — a sure sign of ill-fortune for the infant! She'd said nothing to Blue Beads of its disappearance, and had instead slipped a short, shrivelled strand of dried rawhide into the decoy pouch, and tucked that among the infant's swaddling instead, hoping no one would notice the switch. Blue Beads had almost caught her at her deception! She had asked what she was doing with the second pouch in her hand, rather than in its fork in the cottonwood before their lodge, but she'd made some excuse or other. After all, what good would it have done to worry her daughter, when what was done was done, and could not be changed?

The midwife held the newborn one aloft and blew into its face. A lusty wail of protest tore the breathless, expectant silence asunder. Little fists jerked and flailed out from its body in alarm, and the child turned bright red as it drew its first breath and squalled noisily. The women clapped their hands and crowed with delight and no little relief. A safe birth for mother and child was a true blessing!

"A fine boy!" White Feather cackled, her rheumy old eyes beady and bright, her toothless mouth split in a gummy smile. "A friend for his father!"

Overjoyed, Wounded Doe sank exhausted onto the heap of soft robes the women had prepared for this moment. She lay gazing adoringly at her new little son, while the afterbirth was delivered with hardly a pain. Then the midwives washed her body and packed downy layers of dried moss and cottonwood down between her legs, held in place with a rawhide breechclout, to soak up the bleeding.

Meanwhile, White Feather rubbed the infant all over, cleansing the blood and mucous of birth from his body with soft skins and more handfuls of clean moss. When she was done, she smiled at Blue Beads and handed her the child and a length of soft, pieced rabbit skins, indicating she should have the honor of wrapping the infant for the first time. With a pleased smile, Blue Beads did so, swaddling him loosely before carrying him to his anxious mother.

"Is all well with my son?" Doe asked, holding out her arms.

"Not only whole and well, but beautiful!" Blue Beads assured her softly, laying the naked babe on his mother's breasts. "For a boy, that is!"

He was a big, lusty infant, red-faced, with a thick thatch of jet black hair. Little pads of fat on his shoulders and arms gave him a sturdy look. She could discern none of the fragile loveliness about him that Wounded Doe's first child, her daughter Sleek Otter had displayed as a baby, but then, it was fitting a future warrior of the People should be big and strong, and not slender and pretty like a little girl!

"My son is beautiful," Doe agreed, smiling as she cuddled her baby. "Will you go to the ceremonial lodge and inform his father that he has a new friend, my sister?"

Delighted by this honor, Blue Beads nodded. Softly asking Spotted Pony and Crooked Woman to watch over Red Wing, who'd fallen asleep in a heap with Sleek Otter on a pile of robes across the lodge, their squabbling forgotten, she slipped outside into the cool, starry night.

Gazing up at the heavens for a moment or two, she saw a single star break free of its tether and plummet to earth, trailing a shimmering tail of light in its wake.

"It is fitting that I tell a new father of this falling star that celebrated his son's birth!" she promised herself, and smiling, made her way between the fire-lit tepees to the ceremonial lodge.

She was yet some distance from it when she saw Wolf's friend, Kansaleumko, Rolling Thunder, striding between the lodges toward her.

"What is this magic?" Rolling Thunder boomed in the deep voice that had assured him a permanent position as a lookout in their camp. "I am sent to bring you to our chief, and I find you already on your way! Can it be our camp has ears to hear everything that is said, albeit in secret?"

"Not so, my husband's friend," Blue Beads disclaimed with a smile. "I come to bring our brother, Little Cougar, word of a new friend in his tepee!"

"Ah, thank the Great One, he'll be a proud father once again! But alas, your news will have to wait. Important matters are being decided in the talking lodge — matters that concern you, my sister! I was sent to bring you and Wolf's son before the council."

"Me and — and Red Wing? To the council? But — whatever for? We've done nothing wrong! Why have they sent for us? Won't you tell me?" she pleaded. A sick, dragging

327

feeling weighted her belly. She'd suddenly remembered the way the big pale face's eyes had lit up when he spotted her, and her dread had increased tenfold. *Not again!* she prayed. *Oh, no, Great Spirit, please—not again! Surely he couldn't have asked Black Hawk to trade for her, his own daughter-in-law? And surely Black Hawk would never have agreed to such a thing?*

"It is not my place to tell you anything, but the council's," Rolling Thunder said stiffly, his black eyes sliding uncomfortably away from hers and deepening her fear. "Go before Chief Black Hawk, woman, and I will bring your son to join you."

"But he's sleeping in the lodge of Little Cougar," she divulged, her expression imploring as she added silently, *And safe, with his grandmother Spotted Pony watching over him, as protective as any she-bear!* "Must we wake him?" she whispered.

"We must."

The ceremonial lodge was smoky and crowded when Rolling Thunder returned with a sleepy-eyed, grumpy Red Wing, and nudged them inside the huge tepee, sewn of twenty-four buffalo skins, ahead of him.

A fire blazed in the center below the smoke-hole, and surrounding it on all sides was a circle of seated men; the war chiefs of the village's warrior societies, the elders, and *shamans*—all wearing their finest ceremonial headdresses of animal skins—Chief Black Hawk, and the three white men. All of their faces looked ruddy and unfamiliar in the firelight and shadows, and her throat felt suddenly dry.

"Come before us, my daughter," Chief Black Hawk beckoned, "and bring my grandson with you. You have nothing to fear."

Swallowing her terror, Blue Beads took Red Wing by the hand and hesitantly led him into the circle of light. As the fire burnished her face and glinted in the blue of her eyes, she heard the big white man gasp aloud. He said something in an excited tone to Semanaw, who translated for his chief.

"This paleface, Don-o-van Kell-ee, has ridden many miles to find our winter village," Black Hawk explained. "He has told me he comes in peace to extend the hand of brotherhood to the people of Black Hawk. He has sworn he has no evil in his heart, nor thoughts of war. As Father Sun circles the sky, we have passed the sacred pipe amongst us in the direction Sun follows across the heavens, and have smoked in brotherhood. My heart believes that his words are sincere and without trickery, my daughter.

"He has also told us," Black Hawk continued carefully, "that many winters ago, our enemy the Apache attacked his wooden village far to the south and west. His woman was slain by the attackers, and his little daughter carried off. He has been searching for her ever since that time! Now he believes he has found the one he seeks in the village of Black Hawk. She is the woman-above-all-women of White Wolf, my own son. The mother of my grandson, Red Wing."

In her confusion, it took a few heartbeats for Black Hawk's meaning to sink in. When it did, Blue Beads blanched. "No! This cannot be!" she cried.

Semanaw spoke again in the tongue of the whites, and the tall, husky man rose to his feet and came toward her.

"Mary Margaret!" he whispered hoarsely. "Aye, it's really you, mavourneen! Blessed Mary, it is! I'm yer Pa, sweetling! I've come fer ye, as I always swore t' do! Come, lovie, do ye not know me? D'ye not remember me a 'tall?"

Jerking her head to look up at him, she backed away like a frightened doe, cringing as she dragged a whimpering Red Wing after her. Although she saw that there were tears streaming down the white-eyes' ruddy face in the firelight, the sight stirred no pity in her breast. Rather, when he held out his arms to her, intending to embrace her, she uttered a small, strangled cry of terror and shoved her little son forcefully behind her.

Shielding Red Wing with her body, she stood before the towering white man with her fingers curled into claws, like an enraged mountain lioness defending her cub from attack.

"Get away from me! Do not touch me! I do not know you, white-eyes! You were never my father. Many Horses is my father!"

She darted a beseeching glance around the circle of faces, silently imploring someone—anyone!—to speak up for her, to help her. But all expressions were impassive and closed. Her eyes fell at last on the face of the young white-eyes, and as she gazed into eyes as blue as morning glories, and saw a smile as bright and broad as any Red Wing could summon, something buried deep in her memory stirred and flexed its wings. *Aiee! She'd seen that face before! Its owner had been dear to her once, long, long ago, she knew it!*

"Mary?" the young brave murmured softly, and he too, rose to his feet and came toward her. "You remember me, don't you, little sister? Aye, I could see it in your eyes for a second when ye looked straight at me! Don't be afraid," he urged her softly, " 'Tis Brian, your brother." He pulled open his shirt, to reveal an almost hairless chest marred by an awful scar just below the breastbone. "Ye see? I'm alive! I didn't die that day, Mary, dearling. We've come for ye like we always planned—come t'take ye home, at last!"

"What does he say?" she demanded of old Semanaw, looking wildly from one to the other.

"No!" she insisted hotly again after the medicine man had relayed the young white-eyes' words. Her storm blue eyes sparked. "I am not your sister! I go nowhere with you! Whatever you may say, it can make no difference. My home is here now, not in the wooden villages of the white-eyes. My husband is here. My son is here. My father and mother are here. Here!" She beat at her

breast to give emphasis to her words, adding in a strangled voice, "Aiee, my very heart is here! *Here*, do you understand me, lying paleface? I am of the People now," she insisted proudly. "These—" she gestured about her, "these are my people!"

With that, she turned, her braids flying, swept a startled Red Wing up into her arms, flung about, and fled the talking lodge, leaving astonished mutters in her wake.

"So. You have heard the words of my daughter, Blue Beads," Chief Black Hawk said gently when she was gone, moved by their emotion despite his lifelong mistrust for the clever yet deceptive pale faces. Tears flowed down their cheeks like the tears of women—save for the third man, the pale-eyed one, who'd remained markedly silent and unmoved by the scene. "I promised you that I would tell my son's woman why you have come here, and let her make the choice to go with you, or stay. Black Hawk has spoken truly. He has smoked the pipe in peace, and kept his word to you in this matter. For her part, Blue Beads has listened, and she has chosen. Now you must accept her decision and leave our camp."

Donovan Kelly clenched his huge blacksmith's fists in an effort to control his emotions, but his jaw worked soundlessly nonetheless, and his tears could not be staunched. They flowed in rivers down his cheeks to dampen his buckskin shirt. After all these years, he'd found her, thanks to Cap McHenry! Eight blessed years of not knowing where t' turn, or if she was dead or alive, and then three more hellish, anxious years of tracking the elusive Black Hawk band from camp to camp; three years of what had seemed, at times, like chasing shadows—an' it had all finally paid off!

Mary. His wee daughter, the apple of his eye, his Mary Margaret Rose, was alive and well, and grown in the very image of her poor, sainted mother, his own Kathleen! Aye, and with a wee son of her own now, t'boot, a lad who looked more white than half-breed! His own little grandson, i'faith, and a fine sturdy lad he was, an' all! Blessed Virgin, he couldn't give up, not now that he'd found her! He couldn't return to Agave Flats empty-handed! He opened his mouth to protest, to argue, but McHenry's steely fingers clamped around his wrist to silence him.

"Shut up, my friend!" McHenry rasped in a low voice so that even the eagle-eyed old skunk, Semanaw, couldn't hear and translate. "Whatever damn fool thing you were about t'say, stow it! Our first plan's failed, as I told ye it well might. Now it's time fer the second one. Just tell this savage old buzzard that you're grateful he let ye see the gal, but that ye must have been wrong, and we'll hightail it out o'here."

"But she's my Mary, I know she is!" Donovan groaned like a man in torment.

"Aye, we all know that. But if we try t'take her from them now, against her will, they'll flay the three of us alive! Think of your son, Kelly. Do you want young Brian killed, and my Sarah a widow afore she's scarce a bride? They have our horses, our bullets, man! What the devil could we do against so many of 'em? Now, be sensible, and cool that Irish temper o'yours! Give them the damned pack mules and the trade goods—everything. Offer them your thanks, and say we'll continue the search for your daughter elsewhere. Tell them that that old bastard Black Hawk is a good man. A Comanche chieftain of great honor whose words are true—and fer God sakes, man, look as if ye mean it, or we're dead meat! We'll get the little lass back, never fear—but in our own way and in our own time, agreed?"

Donovan closed his eyes and nodded.

Chapter Twenty-five

"Grow-ler! Growler? Where are you hiding, little brother?"

Red Wing called again and again as he trotted between the tepees that rose like a forest of broad trunks on either side of him. He wandered this way and that through the village in search of his puppy, the little yellow one Grandfather Black Hawk had given him.

The other camp dogs were everywhere, fighting or gnawing at the bones someone had tossed their way, or dozing in the mid-morning sunshine, but of Growler there was no sign, and Red Wing was growing more worried with every passing heartbeat.

Growler always slept with him. He followed him everywhere, like his summer shadow. But when he'd woken that morning, Growler was nowhere to be seen. He'd asked his mother if she'd seen his pup, but Mama had seemed tired and bad-tempered—worried about his father, who still hadn't returned home, Red Wing guessed. She'd sounded cross, and had told him to go outside and look for his puppy and not bother her, and so he had.

He scowled, thrashing at weed heads with the little stick he carried as he trudged along. Everything had gone wrong since Papa went away! Sleek Otter never wanted to play with him anymore. She stayed in her lodge all day, helping her mother with the new baby, that puny Falling Star, who did nothing but suck at his mother's breasts and mess his swaddling, he thought with disgust. Then Growler had vanished, and now his mother—who'd never acted cross like other mothers did until the paleface traders had left their camp three suns before—was as grumpy as a bear wakened from its winter's sleep.

He'd been jolted from a deep sleep himself that night, to go and stand before the council. Only half-awake, everything had seemed blurred and unreal as a bad dream, leaving disturbing half-memories that both confused and frightened him. Why had everyone stared at them so? Who had the palefaces been? Why had Mother spoken so angrily? He'd never seen her like that before! No, he didn't understand what had happened at all! He only knew that afterward, his mother had picked him up and run with him back to their tepee as if the Apaches were chasing them! She'd been trembling all over, and she'd hugged him so tight, he'd thought his bones would break! She hadn't let him out of her sight for two suns afterward—he, a big boy of three winters with the courage of a warrior four times his age! Paggh! Women and girls were such cowards, he thought with disgust, scared of the least little thing!

Stalking aloofly now as he'd seen the hunters stalk game, his bare feet silent on the grass, he left the grassy meadow and padded into the forest.

It was the ending of the Moon of New Leaves. The elm and pecan trees were a pale, fresh green. There was lush grass and pastel-colored wildflowers everywhere under his toes, and birds singing and building their nests above his head. He spotted a mule deer doe and her tiny fawn, peering at him from a hiding place of tall grasses, and he pretended to take aim at them with an imaginary bow and arrow. The doe took fright and bounded away, showing her white tail as she tried to lure him away from her young, just as Grandfather Many Horses had told him

He sighed, and looked about him, the doe forgotten as he called, "Growler! Groooow—leeeeer!" once again. But there was no joyful yelp in answer to his cry; no long, rough pink tongue swiping at his face, and huge paws pushing at his chest to knock him down in the beginning of a fine old romp. There was only the twittering of the birds, the chuckle of the waterfall, the distant laughter of other children in the camp he'd left behind — and a pup-less silence that was awful.

The trees grew closer together here, he noticed suddenly, a little apprehensive now, for he'd never strayed this far from camp before. Their leafy boughs intertwined above him. They blocked much of Father Sun's light, and kept it from shining through and making everything happy. It was an eerie feeling, walking alone through green and gold shadows, and a first twinge of misgiving pinched his belly. His heart hammered loudly, both from guilt and from fear. Grandfather Many Horses had warned him sternly about wandering off, and had told him terrible tales of what had befallen other children in the past who'd disobeyed their parents and done so.

"Little Fox — eaten up by a hungry bear!" he'd told the wide-eyed Red Wing solemnly. "Laughing Water, accidentally slain by a hunter's arrow! Toes Point In, bitten by a rattlesnake! You must never go anywhere alone, my grandson. Always take a friend with you, and never go so far from camp, you cannot be heard if you must call for help!"

But he *had* wandered off alone, and he *had* gone too far to call for help — and now he was very much afraid that he was lost! Which way was it back to the village? This way? That way? He turned full circle, and his lower lip quivered with the beginning of a sob. He didn't know which way home was anymore! Tears brimmed in his eyes, and although he knew only babies like Falling Star cried, he couldn't seem to help them. "Mama!" he whimpered. "Mama, come! I'm lost, Mama!"

It was then he heard the faintest of sounds from deeper in the forest — hiyeeaah, faint, but unmistakably the yelps and whines of his dog-friend, Growler! Sniffing back his tears, he plunged into the undergrowth, headed toward those sounds.

Moments later, he struggled out of the mesquite thickets, his bare little body crisscrossed by red scratches, and found himself in a clearing that lay in heavy shadow. He

could hear the Peewit! Peewit! of a night bird somewhere, the sound one Grandfather Black Hawk had
taught him, and absently wondered why a night bird
would be calling during daylight hours . . .

But then this thought was forgotten as he spied
Growler across the clearing, tied to a tree trunk by a
short length of rawhide and trying frantically to struggle
free!

"Growler, little brother! What are you doing here!
Who tied you to this old tree? Was it that spiteful Sleek
Otter, eh, was it?"

He knelt down to untie Growler, and at once the
puppy yelped and barked and scrabbled to lick his face,
crazy and squirming with joy to see him.

In the same moment that Red Wing reached out to
hug his puppy, two huge hairy arms went around his
waist and lifted him, struggling wildly, high into the air.
He screamed.

"It's all right, me wee boyo, it's all right!" a deep,
strange voice tried to soothe him. "Ye're safe now, ye are!
I'll not harm ye!"

But Red Wing understood not a word, and he whimpered in terror.

"Little Mother, have you seen your grandson?"

"Is he not with you and Crooked Woman? You've kept
him so close to you these past two suns, I was beginning
to fear he'd become a little husband—the kind of boy
who follows his mother everywhere!" Spotted Pony said
with mild reproof in her tone, softened by a smile of
understanding.

"I haven't seen him since he ate this morning," Blue
Beads said, frowning with anxiety now. "And neither has
Crooked Woman. Where can he have gone?"

"Not far, surely? Your father has told him many times
of the dangers of wandering off alone, and he's a good
boy. I expect he'll be in Wounded Doe's tepee, staring at

336

little Falling Star, and teasing Sleek Otter," Spotted Pony suggested.

"Nooo," Blue Beads said worriedly. "That was the first place I looked for him!"

"Then what about Small Cloud's tepee?"

"There, too. His mother hasn't seen him all day, and Small Cloud is helping the herd boys with the ponies."

Now it was Spotted Pony's turn to frown. She cast her flesher aside and stood up, wincing at the stiffness of her joints—a legacy of the past hard winter. "His Grandfather Black Hawk's lodge, then?"

"No."

"The pony herds, then? You know how he longs for a pony of his own? Perhaps he went there to look for Small Cloud."

"I have been there, and he's not with the ponies. I asked the herd boys and Small Cloud, and they hadn't seen him either."

"Then where can he be?" Spotted Pony wondered aloud. "Where else is there left to look for him?"

"I wish I knew! But—perhaps he's found a new friend in another lodge, and has forgotten how quickly time passes. You know how he is when he plays?"

"It could be so," Spotted Pony agreed readily, grateful for a less frightening explanation for her grandson's disappearance than the terrible ones that popped into her head. "I'll go from lodge to lodge, and ask everyone if they've seen him."

"And I'll search along the creek banks and the forest and see if he's there. His pup, Growler, was missing this morning. Perhaps he went there, Little Mother, hoping to find him, and forgot Grandfather's warnings?"

Blue Beads hurried back to her lodge, and took up her skinning knife, tucking it securely into her belt as was her habit now whenever she intended to leave the safety of the village.

Her lovely face tense with worry, she walked quickly, looking from left to right along the creek beds and behind every cottonwood, checking every single juniper thicket for one very small, naughty child in hiding.

As she went, she remembered how she'd snapped at Red Wing and told him to go outside and play, and tears flowed down her cheeks. How could she have been so unkind to her little son, when he was worried about his beloved puppy? She'd never been unkind before! And yet, after two sleepless nights spent worrying about the visit of the white-eyes, and still more nights before that spent wakeful on account of Wolf's failure to return home, she'd been tired and short-tempered, and her tongue had been unusually sharp, she knew.

"If only I can find you—if only you're safe and un-hurt—I'll never speak so unkindly to you again, my son!" she whispered, gazing into the ripples of the pool below the waterfall where the children always swam, but seeing no sign of either Red Wing, swimming like a slippery otter; or, as she'd dreaded, a motionless little body float-ing there. Her heart lifted with belief. That settled the matter. Either Spotted Pony had found him, or he'd gone into the forest!

The forest was cool, dark, and silent, and she shivered with foreboding. Evil lurked here—she could sense it in her bones, feel it prickling like nettles against her skin. Had that evil taken Red Wing? Her relief, so short-lived, abruptly dwindled. Oh, she must find him, and quickly, before Father Sun disappeared over the rim of the moun-tains, taking with him the light that would show Blue Beads her son's trail!

And a trail she found soon after, to her mounting dread and joy. A small heel-print beside a muddy tussock of grass; many tall weeds with their seed-tops whipped off—as if by a small boy's stick, wielded like a grown-up's quirt. Her heart began to race as she halted before a thick tangle of bushes, for hanging from a thorn on one of them was a snarled tuft of long, raven black hair.

Pee-wit! Pee-wit!

She whirled about, alarm clawing through her. A

nighthawk's cry, with the sun yet up? No! She was not such a fool as to believe that! It was the signal of one enemy, calling to another!

She drew the skinning knife from its slim suede sheath at her hip, and held it before her, moving silently into the undergrowth and twisting and turning to find a way through it and out, to whatever lay beyond. She was afraid of what lay ahead, and yet if Red Wing had passed this way, then so must she. He was her son!

As she came out into a small clearing, she heard a terrified cry that struck terror in her mother's heart.

"Mama! Mama! Help me!"

She burst out into the clearing, knife at the ready, all fear forgotten in her fury at her son's attackers. And there, standing before her, was the paleface, Don-o-van Kell-ee, with a squirming Red Wing cradled in his arms! The boy was screaming and trying to escape, but looked unhurt.

"We've not harmed the boy, Mary, never fear," a stilted voice that was somehow familiar said in Comanche behind her. "Nor will his grandfather lay a hurtful hand on him, you know that. But me—? Well, I'm not the little mongrel's grandfather, am I, and I've no softness in my heart for the half-breed whelps of the Comanche! You'll come with us quietly, Mary Margaret. Drop the knife—now!—or the child dies!"

Stifling a sob of protest, of grief, of denial, of terror, Blue Beads swung about to face the speaker. She found herself looking into the hate-filled face of Pale Eyes, the one the white men called Cap'n Elias McHenry.

"Ah! I reckon you remember me from New Mexico, eh, girl?" Cap said with a mirthless chuckle. "Somehow, I figured you might! I remember you, too, Mary, remember you *real* well—jest like I remember poor Mose, and what was left of ole Jonah, too, God rest their souls—! Now, drop the goddamned knife, and be quick about it!"

Her fingers uncurled from the elk-horn handle. She dropped the blade to the grass.

Chapter Twenty-six

Her soul was dying.

She could feel it shrivelling up in her breast like a leaf in the hot desert sun, shrinking and drying and curling in on itself like a child that dies while yet in the womb.

One day, some day, a final blow would crush it, and it would become powder; a dry, gray corpse-dust that drifted on the winds. Then Blue Beads Woman would be gone forever from the face of Earth Mother, would become one of the Star People, and she would never see Wolf again, not in this world. She'd never hold him in her arms once more, nor he embrace her in his. They'd never lie together on heaped buffalo robes under the starry sky, nor share the beautiful dance of mating that created children and bound two whose hearts beat as one together, for all time.

They would never again share smiles or laughter, or tears of sorrow, or whispered words of love, for she was lost to him. Aiee, lost as surely as if she had died; as surely as if she had vanished from the earth! The palefaces had taken her so many, many days of riding from Black Hawk's camp, he could never follow their trail. Spring rains had washed away the small signs she'd tried to leave of their passing—a bent twig here, a bead plucked from her shift there—and those the rains had missed, the one named Pale Eyes had spotted and angrily destroyed, threatening to bind her little son and herself if she didn't cease her tricks, until finally, she'd given up all hope of trying to leave signs for Wolf to follow, and let them carry her away toward the land of the west wind.

For three moons now she and Red Wing had been here, in the land the white-eyes called Arizona Territory, at a small horse ranch called the K & M Corral, a half-day's riding from the sprawling wooden village named Agave Flats. The ranch seemed to be run by the man, Donovan, and his friend and partner, Pale Eyes, the one they called either Cap or Mister McHenry.

For those three long moons, she'd been watched at every turn, allowed little privacy and no freedom, practically walled up alive most suns in a gloomy, suffocating lodge of stone and adobe bricks that, to her thinking, let in no air and precious little light! Surely she would suffocate, she'd thought at first, but she had not. No, she had not. But sometimes—oh, Great Spirit, sometimes she wished she had, and that it was over!

The first sun they'd arrived at the lodge of Don-o-van Kell-ee had been a nightmare. Although the young brave named Brian had been kind to her in his fashion and had seemed to understand something of the misery she must be feeling, his woman, Sarah, clearly had not. She'd wrinkled up her nose when she looked at Blue Beads and Red Wing, as if she smelled something rotten beneath it.

"They must be bathed at once, or I'll not have them in my clean house!" she'd said. "Why, they're probably crawling with lice and fleas!"

Although Blue Beads had not understood her words then, what had followed had made the woman's meaning clear, and her face had burned with shame. The white woman had clearly called them dirty! She, who bathed in the creek each morning with her little son as they gave thanks to the Great Spirit for the blessing of another day! She, who'd always worn clean, tidy garments that she'd cut and sewn herself, and who washed her hair in the suds of the yucca root so that it was always shiny and smelled sweet!

But nevertheless, the man McHenry—oh, how she hated him!—had nodded agreement. He'd rolled up his shirtsleeves and easily overpowered her. He, a man, had stripped her, bared her body and her dignity before the malicious eyes of that hateful Sarah-woman, before dumping her into a wooden half-barrel. Then he'd scrubbed her body with a rough bristle brush, smeared it with some foul-smelling soap, then sluiced her down with jug after jug of scald-

341

ing hot water that had burned so, she'd felt as if she'd flayed alive and the skin peeled from her body.

When they were done with their torture of her, they'd done the same to a screaming Red Wing who, much to his mother's silent glee, had bitten the woman hard on the thigh! But Blue Bead's gleeful pride at her son's bravery and defiance toward their enemies had been short-lived, however. Hateful Pale Eyes had at once upended her little son over his thigh and thrashed his bare buttocks raw with a switch, not stopping until he'd begged and wept for mercy. Little Red Wing, who—raised in the indulgent Comanche manner of child-rearing had never been beaten, and had rarely even been scolded—thrashed like a camp dog! Such treatment was only to be expected for herself, of course. She could accept and understand that, as a woman who'd been captured by an enemy. But to be so cruel to a child—aiee, it was beyond her comprehension!

When the water tortures had ended, Pale Eyes and Sarah had taken their clothing and burned it before their eyes. Tears had flowed down Blue Beads's cheeks as she saw the flames licking hungrily at her yellow doeskin shift, her leggings, her moccasins, for it was as if they were burning her past along with it, trying to erase it from her mind. But it was not over yet! The clothes the woman had given her to replace her own had been yet another great agony to bear.

Smelling sourly of another woman's sweat, she'd wondered if their owner's ghost yet filled them, waiting to work some evil mischief against the spirit of their new wearer, herself. Moreover the shirt, which buttoned high beneath the chin and had tight sleeves that reached to her wrists, was scratchy and hot. The skirt was little better. It was sewn of some heavy, itchy dark blue cloth and pinched her about the waist.

Nothing could compare, however, with what they expected her to wear beneath—long pantaloons that reached to her knees, and layers of more stiff white skirts—so stiff, they stood up all on their own like boards; black stockings with garters, and stiff, confining leather boots that hurt, oh, how they hurt her broad feet, which were accustomed to the soft comfort of moccasins!

Even her hair was no longer her own to wear as she chose. After brushing it until her scalp was afire, then drawing it back severely from her face, the woman Sarah had braided it tightly and pinned it flat against the back of her head each morning so that it gave her a throbbing headache, and made her look as ugly as she felt.

Red Wing had fared little better. Accustomed to going naked and free under the skies, he'd had his shoulder-length hair cropped short to just below his ears, in the style of the white-eyes, and his body confined likewise in clothes. He wore a pale blue shirt buttoned up to the collar that had long sleeves, similar to her own; something he called "draw-ers" covered him from head to toe beneath, and bibbed overalls. He also wore a floppy-brimmed black hat. Dressed in their paleface finest, never had two people appeared so uncomfortable nor so thoroughly miserable, she'd thought, though Don-o-van Kell-ee had seemed delighted by the results.

"Well, Father, what do you say?" the woman Sarah had asked proudly, shepherding the unhappy pair into the main room of the ranch house at supper time that first day.

Donovan's eyes had first widened, then filled with tears as he gazed at them. He'd come forward and taken Blue Beads by the shoulders, pressing his lips gently to her brow in the manner she recognised as a kiss, the way the white-eyes showed fondness for each other.

"Ah, Mary, my own wee Mary!" he'd said. "I can hardly believe it's you, and home with us again at last! Dearling, just look at ye, the spittin' image of my lovely Kat'leen! If your poor, sainted mother's looking down on us from heaven, there'll be singing amongst the angels this evenin', I've no doubt! Welcome home, mavourneen!"

He'd hugged her again, not seeming to mind that she went rigid in his arms.

"And now," he'd said, straightening up and clearing his throat, "your brothers an' sister are here, Mary, love. It's high time they saw you again."

To her amazement, the cabin door had opened, and two of the hugest men she'd ever seen trooped into the room,

343

followed by the one called Brian, and two younger children of about fourteen winters who had—of all things!—hair as red as the fire crackling in the hearth!

"I'm Patrick, Mary," declared one in a deep, booming voice.

"And I'm Mikey. Good to have ye home at last, Mary," said the second.

Both towering, burly men seemed uncomfortable when they looked at her. Their eyes slid quickly away.

"You already know me—Brian—don't ye, sis?" grinned the one with the morning glory eyes that reminded her so painfully of Wolf. "And here's young Seamus, and this is our little Bridget. She's—well, our Bridget's not been much of a one for talkin' since the day you were carried off, have ye, dearling?"

The girl only stared vacantly into space, humming a tuneless song as she rocked a grubby rag doll in her arms.

A long wooden rack had been set with platters of food; a kettle of chicken stew and dumplings, biscuits, boiled squash, and potatoes, served by a pretty olive-skinned Mexican woman named Griselda. To Blue Beads's surprise, all of the strangers had sat down at benches placed on either side of the table, men and women obviously intending to share the meal at the same time.

After a brief prayer to their God, the one called Brian had lifted Red Wing into the empty space beside him, handed him a spoon, and set a platter of savory stew before the boy with a grin and the command, "Eat, nephew!" as he ruffled Red Wing's short hair.

To Blue Beads's chagrin, Red Wing had grinned back at him and tucked in, copying the palefaces and scooping up the stew with the unfamiliar spoon as if to the manner born, and basking under their hearty praises and smiles, which were generously given, she had to admit.

Although she knew her son was still very young, and possessed of a keen appetite that needed satisfying at regular and frequent intervals, she'd been destroyed by his—albeit unintentional—act of treachery. The hurt of betrayal seething in her breast, she'd ignored the remaining empty place

344

alongside the man Don-o-van that he beckoned her to fill, flung away, and went and sat cross-legged on the floor in a corner, stoically refusing to look at any of them.

"Mary, lass, ye must eat, or ye'll fall sick!" Donovan had pleaded with the girl, taking a platter and spoon to her.

"Leave her be," McHenry barked sharply, "and see to your own supper, man. She'll eat—when she's hungry enough. Right, Sarah, my love?"

"Right, Papa," Sarah'd agreed primly, dabbing delicately at her lips, as they'd taught her was proper at the fancy finishing school she'd attended back east until two years ago. She'd smiled fondly across at her young husband, and her sharp features had softened into something approaching prettiness. "Brian, dear, some more dumplings for you?"

McHenry had been right, curse him! After five suns without food, Blue Beads had meekly joined them at the table that evening, dizzy and half-fainting with hunger, and gobbled the food set down before her like a wild animal or the savage creature they considered her, oblivious of the woman Sarah's open disgust.

To her unending shame, her hunger and her will to live—for Red Wing's sake, at least—had proven stronger than her pride.

In the three moons that had followed that first night, Red Wing had quickly adapted to the white man's ways, for he was young enough to adjust. Blue Beads no longer blamed him, nor saw her son's adaption as betrayal. Had she not once adapted herself, and become Comanche in order to survive? Then so must he learn paleface ways, unless they could escape!

Soon, Red Wing was calling the big man Grandpa—the paleface word for grandfather, he'd told her proudly—and trailing after the one called Uncle Brian, whom she admitted in her heart, at least, must truly be her brother.

Her son was starting to belong, to fit in here in the white man's world, but Blue Beads knew in her heart that she could never belong there again. As long as she lived and breathed, she would yearn for the free life she'd known, the freedom to ride the wind and to love the man she'd chosen for her mate. Although she had accepted the clothes they'd forced her to wear, although she did the chores they'd forced her to learn, and ate the food that hunger forced her to eat, they could never subdue the rebellion inside her; never confine or place limits on the endless love and longing she carried for her Wolf!

In the evenings, when the sun lay low upon the White Mountains and the crickets chirped in the grasses that grew about the house, she would go out onto the back porch and gaze out across the still, silent Mother Earth, where only the saguaros and agave, the sagebrush and junipers found root, and silently weep for him, knowing as she did so that one or other of her captors was watching her, guarding against any attempt she might make to escape. Blood kin, flesh of her flesh, seed of their seed — despite knowing that, she still thought of them as her captors — aiee, and always would!

"Who is he, Mary?" Brian asked softly one evening, stepping from the cabin door to stand beside her on the back porch, his pipe in hand. "Who is it that ye mourn for each sundown? Is your man out there somewhere, Mary, lass, searchin' fer ye and the lad? Is that who your eyes seek so sadly in the hills?"

She'd not answered him. Indeed, she'd given him no outward indication that she'd even understood what he'd said — but she had. Like Red Wing, she was relearning the white man's tongue, little by little, willingly or otherwise. Paleface words and phrases had burrowed into her mind like prairie dogs, and now popped up when she least expected them to.

"All right, then. Have it your own way, Mary," Brian had said finally with a doleful sigh. "I can't force ye to talk with me, if ye will not. I was only after thinkin' ye might welcome the chance to unburden yourself, to share your sorrows. We were always close before, you and I, Mary. Don't you remember any of that time?"

He'd started to go. Some inner sixth sense that he, of all of them, might understand and heed her wishes, had forced her to take a step after him, to halt him with her fingertips

346

plucking desperately at his sleeve.

"Please—my white—brother—please—!" she'd whispered, the English words spoken uncertainly but with unmistakable urgency.

Brian had stopped and turned back to face her. His eyes had lit up at what seemed evidence that she was coming around, judging by her efforts to speak her own tongue.

"Yes, Mary, love?" he'd asked gently. "What is it? Ye can tell me. Please what?"

"Please—make—them—let—us—go!" she'd managed to choke out, her voice strangled, her eyes brimming pools of misery.

A knot had formed in his throat. Oh, the poor, poor lass! She was begging him to free her, to let her return to the Comanche brave who'd lain claim to her heart, the one who'd fathered her child! Brian swallowed. He wished with all his heart that he'd resisted Sarah's wiles and pleas for him to wed her, and her father Elias McHenry's urging that he marry the girl; that he'd waited 'til he'd found someone he could love as dearly, as loyally, as Mary loved her man.

"Aye, I know you're hurtin' sorely, lass. But—I can't do it, I'm afraid, Mary," he'd told her regretfully. "I can't let ye go. Ye see, our Pa's been only half-alive since the Apaches killed Ma and took you from us that day. Just a pale shadow of the laughing, lively man he once was! He always blamed himself for her death and your capture, you see—for going gold-panning an' leaving us unprotected. He's spent the last twelve years or so searchin' for ye, off and on. Why, Mary, when he saw ye in Black Hawk's camp, he smiled for the first time in years! So ye see, lass, if I were t' let you go now, why, it'd break his heart, for sure!"

And it will kill me if you do not! she'd echoed silently, and turned away to hide her sorrow.

She never spoke to him in the white man's tongue again.

Chapter Twenty-seven

When she and Red Wing had been with the whites at the K & M Corral for four moons, Donovan Kelly took them into the settlement of Agave Flats with him, along with Sarah and the youngest twins, Seamus and Bridget. They were to buy supplies, he told them, winking at Red Wing.

They rode a sturdy wagon the nine miles into town, Donovan driving the hardy mule team while fourteen-year-old Seamus cradled one of the rifles across his lap, keeping his eyes skinned for Apaches as they journeyed. Two of the K & M's ranch hands rode ahead, while two brought up the rear. All were heavily armed. Eleven years had changed many things, but not the continuing threat the savages posed to the white men who lived in the region. The ones who survived and even flourished in the Arizona territory were hardy souls who did so by never letting down their guard—and even those sometimes perished.

Blue Beads's apprehension grew with every revolution of the wooden wheels over the rutted tracks, but her fear was not caused by the threat of attack by Apaches, but by the knowledge that every turn of the wheels was bringing her closer to the white man's village, and closer to the decision she would soon have to make between the life of a white woman returned to her people and her family, and that of a woman of the Comanche, held prisoner by a very real, if largely benevolent, alien people. Could she ever bring herself to accept the possibility that the past eleven years of her life were gone forever, and that that life could never be hers again? Should she try to live it as best she could, and allow her son to become a white child? Or—should she continue to pray to the Great One that somehow, against all odds, Wolf would come for them, and free

348

her from her captors?

She stared ahead, seeing nothing, her expression outwardly devoid of emotion, although her thoughts teemed. Not even the brilliant blue of the sky or the green verdure of the beautiful, pine-forested White Mountains rising to the east could bring her pleasure, not without her freedom, not without the man she loved!

You will be my woman forever! he'd told her once as they lay together in a nest of fallen leaves, wrapped in the dreamy magic that comes after lovemaking. *Even when our spirits leave Mother Earth and join the Star People, we will never be separated. Our bodies may return to the winds from whence they came, yet our love will never die! We will shine brightly side by side in the heavens, and our children, and their children, and their children's children will look up and see us there. They will wonder how two little stars can shine so brightly, all others pale beside them. . . .*

Sometimes, he felt so close, so very close, it was if he were nearby somewhere, and she had only to reach out and touch him, to call his name, to find him there beside her. It was longing that made it seem so, she knew that in her deepest heart. But it was comforting to close her eyes and imagine she could heard the low vibration of his voice against her ear, so deep, so filled with manly strength; comforting to remember the whispered promises he'd made her, and all the silly, wonderful things he used to say in those quiet times, and believe he could make them come true.

"The Great Spirit brought you to me. From the first, my skinny lizard, you were meant to be the woman of the White Wolf Who Walks Alone!"

"But you are no longer alone, Osolo, my husband. You have me! Our feet share the same path along the trail of life. Now you must change your name, must you not?" she'd teased him gently, stroking his copper-skinned cheek and watching how his bright blue eyes sparkled like falling water in the sunshine.

"Not I," he'd retorted with a wicked grin. *"No, it is you who must change yours! I will give you another name. I think I will call you Mate of the White Wolf."*

"Pah! And I will not answer when you call!" she'd vowed, shaking all over with laughter. *"You may have my body and my heart, my husband — but my name is my own medicine."*

"What are you thinking, Mother?" Red Wing asked.

The memories blew away. They scattered like the seeds of a dandelion puffball as she heard his voice, blinked, and realized her son was staring at her curiously.

She patted his cheek as she'd once caressed his father's. "Only that it is almost the Sun Dance Moon, my son, and that we will not be there in the summer circle to see the ceremonies this time," she told him in their Comanche tongue.

"Oh!" he said with little apparent regret, and with a shrug turned back to his Grandpa Kelly.

So bright, but so very young! she thought sadly. Already his little mind had accepted their new life, and was rapidly beginning to forget the old. Like a blanket of snow spread across a meadow in the mid-morning sunshine, the footprints he'd made during his first three moons of life were melting away. He made new footprints now, in a new blanket of snow that was a fresh new life, and she could do nothing to change it . . .

Her hands, clasped primly in the lap of the new flower-sprigged navy dress she'd been given for the special outing, tightened their grip upon each other. She squeezed them together until her knuckles turned white, in the effort to quell the wail of hopeless, tearing grief that suddenly filled her breast.

Grief? Aiee, truly, it was grief she felt! In that moment, she wanted nothing so badly as to be allowed to grieve for the man and the life she had lost; to hack off her hair, to slash her cheeks and breast wide open in the way of the People in mourning, and by so doing release the bitter gall of heartbreak along with her blood. She wanted . . . she wanted . . . but, oh, what good did wanting do one, but serve to deepen the agony? Wanting could change nothing. Instead, her mind must choose another path — one that led to somewhere else but madness! She must concentrate on the little trail that lay ahead of her and think only of this sun, and how she would get through it. She must forget the choices she had to make, forget all the other suns that yet lay ahead of her, and instead take each sun as it came. If not, the weight of the future would prove unbearable.

Looking down, she realized that her hands were sweaty with nervousness. What would it be like, she forced herself to wonder, to walk among so many palefaces? And how would they respond to her? Would they stare at her with their colorless eyes and point and call her names? Would they openly condemn her for living willingly for so many years among the "Injun savages" they so despised? Aiee! She couldn't begin to imagine an entire village filled with nothing but white-eyes, and nor did she want to! In truth, the idea terrified her.

For his part, however, Red Wing seemed more excited than apprehensive, she noticed. Wriggling about on the driver's perch between the big man and the one called Seamus—who he'd named Little Uncle—he was asking his grandfather so many questions, the patient man finally exclaimed with a pretended scowl, "Why, t'be sure, Rory, me boyo, curiosity killed the cat, did it not?" They called him by the paleface name Rory, Red Wing had carefully explained to her, because it meant red in their tongue—the closest they could come to his Comanche name in their colorless language.

"Aye, Grandpa," Seamus cut in with a grin at Red Wing, "but satisfaction brought it back, did it not, Rory?"

"Ah, but ye've a smart tongue to yer mouth, young Seamus, tho' I dare say you're right! How's a boy t'learn unless he asks questions, eh?" And he'd ruffled Red Wing's dark hair and Seamus's red locks in the same affectionate manner that Brian always displayed.

"Do you think it was wise to bring her to town with us today, Father?" Sarah asked, jerking her pointy chin in Blue Beads's direction.

"By *her*, I take it ye're after meanin' me daughter, Mary Margaret, lass?"

"Why, yes, Father," Sarah acknowledged. "People, however well intentioned, can be careless with their words, and

351

many of the citizens of Agave Flats lost loved ones in the massacre that took my mother and your dear Mrs. Kelly, or have done in others since then. At heart, they've nothing but contempt for women who've lived among the Indians, however unwillingly the poor, unfortunate creatures might have done so." She chose her words delicately. "Sh— Mary's only been—home—with us for four months, Father, and in all that time she's made no effort to adapt. It's obvious she wants nothing so badly as to go back to those dirty, murdering savages, and would as soon kill us all in our beds one night as to try to fit in! I wonder if—if she's truly ready to meet outsiders so soon?"

The rude way the young woman had, of talking about her as if she wasn't there, or at the very least was some dumb animal who couldn't possibly understand what she said, infuriated Blue Beads. She glowered at Sarah with murderous storm blue eyes until hectic color rose up Sarah's fish-belly white cheeks, staining them like red ink spreading across a blotter.

"She's my daughter, Sarah. My flesh and blood. I love her! Would ye have me hide the lass away, like some shameful freak, as if all that happened t'her were her own doing? No! The girl has nothin' t'be ashamed of, t'my thinking. She was a child when they took her, and she did the best she could, Sarah. She *survived!* Where's the sin in that? Our true friends are Christian folk, an' they'll be happy for me, an' treat her kindly. As for those that don't . . . !" He grimaced. "Well, those hurtful, mealy-minded old sods can go t'the divil, for all I care! It's none o'their blasted business who I choose t'have in me own house, after all, is it now?"

"But she had a—a child, by an *Indian!* What will decent people say about us?" Sarah wailed.

"Say? Why, I don't care what the bloody hell they say, woman!" Donovan erupted, his face turning ruddy. "And as her brother's bride, neither should you, missie, I'm after thinkin'. This is Kelly business, and none o'theirs! Geet up there, gal!" He slapped the reins over the horse's rump, and the wagon picked up speed, rocking violently as it careened down the hard dirt trail.

After which Sarah, who was nobody's fool and knew when she'd gone too far, fell silent, and kept her opinions to herself for the remainder of the drive to town.

They drove the wagon to a strange place, rattling between tall adobe walls and into a village built in rows. The lodges were all built of wood and stone and mud bricks, like the Kelly's ranch house, though there were also several clapboard houses and storefronts, their wood grayed almost to silver under the fierce Arizona sun.

The place they finally halted before was huge, and like nowhere Blue Beads had ever seen before—or so she thought at first, looking around her curiously. They'd driven inside the yard of the enormous wooden building where the curious new-moon-shaped metal shoes were fastened to the hooves of the white-eyes' ponies. She guessed this much, for no one said anything by way of explanation, but there were many horses corralled behind the building, and many of the strange metal shoes on racks against its inner walls. And little by little, as she continued to gaze around her, she realized that, after all, the place had a strangely familiar feeling to her. The air was rich with evocative smells from her distant past that stirred long-forgotten memories; leather and saddle soap, horseflesh, and the honest sweat of men unafraid to work, and work hard. She remembered the red hot glow of the furnace fire, the strident ringing of the hammer on the anvil, the sound of neighing horses. She must have spent many happy times about such a place in the forgotten years of her childhood!

To her surprise, her brothers Patrick and Mikey worked there, she soon discovered. They came out to greet the new arrivals, blinking against the harsh sunlight after the ruddy gloom of their working place. Their shirtsleeves were rolled up to expose hairy, burly arms, and leather aprons covered their fronts—to keep away the sparks from the furnace, she guessed. They greeted her in the shy, formal way of strangers that she'd come to expect from them, and introduced her to two plump, pretty young women—

one fair-haired and one darker—and a handful of little fire-haired ones whom she correctly guessed must be their wives and children—and therefore her nieces and nephews—who'd brought them something to eat in the cloth-covered baskets they carried.

Soon after, the women smiled, said their good-byes, rounded up their lively brood, and left for something called a quilting bee, followed soon after by Donovan Kelly and young Seamus, with Red Wing riding high and gleeful on his grandfather's massive shoulders.

They were going, Red Wing yelled over her shoulder, to see a man about buying some new fire-sticks. Meanwhile, Blue Beads was left alone with the woman Sarah, and the silent girl, Bridget, who appeared as frightened by their excursion as she was, she noted, glancing at the girl's pale, apprehensive face.

"Well!" Sarah exclaimed, her lips pursed in annoyance. "It would seem that despite Papa Kelly's lofty words, I'm to be the one to bear the burden of parading you two about before the town! My lord! A witless child and half-savage hellion!" She clicked her teeth. "What will folks think!" She lifted a wicker basket from the rear of the buckboard and turned to the pair with a look that spoke volumes. "Well, come along, if you must—and no dawdling, mind!"

After a moment's hesitation, Blue Beads slipped her hand into Bridget's slender one behind Sarah's back. She smiled. "Come, little silent one. We will hold hands, yes?" she said softly in Comanche. "And if we must be afraid, then we will be afraid together! Fear and joy are like honey, yes? Better when shared with a friend!"

So saying, she led the girl after Sarah's swishing skirts and the military clip of her heels, trying to make her own uncomfortable high-heeled button boots obey the directions of her feet, and wishing she wore moccasins.

A broad, dusty dirt street ran through the settlement, flanked on either side by peeling clapboard or whitewashed adobe buildings that baked in the summer sunshine. Among them was a sheriff's office, a general mercantile, a bank, an undertaker's, a gunsmith's, an assayer's place of business, and a rooming house, as well as the smithy and livery stables run by the Kellys. There were also three busy saloons; the Lucky Lady, the Paloma, favored by the Mexicans, and The Cactus Juice Café, the seedy establishment preferred by the less upstanding citizens of Agave Flats. From the latter's swinging door, tinny piano music and loud laughter erupted in rowdy bursts. Here *vaqueros*, disreputable-looking miners, outlaws, gamblers and drifters, the town neer-do-wells, and a number of "soiled doves," gaudy doxies with painted faces and feathers in their hair and their bosoms half-uncovered, could be glimpsed within as they passed.

Sarah kept up a brisk pace, striding along with her blond head held high. She seemed oblivious to the rude and curious stares the pair trailing in her wake were drawing, offering the townspeople a curt, "Good morning!" and an incline of her bonnet as she swept on down the street.

Meanwhile, Blue Beads's face was burning with mortification as she sensed the hostile stares of the white-eyes they passed, some of whom pulled up short and gaped at her, with no attempt made to conceal either their curiosity or their contempt. They scared Bridget, too, and her grip on Blue Beads's hand tightened to a stranglehold that almost made her fingers numb.

"Why, that must be Donovan Kelly's eldest daughter!" the vicious whispers said. *"I'd heard they found her in Texas!"*

"Found her, aye—and had to drag her home by force, to all accounts! Can you credit that? She didn't want to leave those filthy animals!"

"Well, no decent man'll ever take up with her now, not after what she's been done to. That Donovan Kelly's dreamin' or crazy, he thinks otherwise!"

"Had a redskin's bastard, too, t'all accounts."

"A child—? Why, you don't say! Any decent, Godfearin' woman would have smothered a babe fathered by a—a dirty Injun—at birth!"

"Why, that's just exactly what I said, Miz Travers, but there ain't no accountin' for. . . ."

It went on and on without end, and never had a walk

seemed longer or harder than it did to Blue Beads that day.

By the time Sarah whipped into the general store, her skirts flying out behind her in her eagerness to escape into the gloom and hide from the malicious eyes and sharp tongues of the townspeople, her ears were nearly as red as Blue Beads's face.

"Bridget, dear, come inside with me, right this minute. You," she said sharply to Blue Beads, with a look that threatened hell to pay if she disobeyed, "will stay right here—and don't you dare move so much as an *inch*, girl!"

She grabbed Bridget by the hand and yanked her into the general store after her, leaving Blue Beads outside alone, like a dog set to wait for its master.

Standing there, her head bowed so that her face was hidden by the coal-scuttle bonnet she wore, Blue Beads's heart thumped painfully against her ribs. Her knees hurt and her bladder felt full. Her mouth was dry, and her belly churned. And, although she stared at the dusty toes of her boots and looked neither to left nor right, she could still feel people approaching, pausing, and inevitably, stopping; could feel their pale, hate-filled eyes boring into her.

"Well, howdy-doody, lil' Miz Squaw-missie!" jeered one of the rowdy drinkers who'd ambled over from the Cactus Juice saloon. "You speakum white man's tongue?"

She said nothing, gave no sign that she'd even heard him, but her heart was beating so hard and so fast now, she could hear its thundering in her ears.

"What's wrong, Miz Kelly? Ain't white men good enough t'say howdy to, after them fine, upstandin' red-skinned gennelmens yore used ter?"

"Aw, leave be, Paulie! She's done got herself a taste fer that red meat by now, and ain't no white man what's gonna 'peal t'her now!"

"I surely will leave her be, Saunders, I surely will. See, I'm mighty partickler about my women, and you jest can't rightly tell where this here one's bin, if you catch my meanin'!"

The group of lowlives whooped, and the prim and

proper, back-stabbing townswomen tut-tutted—then snickered behind their lily-white hands.

"Well, you speak for yourself, Paulie. For myself, I surely would like t'get a peek at her face, at least—jest t'see if she's awearin' any war paint!"

Guffaws of laughter followed his outrageous statement as Bowers, a short, stubby man with mean little eyes set amidst a welter of pudgy flesh, peeled away from the rest. Thumbs hooked into his belt, he swaggered cockily across the dusty street toward the trembling girl, who cowered in the shade of the clapboard building like a frightened animal.

With a grin, he shoved back the brim of his Stetson and gingerly reached for the string of her bonnet. Playing to the spiteful mood of the small crowd that had gathered to watch the fun, he slowly pulled the bow loose and flipped the hat away. It fell off and tumbled to the dirt, rolling away like a tumbleweed and exposing her face.

The crowd gasped, for they'd not expected Donovan Kelly's daughter to be such a comely young woman—especially not after all she'd been through. It just wasn't *fair* one of the younger women thought. She had no right to look so—so darned *comely*, not in her situation!

Meanwhile, wild-eyed as a cornered mustang filly, Blue Beads jerked away from Bowers's fingers, stark terror painted on her face. Further retreat was impossible, however, for the wall of the general store was behind her, and Bowers in front. Arms outstretched and flattened on either side of her, head forced back, she looked as if she'd been crucified—or at the very least was trying to melt into the wall and disappear.

"Mite skittish, ain't ye, squaw-honey?" Bowers crooned, reaching out a calloused knuckle to stroke her cheek as he played to his eager audience. "Seems t' me you should be used t' being touched an' such, purty lil' thing like you."

His voice had become a husky, breathless rasp. His small eyes glittered like the cold, unwinking eyes of a snake. "Why, them red bucks musta been all over you, ain't that right, missie—? All over, all kinda *heathen* ways?"

he murmured slyly, winking at the crowd as he ran his hand down over her shoulder in a gesture so familiar, so bold, so — so *intimate*, that some of the watching women came close to swooning, and had to fan themselves with their bonnets. But they kept right on watching nonetheless, uttering not a single word of censure.

Bowers moved to plant his hand on her waist, taking his eyes from her drawn white face to wink lewdly at his audience.

"I knows we ain't bin introduced proper, honey, but might I take the liberty of jest one lil' kiss — ?"

It was a mistake, that moment's inattention, and it cost him dear!

So fast, it was later described variously as a rattler striking, or as "greased lightning streaking down out o' the sky," depending on the source, Blue Beads's hand moved in a pale gold blur for Bowers's waist. Smooth as silk, she whipped the knife from his belt, and brandished it before her.

"Get back! Leave me be, paleface dog!" she hissed in Comanche, her lips drawn back from her teeth in a rictus of fear. Her dark blue eyes were blazing like crazy stars. "You very evil man! I know this! Touch Blue Beads Woman one time more, she kill you!" she added awkwardly in his tongue so there'd be no doubt she meant business.

With a collective gasp, the onlookers fell back. Bowers paled to the color of a winding-sheet, and appeared little more substantial. He held up his hands in surrender, wetting his lips nervously.

"Hey, girl, hey, see here! I didn't mean nothin'!" he whimpered, warily watching her knife hand as if he expected a streak of silver to come flying his way any second, and impale his sagging belly. "Honest, I didn't! I was just — just kiddin' around!"

"Then ye chose the wrong lass to kid with, did ye not, ye worthless scum!" boomed Donovan Kelly's voice, and the crowd parted like the Red Sea to let the girl's father through.

The former blacksmith strode to stand before the man, cutting an imposing figure with his muscles bulging beneath the cloth of his shirt and the black leather vest he wore over it. He gripped Bowers by his shirt lapels, and without apparent effort lifted him clear off the ground, driving a meaty fist up beneath his flabby chin to further elevate him. Bowers flew up, then back, before landing in a lardy heap in the powdery dirt, rubbing his chin and spitting blood and teeth from his broken jaw.

"This young *lady* happens t'be me daughter, Mr. Bowers, an' I'll thank ye to treat her with respect. D'ye understand?" Donovan inquired with deadly civility.

Shaken, Bowers nodded.

"Then seein' as ye do, me foine surr, we'll be after having an apology from ye, I'm thinking, Jedediah."

"I—" Bowers gulped, his mean little eyes darting every which way.

"Come, come, hurry it up now, boyo, before I'm minded t' practice me fisticuffs on ye again! It's been a powerful long time since I boxed the best back in County Cork, an' had me a good old set-to. I'm rarin' t' toe the scratch an' begin!" He scowled, rolled up his sleeves, spat on his palms, and clenched his beefy fists, obviously ready to do just that.

"M-m-my ap-p—pologies, ma'am!" Bowers managed to mumble through a gobful of pink spittle and teeth, and after several weighty seconds, Donovan nodded in grim acceptance of his efforts.

The former blacksmith looked about him, his blue eyes fierce and narrowed, his legs braced apart, his huge fists planted pugnaciously on his hips.

"As fer the rest o' ye," he began, "Why, ye should be ashamed of yerselves, pickin' on me wee frightened colleen, here! And you call yerselves Christians? The divil y'are! Go on about your business, ye shameful louts, and be done wi' your gawpin'!"

The shamefaced townsfolk wasted no time in doing as he'd urged. One by one, they scuttled away.

When the crowd had cleared to the last man—and

woman—Red Wing tore free of Seamus's restraining hand on his shoulder and ran from the doorway where his grandfather'd instructed them to wait, racing to his mother's side. He flung his arms around her knees and held on tight. "Mama! Mama! I thought the white-eyes would kill you!" he sobbed uncontrollably.

"Aiiee, hush, my son, hush! I'm not hurt," she reassured him, slipping the knife down the front of her dress into her bodice, then caressing his dark head. A wary glance at her father over Red Wing's head convinced her that he'd forgotten the knife, if he'd noticed it at all, and would not question its disappearance. "I was just a—just a little frightened."

"Me, too, Mama, me, too! Oh, please, Little Mother, let us leave here? Let's go, this very sun! I don't like it here anymore! I want to see Papa again!" he whispered as she lifted him into her arms and hugged him. "I want Papa—and my grandfathers, and Grandmother Spotted Pony, and—and I want to go home!"

"So do I, little Wolf Cub! Aiee, so do I!" his mother whispered fervently against his cheek as she held him tight and their scalding tears commingled.

Another moon dragged by; another moon in which Blue Beads grew thinner and thinner, until her cheeks were hollows and her eyes ringed with lavender. She never smiled anymore, except for Red Wing's benefit; she never spoke, except to her little son or, strangely, to the young girl Bridget, who'd taken to watching her sister with a fond expression that was almost a smile. Like a shadow, Blue Beads did her tasks about the house and the yard, yet everything she did now, she did by rote, and without a shred of joy.

Her father—watching the bloom of youth and beauty wither from her cheeks—began to despair, and to question his former optimism that one day, his little Mary'd be herself again. He was gradually forced to accept the possibility that Mary—the little Mary he'd cossetted as a child—was gone forever.

One night in early fall, as the menfolk sat about the hearth discussing the German settlers who'd arrived in Agave Flats that morning, only to be quarantined outside the settlement's walls on account of the sickness rampant in their wagon train, and while Sarah applied herself to her mending, they all heard the mournful howl of a wolf, echoing across the flats.

Over and over it uttered its full-throated cry, raising prickles of unease down their arms.

Sarah dropped her sewing and sprang to her feet. "Dear God in Heaven, that terrible creature sounds so close—far too close for comfort!"

McHenry, Brian, and Donovan exchanged startled glances, but only McHenry reacted. He reached for his rifle. "It's probably just a hungry old wolf after the new-born colts, Sarah. A birthing and the scent of fresh blood always brings them down from the hills. Calm yourself, gal. Brian—you go check on Mary Margaret, will you, son, while I go check on our wolf," he ordered ominously, and went outside. *Wolves?* he thought grimly as he went, *Goddamned Apaches more likely than not . . . !*

Brian went out onto the back porch, and saw that his sister was there, as indeed she was each and every night as the sun went down. But this time, instead of standing there, straight and still and with the enormous dignity she possessed, her fingers were clenched over the split railing before her. Her head was thrown back as she looked up at the vermilion-streaked sky, as if in a jubilant prayer of thanks.

"Mary—?" Brian said sharply, alarmed by her stance. "Mary, colleen, what's with ye?"

At once, she spun around to face him, startled by his voice. And in that brief, unguarded moment, Brian saw the wild, boundless joy that filled Mary's face and lit her eyes, and was stunned to the core by its blazing radiance. A scant second later, the look had fled as if it'd never been. Her face was again a lovely mask: composed and utterly devoid of expression.

361

Without a word, she averted her eyes, brushed past him, and went back inside to the room she shared with her son, leaving her brother staring out at the empty foothills — and wondering what had made her look that way.

Chapter Twenty-eight

Blue Beads's twentieth birthday was also the twelfth anniversary of Kathleen Kelly's, and Rachel and Dane McHenry's death. It fell in the moon the white-eyes called August. Donovan and his sons and daughters and daughters-in-law dressed in their sombre church-going clothes and rode in the buckboard to the site of the massacre, the adobe ruins of Fort Agave, which lay some distance outside the settlement. McHenry drank himself into a stupor.

Many crudely fashioned wooden crosses and heaps of rocks marked the spot where the massacred dead had been hurriedly laid to rest that fateful day, just outside the crumbling, weed-choked ruins. It was about these graves that the Kellys and others who'd ridden out from the town for the memorial service congregated, to hear the minister offer prayers for the souls of their loved ones, and to lay wildflowers upon their resting places in remembrance.

The crumbling ruins filled Blue Beads with feelings of melancholy and unease, and she was relieved she'd not brought Red Wing with her.

"There's no need for the boy t' come, colleen," Donovan had told her gently that morning, seeing how tense her expression was, and how her usually deft hands trembled and were clumsy as she started to get him washed and dressed for the services. "He's too young t' understand, anyways. Let the wee lad stay home with young Hans and Wilhelm and the other hands, and play with that great yellow hound of his, as a child should!"

And so she'd left Red Wing in the company of the big blond German youths whom Cap McHenry had hired just last week to help with the heavy work around the horse ranch. Hans, the younger of the two, was a cooper by

363

trade, as had been his father and grandfather before him. He was gifted at carving, too, as well as making barrels. Ferocious bears and wolves from the Black Forest appeared from solid blocks of fragrant white pine under his magical, stubby fingers. Rabbits and perky squirrels frolicked over pine-scented meadows of curly wood-shavings. Goats and sheep ambled in fields of sawdust between tiny fences made with a careful, loving hand, and a huge drayhorse with feathered hooves and massive rump pulled a cunning little wagon with barrels of beer. At the moment, clever Hans was half-finished whittling a white pine copy of Red Wing's dog, Growler, who'd grown from gambolling pup to a huge shaggy beast in the few moons they'd been here, and her fascinated son had been anxious to watch Hans finish it. Gratefully, she'd let him stay at the ranch under the watchful eye of the serving girl, Griselda, and now wished—at least in some ways—that she'd not come herself.

She could sense that many spirits still clung to the crumbling ruins, tied to this place forever by the horror of their deaths and mutilation at the Apaches' hands, unable to take the Star Road to the white-eyes' afterworld. As she stood in the blinding sunlight, long-forgotten memories came rushing back to her. She heard the whispers of the lost ones rustling in her ears.

"Mary Margaret, shame on ye . . . stop that dust raisin', ye hear me? came her mother's reproachful murmur.

"Happy birthday, Mary Margaret! Many happy returns!" she heard Dane McHenry's whisper

I should have been with you! a little voice nagged in her own mind. *I should be one of you now, not here, living and breathing! What was so different about me? What gave me the right to survive, and no other?*

Her flesh crawled until she managed to shrug off the weighty cloak of guilt that surviving such a terrible disaster had burdened her with, and let reason return. She was here because the gods had willed it. She was here because that sun had not been her sun to die. There was no blame in that, no reason for guilt, she told herself with a sudden,

364

fierce gladness to be alive that had evaded her since they'd come here.

People stood quietly in groups of two or three or quite alone, and their expressions were distant as they, too, remembered that day long ago, and maybe heard the whispers of their own ghosts.

Perhaps more than any of them there that day, she understood all too well why they'd come here, the need that drew them, for despite her reluctance to return, she'd known the same need. She'd gone out early that morning while the dew was still wet, and had picked a bunch of late-blooming golden desert poppies, as she'd seen the others doing the evening before. It was the paleface way of mourning and remembrance, this giving of beauty in the form of flowers, and it was thus the dead lived on—in the hearts and memories of the living.

And so, after the minister had ended his prayers, and the other mourners had stepped forward one by one to place their flowers atop the heaps of rocks and faded wooden crosses, she waited until the last of them had moved away, and then defiantly did likewise.

As she did so, she could hear the slow tolling of the church bell carrying from the township, and was suddenly glad she had not stayed away, and missed this chance to say a last farewell.

Her feelings had nothing to do with either Donovan or the Kellys' urgings to accompany them, she reflected, setting her own wilted offering atop the massed blossoms. This was her own token of respect and sorrow, in remembrance of the sweet-faced, over-worked woman she vaguely recalled as the source of all strength and love and comfort for the little girl she'd been back then—more a feeling of security and warmth than a true sense of remembering the woman herself.

Her younger sister Bridget shyly moved to do likewise, giving Blue Beads an uncertain smile as she dropped her little posy onto the heap. She looked like a frightened wild thing, poised for flight at the first sign of danger.

Blue Beads started to smile back to reassure her—but

suddenly heard an ominous rattling sound, coming from the sun-warmed rubble nearby as her younger sister straightened up and turned to walk away. In her mind, that sound meant only one thing!

Sure enough, as she whirled about, she glimpsed the snake, a diamond-backed black streak slithering through the grass. As the rattler struck, it leaped toward the girl like a whiplash of silver black fire!

In the blink of an eye, the stolen knife had cleared Blue Beads's bodice and flashed through the air, but it found its target—the rattler's head—just a second too late!

Bridget screamed in panic and pain. She toppled, clutching at her ankle, and the onlookers reacted in confusion.

"God in Heaven! She tried to kill Bridget!" Sarah's voice rang out, louder and more accusing than all the others. "She tried to stab her!"

"Someone stop her!" cried another panic-stricken woman. "For the love of God, get the knife!"

The mourners surged forward with an enraged buzzing sound like furious hornets, their remembered grief adding fuel to their fury now.

Donovan Kelly shoved his way between the angry mob, thrusting aside the grim-faced townsfolk who were fast bearing down on his daughters, one of whom crouched over the other protectively.

"Mary, girl, no! Are ye mad? Have ye taken leave of yer senses!" he roared, and reached for her shoulder to fling her back, away from Bridget.

It was only then that he saw what her body had concealed from him—the black coil of a rattler lying in the sere yellow grass, its wicked head skewered to the ground by a knife—and the purple marks and white mottled swelling where its fangs had sunk deep into Bridget's calf above her boots.

His ruddy color paled. He drew off his hat and knelt beside them. "Sweet Jaysus and Mary, no!"

"What is it, Pa?" Sean and Mikey demanded, hurrying alongside to loom over them.

" 'Tis our Bridget! She's bin snakebit, an' it looks real bad t' me, lads! Ride for Doc Sullivan, sons, ride jest as fast as ye can!" he urged, drawing his knife from his belt as he drew up his daughter's skirts to bare the wound. He wetted his lips anxiously, finding both them and his mouth suddenly dry with fear. The accepted method of dealing with snakebites—cutting an X across the site of the bite and sucking the poison out—was chancy at best, and no guarantee that his wee girl would survive. But what else could he do? Time was everything in a moment like this!

For their part, his two sons needed no second urging. They were racing for their horses even as Donovan turned back to the child and Mary, his knife in hand, his palms slick with sweat. "Blessed Mary, guide me hands!" he prayed, crossing himself, and bent over his daughter's leg.

"No! Give me knife!" Blue Beads hissed urgently to her father, holding out her hand and fixing his blue ones with her own.

Without hesitation, he gave a small nod and handed it to her, and her heart filled. Her white father trusted her! His actions proved as much!

"No, Father! Don't! Surely you can't mean to put another weapon in her murdering hands?" Sarah exclaimed in horror, pushing her way through the circle of onlookers to reach them. "Isn't one attempt on the poor child's life enou—"

"For once in your life, shut up, Sarah!" Brian snapped curtly, brushing past his wife to kneel alongside his father. "Can ye not see, the wee girl's been snake-bit? Mary only tried to stop the rattler from biting her—not to kill her, ye stupid woman!" he gritted in obvious contempt and no little embarrassment at his wife's foolishness.

Bridget moaned, and Donovan Kelly drew up the hem of his youngest daughter's skirt once again and saw how swollen and puffy her leg had become in just a few moments. Blessed Mary, the venom was travelling like wildfire through her veins! When it reached her heart, she'd die, sure!

"Ye'd best hurry, mavourneen!" he whispered. "Whatever

it is ye're intending to do, best do it fast!"

He saw then that Blue Beads's throw had pinned the rattler's head to the hard ground. It still thrashed its coils, alive, but helpless. Blue Beads rose off her heels and went to kneel by the serpent.

"What the divil are ye after doing, Mary?" Brian exclaimed, horrified despite himself as Mary sliced a portion from the impaled snake's body and quickly split it lengthwise. Opening it out like a filleted fish, she returned to Bridget and clamped the snake-flesh poultice over the wound, holding it there for several minutes.

When she drew it away, the white flesh had turned a pale, sickly green, much to their amazement. The onlookers gasped and murmured surprise as she held it out to show Donovan Kelly, before tossing it aside.

"The—slithering-one's—evil—it go back—where come from!"

With her explanation, her father nodded and squeezed her shoulder. "Aye, lass, I understand! Do what ye can for her, dearling, while I bring up the wagonboard t' take her home when ye're done."

Brian watched as Mary repeated her curious treatment time and time again, until almost all of the rattler's flesh had been used up and had turned from creamy white to poisonous green as it drew the venom from Bridget's body. The swelling on her calf was already greatly reduced now, they saw, and Bridget even managed a wan smile for her savior, who returned it warmly.

As Donovan came to tell them the wagon was alongside, Bridget reached up and gently touched her older sister's face.

"Thank you, Mary!" she said softly, tears in her bright blue eyes. "But then, you always took good care of me and Seamus. You saved us that day, didn't you? I remember it all so clearly, did you know that? You hid us inside the barrels and made us be quiet, but the 'Paches took you away, and we never saw you again! I remember it all as if it were yesterday!"

For the first time since that terrible day twelve years

ago—when her very life had depended on her ability to stay silent—Bridget Kelly had spoken! And, when she'd finished speaking, she wept.

Blue Beads looked up into her father's face, and saw that tears were streaming down his cheeks, down the cheeks of Brian and Seamus and yes, even down Sarah's, who'd been watching them and listening to their touching exchange.

Blue Beads picked up Bridget's hand and gently but firmly placed it in her father's, folding his sturdy, calloused fingers tight about her sister's.

"What is it ye're tryin' t' say, colleen?" he asked, his eyes searching her face.

"This sun, Don-o-van Kell-ee's second daughter come back to him," she said softly. "Something once lost is more precious when found again, yes?"

He nodded gravely, swallowing the giant knot that choked up his throat. "Aye, lass, it is that!" he acknowledged. "Doubly precious!"

"I give you back little sister's life," she reminded him, handing him back the knife by its blade. "Please, Don-o-van Kell-ee, my white father, can you not do same for—for me?"

Bridget passed a day or two in bed following her brush with death, and then was declared well enough by an astonished Doc Sullivan to get up and resume her normal life.

"It's nothing short of a miracle, Kelly," the doctor said, shaking his head as he walked out onto the porch with Donovan. "The flesh taken from the rattler itself worked the cure, ye say? By t' saints, that's a new one t' me! You're damned lucky Mary was there, friend, and knew what Indian remedy would serve! If not, your Bridget would be with the angels . . . But just look at the colleen now—! Why, my friend, she's a changed girl!"

The young woman that rose from her sickbed to join the family was indeed far different from the Bridget they'd known. Though still very quiet, Blue Beads's actions had somehow released her from her terror of speaking after all those years of silence. She spoke to them shyly now, and even smiled once in a while—a smile that her father loudly declared rivaled the sun coming up each fine morning, as he bussed her pale, freckled cheeks in his boisterous, affectionate way.

Sarah, for her part, was astounded by the events at the ruins, and undecided now if Mary were a saint, or a witch! Until she'd settled the matter to her own peace of mind, she gave her sister-in-law wide berth; a circumstance that suited Blue Beads very well.

And then, just a week after Bridget left her sickbed, they heard the eerie howl of the wolf from the foothills of the White Mountains again, even closer this time.

"Damn that savage's soul!" McHenry growled. "I'll stop his damned howling fer him!" He reached for his rifle, but Donovan Kelly stopped him.

"I'll see to it this time, Eli," he said with a voice and a look that brooked no refusal. "Set yerself, down, man."

Scowling, McHenry returned to the fire.

Donovan took his hat from the peg by the door and stepped outside into the night.

As he'd expected, Mary was on the back porch, and his grandson was with her. As he watched, his daughter ducked under the railing and lifted Red Wing down after her. Hand in hand, they started across the dirt yard, stealthily headed for the open gate in the white rail fence that enclosed it.

As the pair passed within feet of him, Blue Beads sensed his presence in the shadows, and turned to look at him.

The breath caught in his throat at the joy—the wild, beautiful joy and love—he saw in her face. In that moment, she looked as his Kate had once looked, on the day they were wed.

She opened her mouth to say something, but he stepped from the shadows and pressed his finger across her lips.

"Nay, mavourneen, there's no need fer words between us, not anymore. By God, your eyes say it all! Go to him now, lass, and quickly, before that damned McHenry comes!"

He kissed her brow, then lifted the lad for a farewell kiss, hugging him tightly before setting him down beside his mother.

"God be with ye, dearlings—both yours an' mine!"

With that, he stepped away.

"Run!" Red Wing's mother told him, the joy singing in her voice like a bow string vibrating. "Run like the wind, my son!"

And then they were running, the two of them racing hand in hand across the yard and through the gate; young woman and little child flying across the moon-washed desert, headed toward the inky blackness of the foothills; headed toward the lonely howl of the white wolf . . .

Brian, watching from the back door that led out onto the porch, realized too late their true intention.

"Mary, no!" he cried softly. "Come back here!"

Cursing his stupidity, he leaped over the porch railing and started running for the corral, thinking to mount up his horse and bring them back.

But he'd taken only a stride or two when a meaty hand snaked out of the darkness and clamped over his shoulder.

"No, Brian lad, no!" came his father's rough voice. "Leave well enough alone, an' let them go!"

"What?" Brian was aghast.

"Aye, ye heard the rights of it!" Donovan rasped hoarsely, and Brian heard the tears that choked his voice, along with the conviction. "Let them go, I say! Enough is enough."

"But Pa—why? Ye've spent a dozen years searchin' after our Mary—!"

"Aye, I did that, didn't I? And I found her, too, thanks to Elias McHenry," Donovan agreed, his eyes glinting mistily in the starlight. "But, Brian, me boyo, sometimes a man gets what he pines for, only t' find it ain't what he really wanted a' tall."

"You didn't want Mary back?" his son asked incredulously, confused.

"Oh, aye, I wanted her, right enough, God knows I

371

did—an' still do. I love the lass, Brian, ye know that! But—more than that—as her father, I needed more than anythin' else t' know that she was safe and happy, after all those years o' frettin' about her! Like a fool, I thought once she were home with us, she'd be both. But I was a fool, Brian, and terrible wrong," he said with a huge sigh. "I finally saw that me little Mary'd never be happy, not so long as I kept her apart from her man. Her will t' live was dying, son—could ye not see it in her eyes, dwindling inch by inch and hour by hour? And so," he shuddered with emotion, "I decided t' prove my love once and for all by—lettin' her go! I decided that if my wee, lost lamb made a run for it, I'd close my eyes and let her run—and say nothin' to Eli.

"Ye see," he continued, "it suited the bitterness and hate inside McHenry t' have the lass kept here, away from the man she loves. Ah, lad, he's a terrible bitter man, is McHenry. It's eatin' him alive, his thirst fer revenge, drivin' out all the joy and happiness he could yet find in his life, if he looked fer it! He couldn't stand that Mary'd taken up with the Indians, after what those Indians did t' his woman and son. He didn't help me t' get her back out of Christian kindness alone, no sir, make no mistake on that score! It were partly to punish her, too, for darin' to love one of their kind! But I—oh, I never wanted to hurt her, Brian, and I couldn't let it go on! So now, Mary's gone, and I can rest easy, knowin' it's what she wanted all along, and that she's happy.

"There's a time t' hate, son, but there's also a time when a man has t' forgive and forget and get on with his life. In pinin' after my wee Mary, I've neglected my other little Irish rose, me own wee Bridget. Mary—well, she made me see that. She gave the girl back to us, lad, an' I don't intend t' forget her lesson again. Ah, now, will ye look at that!" he exclaimed suddenly.

Brian turned in the direction his father had nodded. He saw now that the silhouette of a solitary Indian warrior, astride one pony and leading another behind him, had broken away from the dense blackness of the foothills, and ridden boldly out into the open. Moonlight fingered the ghostly white patches and mane and tail of his horse, and the white plumes he wore in his hair, which fluttered in the night wind.

And, as the pair watched, they saw the warrior dismount and open his arms to embrace the woman they'd called Mary.

She went into them like a ship sailing safe into harbor after a storm, clinging to him fiercely, briefly, before he tossed her up onto the back of the second pony. Then he leaned down and lifted the child, hugged him, and tossed him high in the air, before setting him on his own mount. Then, lithely, he vaulted astride the paint pony and sat there, his head turned in their direction.

For a moment, as he sat his horse as still and quiet as if the two of them were carved from obsidian, it seemed as if the brave was staring straight at them, his eyes piercing the night. They could feel his gaze upon them, could almost feel the Comanche warrior's boundless pride and innate dignity, tangible in those breathless seconds. And then, he slowly raised his arm in salute.

Donovan Kelly stepped forward, and solemnly returned the gesture.

Then, like shadows, both ponies and riders vanished into the light.

The hackles rose on both Donovan and Brian's necks as they heard the howl of a wolf ringing out across the desert soon after, splintering the hush. But this time, it was neither a lonely nor a mournful sound.

It was a high, yip-yipping howl of joy and triumph. The howl of a wolf who'd regained his lost mate!

Chapter Twenty-nine

"It took so many moons for you to find us, Papa," Red Wing complained a little accusingly, as they rode through the silver and black shadows of the starlit night.

Boulders gleamed alongside the old Indian trail that wound through the foothills of the White Mountains, ivory as jumbled heaps of bleached bones where the silvery gray light touched them. Tall blond grasses were bled an ethereal ashy white by the Old Woman of the sky.

A badger scuttled away from their ponies' hooves, and a nighthawk screamed as it swooped over the desert floor in search of prey. An owl glided overhead, its wings a drift of snow, its cry hooting and mournful as any earthbound spirits. But other than for these nocturnal sounds and the thud of their ponies' hooves, the world lay wrapped in stillness.

"I knew you'd come, but—why did you wait so long, Papa?"

From her pony alongside them, Blue Beads laughed softly. The low, sensual sound floating on the hush of night stirred her husband beyond measure. It brought back fond memories of other nights when she'd laughed in just such an earthy, seductive way as they played the mating game! For now, though, he held his lusty memories firmly in check, for after all, there was Red Wing to consider. Later, when their son slept, she would learn of White Wolf's loneliness and longing for his woman; would know firsthand of his great desire, made all the sharper and fiercer by lengthy separation and, at times, seemingly endless fear for her safety! But for now, there remained a question to be answered; one he could not, as a man of honor, avoid. He had been called to account by his little son, and account he must!

Wolf chuckled and clasped Red Wing still more tightly to his chest, as he guided None Swifter up the steep mountain trail, turning his pony's head to the little camp he'd made amongst the whispering pines several suns past.

"When I returned to our village," he answered the boy, "I was told of your disappearance. I went in search of your trail, and deep in the forest, I found your mother's knife, and the single print of a metal moccasin—the ones the white-eyes fix to their horses' hooves. I had been told by your Grandfather Black Hawk of the coming of the pale-faces in search of your mother, and so I knew then what had happened and who had taken you, and I tried many times to follow the path of the palefaces' horses.

"Other clever hunters and trackers joined me—Little Cougar, Rolling Thunder, both of your Grandfathers and others—but we failed! Mother Earth is broad and beautiful, but Red Wing and his mother are very small, you see, and small things are always hardest to find. Worse, the spring rains had washed away even the smallest sign of your passing, and so I and the other warriors returned to our village empty-handed. My heart was heavy, my son, for I was afraid I'd never see either of you again . . ."

"Or Growler," Red Wing piped up insistently. "You musn't forget Growler. He came with us, too, you know, Father?"

"Ah. So he did. How could I forget your faithful dog-friend!" Wolf agreed with a smile that made his teeth flash white in the starlight. "So tell me, little warrior, where is this fierce yellow beast now?"

"I left him behind for . . . for Grandfather Don-o-van to keep. I brought this wooden Growler with me instead. Look, Papa!" He held out a pine carving of a pup with its head cocked to one side, stained and lovingly polished to the color of golden oak by the German youth, Hans, just for him. A yellow beast indeed! "Grandpa will miss me, I think, but with Growler for his friend, he won't be so lonely, will he, Father?" Red Wing added in a small voice that trembled.

"No, my son," Wolf agreed gravely. "He will not.

Growler will remind him always of Red Wing, his true grandson, and they will speak of you often with pride and love in their hearts. It was a brave thing to do, my son, leaving Growler behind to lessen the pain of parting for the man Kell-ee. It was the noble act of a far older warrior, and my heart is filled with pride in my son!"

Embarrassed yet elated by his father's praise, Red Wing tucked the carving under his arm, and snuggled closer to Wolf. "What then?" he coaxed after a few moments of silence. "What happened after you found no sign to follow?"

"Then I returned to our village. I spoke with Grandfather Black Hawk and Semanaw at great length. I told them what I had seen, and that I was certain the palefaces had taken you away. From them, I learned that the white men had come from a village in the land of the setting sun. My father said the one named Don-o-van Kell-ee had talked of a white-eyes' settlement, built close to a place of the long-knives, where your mother was kidnapped by our enemies, the Apache, many winters ago. So it was that I guessed in what direction they had gone, and I turned None Swifter's head to the west wind.

"I rode for many, many suns without end, crossing the desert lands of the Staked Plains, where even our People fear to go in the moons of high summer. From there, I moved on, still riding westward, always looking, always searching for a small warrior and his little mother. But— there are many white villages now, so many! And I did not know to which of them they'd taken you. It took me many moons to find the right place, but at last I did so, close to the land of the Black Mesa, where I myself was born to the Hopituh . . ."

There was no comment in answer to his words. Wolf fell silent as he realized that his son had fallen fast asleep. His little head drooped now against Wolf's chest, and his fist was clamped tight around his father's finger, as if he feared to release it and risk losing him again.

Wolf turned to look at Blue Beads and grinned. His teeth were white against his shadowed copper-skinned face. His raven dark hair caught the moon's light in a bluish sheen, and his blue eyes gleamed.

"Our little one sleeps," he observed in a low, wicked whisper that made her heart skip a beat. The timbre of his voice left her in no doubt as to what thoughts filled his mind; what plans he had made to fill their son's sleeping-time!

Even in the patchy light, Wolf saw color fill her cheeks, and how her hands grew suddenly clumsy and lost the braided horsehair rein that guided her pony. He had to swallow the bubbling urge to laugh aloud with the sheer, boundless joy and relief he felt at having her beside him again, as she struggled to regain the rein.

"So he does," she agreed in a low, even voice that betrayed nothing of her thudding heart, her trembling body, her longing.

"And Wolf and his woman have many nights to make up for, no? . . ."

"Yes, we do," she acknowledged, darting him a nervous glance then looking quickly away.

"The night grows chill. The manroot of White Wolf seeks a warm place to hide himself. Does Blue Beads know of such a place?" he asked boldly, wickedly, each sensual word dripping into her ears like honey dripped from a comb to arouse her further.

"I do, aiee, I do!" she said huskily. Then a teasing smile twitched at the corners of her mouth as his wicked grin broadened confidently. "There are knots in the trees, are there not, my husband? And the burrows of the prairie-dog are everywhere!"

He scowled, the cocksure grin vanishing. "You know it was no such place I had in mind, but a softer, more pleasing one!" he protested, shifting uncomfortably on his pony's bare back, for his arousal was marked now.

"It was?" she came back innocently, and with a trill of silvery laughter that caused his rigid manhood to buck in response.

"Yes," he said grimly. "As soon you shall learn, my teasing one!"

They made the remainder of the short journey in

breathless silence, each pricklingly aware of the other, until finally Wolf reined in his old stallion in the heart of a tiny clearing.

The place was circled by giant pines. They stood dark and tall, and reminded Blue Beads of an enormous tepee. The circle of trunks were the lodgepoles that towered all around them. Their furry needles formed a thick lodge cover to keep out the wind. The rushing sound of water promised a spring or a small mountain river nearby.

Dismounting with Red Wing cradled in his arms, he told her sternly, "You will wait here, my woman. Wolf will return for you."

She waited obediently, quietly sitting Badger and watching as Wolf carried their sleeping son to a bed of young pine boughs, and set him gently down upon it. Tenderness filled her as he drew a robe over the child against the chill night air, then touched his cheek, watching him sleep for a few long moments before turning to a heap of kindling nearby and crouching to light it with the strike-a-light that hung from his belt.

When the fire was crackling, he returned to her, striding soundlessly across the small clearing; moving with the lithe grace of a stalking panther. His black hair swung to and fro over his gleaming bare shoulders. The white eagle feathers that dangled from his braided scalp lock stirred with his movements. His antelope breechclout flapped against his strong thighs.

Desire flooded through her as she watched him draw nearer, for never had any man appeared so handsome, so dear, as Wolf in that moment! The blood began to sing in her veins. Her heart leaped like a fish snapping at dragonflies above the surface of a lake. The tips of her breasts tightened, tingling almost painfully.

His eyes holding hers eager captives, he slipped his arms beneath her and lifted her from her mare, striding back to the fire with her carried in his arms, as if she were a captured prize from an enemy camp—as, in a sense, she was!

Sparks were flying from the crackling fire. They showered up into the night as the flames licked greedily at kindling laden with resin. The orange embers danced in the night breeze, like fireflies swirling against the black and somber pines.

"Well? Do you still bid me find a tree to ease my manhunger, woman?" he growled against her ear as he lowered her to a second heap of pine boughs, softened by another robe, in the circle of its light and warmth.

Her skin rose in tiny, tingling bumps of awareness and excitement as his hot breath filled her ear, followed by the damp, tickling invasion of his tongue.

"Will you surrender, or must I take you by force, and teach you your woman's place beneath me?" he demanded arrogantly, every inch the marauding warrior.

"What can a woman answer, when a brave is so very strong, she cannot escape him," she whispered seductively, her voice a husky purr as she stroked his cheek and jaw and trailed her fingers down over his muscular shoulders and chest. "Sparks fly from your eyes like those from the fire! Truly, you are burning with lust — and I tremble to anger you by refusing. Come, my beloved, I will show you a warmer hiding place for that which is . . . cold!"

Smiling invitingly, she knelt before him and drew the pins from her hair, shaking it loose about her shoulders in a rich, dark cascade. While he watched, his breathing shallow, she turned, and indicated the hooks that fastened her calico gown from behind, asking his help in removing it.

Fingers clumsy with lusty impatience, he began loosening the unfamiliar fastenings one by one. But when his progress was slow, and the hooks and eyes still defied his eager fingers, he grew impatient. Drawing his skinning knife, he uttered a curse under his breath and slit the garment from neck to hem!

The calico fell away, and he grunted in satisfaction as he reached around his woman's body, expecting to stroke her bottom. But his anticipation quickly became dismay as he realized that there were other layers to her garments — far too many of them for his liking!

His thwarted expression in the flickering firelight was

comical on one such as he, and made her giggle. Standing, she unfastened her petticoats one by one, and let them fall in a snowy heap at her ankles, before stepping gracefully from their ruin. Clad in only her camisole and drawers, she stood before him.

"Yet another?" he groaned. "Paggh! I am like a hungry hunter, who must yet skin his kill before he feeds his belly!" he grumbled. "Another layer—and how many after this, by the Great One? Surely the white-eyes men must spend their seed on the ground, before they can mate with their women!"

"Ah, but this 'game' can 'skin' itself, mighty hunter!" she promised, her storm blue eyes sparkling in the light.

She gripped the hem of the hand-embroidered camisole, lifted it over her head, and tossed it gleefully aside. It fell over a small pine bough, and hung there, stirring like a banner in the breeze. Her pale breasts appeared like creamy moons, jiggling a little with her exertions. They were as full and womanly as he'd enjoyed since the birth of their son, the darker peaks standing taut and proud upon full mounds the pale hue of yucca blossoms. She let him feast his eyes for just a heartbeat longer, and then pulled the ribbon bow of her drawers free. They slithered down her hips and thighs to pool at her ankles. Kicking them contemptuously aside, she padded gracefully the two steps remaining to White Wolf's side, then slowly knelt before him. Taking his hands, she drew them to her breasts, her eyes drowning in his as the emptiness and longing of the past moons washed over her.

"Enough playing!" she begged. "My body aches to join with yours!"

She reached out to caress the hard ridge at his loins where, even through his breechclout, she could feel the burning heat of his member. She drew his hands from her breasts down to the soft dark fleece between her thighs, guiding his fingers to the moistness there so that he would know the truth of her words. She'd wanted him for so very long, she'd been ready to mate with him even as she ran across the desert into his arms!

Wolf needed no second urging.

She shuddered as his fingertips delicately stroked and fondled her velvety petals, grazing the tiny swollen bud of her passion between them before slipping deep within.

She gasped uncontrollably and cried, "Aah, Wolf! Wolf! My blood is afire! Take me, take me, beloved one!"

He lifted himself astride her, his mouth playing over the swollen peaks of her breasts as she took his length in her palm and guided him home, pressing his swollen lance to the warm sheath he'd teasingly craved.

With a powerful lunge of his hips, an arching of her pelvis, they came together in a fiery explosion of passion! She opened to him, her love enormous, her desire as fierce and lusty as his. Embracing his lean flanks with her thighs as he rode between them, she arched her body upward again and again to meet his thrusts.

He lifted her. He opened her. He filled her. He plunged deep and swift, thrusting again and again. The urgency of their coupling, the spirited ardor of their movements, made sensual slapping sounds on the hush as bared flesh met bared flesh in joyous abandon. Their mouths met, too, in searing kisses. Their lips remembered old, beloved textures and old, beloved tastes as they meshed together, enjoying feverish little nibblings and sucklings and pressings. Hungry for the taste of each other, they kissed—and kissed—and kissed again, as if unable to quench their raging thirst for each other. Five, almost six moons, spent apart—aiee, they had so many nights to make up for—!

Mouth to mouth, full, aching breasts to hard chest, pliant hips to lean, hard flanks, they mated, giving voice to their passion in contented little grunts and breathy, sighing gasps and mewing little moans. They were all the words needed—for now.

In moments, the agony of their separation, the joy of their reunion, had spiralled their passion to towering heights. Rapture trembled on rosy wings but a heartbeat away!

He clamped his fingers over her upper arms, gripping her so fiercely, so passionately, she felt the bite of his thumbs bruising her flesh. But then the fleeting discomfort was forgotten as he thrust one last, glorious time, and grew taut and still with his rigid body suspended over hers.

The cords stood out like bowstrings down his coppery arms. Sweat beaded his brow and upper lip. More poured in runnels down his throat as a rasping, roaring cry of pleasure tore off his lips.

Blue Beads, too, grew tense as a bowstring beneath him, and then, wordlessly, through the sudden stillness, they felt the wonder of that magical moment together. Felt the full and boundless beauty of creation as his seed leaped from his manroot, its quicksilver tremors filling her with his man-essence, planting it deep in the welcoming, fertile velvet of her womb.

The butterfly contractions of her womanhood answered his pulsing shaft as her body accepted his gift, and drew it deep inside her.

"Aaaaah, my love! My dear one!" she gasped, and held him tightly as the wave of rapture moved through, then over her, leaving her spent and languid in its wake.

His eyes slid closed as he rested his head upon her shoulder. His body slackened with exhaustion. "A child, my woman," he murmured softly. "I prayed for a child from this first mating after so many moons spent apart!"

"And I!" she whispered, her moist eyes shining. "Oh, Wolf, so did I!"

The night wind moaned about their pinetree lodge deep in the mountain forests. Fall was here, and already winter snapped at her heels. The breath of the wind had teeth to it.

Wavering between sleep and waking beneath a thick buffalo robe, Blue Beads heard the soughing of the pine boughs all about them, the creaking of their topmost branches as the wind tousled hem. She burrowed deeper against her husband's body and curled herself protectively about little Red Wing, whom Wolf had carried to sleep

382

between them for warmth after that glorious mating.

Her heart was overflowing with happiness as she embraced her two beloved sleeping ones. She and Wolf were together again, when she'd feared them lost to him forever. Their son was a fine, handsome boy; one who would someday be a brave to bring his parents great joy and pride in his self and in his achievements. And, if the Great Spirit smiled upon them, a new life would quicken from their joy-filled mating this night! Perhaps a girl-child, this time? What more, she wondered dreamily, could any woman ask for . . . ?

But as she slid gently into sleep, a vague, disturbing memory—one almost, but not quite forgotten— stirred in her drifting mind.

It was something . . . something . . . that had happened two suns after little Red Wing's birth . . . yes, that was it. Now, what was it that had scared her? Stirring restlessly, she remembered seeing her mother bending down to pick something up from among the roots of the cottonwood that had grown beyond their lodge that winter circle; a blue-and-yellow beaded something that was almost hidden by her mother's broad brown hand. Spotted Pony's face had paled and looked frightened as she inspected the object, Blue Beads had thought, and her guilty expression as she saw Blue Beads watching her from within the tepee had made her wonder what on earth it could be that she'd found to cause such a horrified look.

"Little Mother? What do you have there?" she'd asked, coming to the lodge flap and poking her head out.

"What? Oh, it is nothing, daughter, nothing at all," her mother had answered quickly, thrusting that something behind her back.

Now what, Blue Beads wondered with a vague feeling of unease as sleep finally claimed her, had made her recall such a silly, meaningless moment . . . ?

It was agreed between Wolf and Blue Beads the next morning that they would remain in the warmer if unfamiliar western lands until winter had come and gone. Their journey back to the camp of the People at this time of year would be a long, hard one, lasting until the snow moons covered the face of Mother Earth with a blast of white, or blizzards howled across the open plains. Lacking pack ponies and a lodge cover, warm buffalo robes and other necessary supplies, it would be foolhardy to attempt it themselves, let alone with a little child in tow. With the first spring thaw, they'd return to Black Hawk's band, they promised Red Wing, expecting him to be satisfied with their decision.

Yet, to their surprise, the child greeted their announcement with scowls and tears, rather than his usual good-natured smiles and easy acceptance.

"But I want to see Grandmother," he whined. "And my grandfathers, Many Horses and Black Hawk! Sleek Otter will have forgotten me by now, Mama, and so will Small Cloud, I know they will! Please, Father, let's go home now?" he fretted. "If not, I'll never see them again!"

"Don't be silly, little one, of course you'll see them in the spring!" Blue Beads insisted gently. "Grandmother—well, she's not so very old, and neither are your grandfathers. Our Old Ones are all healthy and strong, even Aunt Crooked Woman. They'll be there, waiting for you, in the Moon of New Leaves, and will wonder at how tall you've grown since they saw you last!—"

"No, Mama, no! I want to got home now!" He'd persisted stubbornly, stamping his little foot in a rare fit of temper.

"My son forgets himself, and speaks rudely to his mother," Wolf reminded him sternly. "If he is wise, he will not forget again!"

Red Wing's lower lip jutted mutinously, but his father's piercing look and angry expression silenced whatever he'd intended to say. "I am sorry, Mother," he said grudgingly, and whirled away to run and hide his tears.

By the bed of pine boughs where they'd slept, he found his carving of Growler. Hugging it to his little chest, he stomped across the clearing, finding a place to sit and play as far from his parents as was possible without going into the forest alone. That lesson had been well learned!

Blue Beads's mouth twitched with the urge to laugh, for he'd looked so much like his father when crossed as he scowled and stomped away, he'd seemed like Wolf in miniature. "Truly, my husband, he is your cub!" she observed.

Wolf, however, was far from amused. His scowling expression was little less disagreeable than his small son's.

"It would seem to me that he has been too long without a father's teaching," he said softly so that Red Wing could not hear him. "I fear my son has been too much in the company of women, and has learned their pouting ways instead of the ways of men."

"What? No! It is not so! In Don-o-van Kell-ee's lodge, there were more men than women!" she protested, "and your son was their summer shadow, following them everywhere!"

"Perhaps it was so," Wolf allowed reluctantly. "But the ways of the paleface braves are strange, and their knowledge and example of little value to a trueborn son of the People! Perhaps I will take our young one hunting with me today, and remind him of his Comanche blood?"

When Blue Beads nodded agreement, Wolf took up his quiver and long bow, and slung them over his shoulder. He crossed the clearing, coming to a halt a short distance from his son.

"Our parfleches are empty, and soon our bellies will be likewise if someone does not go out from our camp to hunt. But—it is a lonely thing, for a man to hunt by himself," he remarked softly in the oblique way of the People. "Better two hunters than one! Perhaps—perhaps the son of White Wolf will go with him?"

Red Wing looked up, and his blue eyes glittered fiercely with excitement and joy in his pale gold complexion. Vivid color filled his cheeks of a sudden. "He will come," he agreed solemnly, trying to contain his pleasure and behave as a full-grown warrior would as he approached his father, but there was a skip to his walk.

White Wolf nodded, keeping his expression serious.

"Bring up our pony-friends then, my son, while I offer prayers to the spirits of our prey—medicine chants that will make our hunt successful, and thank the four-legged-ones for the lives they will sacrifice on the arrows of White Wolf and Red Wing!"

Father and son returned from their hunting shortly after Sun had climbed to his highest point in the heavens. An antelope buck was slung across the back of Blue Bead's mare, Badger, while Red Wing lolled wearily before his father upon old None Swifter, slumped against Wolf's chest. The excitement of the day's hunt must have exhausted him, his mother thought fondly as she hurried to welcome them back to camp.

"Ul-ul-ul-ul-ul!" she trilled as the women had trilled in Black Hawk's camp when a hunting party returned with a fine kill. "Welcome back to your lodges, mighty hunters!" she sang out, greeting them as if they were truly great providers upon whom an entire camp depended for food. "We will have full bellies tonight, thanks to the cunning of Red Wing and the wisdom of White Wolf! And fine skins to make warm robes for—"

"Wait, my woman," White Wolf cut in tersely, and she realized suddenly that he was grim and unsmiling as he reined in None Swifter alongside her. "Your praises must wait. Our son has a sickness-spirit within him!"

"He is sick? But from what—?" she cried, the merriment fleeing her face. Concern filled her as Wolf lifted Red Wing and leaned down to place him in her arms, for he was limp and heavy.

"Mother," he murmured hoarsely "Mother, I'm so thirsty . . ." Quickly, she carried him to their fire, and lay him gently down upon the bed of pine boughs beside it. She drew off his paleface shirt and breeches, and took the carved dog from his arms so that she could examine his little body properly from head to toe.

Frowning, she discovered that there was not a mark on him anywhere, nor any sign of either injury or insect bite or poison, and yet—his limbs felt so hot and dry! She touched his cheek, his brow, and found them also burning to her touch. Why, his cheeks were red, as if stained with berry juice. And when they fluttered open, she saw that his blue eyes were glittery and bright—*too* bright, to her mind!

"He has a raging fever-spirit within him," she muttered, knowing Wolf had hobbled the horses and was hovering at her elbow now. A great knot of anxiety rose up her throat, lodging in her gullet like a trapped fishbone. "And we have no *shaman* here, nor healing herbs to give him! What must we do, my husband?"

She lifted her face to Wolf's, her dark eyes huge with fear.

He placed his hand upon her shoulder and squeezed it comfortingly. "Do you remember a time when I lay burning with fever, close to death from the poison raging in my blood?"

She nodded mutely. "I remember."

"The spirit of the white wolf came to me in my fevered dreams. It told me that it was time to go with it, and that I should follow. As a gray mist, my spirit escaped my body, and started after the wolf, and yet, my woman would not let me die! She called me back to her. She gave me her strength, her courage, to fight the sickness-spirit. She bathed me with cool water and made a sweat lodge to rid my body of the poison, then bandaged my wounds with poultices of white clay taken from the creek bed. She had no medicine man then, and yet my woman healed me with her love and caring! You and I together are a match for this sickness-spirit. Our love combined will heal our son!"

"I pray that you are right!" she whispered, gathering Red Wing into her arms and cradling him against her breast. If it took but love to heal him, he would survive, she vowed.

Chapter Thirty

Red Wing's fever climbed higher and higher in the next two suns. He tossed and turned on his bed of pine boughs, thrashing as if he fought with demons.

From the depths of his delirium, he begged for water, or called for his mother and father and the grandparents he loved, both Indian and white.

Sometimes, it was as if the Old Ones were gathered about him, visible to his eyes only. Then he would smile and laugh and call to them, his eyes following their movements in a way that made the hackles rise on Blue Beads's neck. Once, he asked Many Horses if he'd soon have a pony of his own, and smiled and clapped his little hands as he heard him answer yes, although his parents heard nothing. Another time, he implored Grandfather Black Hawk to tell him just one more story, "Just one more, before I sleep, pleeease, Grandfather . . . ?"

At other times, his fever brought nightmares rather than dreams. Then the little boy screamed with terror, calling on Wolf to save him from the Thunderbird's cruel eyes and wicked talons, or from the sharp fangs of a mountain cougar three times the size of a pony. He whimpered and flailed his small clenched fists, and in his terror his strength was so great it took his father, holding him fast in his wiry arms, to keep him from hurting himself by falling into the fire, or from leaving the confines of the lean-to Wolf had fashioned them from pine boughs to break the chill winds.

In such moments, even his mother's loving arms and her kisses, her soothing words and lullabies, could not lessen little Red Wing's terror, nor close his starting, horror-filled eyes on the awful sights they saw, for the monsters teemed in his head. Blue Beads could only hold him and rock him, back and forth, back and forth, endlessly rocking until the bad dream ended, or he fell once more into a heavy, unnatural slumber; one so deep and still, that at times it seemed to her anxious eyes like the endless sleep of death.

Blue Beads never left his side, except to answer the calls of nature. She bathed his dry, burning little body with cool compresses of mountain water, which Wolf brought her from the river's source high in the rocky peaks. Crooning tenderly, she swabbed him from head to toe, and gave him sips of fresh water to drink when he moaned that he was hot and thirsty.

When he whimpered fitfully of the pain in his joints, she massaged his arms and legs with bear grease, as she'd once done when he was a tiny baby to make him grow straight and strong. When he shivered violently and complained of the cold, she placed warmed stones against his back, hoping their heat would also lessen its hurting, for he sobbed and clung to her and told her that his back pained him, too. Yet nothing she did seemed to give him ease for long. Even the water she managed to slip between his lips, he'd started vomiting back up.

"We are losing the fight, my husband!" Blue Beads whispered wearily. "Perhaps our love is not strong enough? Or perhaps the sickness-spirit is simply *too* strong. Whatever we do, its evil powers will take our baby from us!"

"No!" Wolf denied, gritting his jaw. "No!" His blue eyes flamed. "Red Wing is the stronger. He will win the struggle, I say! Is he not the son of White Wolf? The grandson of a mighty chief?"

"He is. But—but he is also just a little boy, my husband! A cub of less than four winters, with a very great sickness inside him! How can a small boy fight such a strong fever-enemy? How—?"

She broke down and wept, and Wolf put his arms around her and drew her against his chest, stroking her hair. "Be strong, my dove, be strong, if not for me or for yourself, then for him. He will survive this—I know it!"

Yet there was a dampness in his eyes even as he said the

words, and Blue Beads saw it, and remained uncomforted.

That night, Wolf insisted they take turns to watch over their little son, and feed the fire that kept the chill and the wild mountain animals at bay. He'd spotted the paw prints of a grizzly along the muddy riverbank the day before, a huge male. He knew that in this Moon of Red Leaves before the snow moons when the Big Ones slept, they were often ill-tempered and liable to attack without provocation.

Consequently, he announced that he would stand the first watch, commanding her in a stern voice and with a stern and frosty glint in his eyes to do as he ordered and try to get some sleep. To his thinking, his woman was perilously close to falling ill herself from exhaustion. The moons they'd spent apart had taken their toll, and she no longer seemed strong of spirit. Pining for him, for her freedom, had left her thinner than he remembered, he observed tenderly, wishing it could have been otherwise. Now this new heartache, this fresh worry coming so soon after the unhappy times had seemed well and truly behind them, had quickly drained what little strength she'd regained. Her face, though still lovely, was gaunt and pale. Her eyes were ringed with dark shadows from lack of sleep, and filled with such terror, he could not bear to look in them. He knew if he did, he'd see unspoken questions there—fears he couldn't bring himself to answer, or even dare to guess at.

Accordingly, he let her sleep far longer than she'd wanted him to, waking her only in the darkest hours before dawn of the following day, when his own eyes threatened to close.

As Blue Beads kept her lonely vigil beside her son the remainder of that night, she heard the spitting snarl of a cougar from somewhere close by. Gazing into the darkness, she flinched as she saw a pair of amber eyes staring unwinkingly back at her; cruel and hungry eyes. Gingerly taking a blazing brand from the fire, she held it aloft. Tense in every muscle, she held her breath and waited for the snarling cat to come bounding toward her from the shadows with fangs bared and claws extended. But to her relief, it never came.

A rose pink dawn broke at last. Birds woke. They fluttered and warbled in the forest all about her. A skein of wild geese passed overhead, their formation an arrow, loosed from the bow of the Sun. Another day had been born, but what would the next nightfall hold, she wondered? A turn for the better and their beloved son restored to them, his sickness dwindling? Or the bitter heartache of his loss?

Rousing herself fully from where she'd sat cross-legged for most of her vigil, Blue Beads stood and stretched her cramped muscles. Yawning hugely, she stumbled to throw fresh kindling on the glowing ashes of their fire, then knelt to pour water onto clean cloths—her discarded paleface petticoats, salvaged and ripped into serviceable lengths.

The wet cloths in hand, she knelt beside her son, planning to bathe his face and hands while she sang him the blessing song. They'd sung the song together each and every morning since he'd begun to talk, she remembered fondly, mother and son hand in hand, giving thanks for the gift of another day, and for the Sun's warmth and light. Would he be there in the moons to come, she wondered, her lower lip aquiver, to sing the song with her again . . . ?

The wan, early morning sunshine fell only fitfully between the dense pine crowns as she sang in a husky, broken voice from a throat that had wept too many tears. Yet even in the muted light, she could see the new, angry redness of a rash that mottled Red Wing's cheeks and brow, and his chest and belly where the covering had fallen away from him. The song died on her lips. The wet cloth fell unnoticed from her trembling hands.

With a harsh sob, she tore the robe away, her eyes searching, searching, terrified she would find the thing she dreaded most upon him.

"Aieeee!"

She gasped. Her eyes slid closed. Her heart faltered. It fluttered like a butterfly with broken wings as her last hope died.

Beneath his shoulder was a boil-like pustule, huge and swollen with yellowish poison! The first—but not the last, no, not the last, she knew! Like a black raven, dread swooped down and spread its gloomy wings about her; terror leaped up and engulfed her like a roaring wall of fire!

Her high, ululating scream splintered the forest hush.

Wolf was up and on his feet, racing to her side in the self-same heartbeat. His arms enfolded her. He crushed her fiercely to his chest even as the first, keening wail ended, and another began.

"What is it?" he demanded, his voice a rasp as he looked down at their child. *"Tell me! Is he gone?"*

Yet Red Wing lived, he could see that, and relief overwhelmed him. Then it was not his death she mourned, thank the Great Spirit! His son still tossed and turned on his pine bough bed, and he could hear his pitiful moans.

"By the Spirit, what is wrong with you? Speak to me!"

Yet over and over his woman screamed, until he was forced to take her by the upper arms and shake her roughly to bring her to her senses.

"Our son! Our son!" she babbled, sobbing uncontrollably now. "Can you not see? He has the rotting-sickness! Look at him, Wolf! Look! The rash is everywhere! Soon, the poison-boils will cover his body—! Soon their rot will gnaw at his little face, and then—aiee! aiee!—then he will die!" she shrieked.

She shook her head back and forth like a madwoman, tearing at her hair and beating at his chest in her anguish and hysteria as he tried to calm her.

"My son! My son! Our baby will die! He will die, I tell you . . . !"

Wolf knew then that he could wait and hope no longer. He must not delay, but must take his woman and child from this place. He must go farther west, and seek out his mother's people; find the Peaceful Ones who'd given him birth, and ask their help in saving the life of Red Wing—and the sanity of his woman.

Surely amongst the Hopituh, there would be a *shaman*

whose magic could heal his son?

"Naa!" whispered a long-forgotten voice in his memory; a voice he'd heard only in his dreams since he became a man, and once, while in the depths of fever himself. "Go to him! Go this very sun, and do not linger! Naa, Uncle, knows everything! Lomahongva the Sandpainter will help you, Child of Lightning."

"My beloved, hear me!" Wolf commanded harshly. "Our son will not die! I will find a shaman who can heal him! A great shaman, a mighty shaman, one whose powers are known among all the Hopituh of the mesas," he told her, forcing her to look at him. "By my life, I swear it!"

Yet her eyes were blank and staring. And although she looked straight at him, he knew she saw nothing. She heard nothing. She felt nothing. There was no one there behind those staring storm blue eyes . . .

Her body remained, but it remained as an empty husk, encircled by his arms. A beautiful, vacant shell, left by the woman she'd once been.

The spirit of Blue Beads had fled.

For three suns, Wolf travelled west, riding None Swifter. Blue Beads's game little mare, Badger, was the younger of the pair, and it was she who pulled the travois he'd made, bearing his woman and child.

His heart was heavy in those endless days, for it was clear when he halted their travels to tend to the needs of his son that Blue Beads's worst fears had been founded. Red Wing's little body was covered with virulent pustules now. His whimpers of pain tore at his father's heart, for he could do nothing to ease them.

Was this a punishment, he wondered in the long dark hours of those endless nights? Had the Great Spirit chosen this means to chastise him for taking Broken Claw's life, and for what had come after? For once he'd left Black Hawk's encampment, he'd tracked Broken Claw for many suns, had finally overtaken and slain him, then scalped the body of his enemy . . .

393

"Your spirit will never rest when I am done with you, my *brother!* It will wander the cold earth and haunt the deepest shadows, troubled and earthbound forever!" he'd ground out, filled with rage and hatred as he looked down at Broken Claw's twisted body.

In death, his face, Wolf had noted dispassionately, had registered surprise at the swiftness and suddenness of his defeat with bulging eyes and opened mouth, as if until the very last, Broken Claw had refused to believe his ambush would fail, and that in this, too, Wolf would turn the tables upon him and best him.

But then the image of his beloved's face, bruised and swollen: the innocence and trust in her wide blue eyes muddied by pain and anguish, driven out by shame and terror, had replaced Broken Claw's death-mask in his vision, refueling his rage for his enemy.

"I will lift your hair!" he seethed. "Your scalp will flutter from the lance of White Wolf, so that all shall know you were beaten and defiled by him! Your shamed spirit will never rest — no, it will never find peace in the After World! You have harmed and dishonored the woman I love! You have taken the light from her eyes, and for this you will pay a price more terrible than death!"

Wolf sighed. Truly, his former brother had become his bitterest enemy, and he had relished the killing of him! Was his only son's sickness, his woman's trance state, the terrible price *he* must pay for the breaking of his oath? On the night of his vision-seeking, he had sworn never to take another's life in vengeance or anger; sworn that he'd never ride the warpath again. And yet, he'd done both . . . and without a shred of remorse . . .

But such dark and doom-filled thoughts fled when Father Sun rose again the following morning. He put aside his fruitless soul-searching and self-torture, and forged on, pressing the ponies to the limits of their endurance. By so doing, he covered many miles in a single sun.

Over the following suns, some inner sense drew him on into the harsh, inhospitable lands of the Dine, The People, as the Navajo tribes called themselves, toward the mesas and canyons of the Hopituh, the Peaceful Ones. There were times when he half-fancied he heard the low, gentle voice of his woman telling him the way, guiding him. With hope filling his heart, he'd dismount and go to her side, praying to find her recovered. But he did not. Oh, she yet breathed, and her flesh was yet warm with life, but her eyes, though open, stared vacantly, and her limbs were limp and lifeless when he raised them, like the limbs of a rawhide doll.

Disheartened, he mounted again and rode on, skirting the *wickiups* of the bloodthirsty Apache, avoiding the hunting trails and watering places of his enemies, until he'd left their mountain strongholds behind, and had journeyed farther west into other lands.

From time to time now, he glimpsed *hogans,* the dwellings of the Navajo, built of stone and wood, each one with its opening facing east toward the rising sun. He smelled the scents of sweetbrush and sage rising from their fires, and the mouth-watering aroma of roasting mutton carried on the wind. In the distance, he could sometimes make out the yellow fleeces of the Navajos' sheep herds and sometimes even the bright calico skirts and patterned blankets of their women, flapping about their legs in the autumn wind that blew in chilly gusts across the rocky lands of rose and pink and rust, but he never paused to greet them or to ask their hospitality. He was a man driven by desperation.

On the fifth sun of riding, Wolf halted the ponies at the foot of a rock-littered trail, one that lay deep in a vast land of many canyons and arroyos. The narrow path, fringed by creosote bushes, sagebrush, or an occasional clump of dry grasses, followed the shadow of the stark, canoe-prow shape of a mesa. *What had made him stop here?* he wondered. *Could this be the place? The land of his childhood?*

He looked about him and frowned, unable to fix a familiar landmark from his memories. It had been too long! He'd been so young when he was carried off, and could remember nothing clearly any more. He had only vague impressions and a sense of a certain place: little enough to go by. His spirits, already low, sunk still further. He'd thought—hoped—he might somehow recognize the place with his heart, if not with his eyes, but he did not.

To the east rose towering sandstone buttes, fiery columns of rust, ochre, brown, and red, thrusting upward like giants against the wheeling iron gray sky. Shredded clouds swept in gray mares' tails across the dour heavens behind them, as if the buttes were sacred tobacco pipes, and the clouds their trailing plumes of smoke. The mountains of the high desert country beyond were hazy purple with distance.

To the west there were deep dark canyons and other mesas that reached like giant arms into the windswept plateaus. Beyond them lay the sacred, cloud-wreathed peaks where lived the Cloud People, the holy spirits who brought the rains . . . Was this rugged, desolate place of strange and fantastic beauty truly the place of his birth? Or had his memories—shadowy at best—again played him false? Exhausted, heartsick, he no longer knew!

When he turned back to stare up at the mesa's blunt black shape, he saw, to his astonishment, an old man— unnoticed before now—step from between a cleft in the rocks to stand in his path. He blocked the stony defile that led up to the mesa above with his body.

From where he sat his pony, Wolf realized suddenly that he could hear, very faintly, the rhythmic thump-a-thumps of *manos* thudding on *metates* as the women of a nearby village ground corn into flour; the cries of babes and the shrieks and laughter of children at play, but he forced himself to block out these external impressions, and concentrated instead on the curious old man before him.

He stood far shorter than Wolf, and had the bony gauntness of great age about him. His chest was barrel-shaped, his hips narrow. He wore his gray-streaked hair clipped short across the brow in heavy bangs after the Hopituh fashion, falling loose to his shoulders from a binding of buckskin, tied at the temple. An antelope kilt was his only garment; a gnarled staff of wood his only visible weapon. He leaned on it heavily. Yet for all his great age, his stance was challenging, his expression stern and implacable—yet inexpressibly fond, in some peculiar way Wolf could not define.

"You may come no closer, my son," the old man said softly as he looked straight at Wolf from rheumy dark eyes. "You are forbidden entry to the villages of the Peaceful Ones!"

"And why is this, pray, *Kikmongwi?*" Wolf demanded, calling him chief priest as a mark of respect, though in a tone that was far from respectful. "Are travellers not welcomed here? Are strangers offered no hospitality by the Hopituh?" He was desperate, and his desperation showed itself in unusual curtness, he knew, but he could not seem to help himself!

"Yes, they are welcomed, under different circumstances. Yours, for example, my son! It is forbidden by our wise ones to bring those with the rotting-sickness among the people, you understand? Instead, another place has been readied for your comfort, one a short distance from our village. You will follow me, and there find the welcome you seek for your child and your woman. Come!"

He turned to go, as if there was no question that Wolf would follow him.

"I will come, and gladly. But first, tell me who you are, old Grandfather?" he asked curiously, swinging his leg over None Swifter's neck, and springing lightly to the ground. "And also, tell me how you knew of my son's sickness?"

The old one smiled, amused and mysterious all at once. "How?" he asked. "How? What a question!" He cocked his grizzled head to one side, and his expression grew crafty. "It was once said by a little child of the Hopituh that Lomahongva, Clouds Standing Straight in the Sky, knew everything, Child of Lightning!" he said with gentle reproof. "Can it be that in a few short winters, that child has forgotten all I taught him?"

The years fell away like dried husks from an ear of corn! A great knot of love and remembrance filled White Wolf's throat, and he was a boy of twelve winters once again.

"*Naa?* Can it really be you, my uncle?" he asked, incredulity widening his eyes. But then, who else could the old one be, he asked himself, but his true mother's brother? Who else but the powerful medicine man who'd raised the son of Yoyokee-Mana, Rain Girl, and the Black Robe missionary, in accordance with Hopituh custom? And who but his *naa*, his uncle Clouds Standing, would know his secret war-name, Child of Lightning? No one but Lomahongva, the Sandpainter, for the name was one chosen for him alone by the old man himself for his naming ceremony. It had never been spoken aloud, not by anyone, except in that single whisper at the time he'd been given it!

"My mind has forgotten much, but my heart—ah, my heart remembers all! In my time of great need, I remembered that your magic and wisdom are great and powerful, my Uncle," he said softly, humbly, his tone filled with respect, "and that is why I have come here, in search of you. Although I had forgotten many things these past winters since I was taken away, I have never forgotten the strength of your magic, nor the curing powers of your sand paintings. I came to ask for a curing, wise Uncle. A curing that will heal my son, and restore my woman-above-all-women to herself!"

"Ah, yes, these things I already knew—as I also know that what you ask will be difficult indeed," Clouds Standing acknowledged gravely with a nodding of his old head. "I will do what I can, my nephew—but my success or failure will ultimately depend on you. On you, and on the strength of your love for your woman, and hers for you."

"On our love, *naa?* How so?"

"I have been waiting for you to come here, Child of Lightning! Over the past moons, my visions have revealed to me many things that you yet know little of. In due time, you will know everything, my nephew. Believe. Be patient—and you will see!"

daily and ming his eyes. But then, who else could the old
medicine be called himself, since his true mother's brother,
Who was his the powerful medicine man who had raised the
son of Travokva...

Chapter Thirty-one

The place to which Wolf's uncle led him was an abandoned pueblo of crumbling buildings of adobe, which
huddled against the soaring sandstone cliffs of a deep
canyon.

The magical pictographs painstakingly etched in the
rock walls there told Wolf that this was a place where the
Ancient Ones had lived many winters ago. Perhaps he
should have refused to bring his woman and child there,
for fear of their ghosts, but he did not . . .

Red Wing was still desperately ill, his small body little
more than skin and bones now; his woman lay still and
silent upon the travois, curled into herself like a child yet
unborn curled in its mother's womb. She had neither
moved nor spoken in many suns. Lomahongva, Clouds
Standing Straight in the Sky, was Wolf's only hope to
save them! And so, he lifted his little son from the travois, and, carrying him, followed the old man inside a
small wood and adobe dwelling.

It was gloomy inside, but Wolf could see that the interior was divided into two rooms. One had clearly been
used for storage, the other for living and working. Coiled
pots, a *mano,* and a *metate* used for grinding corn and a
loom were set neatly in their proper places and were
without dust, evidence that the pueblo was still in use,
despite its deserted appearance.

"I will see to the child's needs, and do what I can for
your woman," his uncle promised. "With the gods to
guide my feeble hands, I will make the sacred sand
paintings with the proper symbols for what ails them,
and sing the curing chants for your loved ones in the
sacred *kiva.* I will prepare draughts of healing herbs to
give your little one strength to fight the sickness-spirit.

399

But meanwhile, my nephew, you have other work to do! First, you must purify yourself in a sweat lodge. Then, you must climb to the highest point of our sacred mesa, and remain there, fasting and praying, until the Sky God grants you a vision that will tell you what you must do. Go, my nephew! Tell Him of your love for your woman. Ask His guidance in your time of need!"

"I will, my uncle," Wolf agreed, his handsome face drawn. "I will."

His uncle, Clouds Standing Straight in the Sky, was waiting in the abandoned *kiva* when Wolf returned from his vision-seeking on the high mesa three suns later.

In the dark hours before dawn, White Wolf found the Hopi medicine man still sitting cross-legged before the ashes of a small fire, his chin sunk upon his scrawny chest in sleep. It was as if the *shaman* had not moved since he left, although the sacred sand paintings he'd carefully created and placed the woman and child upon before Wolf's departure had been ritually destroyed. Their colored sands had been buried, along with the evil their magic had drawn from the sick ones.

Lomahongva's eyes, once black as the midnight sky, were no longer bright with health and cunning. Over the past winters of his long life, they'd become cloudy and inward-seeking. They saw little of this world any longer, White Wolf fancied, but looked to the World Beyond. His *naa's* skin had grown leathery, too, dry as the wings of a bat. His fingers were swollen at the joints, like the curved talons of an eagle. Nonetheless, White Wolf knew that despite his frailty, Clouds Standing had the gifts of wisdom and magic, and with them, the knowledge to explain the visions of men. If any man could restore his woman to him, Lomahongva was the one!

Respectfully, Wolf went to stand before him. In silence, his head bowed, the young warrior waited. It was the way.

At length, Clouds Standing's chin lifted from his chest.

With a small gesture of a clawlike finger, he motioned Wolf to seat himself on the dirt floor of the *kiva*, reaching into a beaded parfleche worked with sacred symbols at his side.

He cast a pinch of sacred cornmeal and golden pollen onto the ashes of the dead fire, and muttered a prayer. There was a hiss. The embers rekindled. The air about them was suddenly filled with a sweet, pungent smoke that was intoxicating to White Wolf's starving senses. His weary head reeled as blue flames became yellow. They writhed in the predawn chill, scattering the shadows and spilling warmth over the painted walls of the sacred *kiva*. White Wolf grunted with pleasure as their heat also danced over him.

"By your eyes, I know that Sotuqnangu, the Sky God, smiled upon you, my son," Clouds Standing observed in a low, reedy voice. "Tell me of your dreaming!"

White Wolf grunted assent. He was eager to begin, for his vision had confused and troubled him. But when he spoke, his tongue was as dry as the desert wind, his voice hoarse as the cawing of ravens.

"For two suns, Wise Uncle," he began, "I felt only the heat of Tawa, Father Sun, as he tested my body in that barren, shadeless place. By night, I heard only the cry of the wind and the singing of the stars. I saw only ghosts, the spirits of those who cannot find the Star Path. There was nothing more."

The Old One nodded sagely. "So it is for all men, my nephew. The Sky God tests a warrior's courage before He grants him visions. But, go on!" he urged.

White Wolf wetted his parched lips on his furry tongue, considering how best to describe what had come next.

"On the third night, I stood on the rim of the mesa and raised my hands to the heavens," he began. "I heard a mighty voice asking the Sky God to accept offerings of sacred tobacco and cornmeal from the warrior White Wolf. At first, I did not recognise that mighty voice as my own, and I was afraid," he admitted sheepishly.

The old man smiled and nodded, rocking back and forth very gently, as if nodding his entire body in agreement. "Yes, yes. And then? What came then?"

"I asked for the gift of guidance, as you instructed, Uncle. I asked the Sky God to send me a vision—one that would tell me if my woman would be restored to me. Sotuqnangu's answer came swiftly out of the starry sky!

"A great wind rushed through me, and at once, I felt my spirit soar free of its earthly shell, and whirl away as a leaf is whirled! When stillness returned, I found my spirit-self wandering in the canyon of the little red river, that holy Place of Emergence which is sacred to our People?"

Lomahongva nodded.

"I saw the wisps of orange mist that our legends say are the souls of the unborn, floating between the canyon walls. I saw also the gray mists that are the spirits of those who have already lived and died, and now seek to enter the After World. My heart was heavy, for I believed that the Sky God had chosen this means to tell me my woman would die!"

Looking up, Clouds Standing saw that White Wolf's handsome copper face was drawn with worry. Worry for his wife, Blue Beads, whose spirit had fled her living body, and worry for the little son who also hovered between two worlds.

White Wolf wetted his lips once again, wondering how best to explain the next part of his vision. It was unlike anything he'd heard recounted by young braves about the camp fires of Black Hawk's band after they'd returned from their visions quests; so strange and frightening, he hesitated to tell it aloud, fearing Clouds Standing might call his dreaming false; the fabric woven of an empty belly and a light head.

He continued hesitantly, "Then, in the manner of visions, everything changed! Suddenly, I was no longer floating between the little canyon's walls, but journeying on foot, running through the blackest night I have ever known along a narrow pathway that led to the little canyon's highest ledge. I stood there, as still and silent as if carved from the mountains, waiting for . . . something, though I knew not what! Soon, I heard a great sound in the sky above me—a roaring, screaming sound that was louder than any I have heard before. Truly, my uncle, it was as if the very skies had been torn asunder! Covering my ears, I looked up.

"Darkness had now fled. Out of the mouth of Tawa, the setting sun, flew a mighty hawk! Its wings were silver against the blood red sky, and it screamed as it swooped toward me. My heart—hiyeeah, my heart quaked in terror as its passage fired the sky with a jagged scar of light, for I saw—" he gulped, remembering, "—I saw that on its back rode a great black *beetle!* Hiyeeah, yes! A hideous beetle! It was large as any man, and in its legs—by the Spirit, I swear I do not lie!—in its arms it held my—my woman! I saw this, I saw how she struggled, and yet I, White Wolf, could do nothing to help her! I stood there, and trembled like a cringing coward!" he finished with a grimace of self-loathing.

Clouds Standing saw that as he relived the terrible vision, his nephew had paled beneath his coppery skin. His powerful hands trembled.

"When I'd found the courage to look again, both the monstrous beetle and the silver hawk had vanished! I was back on the mesa, my spirit returned to my body. Only my shame remained—and these!"

So saying, Wolf held out his hand to Clouds Standing. He uncurled fingers that had guarded their secret for many long, lonely hours to reveal their contents.

The fire's light winked off the pair of glass beads that White Wolf held cupped in his palm: the two blue beads that his woman had once carried in a medicine pouch about her throat. He shivered, and the hackles rose on his neck, for the pouch had been stolen by the one named Pale Eyes many winters ago, and he had no inkling of how the beads had come to be there, cupped in his hand!

With a grunt, Clouds Standing leaned over and took them from him. He held each bead reverently to the firelight in a bony pincer-grip, before setting them carefully upon a smooth, flat altar of rock. Again, he delved into his parfleche. This time, he withdrew a pair of sacred rattles, fashioned from the dried scrotal sacs of a white buffalo. They were filled with the humpback's magical powers!

Shaking them rhythmically in his gnarled fists, Clouds Standing rocked back and forth. Then, after what seemed an eternity to the waiting man, he began to chant:

"Hiyeee — aahh! Hiyeee — aah! Hiyeee-aahh! Hiyeee-aahh . . ."

His old voice rose and fell eerily in an ancient, one-word prayer, crooned in an ancient, half-forgotten tongue. Its pitch was part beseeching, part wailing, and his quavering entreaty stirred the hackles on White Wolf's neck once again, although darkness had now fled, taking with it both ghosts and shadows. Golden morning light spilled through the narrow opening in the ruined pueblo above the *kiva*.

Clouds Standing appeared drained when he fell silent again. The power the chanting had suffused him with drained like water poured from a gourd. In return, the blue beads had the lambent glitter of sapphires in the ruddy shadows. They reflected hidden fires and hinted at powers unknown, and as yet unrealized!

Taking up the beads, the old medicine man folded them carefully in a circle of soft doeskin. He added to them pinches of pollen and sacred cornmeal, a small, fluffy down-feather taken from the breast of an eagle, the broken claw of a coyote, and a child's bone whistle. He tied the new medicine bundle with a slim cord of rawhide to form a small pouch, then knotted the cord loosely about Wolf's neck, so that its magic lay close to his heart.

"Your vision tells me much, my nephew," the old *shaman* revealed in a grave tone.

With a start, Wolf realized that the *shaman's* eyes were no longer cloudy. They were black as berries in fall now;

404

brighter than wet stones in the bed of a river.

"Through it, the Sky God has given you a sign," Clouds Standing explained. "As the Great Spirit returned these beads to your hand, so will your woman's lost spirit be returned to her body! She will once again share your robes. She will once again be the one-above-all-women who shares your heart—*if* you have the courage to destroy the evil that keeps her from you!"

"What is this evil?" Wolf demanded hoarsely. "Name it, and it shall be done!"

"The evil is that of one whose spirit—like the Two-Hearts of our legends—cannot enter the After World! It is the evil of one who searches, but can find no peace. This, my nephew, is the Evil One, the beetle of your vision!"

"Broken Claw!" Wolf breathed, knotting his fists at his sides. His jaw hardened. "How can my courage save her from him? Tell me, Lomahongva! Tell me, and I will do it!" he swore, his blue eyes steely with purpose in the murky light.

"How?" Clouds Standing echoed, and shook his head. "How was not revealed in your vision, alas. How is known only to the Sky God! But—of one thing I am certain. What will happen will happen soon! In the coming suns, our people will celebrate the rites of Wuwu-chim—the night when all fires are extinguished in our villages, and all trails but one are closed, until the god Masau rekindles the fires. Is this not the blackest night, the one of your vision? A night without fires to brighten the shadows, and but one road open?"

"Truly, it is so," Wolf acknowledged, dry-mouthed. "But—can you tell me nothing more?"

Lomahongva shrugged fatalistically. "When the moment comes, you will know it in your heart, my nephew, and be ready to do your part. Then your great love will conquer all fear. It will vanquish all evil. You will not tremble then, but will do what is needed. Trust me, nephew. Trust in yourself, and believe that your prayers *will* be answered. I have received many visions concerning you, the son of my sister, Yoyokee Mana, since you were taken from us," he disclosed. *"Haliksa-I!* This is how it is!

"It was revealed to me that you, whom I named Child of Lightning, and your chosen woman would have many offspring; children and grandchildren and great-grandchildren. Through them, the love of Blue Beads and White Wolf would live on forever, and be remembered always in the minds and hearts of men.

"And, many winters from now, it is foretold that one born of your line will become a chief of this land, one of greatness and wisdom. This One Who Comes will have the gift of eloquence, the power to move men's hearts by his words. His talks for peace will be heeded, where the words of other chiefs have been ignored. His voice will soften the hatred of the bitterest enemies, and teach them how to live in brotherhood, be they white or red, black or yellow of skin. This seed of your seed will be called the Peace Bringer, the one to unite all tribes in brotherhood!

"In that time—which comes after the Third Great War of Mother Earth—the red men will be few. Hopituh and Navajo, Comanche and Cheyenne, Lakotah and all others will be scattered to the four winds, as the sands of the desert are scattered. And yet, because of one who carries the blood of White Wolf and Blue Beads, *all* men shall become as brothers. Their tribes will take the warpath no more. This is what my visions told me!

"Do you not see, my nephew? It is in order to fulfill this great prophecy that your woman's spirit *must* be returned to her body. For if yesterday is altered, so must tomorrow also be changed. And if this should happen, the prophecy will never be fulfilled! Do you understand?"

White Wolf nodded mutely, shocked into silence by the old man's telling of his visions. Truly, there was great medicine afoot, for the prophecy of Lomahongva was the same as that foretold him by the *shaman* Semanaw!

"Then, it shall be," Clouds Standing ended simply, tottering stiffly to his feet.

"But—can you tell me nothing more?" Wolf persisted,

unsatisfied with the shadowy promises of future greatness the old one had made him. In his sorrow, he could think only of the present: craved only the recovery of his little son, and the return of his beloved woman to herself. "How shall I find my woman's spirit?" he demanded. "Where does it wander now? If you would have me conquer the Evil One, I must know where she is!"

The old man looked at him long and hard, as if measuring him, before saying in a low voice that sounded like the rustling of dry leaves:

"You must be strong, my nephew, for my visions have shown that your woman will be returned to you from tomorrow, borne on the wings of the silver hawk of your vision!"

"From — *tomorrow?*" Wolf echoed, his heart thudding ominously now, like the hooves of a galloping horse.

"Hiyeeah, it is so, my nephew. Her spirit is lost in the canyons of time. It wanders the world, searching through space. It cannot find its mortal shell, nor return to this moment, as it must to fulfil the destiny for which she was given life. Hear me! The Sky God has chosen one to go after her. I, Lomahongva, will be her Guardian, the one to show her the way!

Blue Beads is the daughter of the future now, Child of Lightning! She is the daughter of days yet unborn, and of dreams yet undreamed . . . !"

Chapter Thirty-two

From a great height, looking down from the topmost crowns of the towering pines, the gray mist of Blue Beads's spirit-self could see Wolf holding her mortal body against his. He was shaking her, gripping her fiercely by the upper arms, pleading with her to hear him. But although she heard him very well, she felt nothing, for she was no longer within her skin. Her hearing was a thing of the spirit now, rather than a physical sense.

"... By my life, I swear it!"

Wolf's words came to her as if from a long, long way off. The wrenching desperation to his tone tugged at her spirit, trying to draw it back to its mortal shell, like a magic rock with the powerful medicine to draw the white man's metal ...

She fought against it, fought strongly, although a part of her spirit-form wanted to return, wanted desperately to be with him. *Aiee,* she thought sadly, *I love him so! How can I leave him with such burdens? How can I go and let him face these heartaches alone?*

But the other part could not bear to go back there! It feared too greatly the pain of returning, feared facing the mortal agony of losing the little one who lay so still beneath the pine bough lean-to to Death!

Instead, she forced herself to look away. She fought against the power that summoned her back, and little by little, won out against its tow.

Higher she floated, until the pine trees and the verdant mountains lay beneath her; the yellow of the sumac made bright splashes of gold below, rather than above. She watched as Wolf, his face etched with grief wounds as deep as any a tomahawk's sharp blade could carve in his flesh, built a travois of long, straight poles lashed together. He slung a pony blanket across them, and carefully placed her still, mortal shell and their son's small, fevered body upon it beneath warm robes, before mounting his pony and turning its head to the west.

For four days, she followed him, her spirit-form hovering, always hovering, lonely and confused, far above him; too afraid to return to the world of men, too afraid to leave it for the unknown world of spirits.

Unknown to him, she guided his path, knowing somehow that he searched for the land of the Hopituh, the people who had given him birth; not knowing how she knew the way herself, but whispering the right path when his own course faltered or his memory failed him.

Sometimes, it was as if she heard her voice, for a look would come into his eyes, and he'd dismount and lean over her mortal body, gently caressing her face and smoothing the hair he'd loved to caress with love — such love! — in his touch and in his tone. At such times, she yearned to feel his gentle hands upon her once again, and the pull of Life was strong, so very strong — almost irresistibly so!

Yet . . . the fear of mortal suffering still remained, greater and stronger. In her spirit form, she recalled the death of her white mother clearly, and the numbing, aching grief that had driven out all feeling and thought for many, many moons. Sadly, she knew she could not bear such a loss a second time. Better to remain like this, waiting, watching, until it was safe to return to her shell . . .

Aiee, yes, she would wait! And if the rotting-face-spirit won, and Red Wing's spirit left his body, she would be there, waiting for it, and mother and son-spirit would take the Star Road together. His little ghost would not be frightened or lonely, not with her to guide him, her love to protect him and take away his fears, she vowed . . .

Soon, after what seemed to her but the blink of an eye, for time no longer bound her fast in one spot, she saw Wolf meet with the one named Lomahongva; saw him follow the instructions of the Old One he called

409

Uncle, and, still floating like a drifting wisp of mist, she watched as he purified himself in a sacred smoke, and climbed to the highest point of the sacred mesa to pray and seek a vision, leaving Lomahongva seated cross-legged before his fire.

Somehow, she knew that if anyone could heal their little son, this Lomahongva—this Guardian of the Lost, this Sandpainter—was the one. He who was called Clouds Standing Straight in the Sky was an old soul, one who had lived and been reborn many, many times before this life he lived now, and would be called on to live still others. He possessed great wisdom and strong medicine—aiee, the strongest medicine and healing magic she'd ever seen! It surrounded him in an unbroken aura, a glowing circle of pure, bright blue light, growing brighter and purer as he gathered his spirit-powers and helpers to him with offerings of sacred pollen and corn-meal sprinkled on the fire.

She looked down and saw that now her mortal form was curled upon a wondrous painting of colored sands that stretched two-arms' lengths across the floor of the *kiva*. The crooked lines of the lightning and other sacred symbols surrounded her body with magical power.

The one named Lomahongva began chanting then, and her soul stirred to listen. His song was ancient, compelling. It rose higher and higher, reaching even her hovering place among the highest clouds. Like a silver lasso looped about her, his chant was drawing her back, commanding her to return to her mortal shell and her loved ones! His soul spoke to hers as a father to a small child, as a mother to her daughter; stern with love, and laden with authority:

Come back, my daughter! it said. *You have a great destiny yet to fulfill. A long and happy life yet to live out. The souls of babes yet to be born are even now waiting to be carried in your womb! They are the seeds of greatness, Blue Beads Woman, the forefathers of the Peacebringer-chief! Your time is not now, I say! Return!*

Oh, she felt the pull, felt that irresistible force like the undertow of some great current in a mighty sea! Her spirit form wavered, yearned.

I long to return, but I fear, wise Guardian! I fear the hurt that will follow!

Fear? No, daughter! There is nothing to fear, I say, if you believe, and love. Return!

His power was great. His words compelled obedience. She started to obey . . .

But then, of a sudden she felt the press of evil all about her; the cold gray nothingness and emptiness of an evil soul that sapped the warmth from her own spirit-self, draining it of strength like a leech drained blood.

No! I return!

Desperately, she struggled to fight off the chill breath of evil; to go back; to follow the Guardian's voice to the safety of her mortal body—

But—the way was now closed to her! The Guardian's voice was faint now. The evil one had blocked her return, forcing her to flee, drowning out the prayers of Lomahongva with its cold, roaring breath.

Drifting faster, faster now, she saw then an opening, a yawning hole in the crisp, cold indigo of the autumn skies; a tunnel that drew her, willed her to enter it, offered her an escape from the Evil One that threatened to devour her in its frigid maw.

A glimmer of brightness shone at the far end of that tunnel, like the blessed sparkle of a single, shining star. The glimmer grew, expanded, became a glorious sunburst of dazzling, white golden light; a shining, wondrous light that was warm and glowing, filled with the promise of joy everlasting . . . and sanctuary from all that she feared . . .

There would be no more pain, not there, not within the warmth and light. Somehow, she knew it! No more heartache. No more hatred. No more fear. No more sickness. No more evil.

There was only love and peace in that golden light!

With a last, lingering farewell glance for her loved ones below, she let the light draw her into its radiance. Deeper and still deeper it drew her, spinning in a slow, spiralling, whirlpooling dance through space and time, until she'd entered and embraced the warmth and the light. And, finally, become one with it . . .

"She is the daughter of the future now, Child of Lightning," she seemed to hear Lomahongva saying from a great way off. "She is the daughter of days yet unborn, and of dreams yet undreamed . . ."

and with deep, soft slow back spinning in a slow, spiral-
ing, whirlpooling dance through space and from out
she'd sensed, hadn't ... the warmth ... to the light.
And finally ...
She sensed the ... of ... of Light,
for, her and ... to ... as ...

Chapter Thirty-three

"Kelly? *Kelly!* For God's sake, Kelly, open this door!"
Devin roared for the tenth time, hammering on Kelly's motel room door with his fists.

Lights were going on in the rooms on either side of hers,
and he could hear the people within them groaning and cuss-
ing at being awakened so early, for it was barely daylight.
Dawn was just coming up over Second Mesa, painting Hopiland in rosy pinks and a thousand shades of pearly gray. The
sun was a blinding flare of gold along the horizon.

Ignoring the neighboring guests and their angry insis-
tences that he quiet down, Devin stepped back and braced
himself to break down the door with his shoulder, television-
cop style. But to his chagrin, although he threw all his weight
and power against it, the sturdy door held—and the lock
along with it.

Grinding out a curse, he stepped back, prepared to kick
the damned door in this time, if that was what it took to get
in there. He was about to do so when he felt a meaty hand
clamp over his shoulder, restraining him.

"All right, my friend, what's the trouble here? You lost
your key, is that it, and the missus is still sleeping?"

Devin turned around to see a brawny Hopi security guard
standing alongside him.

"No, my girlfriend's in there! We were supposed to get an
early start for the Snake Dances at Walpi this morning, but
she's not answering her phone or the door. There's something wrong, officer! I tried calling her first, and when she
didn't answer after it'd rung enough times to wake the dead,
I came straight over here. My room's further down, see?" he
indicated, jerking his head in that direction and brandishing
his own room key as proof.

The security guard nodded patronizingly, his expression

413

unconvinced. "Right, pal, right." Deftly, he tightened his grip and steered Devin about, firmly heading him away from Kelly's door. "I suppose it didn't occur to you that maybe the lady didn't *want* to talk to you, and that that's why she didn't answer the phone, huh? Say, you two didn't have a fight last night, did you, pal? Could be she's still mad at you, eh?" He winked knowingly, and Devin saw red.

"There was no fight, and no damned reason she wouldn't answer the phone — unless something's wrong with her," Devin insisted, livid. "Now, let go of me! I'm going to get into that room, so help me God! If you want to make yourself useful, go see if the night manager has a master key!"

Devin flung off the man's arm and strode back toward Kelly's door, his anxiety even more pronounced now; a tight knot in his gut. If all the racket outside Kelly's door hadn't wakened her, then something *had* to be wrong!

"All right! You asked for this, pal!" the security guard growled right behind him, and simultaneously, Devin felt himself grasped by the shoulder and flung around. He saw a fist coming his way, and feinted left, his right coming up to solidly clip the man with a neat but loaded uppercut to the jaw. There was a cracking sound as his knuckles kissed bone, and with an astonished expression, the guard went down and stayed there. He didn't come back up for seconds, much to Devin's relief. He'd wasted enough time already . . .

The door gave on his second kick, the lock torn from its mounting. Squirming his hand through the ragged hole, Devin forced his way inside.

At once, he saw that Kelly still appeared to be deeply asleep. The drapes were still drawn. The room lay in heavy shadow. Opening them to let in the murky daylight, Devin saw that the bed covers were tangled, the sheets twisted about her as if from the tossing and turning induced by a nightmare. She lay on her side, her knees drawn up, her arms curled around them, in the fetal position.

Something about her uncanny stillness sent chills of alarm sweeping through him, and raised gooseflesh down his arms.

Hurrying to her side, Devin leaned down and felt for the pulse at the side of her throat. It was present, thank God —

but damned slow and faint to his touch. He rolled her over, onto her back, switched on the bedside lamp and shone it full in her face, before raising her eyelids, one after the other.

Her pupils reacted normally, and yet—damn! He shook his head, perturbed. Appearances and his professional instinct suggested she was hypersomnic at the very least—possibly even comatose. A sick sense of dread filled him, coupled with a silent cry of denial. Could her continuing fantasies, and this new symptom—her stuporous state—mean that she had some kind of neurological problem? Had all of her delusions, hallucinations, dreams, whatever . . . been symptomatic of serious disease, rather than the result of prolonged stress, as he'd hoped . . .

"Kelly!" he said loudly, lightly slapping her cheeks in an attempt to bring her around. "Kelly, honey, wake up!"

There was no response.

Louder, he gritted, "Kelly, damn it, it's Devin! Wake up, I say!"

He realized suddenly that his jaw was clenched, the words ground out of him in his desperation to wake her. His heart was hammering. His hands were sweaty. And, in the same instance, he realized just how very much he loved her; how destroyed he'd be if anything happened to take her from him, disease or otherwise . . .

"Oh, God, Kelly, don't do this to me, damn it!" he whispered hoarsely, grasping her by her upper arms and shaking her in a completely unprofessional but human manner. "I need you, sweetheart! Please wake up! Don't run out on me, damn it—! I won't let you run out on me!"

Her head lolled back as he held her in his fierce grip, her hair tossing as he shook her. Seconds that seemed small eternities crawled by on lead-booted feet, and she still dangled limply from his arms.

And then, to his immense and overwhelming relief, she miraculously stirred. Drawing a long, shuddering breath, she sighed, and her eyelids fluttered open.

"Wolf? Aiee, thank the Great Spirit, I have returned to you, my husband!" she whispered, but she spoke in the ancient tongue of the Comanche People, and to Devin, her words sounded like gibberish, confirming his worst fears that she was seriously ill.

"Kelly?" he asked sharply, turning her face up to his by the chin. "Look at me! Do you know who I am? Honey, do you know where you are? *Who* you are?"

She appeared dazed, confused for a few more seconds, but then her dreamy deep blue eyes cleared and focused on his face. She frowned and murmured, "Devin? Of course I know who I am, don't be silly! And what on earth are you doing to me? Please, put me down—you're hurting my arms!"

He wanted to laugh out loud, to weep from sheer relief on hearing her respond so logically! But instead, he released her and settled her gently back on her pillow, smoothing her tangled hair away from her face with hands that trembled with emotion. Her color was returning now, he saw, and she seemed almost herself.

"What am *I* doing? Oh, lord, pretty lady, I could ask you the same question!" he exclaimed shakily, forcing himself to smile so that he wouldn't alarm her. *Christ!* His heart was hammering as if he'd run a mile flat-out! For a moment there, he'd really thought he wouldn't be able to rouse her, and that she was comatose.

"Me?" She smiled, and her eyes slid away, refusing to meet his own. "I was just—sleeping—I guess." At once, her eyes returned to his, and there was puzzlement and a question in their depths, as well as a suggestion of fear. "I *was* sleeping, wasn't I?"

"If you can call being semicomatose sleeping, I guess so," he growled, irritable now in the aftermath of his fear, feeling unused adrenaline still pumping through him. He ran an agitated hand through his hair. "Christ, Kelly, do you know how long it took me to wake you? I called on the phone—let it ring forever—but no answer. Then I pounded on the door like a maniac, waking half the motel in the process. Nothing! And then—as if that wasn't enough—I then had to deck some poor security guard, and break the goddamned door down just to get in here—and you say you were just *sleeping?*" He shook his head, scowling. "Sorry, sweetheart, but I just don't buy that! So? What did you take?"

He fired the question at her out of the blue, hoping to startle her into confessing she'd taken something. Truth was, he was half-hoping she *had* taken something—too many sleeping pills or whatever: anything that would explain the heavy stupor: anything rather than accept the very real possibility that she was seriously ill.

"Pills, you mean?"

"Oh, for crying out loud, don't play the innocent, not now! Yes, damnit, I mean pills!"

"No, I didn't take anything!" she protested. "Not even aspirin!"

"You expect me to believe that?"

"Believe what you want—but it's the truth!" she retorted with a trace of her former spirit.

"All right," he agreed heavily. "Let's pretend for a moment that I believe you. Answer me this; do you usually sleep so damned heavily, it would take a nuclear bomb to wake you, and then some?"

"No, not usually, but I—I was dreaming," she said in a small, defensive voice, drawing the wrinkled sheet up to her chin as if it were a shield to keep at bay this new and alarmingly angry Devin. Her eyes slid away from his in that frightened, evasive way again; one that he didn't care for in the least! Unless he was way off the mark, she was hiding something.

"Dreaming, huh?"

She nodded.

"About your Indian again, I suppose?"

Another nod. He said nothing this time, shrewdly hoping his silence would draw her out, compel her to elaborate. It worked.

"Oh, Devin, I know you think it's all in my head, but it isn't, really it isn't! I lived another life before this one, I'm certain of that now. You see, I know all there is to know! I know what happened, what went wrong, and why I'm—I'm here now."

She sat up, leaning forward in her eagerness to tell him this new installment to her fantasy, encouraged by his very silence. In her pale pink cotton nightgown, which left her arms bare, and with her dark hair tumbling loose about her shoulders, she looked incredibly young and earnest, and so very vulnerable.

"You see, Devin, in my past life, I was a coward—there's no other word for it! I—ran away—left my loved ones alone at the very time they needed me the most, because I was too afraid to face the possibility that I'd lose them. And—when I realized what I'd done—I tried to go back, but—but I couldn't! It was too late! And so you see, my destiny is still unfinished, sort of . . . !" she ended lamely.

She wouldn't tell him about the prophecy made by both Semanaw and Clouds Standing, nor the Evil One, she decided. Nor would she mention that weird sensation of leaving her body that she could recall so clearly from the last few seconds before Devin had jolted her awake—or was it, rather, that he'd jolted her back to the—to the present? No, sir, she'd keep quiet about *that* part of it! That handsome, stern face, those patently disbelieving brown eyes, that clinical, logical, reasoning mind, weren't ready for that part of it just yet!

Accordingly, in a calmer voice she continued, "Devin, I know it sounds crazy and farfetched, but what do we *really* know about death? Or about the moment of dying, or what comes after it—if anything—for that matter, other than the clinical aspects; brain death, the closing down of all the bodily functions, and so on?

"I've been thinking a lot about this since . . . well, since meeting Sam Cloud that first time. Every religion in the world has its own, different beliefs about dying and going to some sort of—of Heaven or Paradise, or maybe Hell or whatever, right? But no matter what the religion, all of those theories are just different aspects of faith, pure and simple, Devin, not proven fact. Shadowy yet comforting explanations that supply what we need as human beings to take away our fear of dying, and to reassure us that leading a good life has a reward, or a bad life, eternal punishment, don't you see?" She drew a deep breath. "And—since we don't—we *can't!*—know for sure, who's to say that Sam Cloud isn't right, and that this life we're living now isn't just one of many

418

lives? Or that I wasn't a woman called Mary Margaret Kelly in a previous existence?"

"Me," Devin said firmly, unconvinced and arrogant in his lack of conviction. His tanned face was implacable. "I say so! That Cloud guy's a dangerous man, Kelly—he has to be! Perhaps he's even more dangerous than I'd figured him for, because somehow, the old coot's got you sharing his delusions!"

Her shoulders slumped. "All right, Devin. I can't make you see things my way, so I won't even try any more. You're entitled to your views—but so am I! You go on back to Phoenix, Devin, and I'll find Sam Cloud on my own. Don't worry about me. I'll find my own way back to Scottsdale."

She tossed aside the bed covers and sprang to her feet, rummaging in her bag for fresh underthings and clothing, her back to him.

"You really mean to see it through, then? You're dead-set on seeing this Sam Cloud?" He scowled, his fists clenched with anger at his sides. Damn! He wished to God he'd never talked her into this wild-goose chase now, but it was too late for regrets! He'd have to see it through to the bitter end.

"More so than ever, after last night," she said without turning around. She spoke so softly, he had to strain to catch her words, and still wasn't certain he'd heard her correctly. A look of abject sorrow and longing shadowed her face as she remembered little Red Wing, his fragile body so still, so drained of life; and White Wolf, her beloved Wolf, his morning glory eyes tormented as he gazed down at her still body, his love for her a potent, tangible force that had almost succeeded in drawing her spirit back to her body, if not for that—that other one!

Pain—as real and physical and hurting as any experienced in her lifetime—gripped her fast like the steely jaws of a bear trap, almost driving the breath from her body. *I'll come back to you, beloved ones!* she promised silently. *If there is a way it can be done, Clouds Standing will know it! He is the Guardian, sent from the Sky God! He will guide me back to you!*

But to Devin, she only added, "Yes. I am."

He sighed. "All right. Then that's that! I guess I'm in this too damned far to back out now. Get your things together, and we'll drive to Walpi. I'll be back in a few minutes, all going well — or else in the tribal calaboose! I can depend on you t' come and bail me out, if need be, can't I?"

"The calaboose! But why? Where're you going?"

"To settle up with the management for that damned door, if they'll let me off that easy, and don't insist on pressing charges for vandalism! And to apologize to the security guard, poor guy," he explained with no hint of a smile.

"You don't have to come with me, Devin, really you don't."

"Oh, but I do, Kelly. I do," he said with feeling, and meant it with all his heart. He loved her! He loved this damned, illogical, crazy woman! And loving her, there was no way on earth he'd let her go haring off to meet with that crazy Cloud character alone. No sir!

The Snake Dances were performed at the conservative Hopi village of Walpi, which was built, for the greater part, from the rock walls themselves, and soared skyward like some fairytale mountain stronghold. The Snake Dances, as Bill had promised, were incredible, and then some!

Along with a crowd of hushed, fascinated tourists, Kelly and Devin watched as Hopi dancers, performing in an open area in the midst of the *pueblo* of mud-plastered dwellings whose style had remained unchanged for over three centuries, reenacted the ancient legend of how a young man, trying to find the Colorado River's source, met many dangers in the course of his travels, all of which he survived with the help of Kokyang Wuuti, Spider Woman, one of the goddesses who helped the Hopi People in time of trouble.

In due course, the youth ran afoul of the Great Snake who had power over the waters. The Great Snake took the Hopi lad to his *kiva,* where he underwent the initiation ceremonies and became one of the Snake tribe.

One year, when the rains failed and serious drought threatened the crops and the lives of the People, Spider Woman instructed the youth to go and teach the Snake rituals he'd learned to the People, so that there would be rain. He had done so, and she'd given him the new title, Antelope Chief.

Accordingly, the sixteen-day Snake Dance ceremonials had been held each summer since that long-ago time.

Many different types of snakes were collected for eight days prior to the performance of the dances, some poisonous, others not. Each snake was blessed as it was captured, then taken into the *kivas* of the village for secret purification rites, which were performed by both the Snake and Antelope societies.

After several days of ceremonies, the Snake Races took place in the afternoon, and it was this part of the ceremonies that drew the most attention from outsiders, for it was an extremely dangerous ritual, and Kelly's heart was in her mouth throughout most of it, fearing someone would get bitten.

While the Antelope society lined up and danced to and fro, singing and shaking their leather rattles, the members of the Snake society paired off, each of them wearing red-feathered headdresses and fantastic masks, and knee-length kilts of antelope hide. One from each pair of dancers would then reach into the cottonwood shelter known as the *kisi*, where the snakes were corralled, and withdraw a serpent, holding it in his bare hands while his partner, known as the hugger, danced nearby and drew the reptile's attention by stroking it with the eagle-feather whip he held, called the snake whip.

When all of the snakes had taken part in this ritual dance, they were piled within a ceremonial circle of cornmeal inscribed on the ground. Before they could slither free, the Snake Society members grabbed them up and ran with them down the mesa, taking them back to where they'd been gathered. The snakes, the Hopi believed, would then carry the People's prayers for rain to the Underworld.

After the dances were finished for that day, Devin asked Kelly to wait with the other outsiders while he went and talked with some of the Hopi elders, and asked them where Sam Cloud could be found.

Along with the other tourists, all respectfully subdued following the powerful, stirring rituals they had witnessed, Kelly took a discreet look about her.

There were many Hopi people here for the ceremonies, naturally; young men in bright shirts wearing Stetsons and denims, their black hair worn either long with bangs in the old way or cut short in the modern one, and several pretty young women in various styles of dress, some selling pottery or coiled-basket work to the outsiders, but she could see no one among the old folks who resembled Sam Cloud. Could he have been one of the masked Snake Dancers, she wondered now? No, surely he was too old for the rigorous rituals! Then was he, perhaps, participating in the secret ceremonies which were closed to the general public? Those took place in the *kivas* below the ground, whose presence was betrayed only by the pole ladders that jutted up from the underground chambers. If he was down there, there was no way to know it. The Hopi, though a warm and friendly people, were very reserved, and maintained strict privacy in regards to most of their religious observances.

"Kelly?"

She turned at the sound of Devin's voice, her expression expectant, hopeful. "Well?" she asked eagerly. "Did you find out where he is?"

" 'Fraid not." He paused and frowned. "Kelly, I don't know how to tell you this, and you probably won't believe me under the circumstances, but I spoke with some of the tribal elders and, well, they've never heard of your Sam Cloud!"

"*My* Sam Cloud? Devin, he's hardly just another figment of my imagination, whatever you may want to believe!" she cried indignantly. "Margot hired him to help out in the boutique, for crying out loud. Barb worked with him and mailed him his final paycheck. And I talked with him. We're not all lying, you know!"

"Calm down, I believe you. But like it or not, his own people have never heard of him, and they know everybody by name, including their mother's people and the people she married into, and so on."

"Well, maybe those old men didn't know him, but he's real all right!" she insisted hotly. Her heart had begun to beat very erratically with Devin's startling announcement. No Sam Cloud? But—there had to be! She had to find him, to learn the way back—!

"All right, so he's real. We both know that. But—just maybe he gave Barb a phony name for some reason? Or maybe he just lives someplace else, and these people simply don't know him in Walpi. It's possible, you have to admit. So. What do you want to do now? You call the shots, Kell, I'll leave it up to you." And perhaps, he thought hopefully, all this nonsense would die a natural death if they couldn't find the old reprobate who'd started it all. No more Sam Cloud, no more wild fantasies, end of problem, happy-ever-after!

She'd been so certain that they'd find Sam here, she didn't know what to tell him. Dejected, she finally shrugged and suggested, "Well, I guess we could take Route 264 and drive on up to the Canyon, couldn't we, as we planned? And—and maybe we could stop and ask about Sam at a few places on the way, just to be—oh, you know!—sure?"

"Okay. You've got it," Devin agreed levelly, and took her arm for the long walk back to where they'd had to leave the pickup.

As they left Walpi and drove on, headed for the Grand Canyon, Kelly looked behind her.

Through the pickup's rear window, she saw yellow white flickers of lightning lancing like zigzag arrows through the dour gray of the afternoon sky; heard the crackle and boom of thunder over the mesas and the soaring cliff village of Walpi. Soon after, huge drops of rain began pelting down on the windshield of the pickup as they sped quickly along Route 264, Devin trying to outrace the summer storm's deluge.

The snakes had done their part. The gods had listened, and the rains were falling on the starkly beautiful, arid lands of the Hopi. *The prayers of the Peaceful Ones have been answered!* she thought, wondering sadly, *Will my prayers also be answered?*

They'd been driving north for half an hour when Kelly suddenly exclaimed, "Stop!"

Devin braked, and the white pickup squealed to a halt. He looked, but could see nothing on the empty road ahead that could have caused her to exclaim that way. "What's wrong?"

"This place, it feels familiar, somehow."

She stepped from the vehicle and looked around. The road was bordered here and there by creosote bushes and an occasional straggly juniper. The broad, black prow of a mesa loomed just ahead of them, and beyond it rose soaring buttes that looked like giant chimneys with charcoal clouds streaming away from their stacks like smoke. The land was a panorama of soft pinks and browns and antique yellows in the fading sunset, which painted some of the smaller arroyos the ruby color of blood. The smell of rain-washed earth was sharp and clean, tangy as the bouquet of a fine wine to her nose.

"Devin, I think we'll find Sam Cloud near here somewhere." She glanced hesitantly across at Devin, who'd also left the car to stand beside her, but if he found her announcement in any way startling, he gave no outward sign.

"All right. You point the way," he said levelly.

They returned to the car, and she pointed him east. Very soon, the rough side branch of the road they'd followed was played out. They had to leave the pickup behind, lock it and continue on foot, following a rocky defile that meandered back and forth down the walls of a little canyon.

Some of the soil was slick after the storm, easily dislodged by their feet, which sent small rocks showering, but at least there was a path of sorts, cut into the stone, and they followed it, scrambling down in some places, able to walk with relative ease in others.

And then, rounding a knobby outcropping of rock, they both gasped at what they saw below; yet another ruined pueblo, hugging the cliff wall. They both pulled up short and stared.

"There's no one here, Kell," Devin said softly, for the place had a quality that engendered low voices and respect. "The pueblo is deserted—must have been for donkey's ages. Look around you!"

Dwellings much like the ones they'd seen back in Walpi

clung to the canyon's rocky walls, yet there were far fewer here. And between the dwellings, Kelly could see pictographs; magic symbols painted onto the cliff faces themselves by the Ancient Ones who'd lived here many lifetimes before. Certain now that this was the place, Kelly started forward, jolting Devin—who'd been almost mesmerized himself by the effect of the dying sunset's colors spreading and spilling down over the canyon's walls—into belatedly following her.

A figure stepped from the shadows that huddled about one of the buildings, and Kelly drew up short, her heart pounding as whoever it was moved forward, into the light. As she'd known it would be, the man was Sam Cloud—and he was smiling.

"Welcome, daughter!" he greeted her in his reed-thin voice. "I prayed, and you have come," he added simply.

"Yes," she agreed. "I'm here. It—it was just as you said, Grandfather. I know everything now, and I want—I want to go back, but—!"

"But what? But you are frightened, neh?"

"Yes!" she whispered. "Very!"

He smiled again, and his brown, wrinkled old face was benevolent beneath its headband of buckskin and his gray white hair. "There is no need for fear. I, Lomahongva, will show you the way. Have you any doubt of that?"

Their eyes met, and she shook her head. "No, Grandfather. If there's a way, you'll show me it."

"Then all is well! Come, daughter. Follow me to my fire. Night comes, and the wind is chill without Tawa to warm it, neh?"

He turned, and she began to follow him. Devin, struck speechless by their conversation, suddenly recovered his wits.

"Hey, just you wait up!" he growled, hurrying after her. "She's not going anywhere alone with you, Gramps!"

Sam Cloud turned, peering intently at Devin. "Aaah!" he pronounced at length, apparently pleased by what he saw despite the man's blatant anger and dislike of him. "So that is the way of it, neh?" He turned to Kelly, and patted her shoulder. "This angry one with you also has a great part in the future, and in the prophecy that rules us all! Come, Father of the Peace Bringer, come with us!"

Frowning in an effort to understand what Sam Cloud had meant, Kelly followed the old man into one of the dark dwellings.

By the light of a small fire, he fed them bowls of corn stew and fry bread. And, when they'd eaten their fill of the delicious meal, he removed the earthenware platters and indicated with an upraised hand that he wished to speak with them on more serious matters now.

"You have come here to me because you believe what I have told you — is that not so?" he asked, and Kelly nodded. "You wish to go back to your loved ones, and mend the broken strand you have left in the cord of life?"

"Yes, more than anything! But . . . how can I, without . . . without . . . ?" It was no use! She couldn't bring herself to say it!

"Without dying? But this is not asked of you! Time, my child, is but a passage between one moment and the next. It is a canyon, leading between what once was, what is now, and what is yet to be. At certain times, the walls of the canyon grow thin. A gateway opens between which one may pass, if one has faith, and the knowledge required. I have this knowledge. And you, my daughter, have found me, you have come here to me. You have the faith!"

"And where is the gateway?"

"It lies in a holy place, one sacred to my People," he told her then. "A place called Sipapu, which lies in the canyon of the Little Red River, the one which is called the Little Colorado by the white men."

"I understand," Kelly acknowledged. "And I must go there, to that place?"

"You must."

"When?" she asked breathlessly.

"Three moons from now, in the month called November, on the blackest night of all, when all fires are extinguished in the villages of the Hopi for the rites of Wuwuchim, when the spirits of the departed are invited to return to their homes. If you are there at Sipapu as the sun dies in the west, the gateway will open to you. You will pass through it, and return to someone who loves you above all others, Little Wanderer!" He paused, regarding her thoughtfully. "Do you understand everything I've told you?"

She drew a ragged breath. "Yes, I think so."

"Then go now, my daughter. Leave me to my sleep, for I feel a great weariness in my bones—the weariness of an old, old man!" His rheumy dark eyes twinkled. "One who is, perhaps, even older than you would believe!"

Kelly rose and went to him, taking his gnarled old hand in hers. Kissing it, she whispered, "Thank you, Lomahongva! Thank you for everything!"

"Well? Is the show over?" Devin hissed when she returned to him.

"It sure looks like it. Sam's fallen asleep," she said lightly. "Come on! Let's get going. It's a long drive to the nearest motel, and I intend to be at Grand Canyon Village bright and early in the morning!"

With a last, fond glance for old Sam Cloud, who sat dozing with his head bowed on his chest beside the fire, she led a disgruntled Devin outside, and back to where they'd parked the truck.

Chapter Thirty-four

"Oh, it's so good to be home!" Kelly exclaimed, tossing her tote bag through the doorway. "If you'd like some coffee, Devin, I'll put the pot on? It won't take a minute," she offered, stifling a yawn after she'd let them into her darkened apartment.

The drive home had been a long one, and she could feel the aftereffects in her lower back and shoulders. For the most part, they'd driven in silence, stopping only when a rest stop was inevitable. Kelly had guessed that Devin was completely at a loss as to what to say to her after their meeting with Sam Cloud, though she suspected he was no more convinced by it than he had been before. He seemed moody and withdrawn still, as he had throughout their visit to the awe-inspiring wonder of the Grand Canyon's South Rim yesterday. *And I guess I can't really blame him, either,* she thought ruefully, arching her achey back.

"Uh uh, I'll make the coffee," Devin offered, much to her surprise.

He sounded as if he'd finally thrown off his brooding silence and was making a concentrated effort to restore their relationship to its former easy, comfortable state, much to her relief.

Coming up behind her, he massaged her shoulders. His strong hands felt wonderfully soothing as they worked out the stiff, cramped muscles, and she groaned shamelessly in pleasure. Whatever else she might be uncertain of in this life, she knew that despite his anger and confusion, Devin still loved her and would never do anything to hurt her.

"I can't let you make the coffee, too, not after you did all the driving!" she protested halfheartedly.

"You're right, I did," he agreed. "But to be honest—I can't stand your coffee!" He grinned and winked. "It's about as invigorating as — as dishwater!"

She stuck out her tongue at him. "Flattering, you're not, but far be it for me to protest! Thanks, Devin, you really are a dear!" Her smile quickly became a frown. "Hmm. I suppose I really should give Barb a quick call and let her know we're back. Do you think it's too late to call her now?"

"No, Barb's a night owl. Go ahead."

She sniffed and wrinkled her nose as she felt her way around the darkened apartment, turning on table lamps to find the telephone. She'd always been sensitive to smells, finding them far more evocative of memories than visual stimuli, and although she'd only been gone for four days, the studio already had a stale, closed-up smell, and a stuffy warmth to it that she couldn't stand, almost as if she were claustrophobic.

His way lit now, Devin tossed his brown leather jacket across the back of the sofa and wandered into the kitchenette. "Where's the coffee, hon?" he sang out.

"First cupboard to your left, right above the counter with the cookie jar. See it?"

"Okay. Got it!"

She adjusted the dial on the air conditioner, and in seconds could feel it working to cool down the stuffy studio. There! That was better! Humming under her breath, she carried the phone across to the sofa, plopped down on it cross-legged, and dialed Barbara's number from memory.

"Douglas' residence," answered a hesitant voice on the third ring.

"Hello, Barb? It's me, Kelly. Sorry to be calling so late, but I thought I'd better let you know that Devin and I are back as planned, and that I'll be at the boutique bright and bushy-tailed tomorrow morning, ready and eager for work. Okay, boss lady?"

She smiled, imagining Barb's curious expression on the other end of the line, silently bracing herself for the inevitable barrage of questions her friend would hurl at her. Tucking the receiver under her chin, she idly turned the silver bracelet around her wrist, admiring the way the silver shone with a soft, mellow lustre, and the dull wink of the two blue stones, as she waited for some response from Barbara. One came, finally, but to her ears her friend's voice sounded somehow strained, her enthusiasm forced.

"I'm—I'm glad you're back, Kell, really I am. H—how was your long weekend?"

"We had quite an—oh, *interesting*—time, I suppose you'd have to call it. I'll tell you more tomorrow. Barb, are you okay? You sound kind of upset or something?"

"I am upset. Very. Oh, Kelly . . . You wouldn't believe what happened!"

To Kelly's dismay, she heard Barb break down and cry on the other end of the line; heard her great, shuddering sobs.

"Barb? Barb, talk to me! What happened? Is Billy all right? Is something wrong with Margot or Big Bill? Barb, please try to tell me?" she implored, a knot of anxiety tightening in her stomach.

"S-someone broke into our home while Bill and I were at work today! Our home—it's a shambles! They slashed the sofas, the chairs, the walls—oh, Kelly, you've never seen such a mess!"

"Oh, no!" Kelly whispered, horrified. "And what about little Billy and your mom? Were they—were they at home?" She hardly dared to voice the question, but crossed her fingers and offered a silent prayer that they were both unharmed.

"No, thank goodness! There was nobody home at the time. Mom arrived back from Illinois on Friday as planned, remember? I dropped Billy off at her apartment on the way to the boutique this morning. She'd missed him—you know Mom!—and wanted to keep him with her overnight, so he's still with her now, thank God. I thought I'd wait and tell her about the break-in in the morning. There's no point in upsetting her tonight, is there?"

"No, of course there isn't. But have the police been there yet? You did call them?"

"Yes, right away. They came and took dozens of pictures, dusted everything for fingerprints and so on, but they're not very optimistic that they'll catch them. And of course, most of the neighbors were away at work all day, too, so there weren't any witnesses to the break-in. Oh, Kelly, I know it's stupid, but I feel so — so invaded! I don't feel safe in my own home anymore!" Sniffles sounded from the other end.

"It's not stupid at all, hon," Kelly comforted her. "I know I'd feel exactly the same way in your shoes. Hey, are you alone? Is Bill there with you?"

"Yes, thank God. But he's wiped out by it all, too. He just keeps walking around, shaking his head, and swearing he'll kill whoever did this if he finds them!"

"Tell you what, I'll come over and spend the night at your place, if you'd like me to, and then I can help you clean the place up. What do you say?"

"Would you really?" Barb asked eagerly. "Oh, Kelly, I hate to accept when you're just back from your trip, and it's so late and everything, but — yes, I'd really like you to be here!"

"Devin's here with me." He was standing over her even as she said it, his expression concerned. Obviously, he'd figured out what had happened from her end of the conversation. As their eyes met, he nodded and held up the car keys. "We'll be right over."

Devin let out a low whistle as they stepped inside the Douglases' beautiful Spanish-style home, for it looked as if a madman had unleashed his fury on the interior.

"Welcome to the Douglas disaster zone," Bill greeted them with grim humor.

Huge earthenware pots of greenery had been emptied, and their potting soil strewn over the off-white carpets or splattered over the walls, staining wallpaper or stucco finishes alike. Sofas and easy chairs had been overturned, their upholstery slashed. Low tables and bookcases had been tipped over and some of them even smashed, their contents scattered and ripped or irreparably shattered. Draperies had been wrenched from their fixtures.

The trail of destruction led from room to room, they saw; Bill's den — with papers strewn everywhere — the guest room, the master bedroom, the bathroom, no room had been spared. The damage extended even to the nursery, where

431

pieces of ceramic from the broken honey-jar lamp had been stomped and ground into the carpet, the gaily patterned teddy bear curtains ripped from their mountings, the crib hurled over on its side and demolished.

"Whoever did this was one *hell* of an angry son of a bitch!" Devin breathed softly, slipping his arm around Kelly's waist to comfort her as he saw tears spring into her eyes. She dashed them away with her knuckles.

"Oh, Devin, how could anyone do something like this to a little baby's room?" she murmured, swallowing painfully. "It's—it's beyond me!"

"That's because you're normal, and those jerks aren't anything remotely approaching normal," he comforted her, giving her a quick, fierce hug. "Whoever did this was carrying a pretty hefty chip on their shoulder. Or at least, that's my guess. C'mon, pretty lady. Let's head back to the family room and see what we can salvage. Poor old Barb! She looks terrible!"

Devin was as good as his word. Although Kelly knew he had to be exhausted, he rolled up his sleeves and set to work straightening the overturned furniture, while Kelly stacked the undamaged books and knickknacks to one side, and set about consigning all of the broken and unmendable items into a large plastic bag for the trash.

After a while, Barbara and Bill seemed to come out of their shock and joined them, although they both still had a stunned look about them, and moved like the survivors of a train wreck.

"Did they take much?" Devin asked over his shoulder as he righted a heavy teak bookcase against the wall, and jockeyed it neatly into place.

Bill shook his head, looking down regretfully at one of his high-school football trophies, the figurine cracked clean in two, before tossing it onto Kelly's pile. "At least, not as far as we can make out. That's the wierdest thing about this! So far, the only thing we can say for sure is missing is Barb's address book! Can you believe that?"

"Oh, Bill, I told you earlier, I probably left it at the boutique!" his wife reminded him.

"Mmm, yes, that's right, hon, you did," Bill acknowledged with a weary sigh, running his hands through his sandy hair. "Then I guess those s. o. b.s left empty-handed. Maybe they heard something, got cold feet, and took off before they were finished. Who knows? That Great Dane down the street is always barking its damned head off, day and night."

"What did the police think they were after?" Kelly asked, rocking back on her heels. She had a throw pillow in one hand, its stuffing spewing out of a huge rent in one side. With a sigh, she tossed it onto the junk pile before resuming the tedious chore of spooning up spilled potting soil from the carpet.

"Well, with me being a doctor, the detectives thought maybe they were after drugs, though naturally I don't keep anything stronger than aspirin at home."

"They didn't take the TV, or the stereo, or maybe your jewelry, Barb? None of the usual stuff these creeps go for?"

"I checked, but nothing seems to be missing. Besides, you know me, I prefer natural jewelry. Wood, pottery, shells, and so on, rather than diamonds and emeralds and stuff. My jewelry chest must have seemed slim pickings, if it was jewelry they were after!"

"That's really strange," Kelly said with a shiver. She shook her head, stymied, then drew a deep breath and stood up, brushing off her jeans. "Well, I guess that's just about all the dirt I can scoop up with my bare hands. Where's the vacuum cleaner, Barb? That should take care of the rest, though you'll have to have the carpets cleaned."

"It's in the hall closet," Barb directed her, and let out a wail as she drew aside a panel of ripped drapes to find yet another casualty of the break-in; her prized collection of miniature houses. "Oh, Kelly, just look at my little houses! Almost every piece of my collection is ruined! And the—the curio cabinet is sm-sm—smashed, too—!"

It was the final straw. She buried her face in her hands and sobbed uncontrollably, mascara making sooty trails down her cheeks, her shoulders heaving.

Kelly started to go to her, but Devin stopped her with a slight shake of his head, mouthing silently, "Uh uh, don't.

Let her cry it out, babe."

Kelly nodded, knowing he was right, and turned back to the job at hand.

By midnight, with the four of them working together, much of the debris had been removed and Barb had regained most if not all of her composure. Although several things would need to be replaced or repaired, the house had been restored to a much more normal appearance, to Barbara's relief.

"There!" Kelly declared, forcing herself to sound positive. "That looks way better! Now, how about some coffee or hot chocolate before we call it a night?" They hadn't waited to enjoy the pot Devin had perked at her apartment, but had left moments after hearing Barb's bad news.

"Chocolate sounds wonderful, Kell. You have no idea how much better I feel, just having you two here," Barbara accepted with a sigh, sinking onto the righted sofa, drained.

"Thanks all the same, kid, but chocolate won't do it for me tonight!" Bill said in a grim voice. "I'll have a stiff Scotch, straight up — and I think I'll make it a big one. Join me, Devin?"

"Will do. But make it a small one for me. I'm driving home, remember?"

"You've got it, pardner. Come on, Kelly. You fix the cocoa, and I'll get the glasses."

Bill followed Kelly out. His tall, husky footballer's body seemed to dwarf the large kitchen, as she bustled about fixing boiling water and arranging two mugs on a tray while Bill took down glasses and wiped them.

"Hungry?"

Bill Douglas shook his head. "No, thanks, nothing to eat for me. Truth is, this whole damned mess has killed my appetite!" He paused and regarded her seriously. "Kelly — ?"

"Mmm?" she asked, smiling as she glanced up at him.

"About Barb's missing address book — it really *is* missing, and whoever did this to the house took it!"

"But you said —"

"I know what I said! I just went along with Barbara about it being at the store, because I didn't want her upset again

434

night. But the address book—I saw it on the nightstand
is morning. We left together, and it was still lying there."

She frowned, wondering what he was leading up to.
And?"

"Well," Bill said slowly, seeming uncomfortable, "there's
mething I think you should know, Kelly. Here, maybe
ou'd better sit down."

Startled, her deep blue eyes widened as he drew out a
hair for her. What on earth could he have to tell her that
as so shocking, he wanted her to sit down? Nevertheless,
he sat, eyeing him apprehensively.

"Now, don't get alarmed, Kell, because I'm not sure that
he two incidents are really connected. But a few weeks ago,
spoke with a colleague of mine, a guy named Royce
ames—he was at your wedding, remember?"

She nodded.

"Well, he's a doctor, too,—a psychiatrist, actually, al-
hough he's with the veterans hospital in San Francisco.
Anyway, we had lunch while he was here in town, and dur-
ig it he mentioned that Tony—your Tony—had been a pa-
ent of his, and that—well, I guess I'd better tell you
traight out, Kelly—that Tony discharged himself from the
ospital back in July."

"*What?*" she whispered in a shaken tone. "You mean,
ony's escaped?"

"Now, please, Kell, don't overreact!" Bill Douglas ordered,
or her face had paled alarmingly. "They'll catch up with him
ooner or later—maybe they already have, and my hunch is
vay off!"

"But—if Tony escaped back in July, why on earth didn't
ou tell me before?"

"Barb and I wanted to, but—well, to be honest, we've
een concerned about you, hon," he said gently, very much
he big brother he'd always been to her in that moment.
You haven't seemed your old self since you came back here,
nd then there're those—dreams, or whatever—you've been
aving. Anyway, we—"

Kelly's eyes snapped back to his face and remained there,
ntent on his expression. "My dreams? But how did you

know about those? I've intentionally said very little abou
them to Barb!"

Bill looked embarrassed now. In fact, he was squirming
"Well, let me see. It was—er—it was Devin who mentione
them, I think." He met her gaze, and turned bright re
under his fair complexion. "Oh, Christ, all right, it wa
Devin. Come on, Kelly, don't be mad at us—and for God'
sake don't look at me like that! We can't help worrying abou
you and wanting to do what's best for you, can we? So w
pooled information—what of it? We did it because we lov
you like a sister, kid," he said in his simple, honest way, an
smiled sheepishly.

"I know you do, Bill," Kelly acknowledged with a heav
sigh. "I know—and I suppose I understand why you kep
quiet about Tony—and why you conspired behind my back
I haven't been exactly easy to get along with lately, I know
It was no lie. She did understand, and it was awful hard t
be angry at the three people she loved most in the world
especially when they'd thought they were acting for he
good, and had been trying to protect her! "But—tell m
more about—about Tony, that is?"

"Well, they've been carrying his description over the radi
all weekend, asking for information on his whereabouts
You didn't hear it?"

She shook her head. They'd hardly turned on the radio a
all, and when they had, it had been to Devin's favorite coun
try and western station.

"Well, apparently, Tony was last seen near Anaheim, but
trucker came forward over the weekend who thinks Ton
may be the hitchhiker he picked up there, who bummed
ride with him as far as the outskirts of Flagstaff."

"Flagstaff! Then he's here, in Arizona?"

Bill nodded. "He could well be, I'm afraid. And there'
more. Barb had a call Friday morning, real early. Th
caller—a man—asked if this was my residence, and if I wa
the Bill Douglas from Colorado. When Barb confirmed tha
it was, he hung up! She wasn't certain, but after we hear
the radio announcement that evening, she told me about th
call and said she thought it could have been made by Tony

Kelly bit her lip. "I see," she said in a small, frightened voice, then added softly, "And you think he's come here, looking for me, don't you?"

"I didn't say that, Kelly."

"You don't have to, Bill. It's in your eyes! Be honest. Didn't that colleague of yours suggest — however indirectly — that he thought I might be in danger?"

"Come on, Kelly! Royce couldn't breach professional confidence, now could he, even if it were so? And I'm not saying he did, or that —"

"Professional confidence, my foot! He did imply it, didn't he? Oh, Bill, don't try to spare me! I'm a grown woman, and I was married to Tony, remember? I know him better than anyone!" She drew a deep, shuddering breath. "I divorced him when he was down and out. I promised — I *swore* the last time I saw him — that I'd wait for him to get well, just to calm him down, you understand? He got really violent when I mentioned the divorce, and I was frightened. I left his hospital room, but I never went back, never saw him again!" She shivered. "If Tony's out there, he's coming after me, Bill. We both know that."

Bill's silence spoke volumes.

"You really think it was him, don't you, Bill? And that it was him who took Barbara's address book, to try to find me through her?"

"Yes," Bill admitted heavily. "I'm afraid I do."

Kelly's hand flew to cover her mouth, to stanch the cry of outrage and shock that she'd managed to contain until now. "Oh, my God, Bill! If Tony did — this — to your home, then he's capable of anything!"

Soberly, Bill nodded. "Anything. Remember, Kell, there's nothing here that's been damaged or destroyed that can't be replaced, but you — well, you're one in a million, kid! For Pete's sake, be careful until they catch him, Kell."

For the first few weeks after the Douglas' break-in, Kelly was a bundle of nerves, shying at her own shadow, half-afraid to answer the phone, wary of strangers around her apartment building, or of anyone remotely resembling Tony as she remembered him.

Bill had confided his suspicions to Devin, and he made certain that he walked her to her apartment after their dates, and checked the studio for intruders before leaving her alone for the night. It was a habit he continued through September and October, and on into November, despite her protests that she was a big girl and could take care of herself, and that Tony was probably miles away, sunning himself in Florida or something.

When his protectiveness seemed to increase rather than lessen with the passing days, Kelly began to suspect that the hunch she'd had was correct. Devin's reasons for keeping a careful eye on her were legitimate, but twofold. Not only was he determined to keep her safe from Tony, he also intended to make certain she couldn't follow through with the instructions Sam Cloud had given her. After all, November was flying past as if on wings, and the Hopi ceremonial of Wuwuchim just a fortnight away.

As inconspicuously as possible, considering her fond jailer, she started putting her few business affairs in order. At the bank, she named Margot, Barb's mother, as her closest relative, insuring that the dear little woman who loved her like a daughter would receive her savings if anything should happen to her. And, on a more personal note, she made a big point of telling Bill and Barbara after dinner one night how very much she loved them, and appreciated everything they'd done for her—a poignant moment that had reduced both her and Barb to tears.

"Oh, Kelly, don't" Barb had wailed. "Really, you don't have to thank us for a thing, does she, Bill? We love you, too, Kelly. Now, enough of this for tonight! I'm beginning to feel like we're all in a soap opera or something—The Bad and the Bawling, maybe! Nothing's—nothing's wrong, is it, Kell?"

"Not that I know of!" she'd forced herself to respond brightly. "Why?"

"Oh . . . it's just my imagination, I guess. But—for a moment there you—you sounded as if you were going away, and were trying to say good-bye!"

Kelly turned her head away and bit her lip, sidestepping Barb's acute observation. "Wow, look at the time! I really should be getting home. Could I hold Billy before I go?"

"Sure, kid. Here, he's all yours!" Handing her gurgling son to Kelly, she eyed the picture they made with an artist's eye. "You know, you look good together, Kell! You should have a dozen, just like him!"

Kell smiled. "Oh, I intend to, Barb, one day . . ." she'd said softly.

The night before the ceremonials were scheduled to begin in the Hopi villages, Devin asked her to spend the evening with him. They returned to the Scottsdale Gardens and her apartment after a wonderful evening of dinner and dancing at a superb Mexican restaurant, with an incongruous but seasonal Thanksgiving motif to the decor.

Outside her door, he planted a palm on either side of her head so that she couldn't escape him, and murmured, "Let me stay with you tonight, hmmm?"

"Why, Dr. Colter, I'm shocked!" she quipped back, deciding not to admit that she knew why he wanted so badly to spend the night with her. "I do suspect you might be trying to take advantage of a poor, defenseless woman!"

Her blue eyes softened with a mist of sadness and honest regret. *If only things had been different!* Beneath the hallway lights, his wavy black hair was glossy and springy-looking, just begging her to run her fingers caressingly though it, and his tanned face was so lean and handsome. He was every inch the hunk Barb had described him from the first . . .

"Damn right I'm trying to take advantage!" he growled, ducking his dark head to hers.

His lips were warm and sweet, loaded with sensuality and sheer, virile heat as they captured hers, silencing her embarrassed laughter and making her shiver violently instead. For once—for this last, sweet time, she surrendered utterly to them.

Oh, lord! His kisses fired a wild response in her body that

439

set her pulse racing and her knees quivering. But then, she recalled Sam Cloud's ambiguous comment the night of the Snake Dances back in August, and knew she couldn't let him continue. *Father of the Peace Bringer!* he'd greeted Devin, and although it had taken several hours of thought on that long drive back home to Scottsdale, she'd finally known what Sam had meant . . .

It took all of her willpower to squirm her hands up between them and gently push Devin away. To her dismay, she discovered she was actually shaking as she pressed her palms against his broad chest, and had to turn her head aside to escape both his searing, hungry lips, and the intimacy of his body's overtly male nearness.

"Don't do this to me, Kelly, honey, not tonight," he groaned huskily, his hot breath rasping against her cheek. "I've been a goddamned monk for too long, but tonight — tonight I want you too damned much to play games anymore! Don't let some crazy dream come between us, not now, not tomorrow, not ever . . . I love you, babe! I *need* you. Hell, I'll always need you . . ."

"Devin, don't!" she whispered, hating herself for hurting him, even while knowing she had no choice. "We've been through all of this already, and you know how I feel." She turned her head, unable to look him in the eyes. "At sunset tomorrow, I'll be there, at Sipapu, and Wolf —"

"Screw your damned Wolf!" Devin cut in, crude in his hurt and bitter with anger. "What about me, hmm, Kelly? What about how *I* feel? Don't I count? I'm in the here and now! I'm real — living and hurting, breathing and wanting — but did you ever stop to think about me, and my feelings in all of this? Give me a real flesh and blood rival, and by God, I'll give the son of a gun a run for his money, woman! But what you're asking of me is crazy! Chrissakes, Kelly, I can't compete with a — a ghost — a — a mirage — with some phantom lover you've dreamed up! Hell, I can't fight a made-to-order fantasy man for the woman I love, now can I — ? Answer me, damnit!"

"I don't want you to fight anyone for me!" Kelly came back in a lower voice, painfully aware that doors had opened

440

up and down the corridor, and that numerous heads had poked out to identify the cause of the argument. "I love you, yes, but as a—a dear, dear friend, or a brother. And Devin, I've never lied to you, I've always been honest about my feelings. I told you not to expect too much from me, right from the first, remember?"

"For crying out loud, lady, let the guy come in, so we can all get some sleep!" came a loud voice.

"Oh, please, Devin, come inside, just for a minute? We can't discuss this here, with everyone listening!"

"Damnit, no, Kelly, I won't come inside! There's no point in prolonging this charade another minute. Fact is, we can't discuss this anywhere, not out here or inside, because there's nothing to discuss! Zilch. Zero. *Nada!*" he ground out through a hardened jaw, his turbulent brown eyes hooded by stormy black brows. "You wanted a friend, you say? Well, sorry, babe, I guess you'll just have to find someone else to see you off on your wild-goose chase tomorrow! See, playing big brother or friend to you hasn't been enough for me for quite some time. Not nearly enough! I look at you, and you drive me wild. I smell your fragrance, and the ache in me's so bad it hurts. I hear your voice, and it's like I'm on fire! I want a woman, Kelly, not a friend. I want a wife, goddamn it! And, since you're more interested in chasing shadows than becoming either, I guess I'll just say adios!"

So saying, he flung about and strode off down the hallway, away from her.

Her desolation was instantaneous and painful. Tears streaming down her cheeks, Kelly rummaged in her purse for her key, finally found it, and let herself into the apartment, fumbling her way through the shadows to the bathroom without bothering to turn on the lights. A long, scalding shower had always been her solution when she was upset. She headed for water now like a thirsty mule to the nearest creek . . .

What did you expect, you little idiot? she told herself as she turned on the faucets and tested the water. *That Devin would hang around like a—like a patsy, while you agonized and poured out every little detail of your relationship with a—a shadow, like some*

441

neurotic old spinster, and then cheerfully kiss you good-bye? Oh, grow up!

Undressed now, she turned on the shower and stepped beneath the stinging jets, letting the hot water cleanse the tears from her face and mingle with the new ones that fell like rain as it cleansed her of her pain. *Poor, poor Devin! He deserved so much better—so much more than she'd been able to give him!*

Logically, she knew she'd had no right to ask him to stay; hadn't had any right whatsoever to expect him to be there for her, day after day, no more than her friend, when all along he'd wanted to be her lover. And yet—selfishly, perhaps—she couldn't bear to think that they'd quarrelled and parted in anger, and that she'd never see him again, nor share the easy camaraderie they'd enjoyed all these weeks. Having a man for a friend and confidante, a companion to laugh with and enjoy doing things with, had been such a wonderful new experience for her, after Tony. And she'd never once stopped to consider that for Devin, feeling the way he did about her, those weeks together might have been tantamount to slow torture . . .

Her tears were all cried out when she stepped from the shower into a fluffy pink bath towel, although the pain of their bitter farewell was far from excised. After vigorously drying herself and winding her dripping hair in a towel turban, she slipped into the robe hanging on the back of the bathroom door, and went out into the living room.

She'd taken only two steps across the carpet, headed to light the lamps, when an alien smell struck her nostrils in the gloom. Frowning, she inhaled, Devin and their argument forgotten for the moment as she tried to pinpoint the faint yet pungent odor. *Cigarette smoke,* she finally identified it, but who'd been in her apartment who smoked? Devin didn't, and nor did Bill or Barbara, so who on earth—?

The answer suddenly popped into her head. Of course, Margot! She smoked like the proverbial chimney, bless her! Kelly remembered, and laughed aloud with nervous relief. Barb's mother had driven her home after work at the boutique yesterday afternoon. Knowing her time here was fast running out, slipping away like sand through an hourglass, she'd persuaded Momma Margot to stay. They'd ended up sending out for Chinese food, and spending the evening catching up on each others' lives, and watching a rerun of *The African Queen* on television together . . .

For crying out loud! What on earth had she expected? To have a wild-eyed Tony leap out from behind the shower curtain wielding a bloody butcher knife, in time to the panicked shrieking of violins à la Anthony Perkins in *Pyscho?* She shook her head in self-disgust, knowing at heart she would have loved to use her edginess as an excuse to call Devin and tearfully summon him back to her side, while having absolutely no right to do so. By this time tomorrow, she wouldn't even be here, all going well. Perhaps it was all for the best that he'd finally gotten angry at her? After all, the sooner he forgot her, the sooner he could begin looking for someone else.

She sighed heavily. *All right, pull yourself together, kid, this is it!* she told herself sternly, blinking back fresh tears that suddenly smarted behind her eyelids, no matter how wonderfully noble and right her decision might be. *You're on your own now, sure, but you can make it! No more running, no more hiding, no more denying the truth for you.*

From here on, she'd be the kind of woman Wolf needed beside him; one with the courage and wisdom—and the love, oh, yes, the love!—to raise the children they would have together. A woman and mother perfectly suited to nurture the little ones who were destined to fulfil Clouds Standing's wonderful prophecy some day . . .

She switched on the lamp.

Chapter Thirty-five

Soft pink light flooded the studio apartment, bathing it in a gentle glow that was kind to the eyes. Nevertheless, Kelly looked about her warily.

Although everything looked exactly the same as it had before she left that evening, she couldn't shake the intuitive feeling that something was wrong, and that she wasn't really alone. She also had the creepy-crawly feeling that someone was watching her, although that was absurd! With the blinds drawn, no one could possibly see in.

She padded barefoot into the kitchenette, and opened the refrigerator, withdrawing a carton of milk and pouring herself a tall glass. Sipping it as she leaned back against the counter, she looked furtively around once again over the smoked rim. Television set in the corner, set at a diagonal angle—check. Glass-topped coffee table set before the sofa—check. The funny little Toby jugs she'd brought back from England, arranged attractively on the bookshelf—check. The bed in the alcove beyond, with the quilted bedspread and sheet turned down—check. In fact, everything seemed to be in place!

Good God, girl! One little fight with Devin, and you start imagining monsters under the bed, you idiot! she scolded herself. What she needed, she decided, was some loud noise—music or a lively talk-show to fill the silence and settle her nerves before she turned in. "The Tonight Show" would be perfect. Carrying her glass of milk, she crossed to the television set and switched it on.

Doc's band was clowning as usual, Doc and Tommy insisting they'd never heard the songs Johnny's volunteers—selected from the studio audience—were challenging them to play. She stood before the TV, and watched while two giggling college students won a dinner for four at a Los

Angeles restaurant, then padded back to the sofa, tucking her legs under her to get comfortable while she watched.

It was then that she noticed the powdery substance on the soles of her feet. She dusted it off, rubbing her fingers together and sniffing it. It felt like talcum powder, almost chalky in texture, but had no perfume to it. Now, where on earth had that come from?

Her curiosity roused, she set her glass down and retraced her footsteps back to the television. For the first time, she noticed the dusting of white powder on its surface and on the carpet before it. Looking up, she inspected the ceiling — a textured acoustic ceiling, she believed the landlady had said it was called. It was white, as were the walls. Well, that explained that! Obviously, the people in the apartment above her must have had a wild party while she was out for the evening, or been hammering or something, and the dancing or whatever had dislodged some of the acoustic. Elementary, my dear Watson. Case solved! Then she frowned. Wasn't that apartment vacant, according to Margot and the bulletin board downstairs . . . ?

She was considering this possibility when the doorbell rang, startling her in her already jumpy mood. Short of some emergency, there was only one person it could be at this hour, she knew. Devin had come back.

Running eagerly to the door and peering through the peephole, she saw him standing there, one palm braced alongside her door, his head bowed. It was a stance she recognized. He was still angry, but had calmed down enough to want to talk things through.

Drawing a deep breath to steady herself, she slipped the bolt and opened the door.

Behind an imprisoning grill, a pair of burning dark eyes blazed with loathing and jealous hatred as Devin stepped through the door and immediately took Kelly into his arms, kissing her hungrily.

The watcher's breathing altered. It became labored and rapid from between clenched teeth, almost feral as he drew a long-bladed hunting knife from the brown paper sack hugged to his chest. Knife in hand, he hunkered down on his haunches, tamping the rage inside him to a smoldering fire. It could well be a long wait until she was alone, he thought, his upper lip curling, but patience was something They had not been able to take from him. Patience—and his hunger for revenge.

Devin released her and closed the door behind him.

"Not going to kick me out?" he asked, brows raised.

She smiled, biting her lip. "No, you dear, sweet idiot!" she whispered. "I'm too glad you came back to do something like that!"

"You know, I really believe you mean that. Fact is, it's because I think you mean it that I came back at all! You see, pretty lady, I've decided to make a deal with you."

"Oh? That sounds serious! Come and sit down, and we'll discuss it."

Taking his hand, she led him across to the sofa. He sat on one end, while she took the other.

"Well?"

"Well, it's like this. Since you obviously intend to go through with your attempt to make a one-way trip to that place—Sipapu, was it?—I've decided to go with you."

"Oh?"

"Uh-huh, I have. That way, if something should happen, it'll happen to both of us. Then again, if it doesn't—and I'll admit that's the possibility I'm betting on!—all this nonsense'll be over, finished with, right? I mean, there'll be no reason for you to keep pining for this Wolf guy anymore, because you'll know once and for all then that it was nothing but a fantasy, am I right?" He grinned, obviously pleased with his reasoning. He sidled closer on the sofa, and took her hand in his. "Now, here comes the deal—though it's real hard to talk business with someone wearing a milk-moustache!" His grin deepened as she blushed, tore her hand free of his, and scrubbed furiously at her mouth. "I'll come with you, and *when*—notice I didn't say if, ma'am!—we get back, we are going to get married, and live happily ever after. Deal?"

She hesitated for a moment before answering softly, "Deal!" and leaning forward to press her lips to his cheek.

But even as she made the promise, she knew she couldn't possibly let him go with her tomorrow. She had to do what must be done alone. Besides, in her heart of hearts, she was convinced that she wouldn't be coming back . . .

"Feel like watching the late movie?" she suggested.

"Only if there's popcorn," he bargained, cocking a twinkling brown eye at her. "Nacho flavored."

"What else!" she joked.

"Better set your alarm, then, if you plan on making an early start tomorrow after staying up half the night."

"It's already set," she told him, smiling fondly. "Just relax, and put your feet up."

He didn't see the tears in her eyes as she headed for the kitchenette.

It was daylight when Devin woke, still stretched out on the sofa in Kelly's apartment. He opened his eyes, and saw the bed in the alcove beyond, still neatly made. The second thing he saw was the note Kelly had left him, propped up on the coffee table. The black ink looked stark against the white notepaper as he snatched it up.

Dearest Devin, it began, and a dull throb of pain began behind his eye sockets,

'I hate saying goodbyes to people I really care about, so I'll just say So long. You've been the best friend I ever had, Devin, at a time when I needed a friend more than you knew. I know the practical guy you are could never accept the wild possibility that I've lived before, but then sometimes, I can hardly believe it myself. For standing by me even when you thought I was crazy, and for all the wonderful times we shared, and most especially for loving me in your gentle, funny way, *thank you*, Devin, from the bottom of my heart. I'm wearing the silver bracelet you gave me, but with or without it, I know I'll never forget you.

'I don't know whether you'll ever figure out the truth for yourself, or even if you'd believe it if you did, but I know from something Sam said to you that night back in August that you and I were never meant to be together—or at least, not in *quite* the way you wanted us to be. Still, I have a strong hunch that you'll meet someone someday soon, and that she'll be everything you'd hoped for. Love her, Devin, and don't mourn me. There's a wonderful future waiting for you, I just know it.

"By the time you read this, I'll be well on my way to finding out if my friend Sam is really just a senile old man with an imagination that won't quit, or something else entirely—! If what I'm hoping for really happens, I'll try somehow to find a way to let you know I'm okay, and that I made it. And if not—well, we can read this note together some time in the future, when we're old and gray, right, and laugh about it all?

"Take care of yourself, Devin, and God bless. Say a prayer for me, would you?"

It was signed simply, Love always, Kelly.

"No!" he ground out, smashing the note into a ball and flinging it from him. "I won't let you do this, Kelly . . ." he muttered, pacing as he looked around him.

She was definitely gone, but the room was still filled with her presence. The lingering fragrance of her perfume and her own unique, delicate scent teased his nostrils and filled his mind with unwanted memories. Her belongings scattered here and there seemed to be waiting, as if expecting her to return at any moment and take up the threads of her existence: the oversized beige jacket she'd worn the evening before, tidily folded across a chair back; the opened phone book on the coffee table; a half-emptied cup of cold coffee on the table; a pale pink hairbrush, all waiting. . .

Pain made a hard, tight fist in his gut, squeezed clawing fingers about his heart. *No, sweetheart, I won't make it so damned easy for you to walk out on me! Sure, I was sweet, I was understanding as all damned get-out last night, but that was because . . . because I love you, damnit, woman! I want to spend the rest of my life loving you, no matter what crazy fantasies you might have. Oh, for God's sake, Kelly!* he groaned in silent anguish, *Don't do this to me! Where'd you go? How can I find you, honey? How can I stop you . . . ? Because I have to stop you somehow, you know that, don't you? What you're hoping for is . . . hell, it's nothing short of crazy!*

Wuwuchim! he thought contemptuously, shaking his head. A harsh bark of a laugh escaped him. What did she expect would happen, if anything? Surely Kelly, an intelligent, reasoning woman, couldn't really believe that if she went to that place tonight—what the devil had Cloud called it? Sipapu?—she'd somehow be transported back through time, courtesy of some fantastic time machine? She couldn't logically believe she could return to some airy-fairy damned past life, complete with her fantasy Indian lover?

He wanted badly to laugh, to tell himself it wasn't true, it couldn't be true, but somehow he didn't have the heart even now, for he knew with chilling certainty that that was *exactly* what she believed—or rather, hoped with all her heart.

Acting on a sudden hunch, he swung sharply around and strode across to the coffee table. He scanned the open pages of the phonebook there, noting that as he'd half-expected, it was opened to the yellow-page section offering scenic tours of the Grand Canyon and other popular tourist attractions. Relief filled him as he saw that one of the tour companies had been circled in the same black ink Kelly'd used to scribble her note to him, along with a scrawled name. Grand Canyon Scenic Tours. Hardly original, he thought with a wry grimace as he savagely dialed the numbers.

The phone rang again and again. Devin cursed foully under his breath, running his hand through his hair. "Come on, damn you, answer!" he swore. He slammed his fist down on the table in frustrated rage as someone finally answered, absently noticing the fine film of white powder coating the polished surface of the table as he did so.

"Hello?" he barked.

"Grand Canyon Scenic Tours, Lillian speaking. Can I help you?" a woman's smoky voice had finally answered.

"Yes, ma'am!" Devin almost shouted. "Listen up! I'm trying to get a hold of someone who booked a tour with your company—probably sometime early this morning. Her name is Kelly Michaels, and she was scheduled to take the er—the Grand Canyon tour, I think, probably with a pilot—" he glanced down at the circled ad and the name scrawled alongside it, "—a pilot named Terry, or maybe it's Jerry, or Lenny something-or-other. I can't quite make it out—"

"We do have a pilot called Jerry who's scheduled for a forty-five-minute sunset tour of the canyon this afternoon?"

"What time would that be?"

"If you'd care to leave your number and hang up, sir, I could call you back with that information as soon as it's available?"

"No, damnit, I can't wait! Look, can't you check your books and hurry this up, miss? It's an emergency! I must talk to Mrs. Michaels before she gets on that plane! It's—well, it's a matter of life and death." Even to him, the words sounded lame and absurdly melodramatic.

"Very well. Just one moment, sir." The woman's voice was infuriatingly calm but frosty now. "I'm checking our computer flight schedules and booking records."

Seconds that seemed like hours passed before he heard her voice again, though the beeps of a computer reached him over the line. He noticed then that the white powder was everywhere about the room, dusting the carpet and the television set. Devin frowned as he looked above him for its source, wondering what the hell it could be . . . ?

"Sir?"

"Yes, I'm still here," he growled.

"Sir, Ms. Michaels's tour is scheduled for five-thirty this afternoon. Is there a message you'd like to leave for her?"

He considered telling the woman to do anything she had to in order to keep Kelly from taking that scenic flight, but knew that she'd be too determined to listen to reason, even coming from a stranger.

"No—but thanks anyway."

Shit! he thought as he slammed the receiver down. In his agitation, it missed the cradle and toppled to the floor. Crouching down to retrieve it, he noticed a long screw caught in the fibres of the deep carpet, the threads coated with a hard, white substance that crumbled under his fingers. Looking up, he saw the air-conditioning unit directly above him. There were dark scuff marks on the newly painted walls, and the filter looked a little lopsided, to him . . .

Feeling cold sweat bead on his brow, Devin dragged a chair across the room and climbed up on it, easily lifting down the grill, for it was no longer bolted in place, as it should have been.

Bracing his hands on the edge of the opening, he levered himself up into the air-conditioning duct, which was like a tunnel leading from apartment to apartment—easily wide enough to allow a man to crawl through, he realized with a mounting sense of dread.

Hunched over in the duct, he sniffed, a strange odor assailing his nostrils. Tobacco smoke—and something else. Some sort of animal fat, mixed with the pungent odor of human sweat, he thought, and maybe—the reek of fear? Or more likely, hatred! It was then he saw the crumpled, stained paper sack, forgotten at the rear of the duct. He picked it up, surprised by its heaviness, and looked inside.

There was a hunting knife within it, a wicked son of a gun with a pointed blade, honed like razors along both its edges. The handle was made of some kind of bone—elk, probably—and worked with pin-figure symbols. *Indian?* he wondered, and as the thought entered his head, his blood ran cold. He knew without a shred of doubt who'd hidden there, watching, listening to everything Kelly said and did in her apartment, biding his sweet time for God-only-knew how long, until he judged the moment was right . . .

"The radio report said they called him Injun Joe at the veterans hospital," Bill had told him soon after the break-in at the Douglas' house.

"Kelly mentioned that the doctors had said Tony was suffering from a split personality—he believed he was a Comanche war chief, I think she said. Isn't that a strange coincidence, under the circumstances what with Kelly's dreams and everything?" Barb had confided at an earlier date.

And Tony had been hiding here . . . must have heard the call Kelly made . . . could even now be following her!

451

Springing down from the duct, Devin grabbed his car keys and raced for the door. He glanced at his watch as he tore through it and outside to his pickup. Goddamn it! He was hours too late! Even if he drove like the devil, it was a five- maybe six-hour, drive to the Canyon. Dully, he realized that there was no way on earth that he could stop her or Tony now, not by car! His only chance to catch up with her, to warn her, was by taking a plane.

Yanking the pickup's door shut behind him, he turned the keys savagely in the ignition. The engine came to life with a growling burst of power, and he roared out of the parking lot, doing a rubber-burning U-turn on two screaming wheels that turned heads for a full block as he raced for the freeway on-ramp, headed for Sky Harbor International.

His handsome face grim but undaunted, he switched lanes back and forth, weaving his way relentlessly to the front of the early-morning rush hour pack, before pushing the accelerator clear to the floor. The white pickup hurtled down the road, headed south-west at speed; seventy-five — then eighty — eighty-five — ninety — its red hazard lights flashing.

Scenery and buildings flew past the windows in a blurred, streaming band of rusts, white, golds, and browns, but single-minded in his futile pursuit of the unattainable, Devin saw none of it. Jaw squared, lips a tight, hard slash, his tanned knuckles white where they gripped the steering wheel, he drove with an intensity of purpose that made slower drivers change lanes to get out of his path, and rant frightened curses after his receding tailgate as he roared past them.

Ten miles down the freeway, he was rounding a curved stretch of road at suicide speed when he saw a station wagon some distance ahead in his lane. Luggage was strapped to its roof, and an assortment of vacation gear was stowed up against the back window. A number of small heads were bobbing about like owlets in the rear passenger seat. *Kids.* A family group on vacation, or returning from one. *Christsakes, Colter, slow down!*

His subconscious registered the alarm, and he lifted his

foot off the accelerator and stepped on the brake.

Nothing happened.

Again, harder this time.

Still nothing!

A frantic knot tightened in his gut when the brakes still refused to respond. The white pickup was hurtling over the straight black road, out of control; the rear of the yellow station wagon was flying toward him now!

Goddamn brakes! He'd had the truck serviced just last week, so how the hell could this happen—!

He jammed his foot down again, but there was still no lessening of speed.

Oh Christ.

Oh sweet sweet Jesus!

He couldn't stop.

He could see the ribbons in the little girl's blonde hair now—sassy green bows; see the thick, round prescription glasses on her little brother's pudgy freckled face. He saw their mom turn around to point out something or other. Saw her open-mouthed, silent scream of horror as she saw his pickup bearing down on them like a ravening monster.

Those poor little kids—!

Somehow, he had to stop, but . . .

playing in the backseat—

Jesus Christ, the goddamned brakes . . .

They wouldn't know what hit them until—

were *useless* . . . !

it was way too late—!

Wrenching the steering wheel hard to the left, he took the only way out he had, the only way out he could take without ploughing into the other three lanes of traffic to his right, or turning that station wagon with its precious cargo into a twisted lump of mangled metal.

The white pickup screamed as it skewed violently sideways into a skid, its tires smoking, rubber burning, metal grinding and sparking. The truck left the freeway and began a heavy, graceful roll as if in slow motion, flipping end over end once, twice, three times, before climbing an embankment and leaping over it to the other side.

The last thing Devin saw was the telegraph pole as it rushed up to meet him, and the crazy, crystal beauty of the windshield as it shattered before his very eyes. Like frost . . . ! Like sparkling frost on a window pane . . .

It was his last conscious thought.

And, of course, there was the yawning black nothingness that came after it.

Chapter Thirty-six

Strapped into her seat in the Piper Chieftain behind the pilot, Kelly risked a peek out of the side window.

They were flying awfully low, she thought uneasily. And the sky seemed such a threatening, gunmetal shade from up here—almost as if a summer storm were brewing, though that was impossible, of course, in November! she reminded herself with a silent, nervous laugh. She could make out the Colorado snaking like a gleaming brown thread far below, between soaring turrets and chimneys of red and rust sandstone. The river looped back and forth, forging its serpentine course between great orange crevasses and lofty yellow castles of frozen stone that appeared fashioned by a demented artist—or an inspired genius—into the wonder that was the Grand Canyon. Awe-inspiring as it was by day, with sunset fast approaching and the dying sun drenching everything with blood red color, the canyon was breathtaking!

Little wisps of mist floated between the walls like tiny clouds, tinted a rosy pale orange and pink in the sunset—the spirits of the dead, Sam had once told her was the Hopi people's belief. Sam Cloud had also told her that it was from the place called Sipapu, a yawning chasm deep in the canyon of the Little Colorado, about four and a half miles above its junction with the main river—that the spirits of the newborn emerged, and the spirits of the dead returned after death. It was to that place she'd asked the pilot to take her.

She'd never been overly fond of flying, and would certainly never have chosen to become airborne in such a tiny, fragile plane as the silver Piper Chieftain, given an alternative, but she had no choice. None at all! Sam, in his oblique fashion, had made that much clear that night back in August, when she and Devin had gone looking for him. Time was of the essence now, according to the old *shaman*. The

Hopi began celebrating the rites of Wuwuchim with the return of the dead to their darkened villages at sunset this very evening. It was now or never . . .

Despite her queasy stomach, Kelly felt a mounting sense of anticipation, too. If—and admittedly, it was a great big if!—the crazy, improbable things Sam had told her were all true somehow, her dreams truly memories of a past existence left unfinished, she'd soon be with Wolf again, held in his loving arms, never to leave them again in their lifetimes! She'd said her final good-byes to Barbara and Bill and to baby William—though of course, they didn't know it—and had left a note to Devin. There was nothing else to keep her here now. If it happened, it happened. And if it didn't—? She bit her lower lip and her eyes filled with tears. Well, if it didn't, she'd never see Wolf again! She'd know that everything Sam'd told her, promised her, had been lies—empty, fantastic lies! Or simply the senile ramblings of a crazy, overimaginative old man who imagined himself possessed of mystical powers. And White Wolf, the little son she loved, everything she'd finally, painfully come to believe and hope were truly memories of a former life they'd shared together, would be nothing more than dreams; her Wolf a fantasy man woven from her own innermost, secret longings. A mirage who vanished on waking, leaving her with an aching loneliness in her breast that nothing in this life could ever fill, and a boundless love she knew she could share with no other man . . .

"How much longer?" she asked the pilot, Jerry, yelling so he could hear her above the throb of the engines.

"What?" he yelled back over his shoulder.

She repeated her question, louder this time.

"We'll be banking and following the course of the Little Colorado south in just a few minutes. We should be directly over Sipapu in . . . oh, roughly twenty minutes, give or take a minute or two."

"That long? Can't we go any faster?" From the position of the sun, time was fast escaping!

"You're real anxious to get there, aren't you, honey?" The pilot chuckled. "This archeologist boyfriend of yours must be quite some guy, t' get a pretty little thing like you so damned het up over a few minutes, more or less!"

The pilot twisted in his seat to look over his shoulders at her, grinning broadly as he shoved back his hat, revealing a cowlick of thick black hair.

The embarrassed smile died on her lips as Kelly's heart gave a tremendous lurch of shock. The blood drained from about her lips. A keening cry welled up from somewhere deep inside her, but never made it from her mouth. The pilot—he wasn't Jerry—he wasn't the man she'd hired to fly her to Sipapu!

Oh, God, no, it was him!

Despite the distracting mirror sunglasses, the blue baseball cap set at a cocky angle on his thick black hair, the new growth of black moustache hiding his upper lip that made him even more wickedly attractive than the day they'd first met, she would have known him anywhere.

"Tony!" she breathed, feeling a sick twist like a knife blade deep in her belly.

"Right first time, babe. Give the little lady a kewpie doll!"

"Oh, my God, Tony! What the devil are you doing here!" She managed to choke the words out.

"Believe me, honey, I've been asking myself the very same question!" Tony drawled. "But then, I think we both really know the answer, eh, Kelly? Some things you just know inside you, without needing to be told. You and me—well, we're like bacon and eggs. Peaches and cream. Romeo and Joo-li-et." He chuckled again, and the mirthless quality to his laughter iced her blood. "You know, doll—meant to be together!"

He drew off the mirror sunglasses then, and considered her thoughtfully, a faraway, glazed look in his eyes. The deep brown irises she remembered seemed to have shrunk. They were dominated by huge, dilated black pupils now.

Was he on something, she wondered, wetting her dry lips. Or—crazy?

Then she noticed his left hand, the fingers hooked over the back of his seat as he skewed around to look at her, the ring finger on his left a stubby, malformed stump. He'd

457

joked about that before they'd been married, brushing off her gentle questions about its cause with a casual, "You mean, this old finger right here, babe?" His eyes had twinkled, full of mischief. "Don't tell me I didn't mention I was married before? I wore a wedding band right here, on this bust-up old finger. Big gold band, it was, too, twenty-two carat, with a diamond as big as a marble. Heck, I near cut off my goddamned finger to get that wedding ring off, when me and my last old lady split up! See, it'd had gotten t' feeling like a ball and chain!"

He'd winked, just to reassure her and let her know that he was really kidding her about being married before, and she'd been touched, thinking he'd used humor to cover up his embarrassment about his minor handicap. It had endeared him to her, as had so many other little ways he'd had about him. Ways she'd later come to realize were nothing but an act — or more accurately, a symptom of his mental problems.

But now . . . now that stump of a finger wasn't nearly so innocuous, not a minor handicap at all. Oh, no! She swallowed, her heart thumping painfully. Dear God, why hadn't she figured out the connection before? *Why?* How could she have been so blind, so — so damned stupid?

For either she'd dreamed up Wolf and their enemy, Broken Claw, from the real-life fabric of Tony, his violence and their broken marriage, or else Tony was . . . was Broken Claw! A reincarnation of the . . . the Evil One . . . the one whose troubled spirit would not rest!

". . . just you and me, forever, babe!" Tony was still speaking with that eerie calm to his voice, his tone measured and reasonable, and so terrifyingly at odds with that dark glitter in his dilated eyes. "To the end of time, etcetera, etcetera . . . You can't change something like that with a goddamned piece of paper, doll. Divorce or no divorce, Kelly, you're still mine. Always were, always will be! Soul-mates, baby, that's what we are! I tried to make you understand, that time at the hospital, but you just couldn't see it. So, I watched, and I waited, and I followed you, and I finally got lucky. It all worked out perfect! I've got you all to myself now . . ." he finished with terrible finality, and she saw that the smile had fled his lips now, leaving them as thin and cruel as she remembered in her worst times with him, in both the past and present.

Shock had made her mouth dry. It was a struggle to speak, to make her lips and tongue form the words. "What are you saying, Tony? Whe-where are you taking me?" she asked in a hoarse whisper that sounded more like a croak than words. "And wh-what happened to the—to the real pilot? He's not—"

"Dead? Ole Jerry? Hell, no, babe, ole Jerry's having himself a nice little catnap back in the hangar! Don't worry about him, hon—not about him, or that fancy doctor fellow you've been runnin' fast and loose with. I took care of both of 'em for you!" Jealousy blazed in his eyes, and his jaw hardened. "All you have to worry about from here on in is little ole Tony. You ain't going anyplace, not anymore, so c'mon, doll, come along up here and sit beside me in the copilot's seat. We'll get cozy and enjoy the view! It's really something, isn't it?"

On that score, he was right. A panorama of rock formations spread out below the cockpit windshield like cake batter dripped from a giant's mixing bowl, then baked hard. Rusts, ochres, browns, black, grays—the palette of swirling, soaring colors was dizzying and endless. She glanced through the cockpit window, saw the horizon lurch and exchange places with the canyon's rim, and quickly jerked her head back to Tony.

The Piper Chieftain was flying erratically now, the engine coughing, the little plane losing and gaining altitude as if trapped in a series of pockets of turbulence. Her stomach heaved. Nausea and vertigo made her ears ring. Oh, God, she had the awful feeling she'd throw up if it didn't end soon . . . but she daren't let that happen! She had to keep her wits about her, or else.

"No," she insisted, forcing a shaky smile. Her face was the color of ashes, a chalky grayish white. "Really, Tony, I—I'm fine sitting right here. You know how I feel about small planes like this—about flying in general—remember?"

459

He shrugged, still smiling that sinister, all-knowing smile that never warmed the snakelike coldness to his eyes. "I remember. I remember everything. You suit yourself, honey. Stay right there. Either way, it's gonna turn out the same."

The unspoken menace behind his flatly uttered words sent chills of fresh terror swamping through her. Goose bumps sprang out on her arms. Her hair prickled on her scalp and down the back of her neck.

"What is, Tony? What's going to turn out the same? *What?*" Her voice rose to a shrill, panicky pitch as she gripped the sides of her seat until her knuckles were blanched. She felt herself straining forward for his answer, almost lifting herself from her seat.

"You and me, baby doll," Tony answered casually. "What else? We're going on one last little trip to the moon together, and after that—why, honey, it'll be just you and me—forever."

Her head reeled as the underlying meaning of his words sunk home. She felt burning hot and icy cold all at once. Dear God, he meant to kill them both—that was what he was saying!

"Maybe—maybe that's a good idea, Tony. You know, spending some time together up here, away from it all," she said, forcing her voice to sound calm as she deliberately misinterpreted his chilling meaning. "Then again, maybe you were right all along, about everything, and I was wrong," she continued, bargaining frantically for her life now. The words spilled from her in a hectic rush. "Maybe we can work things out after we—after we land. Maybe all this—" she indicated the enthralling view below with a nervous wave of her hand, "can—oh, you know!—help us to get our problems into proper perspective? I don't know about you, Tony, but our differences seem so—so small and petty, weighed against all this grandeur," she lied, trying with all her heart to sound sincere and convincing.

"Oh, yeah?" he jeered. "Come on, then. Don't stop there. Tell me more, baby! Let's hear all your pretty little lies! Like—why the hell you ran out on me, bitch—!" His voice rose, became a raging snarl. Spittle flew off his lips. "Ex-

460

plain that away, damn you, woman!"

"You're right. I shouldn't have left you. I was wrong, Tony, I see that now—I really do, darling! I—I shouldn't have been in such a hurry to end it between us, not without giving you another chance. But I'll make it up to you, darling, I promise! When we get back to—to Phoenix, we'll have Bill find you a good doctor. What do you say, Tony? The very best! Someone who can really help you this time around—not like those quacks at the military hospital. You'll see, Tony, I'll—"

"No!" he rasped softly, his voice a dangerous purr. "No goddamned doctors. No more broken promises. It's too late. Way too late!"

"It's not, Tony—really it's not!" she pleaded, almost sobbing now. "I'll get some counseling, too. It'll work out, you'll see. We'll be happy together, Tony—! In a few months, you'll be better, and—and I'll be waiting for you this time, Tony—I swear I will!" she lied desperately.

"Like you waited the last time?" Tony laughed, his voice harsh with bitterness. "Hell, no, baby! I'm not taking any chance of losing you again! It'll be just you and me this time around, Kelly. No more White Wolf," he sneered, his lip curled with contempt, and she gasped, for how else could he have known—unless her guess was right? "No Dr. Devin Colter. It'll be Tony Michaels *and* wife, here on in. We'll ride this little bird all the way to the ground—together."

As if in response to his ominous tone, lightning flashed in the brooding sky that surrounded the small plane, winking off its silver wings and lighting Kelly's ashen face and frantic blue eyes with stark white light . . .

"It is time," Clouds Standing said.

He rose stiffly for the first time since kneeling there, just after dawn that morning.

Before him on the smooth rock floor of the sacred *kiva* stretched a huge sand painting of marvelous design, showing figures and animals carefully drawn in lines and swirls of colored sands. Here a great hawk had been picked out in

461

white grains that sparkled in the torchlight: there, four crooked serpents, the symbols of lightning; sacred tobacco and corn designs, and above them all, the red disc of Tawa, the sun—or was it the red of the mighty fallen star, whose tail had stained the skies with color for many nights now? White Wolf did not know, and would not ask.

"Soon, the rites of Wuwuchim will begin in the pueblo. All fires will be extinguished until the god Masau rekindles them at dawn tomorrow. And before the sun dies in the west, the magical painting I have created must also be destroyed, for its powers heal only between the rising and setting of the sun. Here. You will have need of this," Lomahongva commanded, and the *shaman* held out his arms. "It has been blessed."

Lying across the *shaman's* frail arms was a heavy war lance, the blade finely honed. The wooden shaft was painted with zigzagging designs. Wolf took it from him and nodded his gratitude. The weapon felt smooth and right in his warrior's knowledgeable grip, its balance perfection. It almost seemed to hum with a life of its own.

"My part in your destiny is now finished, my nephew. I have done all I can, and may help you no longer. I have shown the Daughter of Tomorrow the way back—the rest is up to you and to her. It is time now for me to bid farewell to this life. You will see me no more.

"All paths leaving this pueblo and those from the mesa above have been closed with sacred cornmeal. You must take the only open path remaining; the spirit road that leads to our place of burial. From there go swiftly to our holy place, Sipapu, Gateway to Yesterday and Tomorrow. Go now, my son, and do what you must to return your woman's spirit!"

White Wolf nodded silently, unable to give voice to the gnawing doubts in his breast and the questions that teemed in his head, clamoring to be answered. What was it he must do? And how would he know? he asked himself, but he asked no questions. His uncle Lomahongva had asked for his trust, had he not? And he had assured him that he possessed the courage and the love to do what must be done.

When the time came, he would know it, somehow, or Loma-hongva would never have sent him on this quest.

Giving the medicine man a fond farewell glance, he turned to look once more at Blue Beads, whose body was curled motionless in the center of the sand painting. His heart swelled with love as he gazed down at her beautiful, empty face. For her, the woman he loved above all others on the face of Mother Earth, he would sacrifice his own life, if needs be! Hiyeeah, truly, he would sacrifice his own life in return for hers, if such a price were asked of him — and still consider it a trade cheaply won, so great was his love.

"Soon, everything will be as it once was between us, my woman!" he vowed softly. "I, White Wolf, have spoken!"

With that, the tall young warrior turned proudly, took up the feathered war lance Clouds Standing had blessed for him, and climbed the ladder leading out of the *kiva* into the pueblo above.

In the glow of the dying sun, the adobe and stone were stained red, as if with blood.

Chapter Thirty-seven

"Please, Tony, pull out! Oh, God, Tony, no! Don't! *Don't!*"

But Tony only laughed as she struggled to wrest control of the joystick from him.

"Beg all you want, Kelly," he told her gleefully. "But you can't do a damned thing about it, not any more, honey! The controls are locked on autopilot, see? This little bird doesn't even need ole Tony anymore! But me? Oh, I sure need you, darlin'. Always have, baby, I guess!" he grinned. "When we met, it was like I'd been waiting for you all my life, and then some. Come on, Kelly, one last little kiss before it's too late. For old times sake, mmm?"

Tony slipped his seat belt off and stood, lurching like a drunk as he left the controls unattended to reach for her and drag her against him. Kelly sidestepped to evade his hands, her head and shoulders bowed in the plane's cramped cockpit.

She was frantic to get at the controls, desperate to do *something* to regain control of the Chieftain! The rocky rim of the Little Colorado's sacred canyon was rushing toward them! In another second, it would be all over for her, and for Tony — sick, twisted Tony — too! It was too late to stop it now, she realized with a gut-churning feeling of dread; too late to pull out, even had she known how. Too late to change anything! Only another moment, another fleeting, precious bittersweet instant of life, and they'd hit the canyon wall. The plane would explode on impact, and she'd be — she'd be — ! Oh, no, it couldn't end like this! She wouldn't let it end this way, not now, when she was so close!

Somehow, despite the vibrating of the plane that threatened to slam her against the cabin walls, Kelly managed to shove at Tony's chest, thrusting him away from her. She fell backward with the effort, lurching into the pilot's seat herself. With trembling hands made clumsy and stiff with terror, she tried to fasten the safety harness about her waist and prepare for the impact, while Tony, giggling crazily now, took her rear seat instead, taunting, "C'mon, woman, give it up! It's too damned late to play pilot now, Kelly, honey! There's no way you could pull us out of this one, not even if you were Amelia Earhart or the Red Baron himself!"

"Shut up! For God's sake, just shut up and hel-help me, *please!*"

Frantically, her hands shaking so violently she couldn't still them, she checked all of the dials and controls, searching for the one that would unlock the autopilot. There was so damned many gauges and switches! All of them leered at her like spiteful goblin eyes, red and green and amber. Oh, God, where was it? Which one could it be?

"Damn you, you bastard, help me!" she screamed at Tony. "Tell me which one, for God's sake!" she sobbed hysterically.

"No!" Tony suddenly cursed behind her, pressing his face to the glass as the careening world below raced up to meet them—but he hadn't spoken in answer to Kelly's plea! "No, it cannot be!" he spat, his lip curled with loathing, his knuckles white where they clutched the seat. "He will not take the woman from me a second time!"

He blinked then, flicked his head to clear it, and giggled. "All right, White Wolf, old buddy, if that's the way you want it, here goes nothin'!" he crowed. "You're headed for the happy hunting grounds this time, pal, make no mistake, and this time around, the gal's all mine—!"

Tony's startling exclamation froze the frantic sobs on Kelly's lips.

Looking down, she saw the rocky red rim of a smaller canyon hurtling toward her through the cockpit windshield; the snaking glint of the Little Colorado like a river of old blood in the sunset, and the yawning black mouth of Sipapu below.

And there, standing upon the canyon's very edge, his tall, muscular copper body brazed by the dying sun, she saw what Tony had seen. She saw White Wolf, *her* Wolf standing there, painted gloriously for war! His powerful arms were raised to the sun, his feathered war lance brandished above him.

As he saw the small plane swooping toward him out of the sunset, he flung his head back to issue a thundering war cry, and she knew in a single, heart-stopping instant that Sam Cloud had been right, after all. He'd been right about everything!

"I am coming, my husband!" she cried, her heart swelling with joy. "I return to you!"

"*No!*" Tony screamed, lurching from his seat with his arms outstretched for her. Yet the plane dropped suddenly, and he was hurled aside.

The mindless panic of moments before left Kelly. It floated away like the fleecy wisps of mist that rode the air between the canyon walls. Her terror was replaced by a sense of utter calm, by serene acceptance—and with joyful anticipation.

The tension left her body as, settling back in the pilot's seat, she smiled with joy as the silver hawk carried her home on its wings.

Carried her through the Gateway to the man she loved, to fulfil her destiny . . .

White Wolf saw the silver hawk of his vision and knew that Clouds Standing had spoken truly. Power sang through his body, filling him with strength and courage.

Hiyyyeaaah! It was time!

The silver hawk rode the wind, came swooping out of the mouth of Tawa, out of the dying sun, to slay him! The hackles rose on his neck as, screaming its terrible challenge, it hurtled toward him. The hawk seemed bent on streaking out of the sky, on plucking him up in its steely talons. The bloody glow of sunset flashed off its wings. Arrows of white lightning flickered and danced about its body.

And there, upon its mighty back, struggling to escape the hideous black beetle that was the twisted spirit of Broken Claw—was his beloved woman, her face a pale moon of terror!

Power surged anew through Wolf, coursing like peyote through his veins. Love added strength to his throwing arm. Danger lent a tingling, icy clarity to his thoughts and his aim. Suddenly, as Clouds Standing had promised, he knew what he must do . . .

Uttering an ululating, thundering whoop of challenge, he threw back his raven dark head and raised his snake-painted lance to the sky. With all his might, he drew back his arm, and hurled it.

"Child of Lightning—!" he cried in his loudest voice.

The mighty war cry echoed through the canyon walls as White Wolf's lance struck home with a terrible booming, cracking sound that deafened his ears, lodging deep and true in the glassy red eye of the hawk . . .

The plane exploded in an orange ball of fire before, tail over nose, its wreckage tumbled to the Little Colorado below, into the cavernous mouth of Sipapu.

The wisps of mist still drifted by; the soft gray mists that were the spirits of the dead.

But now—now there was another wisp among them.

Epilogue

Phoenix Sun, December 6

GRAND CANYON NATIONAL PARK—The charred remains recovered from the wreckage of a hijacked Scenic Tours plane just a week ago have been tentatively identified through military medical and dental records as belonging to former Air Force pilot, Major Anthony Michaels, twenty-eight, of no fixed address.

Scenic Tours' pilot, Jerry 'Mitch' Sczczkutek positively identified Michaels from photographs as the assailant who overpowered him on the afternoon of November 31, and later hijacked his company's Piper Chieftain plane. Sczczkutek reported having been hired by Michaels's former wife, Kelly Michaels, for a scenic tour of the Little Colorado canyon some hours prior to the crash, but Sczczkutek added that Mrs. Michaels had failed to keep the appointment as scheduled.

Michaels, a former Air Force pilot stationed with the Eighty First Tactical Fighter Squadron in Europe, had been undergoing psychiatric care at a San Francisco military hospital since his medical discharge from active duty eighteen months ago. A spokesman for the facility reported that Michaels had been diagnosed as severely depressed following his divorce from his wife, Kelly Michaels, and that the possibility that Michaels's death had been a suicide could not be ruled out.

White-water kayaking enthusiast Don Washington who witnessed the plane crash, however, testified at the coroner's hearing to having seen lightning strike the plane immediately before its explosion. Although National Weather Service spokesmen have cited lightning as an unlikely cause for the plane crash at this time of year, FAA investigators will be examining the wreckage to determine its cause.

There were no other remains found aboard the wreckage, and in the absence of further testimony, the coroner's office recorded a verdict of accidental death, incurred in the commission of a felony.

The fires of Clouds Standing's pueblo had been rekindled by the god Masau when White Wolf returned from the canyon. Their light offered a welcome relief from the cold, oppressive darkness. Now, countless stars pulsed icily in the dark skies above, singing their star songs as they reflected the sparkling frost on the hard earth and rocky wastes below. Yet even the promise of warmth from the fires and the welcome starlight could not brighten Wolf's heavy heart. It lay as a stone upon the ground!

He had tried, and he had failed, the cry of the screech owl seemed to mock him. He had slain the silver hawk, as instinct had commanded him. With it, the hideous black beetle—the evil spirit of Broken Claw—had been consumed in the inferno. But so, too, had his woman's spirit been swallowed up by the flames of the silver hawk's dying; lost to him forever in the yawning black mouth of Sipapu, Gateway To Tomorrow and Yesterday. And now, with dawn imminent, the rites of Wuwuchim would end, and the Gateway would close . . .

He skirted the ceremonials in the plaza. He ignored the whirling figures of the weary dancers, fantastically robed and headdressed like sacred animals as they reenacted the People's Emergence from the Underworld; turned a deaf ear to the singers and the throbbing drumbeats.

Instead, he passed through the pueblo and left the mesa, making his way to the other crumbling pueblo below it. Once there, he sought out the *kiva* where he knew Clouds Standing would be awaiting his return. Perhaps the *shaman* could tell him where he'd gone wrong? Perhaps he would know of some way to mend the terrible thing he'd done?

He clambered down the ladder into the *kiva* and stepping

from it, saw as he had expected that old Clouds Standing was still sitting cross-legged before the fire. His head was bowed, and he had drawn a blanket over it and his bony shoulders to warm himself against the cold.

Shadows danced over the painted *kiva* walls as Wolf moved away from the ladder and crossed the *kiva* floor. Firelight caressed the planes and angles of his savagely handsome face and glittered in his blue eyes as he strode to stand before the old *shaman*.

He was no coward, he reminded himself, gritting his jaw. Cowardice was for women and little children and old, toothless men! He would confess his failure and bear the weight of Clouds Standing's disappointment in him, as somehow—*somehow!*—he would bear the great sorrow of his loss.

"I have failed, my uncle," he announced in a deep voice laden with grief and shame. "On this one, the gifts of your wisdom, the great powers of magic you possess, were squandered!" he rasped, furious at himself. "You showed me the way. And yet somehow, when the time came, this weak and foolish one failed his woman! I slew the silver hawk of my vision. I watched it die in a ball of flames. And now, my woman's spirit is no more! She will sleep the deep sleep that is neither death nor life forever!"

Silence followed his words, which trembled upon the darkness with his emotion.

"Failed?" came a low, musical voice, one of infinite sweetness to his ears. His heart gave a great leap. "Can you have failed, mighty White Wolf, when your courage and love have brought me back from—tomorrow?"

With these words, the figure by the fire drew aside the blanket that covered its head and rose gracefully to standing.

White Wolf gaped, his jaw dropping. He saw now that the person was a woman—not Clouds Standing at all! She was both young and shapely. Her fringed gown of soft doeskin was the creamy shade of clouds at first light. The quills and beads that adorned it were yellow as pollen, as golden

470

as cornmeal. Her hair was a dark swathe that fell to her waist like a waterfall. Her cheeks were the blushing pink of the wild roses that hide their faces in the mountains. All this he saw, and yet he could not—dare not!—believe his eyes!

The young woman raised her face shyly to his, and a thrill ran through him as he gazed into eyes as blue as the sky before a summer thunderstorm; as blue as the two blue beads he wore in the medicine bundle at his throat.

"So? Do you not recognize me, my husband?" Blue Beads asked softly, stepping gracefully toward him. "Have you already forgotten me?"

The soft tinkle of her cone ornaments as she came to him were songs of gladness to his ears!

"I was once the daughter of tomorrow," she continued, "the daughter of days yet unborn, and of dreams yet undreamed. But now, I am again the woman I have longed to be, even in the spirit world of shadows and mist—and yes, even in the canyons of tomorrow! I am the bride of White Wolf. I am the mother of his children," she added, caressing her belly and the secret that lay hidden within, waiting to be born. "I am again Blue Beads Woman, the one who fills his heart as he fills hers—with gladness and love! I am she who will again give him pleasure upon their buffalo robes, and help him to forget the cold sleeps of winter in the warmth of their lodge! Smile, my scowling husband," she teased him gently, "or I will think you're not happy to see me—that you've found another amongst the Hopituh maidens who can make you smile as I once did!"

"Never," he murmured, taking her in his arms and holding her tightly with a fierce, sweet joy that thrummed through his veins; that sent his very spirit leaping like a buck in spring when its blood ran hot and swift.

"No, never!" he repeated in a stronger voice, and threw back his raven head and whooped aloud with joy, "Hiyeeeeah!" His shining sky eyes and his sternly handsome features softened as he stroked the gentle curve of her cheek and traced the margin of her smiling lips.

471

"And our son?" he asked finally.

"Come, we will go and see him together," Blue Beads suggested. Taking his hand in hers, she led him to the ladder, climbing up it and from the *kiva* ahead of him.

In the two-roomed dwelling that Clouds Standing had prepared for them, Red Wing slept, warmed by a small fire and antelope and buffalo pelts. Blue Beads pressed her hand to his brow and found it warm, but without the dry, unhealthy heat of fever. The pustules had dried and become scabbed over now. Their son would bears the scars forever, but he would survive, and that was all that mattered!

As they exchanged tear-filled glances, Red Wing stirred and his beautiful long-lashed eyes fluttered open.

"Papa?" he questioned, yawning and rubbing his eyes sleepily. "Mother—is it you?"

"It is, my son. We are both here, watching over you," Blue Beads reassured him, and leaning down, she pressed her lips to his brow and stroked his little head. "Go back to sleep, my dear one. There is nothing to fear."

No, Wolf thought. *There is nothing to fear, not any more.*

Together, they would live and love as man and woman. Together, they would see the great destiny that Clouds Standing and Semanaw had prophesied for them fulfilled. Together, they would raise Red Wing and the girl-child, Hope for the Future, the babe who was even now waiting to be born. These two little ones would be the first of Wolf's seed, the son and daughter of White Wolf, Child of Lightning, and his woman, Blue Beads. And someday their line would give birth to the one called Peace Bringer-Chief, the one whose wisdom and eloquence would bring peace to Mother Earth. Truly, it was a destiny worth fulfilling!

"You are my beloved, my woman-above-all-women," Wolf murmured, tilting her face up to his. In the fire's light, her eyes shone like deep blue stars, radiant with love, sparkling with life. She was his, he thought, and his heart swelled with joy. "I will love you forever, Blue Beads!" he whispered fervently. "Forever—and still beyond . . . !"

"As I will love you. Always . . ." Blue Beads murmured

simply.

Pressing her cheek to his chest, curling her arms about his throat, she silently offered up two prayers of thanks. The first was to the Sky God, Sotugnanga, the Great Spirit Above. The second was to the spirit of Lomahongva, the Guardian of the Lost; to Lomahongva, Clouds Standing, the *shaman* whose medicine had brought her back from tomorrow, so that she might walk in beauty and love, always . . .

South Rim, Grand Canyon National Park, July 1987

It was a hot day in July, exactly one year to the very day since he'd first met Kelly at Barbara and Bill's, Devin recalled with a heavy sigh and a stab of pain that was so much a part of him now, he'd almost grown accustomed to it.

Leaning on his cane, he forced his healing legs to obey him and started toward the overlook point near Hopi House, slowly weaving his way between the oohing-and-aahing tourists thronging the visitors station to stand alongside them and look out on Mather Point.

Yet his eyes were dark and distant with memory, seeing nothing as he gazed out over the awe-inspiring wonder of the Grand Canyon and the Colorado River a full mile below, snaking like a silver thread through its wondrous rocky minarets and towers and sweeping formations.

All he could see with his mind's eye was Kelly's lovely face, her deep blue eyes, her smile. Christ! All he could think of was Kelly; of how she'd vanished from his life somewhere not far from here, probably, just eight short months ago, leaving behind only the unsolved mystery of her disappearance.

He'd talked to the pilot from Scenic Tours, a man named Jerry, who'd only confirmed what the police had already told him; that he hadn't gotten to meet Kelly Michaels in person at all; that she'd booked the tour over the phone, but had failed to keep the scheduled appointment, and that instead, Tony Michaels had surprised him while he was performing a preflight inspection of the plane, laid him out cold with a wrench, and so on. Kelly's Hertz rental car had been found, apparently abandoned, at the Grand Canyon National Park Airport lot, though, which clearly implied she'd made it that far . . .

The mystery remained about where she was now, and as long as it was unsolved, Devin doubted he'd ever be able to grieve for her properly, and get on with putting his life back together.

Had she really done it? he'd wondered a hundred times a day since waking up to find himself alive but badly injured in a hospital bed, and hearing Barbara tearfully explain how Tony Michaels had crashed to his own death, and that Kelly had vanished. Had she somehow found her way back to her White Wolf—or had Tony contrived to keep her his forever before the plane crashed, without leaving a trace?

It was a question he'd pondered long and hard during most of his lengthy hospital stay, while they tried to put the fragments of his legs back together after the pickup crash, and then again as he underwent intensive physical therapy. It would be a long hard road, the doctors had told him, and an uncomfortable one for quite some time to come, but they cheerfully anticipated a full recovery with little or no loss of function in his legs. Whoever had cut his brake lines had failed to kill him, as they'd intended.

He'd thanked the doctors, but hadn't shared their ebullient optimism, for he'd discovered by then that—almost masochistically—he welcomed the physical pain his shattered legs still gave him from time to time. It helped to drown out the emotional agony.

"What happened to your legs?" piped a curious young voice, echoing his own thoughts.

Dragged back from his moody reverie, he looked down into a pair of curious gray eyes belonging to a towheaded tyke of about seven, judging by the gaps in his front teeth.

"These wobbly old things?" He managed a wink and a

474

wry grin. "Well, son, this here's what happens when you don't listen to your Momma, and stray too close to the edge!"

"You fell over?" the boy whispered, round-eyed and awed. "Way down there?"

"Ryan! You come back here, and stop bothering people!" his mother scolded before Devin could answer the boy with a whopping great lie. The woman darted him an apologetic and embarrassed smile, her eyes sliding away from his cane with pointed tact as she shepherded young Ryan back into her fold.

Forcing a smile which faded the minute his back was from her, Devin turned away. He might as well go. It was a trip wasted. There was nothing here to remind him of Kelly, he reluctantly admitted to himself. For weeks he'd fostered a desperate hope that by coming here, by reliving the days they'd spent together last August and by going to all the same places they'd gone together then, he could make her real; living and breathing, alive and warm again in his memory of her, which time—that great healer, that cheating son of a bitch—was already starting to dim. But he'd been wrong.

"Dr. Colter?"

He glanced up, and for a minute, he stared open-mouthed, his heart erratic and skipping beats all over the place.

The brilliant summer sunlight dazzled him as he looked directly into it. It had thrown the features of the young woman standing before him with her back to it into inky shadow. She was quite tall and slenderly built, in silhouette. Her hair fell to her shoulders in thick, glossy dark waves. And, something about her casual grace as she took a step toward him had convinced him—just for a fleeting, heart-stopping second—that she was Kelly.

"It *is* Doctor Colter, isn't it?" she asked, uncertain now. "Devin Colter?"

"Guilty as charged," he admitted, smiling uncertainly himself now as his shoulders relaxed. It wasn't her. He'd been crazy to think it was. "I'm afraid I don't—?"

"—remember me? No," she laughed, and it had an attractive, warm sound. "I don't suppose you would. Let me introduce myself. My name's Hope, Hope Dallas. We met once, briefly, a few years ago. Of course, I was just a student nurse then, so I'm not surprised you don't recognize me. I attended one of the lectures you gave—on neo-natal nursing care, and the special problems of preemies. Your speech was fascinating!"

"I'm glad to hear it," he acknowledged, and she turned just a little so that the light revealed her features.

She was lovely, he saw.

Warm brown eyes fringed with impossibly long lashes twinkled up at him from a striking oval face of obviously part-Indian ancestry, judging by its high cheekbones. Her complexion was a clear, golden brown, her hair loose and thick and dark, reflecting reddish rather than blue lights. She had full, generous lips, curved now in an infectious smile. The dimples at their outer corners promised that she was a woman who laughed often, and despite his introspective mood, he found himself smiling back.

"Please, don't be embarrassed," she continued. "I didn't expect you to remember me, really I didn't. After all, I was just one giggling student nurse out of lord-knows-how-many who must have attended your lectures!" She rolled her eyes and shrugged, dismissing the matter as unimportant.

The graceful way she moved her willowy yet femininely rounded body stirred Devin's senses, making him feel wonderfully alive for the first time in many months. He noticed the way her golden throat disappeared into the shirt collar of her crisp white blouse, the pretty turquoise and silver necklace at her throat off-setting its graceful column; her slender arms, and the way her small breasts thrust against the cloth of her shirt, mounding it in gentle, undeniably female curves.

"I'm sure I'd have remembered you if I'd met you, Miss Dallas," he said gallantly, but meant it nonetheless. His eyes were warm and appreciative as they returned to her face.

A pretty blush of color filled her cheeks. "Thank you."

"So. Are you still nursing?"

"Oh, yes. And I love it," she confirmed with unvarnished sincerity.

"Here at the visitors station clinic?"

"No, not quite! Today, I'm playing tourist, like everyone else here — on vacation and anxious to see the sights! My family lives in Hotevila, you see? But in two weeks, it's back to work, I'm afraid. I'm with the Peace Corps, you see — assigned to a disaster relief clinic in South America."

"Really?" He nodded approval, genuinely impressed on more levels than the obvious physical attraction she'd subtly generated in him. "It sounds like a fascinating assignment! To be honest, Miss Dallas, I've been thinking a lot lately about trying something along those lines myself. You know, getting out of private practice, tackling a challenge I can really get my teeth into?"

"You have? Well, they could use someone with your pediatric experience down there! Oh, those poor, sick babies! And the little children suffering from malnutrition and disease — it's just heartbreaking to see them, Dr. Colter." Her eyes filled with tears.

"It's Devin," he insisted softly. "And you can't very well keep calling me Dr. Colter if we're going to have a fascinating lunch together, now can you?"

"Oh, we are, are we . . . Devin?" she said with a slow, delicious smile that spread from her lips to put a sparkle in her eyes.

"I surely hope so! Well? Would you? Join me for lunch, I mean?"

"I think I might enjoy that, yes," she agreed after a moment's deliberation. "Thank you. And please, won't you call me Hope?"

It was over a long and enjoyable lunch in the dining room of the El Tovar Hotel with its rustic decor and huge fireplaces that Devin first noticed the bracelet encircling her slender arm below the folded back cuffs of her blouse.

477

A wide silver crescent bangle, it was set with two cabuchon cut blue stones that looked like sapphires. The silver was decorated with sun and hawk designs that he knew as intimately as if they'd been etched into his memory, rather than into the silver.

"Where did you get that?" he demanded sharply, staring at the bracelet.

"This?" Hope asked, twisting the bangle around her wrist to remove it. She held it up to the light, and it gleamed with the gentle lustre of aged silver. "It's a family heirloom, I guess you could say. It's been in our family for over a hundred years. My mother gave it to me, and my grandmother gave it to her, and so on. One day, I hope to give it to my daughter, too, if I have one. It's quite unusual, isn't it?"

"Very," he agreed, hardly able to keep his voice level in his excitement. "Could I—that is, would you mind if I took a closer look at it?"

"Of course not," she denied, smiling. "Here you go."

She handed the bracelet to him, but even without looking, he knew the minute its warmth filled his hand that running around the inside surface he would find the delicately worked paw prints of a wolf.

Sure enough, they were there, just as he remembered, and he realized with a tingling flood of awareness rising through him, that Kelly wasn't missing after all! She'd found her way back through the canyons of time, had returned to the man she'd always loved! He knew she'd chosen the bracelet as the means of letting him know it, to set his mind at rest.

"It was made for my great-great-grandmother," Hope disclosed, seeing the interest in his expression. "According to the family stories my mother and grandmother told me, she was a white woman, taken captive by the Comanches as a child. My great-great-grandfather was of mixed blood, sold into slavery when their pueblo was attacked by Apache, then raised by the Comanche. It took him years to get back to his mother's people, but when he did, he brought my great-great grandmother with him. In later life, he became a highly respected *shaman* among our People," she added with pride in her tone.

Devin was staring across the table now as if her casual recounting of her family history had utterly riveted his attention. The piercing intensity of his brown eyes and handsome face was disquieting. It made Hope feel a little uncomfortable, but by the self-same token it was also—she had to admit!—rather flattering to have such a striking, handsome man gazing at her with such complete absorption! "It's the only bracelet of its kind, my brother tells me. You see these stones? They're sapphires. We've always assumed it was sort of a good-luck talisman, made just for her, because my great-great-grandmother's name was—"

"—don't tell me," Devin cut in in a tone that was gravelly with emotion. "Her name was Blue Beads Woman."

"Yes!" she exclaimed, then grinned and made a face. "All right, Doc. I'll bite! How did you know?"

"Just a lucky guess, honest," Devin disclaimed innocently, drawing a deep, shaky breath.

"Oh, I'm sure it was!" Hope teased back.

"Okay, you're right. It wasn't a guess! And maybe I'll tell you how I knew some other time—like, over dinner tonight, say?" His dark brows rose in query.

"But we haven't finished lunch yet!" she protested, smiling nonetheless.

"I know," he agreed with a wicked little grin. "But I've decided to monopolize your time, Miss Dallas, if you'll let me. Any objections . . . ?"

"Nooo, I guess not. Besides, what choice do I really have? You're a very persuasive man, and I was born nosy! I really want to know how you knew my great-great-grandmother's name!" Hope agreed softly.

Laughing, Devin reached out and took her slim, warm hand in his. To his delight, she didn't pull free.

"All right, pretty lady, I'll tell you," he promised "But—I seriously doubt you'll believe my story."

"Oh, I'll take that chance," she said huskily, and both of

them knew she was talking about something more than the story he intended to tell her.

Their eyes met across the table in an electric exchange.

That exchange was only the prelude to many more such looks to come down through the years . . .